Scanda

Books by Lance Horner in Pan

Santiago Blood
Rogue Roman
The Mustee
Heir to Falconhurst
The Mahound
Flight to Falconhurst
Mistress of Falconhurst
Six-Fingered Stud

Books by Kyle Onstott and Lance Horner in Pan

The Tattooed Rood
Child of the Sun
The Black Sun
Falconhurst Fancy

Books by Kyle Onstott in Pan

Mandingo
Drum
Master of Falconhurst

Lance Horner novels by Ashley Carter in Pan

Master of Blackoaks
The Sword of the Golden Stud
Panama
Taproots of Falconhurst
Secret of Blackoaks

Ashley Carter

Scandal of Falconhurst

Pan Books London and Sydney

This novel is based on themes, settings, character, atmosphere, and situations created by Kyle Onstott and Lance Horner in *Mandingo* and the Falconhurst novels and has been prepared for publication by Ashley Carter through special and exclusive arrangement with the Kenric L. (Lance) Horner estate and the estate of Kyle Onstott.

First published in Great Britain 1981 by W. H. Allen & Co. Ltd
This edition published 1982 by Pan Books Ltd,
Cavaye Place, London SW10 9PG

ISBN 0 330 26665 9
Printed and bound in Great Britain by
Hazell, Watson & Viney Ltd, Aylesbury, Bucks

for my daughter, Harriet Kathryn,
with all my love . . .

part one

Falconhurst, 1844

1

Late in April of that year Ellen gave birth to the mustee's git. Parturition set in on a bitterly cold night, the last snarling bite of winter rasping in an unbroken spring downpour. Though the countryside was calf-deep in mud when Ellen began to writhe and scream on her bed, Miz Lucretia Borgia yelled for Mem.

"You git dressed. Fast," she told him.

He stared at her, groggy with sleep. "Hit the dark o' night, Miz Lucretia Borgia, ma'am."

"I ast you what time is it? I didn't no-way ast you what time. I say git dressed. Fetch Doc Redfield."

"Doc Redfield? Way over to Seven Mile Road?"

Lucretia Borgia nodded, jaw hardening. "He the one. That the place. Now quit whinin' or you gits the flat of my hand 'gainst the side of your burr head."

He stared at the storm-riven windows, fiery with lightning. "Why, hit's rainin' cats and dogs out there."

"I know it's raining."

"I purentee scairt of lightnin', Miz Lucretia Borgia."

"You scairt of your own shadow. Only thing you ain't got sense enough to be is scairt of me. . . . Now git."

He trembled, terrorized by the storm, afraid to oppose her. "How I git way over there?"

"Git a mule, nigger. And ride. Now."

Memnon burst into sudden helpless tears, but even as he wept, wiping at his runny nose with the back of his hand, he dressed. Lucretia Borgia waited only long enough to make sure Mem got on his way; then she hurried into Ellen's bedroom, where she struggled in her first labor though she was at least twenty-four plantings old.

"Oh Gawd, Miz Lucretia Borgia, ma'am," Ellen wailed. She clutched the big woman's hand, fingernails digging into her flesh. This third-floor room of the old farmhouse was as well furnished as the finest guest room on the lower floors, but none of this comfort and privilege had reality for Ellen now. Fear and pain reduced her to the level of the least slave over in the quarters. The room spun before her eyes and she shuddered, dizzy with pain.

"I in misery. I in terrible misery."

"That sucker on his way." Lucretia Borgia nodded. She was, in fact if not in name, mistress of this enormous slave farm. In the years Master Hammond had been away across the Texies, she had managed the estate to its greatest profits. Catlike curiosity, exuberant happiness, good health, unflagging vigor, and an inborn desire to take charge were her birthrights. They were as much a part of her as was her large-boned body. She was within two inches of six feet tall, with magnificent breasts, rounded hips and sculpted thighs to make her stand out in any company. She was in no way corpulent, she was massively beautiful—a light tobacco-brown skin, brilliant and flashing brown eyes and thick lashes, an amazon of a woman, yet strikingly attractive, even in her late thirties.

"I agonizing, Miz Lucretia Borgia."

Lucretia Borgia held the lamp high in her left hand while she pushed Ellen's legs apart and inspected her, squinting. She nodded again. "You startin' to dilate, all right."

"It hurts. In my belly." Ellen cried out and bit at the back of her hand. "It hurt terrible fierce, Miz Lucretia Borgia."

"I know. I know. I been in yo' place four—five times now—not countin' that once I drapped twins. It just that sucker of yourn a-droppin' down. He just a-slidin' into the chute."

"It hurt! Oh Gawd, it hurt. I wishes Masta Herman was here."

"Masta Herman done all for you he can do."

"He promise. He know I scairt—"

"From here on, it all up to you—and the sucker. He a-tryin' he best. Now you got to help him. You just got to strain, and strain hard, and bear down, and then you got to let up and take it easy. Let that li'l ole sucker rest . . . he let you know in plenty time when he ready to try again."

Ellen screamed suddenly. "I on fire . . . I burnin' down there. Oh Gawd, Miz Lucretia Borgia, please! Please Gawd, make it stop . . ."

"Too late fo' that, too. You likely decide a hundred times 'fore that sucker fights his way out'n yore guts that you don't want him . . . but you gon' have him . . . you might just as well settle your mind to that."

Ellen screamed again until Miz Lucretia Borgia clapped her hand over the pale-tan girl's mouth to silence her. "I swear if you ain't somethin' else, Ellen gal. I didn't hear you screamin' and carryin' on like that when Masta Herman was a-sneakin' in here nights plantin' them seed."

"I didn't know. I didn't know . . . oh, my Gawd, I didn't know."

Miz Lucretia Borgia's voice remained low, level, but in no way vindictive or judgmental. "You knowed Masta Ham was comin' back home."

"When?" For a moment, Ellen's olive-black eyes washed clear of pain. Fear swirled in them and tauntened the soft, sharply hewn features of her tea-rose face. "When Masta Ham comin' home?"

Miz Lucretia Borgia shrugged. "Don't know. Don't nobody know. But he comin'. Sometime. Soon enough. Too soon for you, now you drop the mustee's git. . . . You knowed when Masta Ham left here what he say he do to you an' you let nobody git to you 'twixt yo' legs whilst he was away across them Texies. . . . Thank God, he ain't here."

"Thank Gawd," Ellen whimpered. She clutched Miz Lucretia Borgia's hand tighter than ever.

Miz Lucretia Borgia closed her eyes and lifted her head as if gazing through the ceiling, the roof and the dome of the sky to heaven. "I do thank you, God. I thank you that Masta Ham across the Texies an' don't see what's got into his li'l bed wench Ellen whilst he was away." She glanced down at the girl writhing on the rumpled bed. "What Masta Ham told you 'fore he leave here? Don't you let no other man—white or black—get at your pretty. That *his* pretty, he tell you. I heah him say it. And I know Masta Ham well enough to know he not speakin' idle. They some things Masta Ham don't joke about—and his slaves belongin' to *him* alone is one of them things he plumb dead serious about in his own mind."

Ellen writhed back and forth on the bed. She was in her earliest twenties, born to an octoroon mother by a white sire—likely old Warren Maxwell himself, in his randy years, or some favored friend on an overnight stay. Hospitality demanded a bed wench be furnished overnight guests, and at Falconhurst when a girl got pregnant, the mustee git could be sold as a Falconhurst fancy-grade slave.

Ellen's teeth chattered though she burned with fever. She was slender, except for that descending bulge where she carried her child. Her features were dainty, her wrists small, her bone structure frail. One thought her olive-dark eyes her single most prominent feature—easy to laughter, quick to reveal hurt. Her thick black hair was crisp and shone with sweat in the lamplight.

Lucretia Borgia soothed that hair back from the girl's straight forehead. If there were anything on this earth Miz Lucretia Borgia found to envy about the thin, weak-looking little Ellen, it was that lack of kinky curl in Ellen's hair.

Miz Lucretia Borgia's lips pulled into a sour smile. She was forced to wear a red bandanna every waking moment to conceal her own hair. Maybe, when she was cruel to Ellen, the secret explanation was jealousy. She had much Ellen would never have, experienced joys Ellen would never even dream about, but she did hate Ellen's straight hair.

Ellen wept, clinging to Miz Lucretia Borgia's hand. "But Masta Ham . . . he gone so long, Miz Lucretia Borgia, ma'am . . . can't you understand? Can't you?"

"I understand all right." Miz Lucretia Borgia's mouth twisted. She understood only too well. More than a couple nights without a man between her thighs, she got the mollygrubs. Masta Ham had been gone almost eight years. "But me understandin', that ain't your problem. You got to pray Masta Ham gon' understand when he comes back home from them Texies."

Miz Lucretia Borgia placed the lamp on the old table beside the girl's bed. She sat down on the mattress and massaged Ellen's swollen belly, marked with the faintest lines of blue stria. Woman wasn't ever truly the same after her first git. She could never be a girl again, ever look like a girl any more. Miz Lucretia Borgia sighed.

Like Ellen, she wished Master Herman Hengst were present at Ellen's labor and delivery, but for widely divergent reasons from Ellen's. She didn't want the responsibility for this child. One might almost wish it a stillborn. That would solve a lot of problems. But she shook this thought from her mind. She was too full of the joy of life to deny the opportunity for living, even to an unwanted brat that might be the death of them all.

No, Miz Lucretia Borgia wanted the mustee—masquerading as a purentee white man—to witness what his unbridled passions had produced, the hell that was ahead for all of them. At the same time, she thanked God that Master Hammond Maxwell was not present. She would need time to straighten out this mess. They had all the problems they could handle right now without having to face the consequences of Master Ham's violent and ungovernable temper, which flared into madness when he felt himself wronged or deceived. She quivered, seeing—as she saw in her nightmares sometimes—the way Master Ham had boiled the flesh off the Mandingo slave Mede. Boiled Mede alive, he had. God alone knew what he might do to Ellen, and to Herman Hengst, though they all owed Herman so much. She couldn't believe Master Ham would be much moved by the morality of debt when he learned what Master Herman and Ellen had done. . . .

The baby was delivered and wrapped in a much-washed cotton blanket by the time Mem returned with Doc Redfield from Seven

Mile Road. Doc Redfield stomped into the bedroom, dripping with rain. He tossed his soggy black hat behind him. He did not wash his hands before inspecting Ellen, but he did scrub them dry on his trouser legs.

"Couldn't wait, huh?" Doc Redfield appeared to be withering on the vine. Each time he arrived at Falconhurst, he seemed thinner and more dried-up than before. His hands were gnarled, liver-spotted. A thin line of black edged his fingernails. His narrow-shouldered frame shrank in upon itself, melting down to a melon-like potbelly at his flowered waistcoat. Tobacco stains discolored the sparse, gray-streaked, red whiskers about his mouth. His few teeth were blackened stubs.

Straightening from his inspection of Ellen's pelvic area, Doc Redfield nodded and grinned at Miz Lucretia Borgia. "You done fine," he said. "The gal will be good as new in a few days. . . . Let me see the git."

He took the infant in his arms and turned back the coverlet. His faded blue eyes widened, and though he often said he'd been down all roads at least twice, he bit back an audible gasp of shocked surprise. He stared at the newborn baby, its skin creamy and whiter than his own, and at the rosebud between its thighs designating it a female, then he lifted his gaze to Ellen's face. "Ain't you Masta Ham's private bed wench, girl?"

Sweated, pale, her eyes stricken, Ellen nodded.

Doc Redfield grinned like a briar-eating mule. "Don't have to count on my fingers to tell this ain't Masta Ham's drop. . . . What you gone tell him?"

"We think of something," Lucretia Borgia said.

Redfield shook his head. He studied Ellen's face without compassion. "Looks plain to me you been messin' round with that handsome Masta Herman Hengst. . . . Reckon I cain't no-way blame him for wantin' you—I hankered after that pretty 'twixt your legs many times myself. But me—I knowed better. Could've fetched a real scandal—or a killin'—Hammond Maxwell catch airy other man—white or black—pesterin' his own favor-rite bed wench."

"We think of something," Lucretia Borgia said again.

"You got my prayers," the vet said, laughing. He hefted the infant in his hands. "Say she weighs six, six and a half pounds. Seven pounds of scandal. That's shore to God what you got on your hands.

"Scandal," Lucretia Borgia whispered.

*

The baby's crying wakened Ellen. She lay for some moments disoriented. She was exhausted. It seemed to her the infant slept spasmodically during the day and then cried all night. In the four nights since its birth, she thought she had not slept one full hour.

"Damn you, Rachel," she whispered. "What do you want now?"

She felt sweated, weak and trembling with fatigue. And there was the fear with which she lived now, twenty-four full hours every day.

Time seemed rushing forward, like a runaway horse, an avalanche. Nothing could stop it. Lucretia Borgia promised to think of something to say to Master Ham Maxwell when he returned, but she had come up with nothing workable. Lucretia Borgia's mind was too numbed with fear, she was unable to think clearly. They all were.

The child went on crying, demanding, imperious. Ellen bit her lip and pressed her hands over her ears. Lying there, breathing raggedly, she heard a wagon rolling across the yard.

Her heart flagged, seeming to stop for an instant. Wasn't this the way Master Ham would return from the Texies? Late in the dark night, before any of them were ready for him. Unexpectedly. Suddenly. Catching them in the night.

She sat up in the bed, listening, infuriated because the baby continued to wail. She needed to hear every sound. She needed to know if that was indeed Master Ham. If he came back tonight, found her with this infant in her bed, what could she do, what could she she say to him?

The wagon rolled away across the barnyard toward the fields—some of the hands going out to chop cotton. They would be at work in the first light of dawn. Relief flooded through her. And yet she could not escape the thought that some moment like this—long before she was ready—Master Ham would come back, and she must face him.

She gazed down at the crying child in the darkness. She hated it. She felt no twinge of mother love. She felt only the fear and the trouble this child had brought her. It had torn her open, but that pain was nothing compared with what lay ahead for her.

Her hands trembling, Ellen touched one of the goosedown pillows. How easy to press it down over the infant's face and hold it there until those screams ceased forever. If that baby were dead, it would be easy to lie to Master Ham. But even with the child out of the way, she dreaded facing Master Ham. He would read the truth in her eyes. He would know what had happened, that she had not been faithful. He would force her to speak

Herman's name. She could not deny that she loved Herman, as she had never loved Master Ham—she had been a child of thirteen when he first took her into his bed. She hadn't known about love; she did what he ordered. Sometimes it hurt her badly, once in a while she cried out in pleasure, but it never mattered to him whether he hurt her or enthralled her; he had what he wanted.

Her eyes filled with tears. If only Herman would come back from New Orleans. He would see the baby, know it was his own. Perhaps he would love it enough to want her as his own. Perhaps Herman would take her and the baby away. But even as she thought this, she knew better. Herman had never promised her anything. Though she quivered with desire and ecstasy in his arms, she always had the heartbreaking sense that he had possessed dozens of girls who thrilled him far more. No matter. I love him, she thought. I love him, no matter what happens I love only Herman, and nothing will change that, even if I never see him again.

"Herman," she whispered aloud, her voice pale against the child's crying. "Whatever happens, I'm *glad* for what we had . . . what we did. Please, Herman, come back . . . take us away with you."

The crying of the baby mocked her. The corridor door was thrown open, blades of lamplight slashed away at the darkness, and Lucretia Borgia strode in, like an avenging angel in her ankle-length cotton nightgown.

"Damn you, Ellen girl." Lucretia Borgia's voice battered at Ellen, like fists. "What are you doing with that pillow?"

Ellen stared at the pillow which she'd taken up in her hands. She let it drop back and shook her head, staring at the ceiling, breathless. How close she had come to suffocating her baby! She hadn't even known how close. She shuddered. She was losing her mind. She could no longer even be trusted alone with the child.

"Why in hell don't you feed that baby?" Lucretia Borgia said. "You afraid your pretty tits lose their shape and Herman Hengst won't want you no more?"

"I'll feed her."

"Why do you let her cry like that? Don't you even have sense enough to know when your baby is hungry?"

"I hate her. Dammit, I hate her. She cries all the time."

"She's hungry all the time. Poor little Scandal."

"Don't call her that."

Ellen reached inside the bodice of her gown, lifted her golden breast out and pressed the child's mouth to her nipple. She gazed down, watching it eat. She felt no maternal love. She was too numbed with fear and dread to feel anything.

"You'll change," Lucretia Borgia said, watching her, watching the perfectly formed child suckle. Lucretia Borgia laughed. "Lot of women ain't borned mothers. But most of them change. This here baby will change you. Having a baby, feedin' it, watchin' it grow—that changes every woman."

"Not me," Ellen said. "Nothing will change me. I hate her. I'll always hate her."

Finally, Lucretia Borgia was gone. The room was dark again. Ellen placed the baby on the pillow near the wall as far from her as she could. She lay breathless then, waiting. After a moment, the child whimpered and then wailed lustily.

Crying, Ellen put her pillow over her own head and pressed it against her ears, trying to shut out the grating wail of Scandal's weeping.

Lucretia Borgia walked into the kitchen. The place was quiet, scrubbed and spotless in the middle of the morning. A few flies buzzed over the cheesecloth-covered pine table. She walked to the stove and poured hot black coffee into her own large tin cup. Steam rose up about her face.

She walked to the back door, sipping at the coffee. She watched the men at work near the barns. No coffee was going to soothe her this morning. She had been too long without a pestering. She needed a man.

She watched the men working near the barns. Huge Plymouth Rock and Rhode Island Red roosters pursued squawking hens. Pigeons, sparrows and mourning doves, tamed by hunger, fed around the horse pens. Children, half-naked, raced and played, laughing in the morning sunlight. Her gaze narrowed and focused upon one man.

Her heart beat faster and she felt herself grow heated. One man, but what a man! Jingo Jim was man enough for any two ordinary women. Which makes him just about satisfactory for me, Lucretia Borgia told herself. She smiled and licked at her lips.

She called to one of the small boys playing in the shade of the tupelo tree. The boy came to the door, his head hanging. He wore Osnaburg britches and linsey shirt—one of the children assigned each morning to watch for company on the trace to Benson. Lucretia Borgia said, "Which chile is you, boy?"

"I Ursa," the boy said. He was far too polite to lift his head far enough to meet her gaze.

"Ursa. How you like a nice warm bun, made with cinnamon, sugar and raisins?"

The child salivated, eyes and mouth widening in anticipation. Lord, how little it took to please a child. "Yes ma'am, Miz Lucretia Borgia, ma'am. I shore do fancy one of your buns."

Lucretia Borgia nodded. She brought a cinnamon bun from the screened sideboard. The child clutched it, already backing away. "Wait a minute," she said. "Somethin' I want you to do for me, Ursa."

"Yes'm?"

"You go down to the barn. You find Jingo Jim. You know Jingo Jim?"

"Ev'body knows Jingo Jim, I betcha."

"All right. You tells Jingo Jim I say to meet me over at the tack room. Tell him it's important. He to wait there. I be there, soon's I can."

She watched the child race across the sunstruck yard toward the barn, already feeling breathless with anticipation and sharp-honed desires. Jingo Jim was a right fancy boy. He was young, yet he knew how to pleasure a lady, how to hang on to his own raging emotions until she had been pleased and satisfied. Her heart battered in her rib cage. Her large nipples grew rigid, like gold pieces against the fabric of her dress.

She delayed a moment, giving the child a chance to deliver her message, giving Jingo Jim time to walk over to the shadowed tack room. And give him time to think on her coming to him. Let him wait a minute or two. Let the juices steep and simmer. She smiled. Now that she had her morning chores out of the way, she had time for herself, and she meant to humor her needs. She had been so involved with Ellen and that new baby, she had neglected herself.

"Miz Lucretia Borgia, ma'am?'

Lucretia Borgia flinched and turned, impatient. Ellen stood at the foot of the rear stairwell. The girl wore a gown and a lacy robe which once had belonged to Master Hammond's late wife. Ellen looked as flimsy as a reed, still unsteady on her feet. Damn her. She was seldom steady on her feet. She found whatever strength she possessed when she lay on her back. "What you want, girl?"

"Reckon Masta Herman be home soon?"

"How I know?"

"He's been gone a long spell."

"Yes. He's got work to do, selling our slaves for us down in New Orleans. He be home when he can."

"I want him now." Ellen looked ready to cry.

"You want horns, gal. But you gon' die butt-headed."

Ellen drew a deep, ragged breath. "Maybe he'll take me away from here."

"Where would he take you?" Lucretia Borgia's gaze strayed to the doorway. Jingo Jim was no longer in sight at the barn. Her breath quickened. She had no time to waste on this foolish girl's stupid problems. Ellen didn't regret her sin, but she sure as hell despised the idea of being caught. "You git back upstairs to your chile and stop thinkin' foolish things that ain't never goin' to happen. You ain't goin' nowhere. You a Falconhurst nigger—no matter your fine airs, that's all you is—and that's what you stay."

Lucretia Borgia set down her coffee cup and moved toward the rear door. Ellen cried out, like a child afraid of being left alone in a dark place. "What ails you now, girl?"

"Miz Lucretia Borgia, I cain't no-way face Masta Hammond when he come home. He see that baby, he kill me."

Lucretia Borgia's voice raked her. "I done tole you, and I done tole you. I think of something. Whatever I tell Masta Hammond, he believe." To herself Lucretia Borgia admitted she was less positive about this than she sounded. But at the moment all she wanted was to get away to that tack room.

"What if'n he don't believe you? He whup me—"

"You lucky an' whuppin' all you git."

"Oh Gawd, Miz Lucretia Borgia. Help me. I scairt."

"I got no time to listen to you now. Masta Hammond done gone all the way across the Texies. Been there fo' years. May be years 'fore he git back. Mayhap that chile of yourn half-growed 'fore Masta Hammond gets back here . . . your thing be back in shape and healed up—maybe *it'll* lie for you—maybe he believe *it*."

But Ellen was inconsolable, sunk into deep depression. She sank, desolate, to the chair at the pine table. Lucretia Borgia stared at her without compassion. She saw Ellen only as obstacle in her way at this moment. Jingo Jim and that rigid mast throbbing and waiting in the tack room while she played wet nurse to this mealy-mouthed little sop.

Lucretia Borgia propelled her bulk toward the rear door again. When Ellen cried out, Lucretia Borgia heeled around. Her voice lashed out savagely. "Now, Ellen, I don't care to heah no more from you. You start pullin' yo'self together. You start gettin' ready to be a woman, not a mewlin' chile. You a mama now . . . time you acted liked one. You had it easy all yo' life. Hardest work you ever done was hot-iron a bit of lace. Too easy . . . living like a house pet 'round here since you was twelve, thirteen year old. I tole you. When Masta Hammond come home, I take care of it. I will. Till then, you straighten up."

Lucretia Borgia stopped talking. Ellen was no longer listening to her. The girl had slumped in her chair as Lucretia Borgia castigated her, pressed back as if the big woman were physically abusing her. Maybe nobody had ever spoken to her so harshly before. But then, as Lucretia Borgia spoke, Ellen straightened. Her tea-rose face suffused with blood, and she sat forward, listening to something outside this house, staring beyond Lucretia Borgia to the yard.

"Somebody a-coming." The lookouts were screaming, jumping up and down as they scrambled along the lane toward the Benson trace.

Lucretia Borgia stopped talking. She pushed through the door, let it slam behind her. She stood, legs apart, on the stoop. She watched the buckboard come up the lane. Behind her, Ellen pressed against the screen door. "Maybe it be Masta Herman," Ellen whispered. "Please Gawd, let it be Masta Herman."

Lucretia Borgia did not speak. Her gaze was fixed on the buckboard rolling up the lane. She could see the man driving it. She shook her head. It was not the blond-headed Herman Hengst.

"Glory be to God," Lucretia Borgia whispered. She forgot Ellen, forgot Herman Hengst and Ellen's unwanted baby, even forgot Jingo Jim awaiting her in the shadowed and heated tack room.

She felt the hysteria of delight and disbelief rising inside her, the flooding of uncontrollable joy. She began to laugh and cry at the same time, her magnificent body shuddering under the violence of her emotions. Her arms reached out, even before she could move down the steps and run toward the graveled driveway.

"Lord in heaven!" She wept, choking on her words. Tears coursed down her cheeks. "It's my own Masta Hammond hisself. My own sweet Masta Hammond! Oh, praise be, it my Masta Hammond what come home. Praise God. Oh, praise God's dear name, my own Masta Hammond."

Ellen staggered away from the door, retreating into the dim kitchen. Her legs trembled, weak. Sounds gushed in from the yard, battering at her. Her mind went blank. Her heart sagged in her chest and pounded erratically—slowly, and then at terrible, uncontrollable speed. She felt cold sweat bead across her forehead. She felt as if she would faint, but knew she could not. She couldn't fall helpless, here, for Master Hammond to find her like this.

She shook her head, backing across the room. She tried to close her ears against the confusion and uproar of screaming, laughing and yelling in the yard. Slaves came running from every cranny of the huge farm. Bells rang. Dogs barked wildly. The whole place was possessed with madness. Masta Hammond had come home.

Ellen turned and ran toward the rear stairwell. She went up the steps, frenzied, stumbling, falling, crawling and clawing her way upward toward her third-floor room. To escape. To wait. To hide.

2

Ellen crouched in her chair, withdrawn, chilled with terror, in her third-floor room. Around her were piled the fine knitting, the intricate crochet work, the quilting she'd learned to while away lonely days. She stared at the fabrics and frames and yarns, unable to think about them, unseeing.

Her infant's crying assaulted her, but she did not move. She heard the bells, the clang of iron against the smithy's metal ring which summoned slaves from the farthest reaches of the farm. Dully, she thought about the slaves lining up to welcome Master Hammond Maxwell home, groveling, grinning, crying to show their joy. Many of the younger ones had never seen him, had no memory of him.

She shivered. She had no memory of him, either. Not any more. Her faded recollections of his love making had been long burned from her mind, seared from within by the fire and fury of Herman's passions for her, by the trauma of her childbearing. She hugged her arms across herself and huddled, unmoving.

She hoped that perhaps Master Ham had forgotten her over the long years, put her from his mind. He had been so far away, for so long. She kept praying that somehow Herman Hengst would return and take her and her baby away. Lucretia Borgia had warned her against such futile dreams, but she could not abandon this last hope.

After a long time, she heard Master Hammond's footsteps on the stairs. The sound brought old memory flooding through her. She recognized his tread, the awkward pound-and-drag of his lame leg.

Her teeth chattered. It was as if she awaited the hangman,

rather than her old master. Sweat broke out across her forehead and dried, fevered.

He came along the narrow hallway, his footsteps louder. He hesitated a moment outside her door, then opened it without knocking. It never occurred to Hammond Maxwell to knock on any door in his own house.

He stepped inside the door, closed it behind him. He limped slightly, his game leg rigid at the knee and awkward. It had been broken when he'd been thrown by a gelding in his childhood and had never been set or repaired properly. He had learned to live with his lameness. He moved in an ungainly way, but he could move quickly and he could keep going at hard labor or on forced marches when younger men fell aside. He could work or ride horseback all day.

Ellen stared at this stranger, trying to recall him. He was thick and tall and broad, and about him was an inborn arrogance, acceptance of his God-endowed superiority over most white people and all blacks. His face was sun-reddened, as his father's had been, and he had the light-brown hair with the sandy-red highlights also inherited from his father. His skin was coarse and weather-beaten, cooked a deep tan by Texas suns. He carried a planter's wide-crowned black hat; his clothing was expensively made, as were his hand-tooled boots, though they were travel-scuffed and dusty.

Ellen felt the nauseating sinking of despair and hackles prickled at the nape of her neck although Master Hammond was smiling down at her.

"Ellen," he said. His voice was unnaturally soft and warm. "You didn't come down with the others to welcome me home."

His smile widened. He tried to put her at ease. He had not taken his eyes from her face. "I missed you, Ellen gal. Never thought I could miss a nigger wench the way I missed you." He cleared his throat. "I've felt right starved—for a long time."

She nodded, feeling a slight upsurge of hope. She read the hungers in his sun-seared face. No matter what women Master Hammond had known in those long lost years across the Texies, he had not forgotten her. She had trailed after him, like an unending need, like a yearning for home, like the faint scent of some unforgettable musk.

"Was you afraid to see me, gal?" His eyes searched her face. When she shook her head, he smiled again. "Just shy, eh? After all these years?"

She nodded again, and lowered her dark eyes under his. He

stepped toward her. She forced herself to rise to her feet, her heart hammering wildly. Her legs felt buttery. He smiled and put out his arms.

At this instant, the baby wailed from its crib.

Ellen stopped, as if numbed. *Herman*, she thought, frantic. *Oh God, Herman.* Her hands tightened into fists as if she could physically keep herself from flying into pieces.

She watched Master Hammond's face change. His head jerked up as the infant cried out. He stared past her at the old wooden crib, the lace coverlet, the red-gold hair of the pale-tan child, kicking and squirming and screaming.

Hammond's mouth twisted as if he were in sudden physical pain. But it was the torment, the darkening shadows that swirled in his eyes, that frightened her.

He moved his gaze back to her face. He did not glance again toward the child crying in that crib. "That sucker yourn?" he said.

She was unable to speak. She barely nodded her head, affirmatively.

His bleak, sun-faded blue eyes impaled her. He stared at her coldly for a long time. She could not guess his thoughts. His face was a stranger's face. It was as if he had never seen her before, did not even know her and, as far as he was concerned, the crying infant did not exist.

After an eternal moment of taut silence, he turned and limped from the room. He closed the door behind him. For a long time, Ellen stayed where she was, unmoving.

Days passed slowly after that for Ellen, the dread and terror building inside her. She began to feel as if she herself no longer existed. Master Hammond never came near her. She never saw him inside the house, except by accident—on the stairs, passing in the cavernous upper hallways. She waited, each time, holding her breath, but he did not speak to her. He seemed not even to see her.

The first night Hammond was home, Ellen bathed in hot water steaming in a galvanized tub. She soaped herself, washing away any trace of musk which might offend her master.

She dressed in her nicest hand-stitched gown, and she waited. She paced her bedroom as if it were a cage, waiting. Her heart pounded—her future depended on her pleasing her master in his bed; she dreaded his accusations. She had no idea what she could say to Hammond when he demanded to know the truth about Herman Hengst. She waited. Hammond did not send for her. . . .

Candles and lamps and woodfires were extinguished in the

manor house and across the quarters. The farm grew dark and silent. Silence spread blanketlike over the estate.

She shivered. The waiting was unbearable. It had been many years since Hammond Maxwell had lived in this house, since she had lain, his concubine, beside him on his bed. But now she recalled suddenly and desperately what had happened to those girls who had preceded her in Hammond's favor.

He used these bed wenches until, pregnant and bulky, they became repugnant to him. Then he returned them to the quarters, where they either delivered a mustee sucker to be sold as a Falconhurst "fancy" or, thick-bellied with child, the girl herself was sold off on some slave vendue in New Orleans or out at Natchez. Pregnant dams brought a better price than empty vessels.

She shuddered, gazing about the candlelit room. Every dark corner loomed black, a threatening cavernous pit.

Hammond was angered, enraged. But if only he would allow her in his bed, she would make it up to him—somehow! But she couldn't go on waiting like this to learn his judgment upon her. The silence was as terrifying as the dark rages she saw in his eyes.

She looked about helplessly. She didn't know what to do. She had been almost ten years a part of this household, in status far below the white people—poor old Warren Maxwell before he was slain, Cousin Charlie Woodford, Doc Redfield, all the whites who came as guests or buyers, lower even than the mustee Herman Hengst. Yet she had become accustomed to a life many levels above the existence of field hands or slaves awaiting a coffle to market.

She had lived in a half-world of her own, waited on by the house servants, deferred to, slightly above them—all except Lucretia Borgia, who bowed only to God Himself.

What was her place now? Could she become a kitchen drudge, an upstairs maid, a cleaning slavey? Would she be exiled to the quarters—sold to some passing itinerant slave trader? And little Rachel—what would Master Hammond do to *her* in his rage?

She walked to the window. Not even the softly shadowed outside world of night looked like a place of freedom to her now. Only a wall of darkness reared before her.

But she was youthful, still buoyed by hope peculiar to the young. She was confident of her charms. Hadn't Herman Hengst chosen her above all the other slave women at Falconhurst? Herman was a handsome, virile, powerful young man who could have any woman he wanted, white or black—and he had wanted her all these months.

Thinking about Herman, she felt her heart sink. Where was he?

When was he coming back to Falconhurst? She was fevered with the need to know and yet there was no way she could find answers to any of her questions.

At last, after waiting night after night, she made up her mind to face the moment of truth with Hammond. She could beg for another chance, she could make him listen, enraged as he was. She had confidence in her physical charms, in the wiles she'd practiced in Herman's loving arms. She had no desire for Hammond, but her chance for existence lay in her appeasing him.

She brushed her hair until it gleamed in the lamplight. She chose the prettiest of the gowns she'd inherited—eight years ago!—from Hammond Maxwell's deceased young wife. She let herself out of her door, closed it quietly behind her. She did not need a candle to light her way down the steps—her service in this house had begun in Hammond's bedroom, and it had become Herman's room while Hammond was away.

Her heart pounding, her stomach empty and queasy, she went slowly, cautiously, down the dark, narrow stairwell. Silence pressed in upon her like a suffocating mask.

Holding her breath, she tiptoed along the corridor to the bedroom prepared for Hammond's return. She inhaled deeply, reached out, touched the knob, tried to turn it. The door was locked.

She retreated a step. She felt as if she had been struck across the face. She gazed around emptily in the darkness, far more frightened than she had ever been before.

The next morning Ellen woke sick at her stomach.

The baby's crying set Ellen to trembling. "Be quiet," she whispered, pleading. She dreaded it when Rachel cried, afraid the sound would enrage and offend the master. All she could hope was that perhaps if Master Hammond didn't see or hear the baby, he would forget her. "Oh God, Scandal . . . please be quiet."

Ham did not send for her this morning. He did not come near her.

Ellen waited in a hallway until Mem shuffled near. "Mem," she whispered.

Mem paused, looking at her vacantly, filled with his own woes, barely able to concentrate on her. "What you want, Miss Ellen?"

"What does Masta Ham say, Mem?"

" 'Bout what, Miss Ellen?" Mem trembled, checking over his shoulders both ways along the morning corridor. He had learned, to his distress, that the very walls of this old farmhouse had ears.

"About me." Ellen dug her fingernails into Mem's wrist.

"Ain't heard him say nuthin' 'bout you, Miss Ellen. I swear."

"What about—my baby?"

Mem shook his graying head. "Ain't heard."

"When's Masta Herman Hengst coming home?"

Mem tried to pull away. "Ain't heard a blessed thing 'bout that neither. Swear, I ain't heard nuthin'."

Trembling, Ellen released her grip on the aging butler's arm. He sighed heavily and hurried away, anxious to be away from her, as if afraid to be seen in her company.

Ellen bit back the sickness that rose up in her throat. She looked about, distracted. Even the slaves felt the tension. They were afraid to be seen near her, afraid to be caught talking to her. She looked around, feeling trapped, wanting to run, but knowing there was nowhere to run.

Fear. Uncertainty. Silence. She lived with a sense of unknowable doom hanging over her.

She lived in terror magnified inside her own mind. She raced around the same thought interminably, as if on a treadmill. She was reduced to a jittery wraith, slinking across rooms, hiding in corners, listening at doorways. She jumped at shadows, shivered convulsively at sudden noises. She was unable to eat, unable to sleep.

She watched the faces of the others furtively, convinced a conspiracy of silence existed against her. The worst possible fate was planned for her—Hammond Maxwell was vengeful, intolerant, without compassion, violent in rages. They knew all the details of her fate, but no one would tell her anything.

Then one morning as she crossed the empty kitchen, she heard voices from the front of the house—Master Hammond's voice riding over Miss Lucretia Borgia's. She was drawn toward the sound as filings to a magnet.

Her heart sinking, Ellen slipped into the dining room and crossed it stealthily. She went into the shadowed corridor. The voices were clearer now, close by; she could understand everything they said. She pressed against the wall, listening.

"We is all truly happy you is home, Masta Ham. This be the happiest time of my life," Lucretia Borgia was saying. Her tone was placating, as if Master Hammond had been finding fault.

"It ain't the same," Ham said. "No . . . Papa's dead . . . and Ellen . . . ain't nuthin' the same."

"Ellen be the same, Masta. Same sweet chile as when you left. Ellen, she loves you, Masta. Like always."

He swore, his voice rising, then subsiding. "No. Ellen, she git herself knocked up . . . by that mustee Hengst."

"You knowed?"

"I knowed. Anybody'd of knowed. Cain't no way nobody look at that sucker of hern—that light-colored hair on a nigger's drop! Who could not know?"

"It was a long time you was away, Masta. Ellen, she was a young wench. She'd knowed nobody but you . . . for many years she waited quiet—"

"Like I warned her—"

"Like you tole her . . . but she was hardly more'n a chile when you went away."

"Yes . . . I try to recollect that . . . when I think what I got to do . . . But it ain't easy forgivin' that wench what she done, Lucretia Borgia. She *mine* . . . I done tole her that plain and clear afore I left here."

"I know you did, Masta. Can't nobody ever say you didn't tell her plain. . . . But it a long time. That Masta Herman a powerful handsome young dude . . . he took over like he purentee white after yo' pa died."

There was a brief, taut silence. Then, "Pa—didn't die. Pa was murdered, wasn't he?"

Lucretia Borgia did not answer. Ellen remained pressed against the wall, sweated. They had veered away from discussing her directly, yet all they said concerned her, her life and her baby's life, from this moment.

Ham's voice came to her from the front room, low but distinct and insistent. "I see Masta Cousin Charlie Woodford is buried out there in the Falconhurst burial plot—along with my folks." This was an accusation.

"He was your own cousin, Masta. Your daid wife's own brother."

"Cousin Charlie, he kilt my pa, didn't he?" When Lucretia Borgia did not reply, he persisted, though he knew it unseemly, even fatal, for a black to speak against a white person. And Lucretia Borgia knew the rules. She knew her place. "You can talk straight to me, Lucretia Borgia. You know you can."

Lucretia Borgia's sigh was massive. "Cousin Charlie, he choke your pa. Tryin' to make him tell where them pots of money was buried. . . . Cousin Charlie would of kilt poor Masta Warren, but Masta Herman, he stopped him—"

"Masta Herman! My God. That damned white mustee. Brass Door. That's his true nigger name. Seems like Herman is mixed up in everything that went on round Falconhurst whilst I was away."

"Don't know what we'd done here at Falconhurst, Masta Ham, if it wasn't for Masta Herman—uh, Brass Door. If'n he don't pretend he purentee white—them powerful and greedy white men—they could've took over Falconhurst whilst you was away. They could have come in an' taken over. None of us black folks could've stopped them white people from takin' this place. . . . Masta Herman, he saved Falconhurst for you." She exhaled heavily again. "Hate him or not, you got to credit him that."

Ham's voice was low, but chilled and savage, without a trace of gratitude. "I credit him. I do. I take what he done in my considerin', whatever I do. . . . But for now, I tell you this, Lucretia Borgia, I don't want that Masta Herman's name mentioned at Falconhurst, ever again. . . . You understand me? Won't have no biggety nigger actin' like he purentee white, bossin' this place, no matter what the color of his skin."

"Yassuh, Masta. You kin straighten all that out when Brass Door come back home."

"Come back? He ain't nevah comin' back to Falconhurst. He better not nevah set foot on my land, or I whup his bones bare and bleedin' . . . God knows that's what my insides tell me to do anyhow. But he ain't coming back."

Lucretia Borgia sighed again. "Yassuh, Masta Ham. I purely understands."

"I met him in New Orleans. On my way home from the Texies. He lucky I didn't kill him there—pretendin' he good as a white man, turkey-struttin' around in fine clothes, representin' Falconhurst and Hammond Maxwell. . . . Well, I paid him off for what he done here. And he nevah comin' back. And his name ain't nevah to be spoke on this farm. You understand me?"

Ellen sagged against the corridor wall. Her eyes burned, welled in tears which did not quench the fire. Her throat felt choked. Her fists locked at her sides. She felt bereft as if by death itself.

She heard a whisper of sound behind her and heeled around, gasping.

She stared helplessly at Mem. He limped in from the kitchen on tender feet, smelling of corn whiskey. He opened his mouth to speak, his face contorted in disapproval at finding her eavesdropping in the shadowed hallway.

She slapped her fist against her lips, motioning Mem to silence, pleading. He closed his mouth, but continued to shake his head, gaze jaundiced.

Ellen ran to him, her dress rustling in the silent house. She caught Mem's arm, pressed him back into the dining room. Standing there, sick with panic, she waited for Master Hammond's heavy tread. But the two people in the living room were too intent upon their own dialogue, they had not heard her rustling clothing. She breathed out, sighing as if she'd been holding her breath for hours.

More questions than ever swarmed in Ellen's mind, questions she was compelled to ask, questions for which only those two people in that front room had answers. But all doubts would remain unanswered now. Despondent, she followed Mem into the kitchen.

Mem trembled. His voice castigated her. "Lawsy, Miss Ellen. What you doin'? You could git yo'self stripped naked and whupped, sneakin 'round listening on white people. . . . You git *me* whupped—for not sayin' against you."

"You won't say against me, will you, Mem?"

Mem hesitated. He licked at his thick lips. This was too deep a question for him to answer easily. Like the ancient Romans, Hammond Maxwell often punished the bearer of bad tidings. Mem had learned, too, however, the terrible punishment meted out to the nigger who did not speak up when some matter concerned the master. He'd swung often by his heels and felt the merciless cut of the whip. His back was scarred in mute testimony. He shivered, in a no-win situation.

"You gits up to yo' room," Mem said at last. "You stop that sneakin' round. Listenin'."

"I will, Mem. I swear. But I so scairt. Fo' me and my baby. . . . What's Masta Ham gone do, Mem? What will he do to me?"

Mem winced. "Done tole you. I don't know that, Miss Ellen." He shook his head, his eyes grave. "Can only say—whatever it is, ain't likely to be pleasant. Masta Ham's right fearful when he's riled up and roused to rage . . . and that's the truth."

3

In the living room, Hammond Maxwell sat in his father's old easy chair, his game leg stretched out straight and awkwardly before him. A fire leaped and lunged in the fireplace, blazing desultorily in a deep bed of gray ashes. That damned Mem had neglected another chore. One more mark chalked against the lazy nigger;

that Mem was begging for the whip. All of this added to Hammond's sense of acrimony. Inside, he seethed with rages, but his anger was all mixed with sadness and pain and self-pity. For one of the first times in his life, Hammond Maxwell was less than totally sure of himself. He continued to stare into the fire in silence, aware that Lucretia Borgia remained unmoving beside his chair.

At last he glanced up and tried to smile at Lucretia Borgia, in white apron, the bright-red bandanna knotted on her head as old as his earliest memories of her. He pointed to a straight chair facing the hearth and blue-tinged flame. "Set."

She hesitated. "Tain't seemly, Masta."

"Set. You can set when I tell you to set." He forced his lips to smile. But agony swirled in his eyes and pulled his mouth taut. Lucretia Borgia felt a rush of pity for her master. She sat down and folded her dark hands against the snowy whiteness of her apron.

For some moments they sat without speaking, watching the faulty flaring of the fire in deep ashes and damp wood. Lucretia Borgia made a mental note to skin Mem's hide, but she did not speak.

Ham said, "Want to say, Lucretia Borgia, you done a tol'able job runnin' Falconhurst whilst I was away. Papa sick and dyin' an' all. You did good. Did better'n anyone else could've—white or black. I proud of you. You a smart nigger wench. Sometime I swear you almost human, Lucretia Borgia."

"Thankee, Masta Hammond, suh. Knowed I had to keep Falconhurst goin' for you. I knowed that. Couldn't bear to see it go to ruin—or taken over by some no-good—fo'give me—greedy white man. . . . I *knowed* you was comin' home. . . . I meant and determined you to have Falconhurst to come home to."

Ham watched the listless fire. "Reckon that Mem ain't been much help."

"Mem's gittin' old, Masta. Mem do what he can. He got plenty houseboys round here to help him—he jus' plain forgetful, and them nigger boys, they wuthless less'n you after 'em all the time."

"That Mem. He stay drunk all the time. Think I don't know. All the time sneakin' good corn whiskey. Thinkin' I can't tell. He needs a tech of the lash, that what he needs. That's what he gits—soon's ever I get round to it."

Lucretia Borgia wanted to protest—whatever lack was in Mem was innate; the lash had never improved him, it had only broken and scarred him. But she said nothing. She searched

Master Ham's face, saw the pain and hurt and rage at war in it. She was wise enough to know that inner agony had to come spewing out—like the pus and putrefaction festering in a skin boil—or a man couldn't live inside himself. Especially a proud and lofty white man like Hammond Maxwell.

"That Mem's a goddam disgrace to Falconhurst," Ham went on. Lucretia Borgia saw that though Master Hammond vented his rage on Mem, his true anger was directed elsewhere. He would come to it. She nodded and waited.

Ham spat toward the fire. "Mem, he lackin' in respect, too. . . . I shorely gon' have Mem stripped and spanceled in the barn—no less 'n twenty lashes. Do him good. Do the rest of them wuthless niggers good to see the master is back. That black bastid Mem, he got to learn his place."

The master of Falconhurst lapsed into silence and Lucretia Borgia waited for him to speak again. When the silence persisted and stretched taut in the room so that the buzzing of a bottle fly at the window was annoyingly loud, she said, "Lawsy, Masta Ham, suh, it's sho' good to have you home. Goin' to git them niggers steppin' high round here now you home."

"Whoa up," Hammond said. "Yo' still runnin' things, Lucretia Borgia? You mighty biggety, me home an' all. Don't you fo'git, you jus' a nigger, too. You can feel the tech of the lash same as the blackest nigger in the quarters yonder." His words were cold, but he smiled through the pull of sadness in his face.

Lucretia Borgia lifted her eyes toward heaven and shook her red-wrapped head. "Lawsy. Jus' plumb got in the habit, Masta. All these years. Had to give orders when they ain't nobody else here to give 'em. But you home now. My own dear Masta Ham done come home. Ain't no need of me a-bossin' this place no more. No suh. Masta Ham, he home to stay."

"Yes. I am home to stay. . . . But they got to be some changes, Lucretia Borgia. You know that. A lot of changes."

"Yas, suh?"

Hammond gazed around the old familiar room, the aged furniture, odds and ends from other years and other plans, a texture without any design any more. Old, ugly, useless. Falconhurst seemed to have altered little, all the years he was away.

"But you people has changed," he said aloud as if Lucretia Borgia followed the tangled skein of his thoughts. "Little Miss Sophie. My own flesh and blood. Nine year old and hardly know her. Growin' up wild as a weed." He shrugged. Little Sophie had gazed at him from her crossed blue eyes—so like Cousin Charlie Woodford's—without interest. These people had changed in ways that discomfited him. It hurt him to admit it, but Lucretia Borgia looked older, tireder, her eyes dulled with ancient sadness, old as her race. Her dulled eyes added years to her age. He wouldn't have it. She had been a monolith of strength and comfort since his own childhood. He *needed* her.

His mouth twisted bitterly. Other things had changed, too. Ellen was no longer the lissome bed wench he had dreamed back to sometimes across the Texies. He had no desire for her now, though he had walked into her room that first day meaning to crawl her within the first five minutes, so much built-up hunger, pent-up need. But Ellen had betrayed him with another man. And not even with a human being, but with a mustee nigger. Mustees were still black animals, no matter how white the skin. And whenever he was near Ellen now, there was the sour stench of fear about her, as if she sweated fear from her pores, from her armpits. He shook his head. He had been a long time away from nigger musk. And now Ellen offended his nostrils, as she offended his sense of morality.

His hands clenched on the chair arm. There was more than a sense of physical repulsion toward Ellen. There was the agonizing knowledge that she had gone naked to that mustee's bed. That blond-headed mustee sucker in that crib up there was the nigger's git. He had never taken seconds, and damned if he would take them now. He would never stand in a line for any woman—and certainly he would never share her with a white-skinned nigger.

He returned his gaze to Lucretia Borgia. Though she looked older, fatigued, she remained the solid base on which his whole life rested. She had nursed him when he was a child. Her tenderness had helped him through the agony of a broken leg which never healed right. The years had added inches to her girth, swollen her massive breasts, but inside surely to God she had not changed. Nobody in this world loved and cared for him as this black woman did.

He bit his lip, feeling the tears well in his throat and aching. He yearned to bury his face on her bosom and weep as he had when he was a child. There was so much more sadness to wail out now. His father dead. Ellen faithless and suckling some nigger's git. But he remained where he was, his face cold and set. He said, "You ain't tole that Ellen gal that I be a-wantin' her for my bed wench any more, have you?"

Lucretia Borgia rose to her feet and stood before him, firelight warm on her light-chocolate-colored face. "Oh no, Masta." She shook her head.

"Well, I ain't wantin' her." His voice was adamant. She recognized the tone. He had made up his mind. This was an irrevocable decision.

She waited a long time, watching the guttering flame, then she said, "What 'bout Ellen, Masta?"

Ham shook his head. "I don't know. I ain't made up my mind yet. It ain't easy for me. I ax myself what 'bout her. And ax. And ax. I don't know. For now—she can stay on here in the house, I reckon. Leastways till I make up my mind what final to do with her. She been here too long to send back out to the cabins. Reckon she got to keep her mustee sucker with her, too—whilst I make up my mind. Don't no-way believe in lettin' a sucker stay with its dam past weanin'. They gits attached. You know that, Lucretia Borgia. But they's good blood in her sucker. A fancy, light-skinned wench when she's growed. Bring a right fair price if I put it on the market."

She started to speak, but did not because she dared not oppose her master in any way. Somehow it seemed wrong that the daughter of Herman Hengst be sold as a common slave after all Herman had done for Falconhurst. But she also knew this is what would happen, and her protesting would only speed the matter.

Ham watched Lucretia Borgia narrowly. When she did not protest his decision, or speak against him, he exhaled heavily. He purely would not abide an uppity nigger. She might as well be reminded of that, right off.

At last he said, "You done a good job here whilst I was away, Lucretia Borgia. Everything fine round here. Got a good crop of bucks comin' of age to market. I won't never fo'git all you done."

"Thankee, Masta Ham."

"Yes sir. Things are good here at Falconhurst. On account of you and the good work you done. Got us money buried in them pots. Got us a good herd of blacks to sell. An' a good crop comin' fo' next year."

"Yassuh. Things is good at Falconhurst."

"Except this here ole house. Papa always a 'tellin 'bout buildin' a new house but he never did git round to it. His grandpappy built a log house in this clearin' right here. An' my grandpappy built this nine-room clapboard. Hit good enough. Plain and common house for its time. Right fancy, as a fact, for these parts in them olden times. When Papa married my mother—from the Hammond family of Anglebranch Plantation—he planned to build something fine for her. Might've too, could've afforded it easy an' all, but when Ma passed away, Papa jus' kinda lost interest in a new house."

"This ole place mighty comfortable."

"Comfortable. But plain. An' old. I aim to build the kind of house Papa planned—only bigger and finer. If little Miss Sophie is to grow up to be a fine white lady she ought to have a great lovely house where them fine young gentlemen can come callin'. House so lovely they fo'git all about the cross of Sophie's pore li'l eyes." He stood up beside his chair and pointed through a window to a knoll which reared against the sky, the highest elevation on the estate. "Yonder. Past the buryin' ground. Over there on that risin' hill, we a-goin' to build us a new house, Lucretia Borgia. Goin' to be the best goddam house in all Alabama. Folks come from far away as Charleston jus' to look at it. Goin' to be a brick house and have big white pillars out front. Goin' to have fifteen—maybe twenty—big rooms and new furniture from New Orleans—all covered with silk and velvet—grand enough fo' li'l Sophie—maybe even grand enough for some white lady . . . in case I decide to take me a new wife."

Lucretia Borgia stared at her master, thunderstruck. Too often she'd overheard his confessing—bragging—to other white planters of his decision never to marry again. His first marriage to his cousin Blanche had been disastrous from the wedding night. He couldn't stomach the pale sickly lily-white flesh of naked white women.

Lucretia Borgia shook her head, awed. "What you say, Masta?"

He laughed. "Say I goin' to build the grandest goddam mansion in all Alabama."

"Not that part. That other part—'bout some white lady you might marry."

He struck fire with a sulfur match to a hand-rolled cigar. His face was briefly illumined and shadowed. His smile was almost gentle. "It ain't to be talked about. Might fail and I won't have people laughin' at me. But I has met a white lady. In New Orleans. Nuthin' settled, you understand. Name of Miss Augusta. . . . If ever I do marry again—it be Miss Augusta—or nobody. . . . But I couldn't never bring a fine, gentle lady like Miss Augusta to a place like this ole farmhouse. Ain't nearly grand enough."

Tears of happiness welled in Lucretia Borgia's eyes. She dabbed at her cheeks with her apron. "Oh, Masta Ham, my heart jus' bustin' full of happiness to hear you say that. Miss Sophie need a mother an' you needs yo'self a lovely lady."

He nodded, drawing deeply on his cigar. "Yes. But that got to wait. Got to be some changes round here first, Lucretia Borgia. Some big changes."

Ellen waited until she heard Miz Lucretia Borgia ordering her kitchen help about, then she slowly descended the rear steps.

Ellen stared at Miz Lucretia Borgia hopefully, but the huge woman ignored her. Ellen's sense of nonexistence was magnified inside her mind. She wanted to ask her questions of Lucretia Borgia. If anyone had the answers, Lucretia Borgia did. But watching her, Ellen hesitated. She wanted to pour out her questions, but did she want to hear Lucretia Borgia's answers?

Ellen caught Miz Lucretia Borgia by the arm. Lucretia Borgia shook free impatiently, her face darkening. "I busy, gal. What you want?"

"I can't stand this no more, Miz Lucretia Borgia."

"You stand what you got to stand. We all do. You can't stand what?"

"This silence . . . this not knowin' . . . what goin' to happen to me, Miz Lucretia Borgia? My baby?"

Lucretia Borgia hesitated. The stern look in her creamy chocolate face softened. She gazed at Ellen, if not in love—she was far too honest to pretend anything she didn't feel, except toward white people—at least with vestiges of compassion. "What make you think anything gone happen to you, gal?"

"Masta Ham. He ain't come near me, Miz Lucretia Borgia. He ain't sent for me. . . . I heard him a-talkin' with you. . . ."

"Nigger listens, nigger deserve what she hears."

"I'm going crazy like this."

"You is gettin' addle-pated an' you listen when Masta Ham a-talkin' in private."

"I know I crazy. I feel crazy inside. Scared. 'Cause I know Masta Ham he mad. He raging mad. About me. And my baby. Do he know Masta Herman is the papa?"

"I reckon he do."

"Oh God . . . I fell in love with Masta Herman, Miz Lucretia Borgia. Wasn't something I wanted. Couldn't help myself. Masta Herman so brave. And strong. And handsome. And he did save us all. . . . I couldn't fight against what I felt. I loved him."

Lucretia Borgia shook her head. "Nigger wenches got no right fallin' in love. Love. That's for white people, not for folks like us."

Ellen nodded, sagging without hope. "But what am I going to do, Miz Lucretia Borgia? What can I do?"

Lucretia Borgia shook her head slowly. "That's all up to Masta Ham now. Ain't no sense a-lyin' to you. I been here at Falconhurst a long time. Most of my life. I seen everything happen that can happen—sometimes twice. I has seen Masta Ham, and his pa Masta Warren too, sell off his bed wenches when he tired of them. . . . I seed Masta Ham kill his prize Mandingo when that nigger boy went against him. . . . Masta Ham a good man—good as airy white man I ever see. But when he ragin' inside, he different. When his heart broke, he different. . . . He plumb go out of his mind, and nuthin' you can say can git in to his heart. You cain't no way reach him or make him listen. God knows, in my time I tried."

"Oh God."

Lucretia Borgia nodded and smiled in a sour way. "Maybe God will help you, gal. . . . I can't lie to you and say things a-goin' on jus' like they been. We both know better. All I can say is fo' you to face the truth. The truth is, life ain't easy, an' life ain't fair, and the truth is, yo' is black. You is a slave. You Masta Ham's slave. You done gone against him . . . you had yo' fun. Now, one way or another . . . you got to pay for it."

4

"Pack yo' belongings, Miss Ellen," Mem said. "Pack whatever you want to take with you. Masta say."

Ellen stood as if at bay in the middle of her bedroom and stared at the aged butler, at the retinue of houseboys and maidservants in his wake. She shook her head. "Where I goin', Mem?"

"Don't know," Mem said.

"Masta . . . he done sold me?" Ellen could barely whisper the words.

Mem spread his hands helplessly. His face showed how troubled he was, but he had his orders, directly from Master Ham himself and reinforced by Miz Lucretia Borgia, who kept reminding him all the way up the stairwell that the master said Ellen was to take anything she wished from her room. Mem sighed raggedly. "Masta sent us up heah to help you pack, Miss Ellen. Masta say."

Ellen gazed at the bleak faces of the other slaves. They looked as helpless as she felt. She stood in the middle of her room, unmoving, unable to move or think clearly.

"Tell us what to pack, Miss Ellen," Mem urged her. "We do it all fo' you, Miss Ellen." The maids and houseboys nodded in agreement.

But Ellen remained immobilized. They all remained helplessly until Miz Lucretia Borgia pushed her way into the room. Her voice lashed them. "What you-all a-doin'? You heard the Masta, Mem. He say he have the buckboard ready, soon's ever Ellen is packed."

"Where-at he takin' me, Miz Lucretia Borgia?" Ellen whispered.

"Don't know." Miz Lucretia Borgia shook her head emphatically. "An' that's gospel truth. No sense naggin' at me 'cause I don't know. . . . But Masta say kindly, you is to take anything you want. You want all your clothes?"

Ellen managed to nod her head. Miz Lucretia Borgia swung her arm in a silent command and maids took the dresses, petticoats and gowns from the closets and piled them on the bed. Then, under Miz Lucretia Borgia's direction, they folded the garments carefully and placed them in an old steamer trunk. A pinewood box was neatly stacked with the needlepoint quilts and sewing Ellen had created and accumulated over the years. The houseboys began removing the articles from the room, taking them down the rear stairwell and out to the kitchen stoop.

In a few moments, the room looked bare. "You kin take your bed along if'n you want, Ellen," Lucretia Borgia said. "Masta say—whatever you want."

Ellen nodded. The old bed with rope springs was dismantled, carted out. Finally, Miz Lucretia Borgia took the infant Scandal in her arms and the crib was carried from the room.

Ellen stood as if in a catatonic trance gazing about this room which had been her prison, refuge and haven since she was twelve years old. Her throat ached, her eyes burned, but she was unable to cry. She was too numbed with fears of the unknown and unknowing to weep.

And now the room was bare. It appeared slightly larger with the curtains down from the windows and morning sunlight steaming in, etching a mishapen gray rectangle across the lye-scrubbed flooring.

"We best go now," Miz Lucretia Borgia said, voice gentle. "Masta Ham, he be waitin'."

Ellen nodded but was unable to move. Mem put his arm about her and they followed Miz Lucretia Borgia, who carried the infant into the hallway and down the stairwell.

Ellen did not look back, but she clung to Mem's arm, afraid she would fall.

When they crossed the kitchen and went out on the stoop, Ellen hesitated, unable to go farther. Her belongings had been piled and secured in the rear of a buckboard. Master Ham sat on the box, lines gripped loosely in his fists, awaiting her. He did not meet her gaze; he didn't glance toward her. He sat calmly, neither impatient nor any longer uncertain. Whatever it proved to be, his decision was made and nothing would alter it. His face was set, but not cold, angered or unkindly.

Staring at Master Ham, Ellen sobbed and sagged against the doorjamb. Mem tried to urge her forward, but she was unable to move, afraid her legs would not support her.

"What's wrong with her?" Master Ham said to Lucretia Borgia, who waited beside the vehicle with Ellen's baby.

"She all right," Lucretia Borgia said, nodding. "She jus' all worked up, Masta Ham, suh. First time she evah been off this place. She a little scairt. She be all right."

"Nothing to be scairt of," Master Ham said loudly, gazing up at Ellen now. "Come on, gal. Don't be wastin' my time. We got a ways to go."

Mem caressed Ellen's arm reassuringly and urged her forward. Ellen walked slowly across the narrow gray-scrubbed stoop and down the wide planked steps. She moved toward the rear of the carriage, but Master Ham said. "You can set up here."

Mem helped Ellen up into the front seat beside Master Hammond. Lucretia Borgia passed the baby up to Ellen. Ellen took the child, afraid her arms would sag, allowing it to fall.

Master Hammond wasted no more time. Many slaves had gathered around the rear of the house, the curious, those who loved Ellen, and those who disliked her uppity ways. They stood silently, squinting in the sun, troubled, watchful. They had never seen one of the slaves leave Falconhurst in quite this fashion.

Master Ham slapped the reins across the rumps of the horses, and the loaded buckboard rolled forward along the lane toward the main road.

Ellen knotted her fists in the baby's coverlet, fought to keep her mounting hysteria under control. Deep in the pit of her stomach she felt herself shaking and sobbing and laughing wildly, all these conflicting sounds and emotions threatening to rage upward out of her, spewing like vomitus.

She heard some of the slaves calling farewells to her. She turned on the seat and looked back at the old house, the familiar surroundings where she'd lived all her life. She was certain she would never see this place again. She shivered convulsively and gritted her teeth together tightly.

"Thought a lot on comin' back home to you—takin' you ag'in as my bed wench, I did," Master Ham said. Regret chilled his tone. "Recollect how I got mighty fevered thinkin' ahead to how it would be. . . ."

"Yes, Masta." Ellen stared straight ahead, seeing nothing, her eyes blurred with tears.

Master Hammond glanced at the whiteness of the child in her arms, the light-yellow hair, the delicate cut of its features. "Didn't no-way count on this—you droppin' the Dutchman's git an' all."

"No, Masta." She managed to whisper the words through her constricted throat.

"Know all about it, I do. Can't help hatin' him. Not only for pesterin' you like he done. Passin' hisself off as a white man. That I can't no-way stomach. Ought to be strung up, he ought." He nodded his head with cold emphasis. "I string him up, if ever he comes back here." Then he waved his arm. "But ain't no sense lyin' to me now. I know how you pleasured him, birthed his git. I see now that Lucretia Borgia lied to me that first day I come back. Sayin' you was jus' takin' care of a child what belong to a wench who died birthin' it. . . . But I knowed—minute I seed the sucker—an' its fair colorin' an' all—I knowed it was the mustee's git out'n you, a octoroon. . . . But I got to credit you, Ellen. You didn't try to lie to me."

"Where-at you-all a-takin' me, Masta?" the slave girl asked, terror making her teeth chatter.

"Ain't none of yo' goddam business what I intends to do," Ham answered. "I dŏ, what I think is best. Ain't yo' place to question me." He shook his head. "You nevah did truly learn yo' place, Ellen. . . . Reckon I partly to blame. Pa said I spoilt you. Treated you too easy. Tech of a buggy whip now an' ag'in, maybe none of this would of happened."

"I ain't nevah had no home but Falconhurst, Masta."

"Dammit, gal. There you go ag'in, talkin' up to me like you white. You ain't white, dammit. You got nigger blood. You a nigger. Don't give a damn in hell the color of yo' skin. My pa always did say he preferred a black nigger to a light-skinned one ever' blessed time. Don't know but what I agrees with him total. . . . Now you listen to me, Ellen gal. I don't no-way have to explain myself to you. I the master. You jus' a slave. A black slave. You ain't nuthin' else—till I say you somethin' else. You understand me?"

Ellen nodded, trying to appease him, but she had no inkling of what he was talking about. His words were merely jarring and discordant sounds rattling around inside the confusion already moiling in her mind.

They rode in silence into the village of Benson. Men spoke warmly to Hammond, welcoming him back from Texas. They stared at the mulatto woman on the seat beside him, the meager furnishings roped in the rear of the buckboard.

Ham wiped the back of his hand across his mouth as they passed Pearl's Tavern, but did not slow down though the sight of the place made him thirsty and stirred old memories of the days when he'd fought the Mandingo Mede against the best fighting niggers in the country. The tavern owner, Pearl Remmick, stood in the doorway. He smiled and nodded, greeting the plantation owner.

Ham pulled the buckboard in before the old county courthouse building. The courtyard was scabbed with grass straggling in bearded patches under a dusty miscellany of trees, tupelos, maples, chestnuts, oaks and elms. Men lounged on plank benches in the shade. None spoke. They were beneath the slave breeder in status and it was unseemly for them to speak unless he spoke first. He barely glanced toward them. They touched their hats when he passed and bobbed their heads, but they did not speak and kept their gazes lowered.

Ham said to Ellen, "Now you wait quiet here. You understand?"

Ellen nodded, rigid. She sat, too fevered to perspire even in the midmorning heat. She felt the gazes of the white men gouging at her. She heard their whispered voices but not their words.

At last she saw Ham emerge from the double doors of the lower courthouse hallway and come down the wide stone steps. He was smiling.

He came to the side of the buckboard and held out something toward her. Ellen stared at the official document, sealed and printed with portentous black ornate border. She dared not touch it. "Take it," Ham said. "It's yourn."

Her lips quivered. "What is it, Masta?"

"It's your freedom papers."

She shook her head. "What?"

"That's what it is. I went in there and got yo' manumitted. . . . You know what that is—manumitted?"

Ellen trembled. "No, Masta."

"You is free, Ellen. You ain't a slave no more." He gestured with his outflung arm toward the men lounging in the shade. "Yo' is free. Free as any white man you see."

They left Benson and drove east on a miserably rutted road through farm lands and deepening forests. The roadway was wretched, infrequently traveled, overgrown in places. Silence hung oppressively in the thick hammocks.

A rattlesnake slithered across the trace ahead of the horses. The animals reared in their gear, but Ham's firm hand on the lines kept them under control. A deer crossed a few yards in front of the trail, either terrified or curious, staring at them with round doe eyes, head tilted. Ham took up his rifle, but the animal lurched about suddenly and darted into the underbrush. Somehow, Ellen felt an unexplained sense of relief and she sighed aloud.

She gripped in her fist the manumission papers which Ham had given her. She had her freedom, but freedom was a word with little meaning for her. There was room in her mind only for a sense of terror—fear for the future, of the unknown, of what was to become of her and Scandal now that she was free—in exile from the security of Falconhurst. She had never even seen a freed black person. She'd heard from Mem and from Miz Lucretia Borgia that many thousand free persons of color lived in New Orleans. But all this seemed distant, unreal.

"Reckon it all going to work out best this way," Ham said. "You the first slave I ever set free, Ellen. Hope you appreciates what that means. Never thought it would happen in this world. My pa never manumitted a single slave long as he lived. Didn't hold with it. Don't say as how I believe in it, either. . . . Sons of Ham born slaves, die slaves, like beasts of burden in the fields. Bible say. . . . But it different with you, gal. I give it a lot of thought."

"Yes, Masta."

He smiled tautly and shook his head. "I ain't yo' master no more, Ellen. You ain't got no master . . . you free. Long as you live—your chillun and they's chillun's chillun free forever. Cain't nobody enslave you no more. You got your papers, and it's on the record books, legal, back at Benson courthouse."

"Thankee, Masta." There was little emotion in her tone. She saw nothing ahead but the gloom of fear and loneliness and danger—and no one to turn to.

Ham shook his head. "Maybe I makin' a gyascutus mistake. Could've sold you and yo' sucker—pretty white-lookin' mulatto like you—for two, three thousand dollars, market like it is and white men yearnin' for a slave that looks like you."

She nodded, watching the deep forest slide slowly past on each side of them. All she could think was that each turn of these wheels took her farther from the security and familiar surrounding of Falconhurst. Fear fed on itself inside her empty belly.

"But that was part of it. Didn't hanker on sellin' you when I knowed what them white men what bought you wanted. They'd be buyin' you for a bed wench. . . . Didn't want that. Don't want you no mo' myself—"

"I sorry, Masta—"

"But I don't want you sold to be a bed wench. . . . Could of kept you on at Falconhurst—"

"Yes, Masta—"

"You could've tooken care of the younguns that we takes from their dams when they weaned. Along with your own. Thought 'bout that a lot. . . . But then I think if I marry this Miss Augusta, she might hear what you been to me—before. An' she might not like it. Might upset or disturb her. Make her unhappy. Reckon if I wasn't hopin' to marry Miss Augusta, I'd've done different by you. You might thank Miss Augusta. You might say yo' freedom is my weddin' gift—to Miss Augusta."

"I glad you gittin' married—"

"Don't know an' I am gittin' married. Thinkin' 'bout it." He sighed. "Miss Augusta a purentee genteel lady. She might turn me down. . . . But I'm makin' changes so maybe she won't."

"I glad, Masta. Fo' you."

"Buildin' a fine new house at Falconhurst. Want things nice for her. . . . Don't want nuthin' or nobody around that might upset her or remind her of unpleasant things—ladies bein' so genteel and all."

"Yes, Masta."

"So it come down to what I do with you. You nursin' the Dutchman's git an' all. I know I got to git shed of you from Falconhurst. Could sell you. Could even give you away if'n it please me. You be a fine breedin' nigger. . . . But then I think—this here baby—she belong to the Dutchman. The mustee. Brass Door. That Herman Hengst. No matter what else, he did save Falconhurst for me—"

"He did, Masta—"

"All right! I don't want to hear no more about it. . . . So Lucretia Borgia say Herman, he kindly taken with you. And he shore plant his seed in you. . . . So part of what I doin', I doin' for Brass Door and his git. . . . This way I got nuthin' on my conscience. I don't owe that mustee nuthin' no more. I don't owe nobody nuthin'."

The pale sun westered, flinging ragged and limber shadows across the trail when they rode into a settlement. A crude sign named the place Wilkes Corners. A general store, tavern and inn sat on the intersection of crossroads. Outside, a weathered sign held the single paint-scabbed word: Wilkes'.

A half-dozen houses and shacks clustered near the tavern. The lowland swamp seemed to grow heavily on all sides, bearding the village, encroaching and reclaiming with vines and tendrils and limbs. The place was somnolent. A few dogs ran out to bark at the buckboard but quickly lost interest and slunk back to the shade.

Ellen held her breath, disliking the quiet and isolation of the settlement. They had not eaten since breakfast, but Ham did not stop at the inn.

Less than a quarter of a mile from the tavern, he did turn off the main road into a cleared farm of twenty acres. "This is yo' home," he said. "I bought this here farm for you. It where you gon' live."

"Alone, Masta?"

He gazed at her, laughing, sad and faintly sardonic at the same time. "That's up to you," he said.

Ellen stood desolated as he loosened ropes and unloaded her belongings from the wagon. After a long moment, Ellen placed the baby in its crib on the front stoop and helped.

They carried in the trunk, boxes, the chairs, the bed, mattress. Ham set up the bed, tossed the mattress upon it. The afternoon was dreary but not chilled. He struck a fire in the fireplace.

He stood gazing into the flickering flames. "Send Mem and Jingo Jim over with some odds and ends from Falconhurst in a day or two. Stove. Table. Some chairs make this place look homey. Can give you some good things from the big house. Ain't takin' none of that furniture to the new mansion I'm building."

He knelt beside the stone hearth, his bad leg stretched uncomfortably behind him. From long habit, he took no notice of the physical discomfort. With his long-bladed hunting knife, he scratched out the mortar around an old brick. Then he took a pouch from his pocket. He shook it. Gold pieces rattled.

"Gold eagles," he told her. "Each one worth 'bout twenty dollars. Keep you for a while. You can buy supplies from Wilkes' store. Them Wilkeses, they white, but they treat you fair, likely—'cause you pay cash, you be a good customer."

He dropped the pouch of gold pieces into the hole, replaced the brick. He stood up, bracing himself against the mantel, and mashed the brick into line with the heel of his boot.

He stood then with his heel pressed down on the loose brick. "Reckon this be all I can do for you, Ellen. . . . You not far from Miss Dovie Verder at Dovecote Plantation. You need something, you tell her—she send word to Falconhurst. . . . It best like this, Ellen. We shed of you at Falconhurst—an' you free . . . free as long as you live."

5

Slowly, Ellen learned to live free. . . .

Loungers stood or sprawled on their spines across the stoop of Wilkes' store and laughed, nudging each other and winking, as they watched Ellen approach along the rutted clay road pushing her baby in a wheelbarrow. She wore a plain cotton dress, unprinted gray material that hung sacklike upon her, heavy shoes and a wide-brimmed straw sun hat that almost concealed her face.

The laughter was not taunting, amused but less than cruel. Ellen presented a comic sight, yet her baby carriage was utilitarian, practical and unaffected. Even Mr. and Mrs. Wilkes came out on the stoop to see what the commotion was.

Trout Wilkes stood medium height, with large balding head and quick, cunning eyes that darted like a ferret's and seldom rested anywhere for very long. He wore black worsted trousers, denim shirt, open at the collar with pink sleeve garters at his biceps, and a soiled apron like a baronial shield. He was proprietor of the general store, the leading business entrepreneur in the community, a man of status.

Portia Wilkes, at his side, her arm lifted to shield her eyes from the glare of the sun, was slender, a tired-looking woman about Ellen's age. She wore shapeless colorless dresses which she sewed herself from sack linings and bolt ends which Trout allowed her to use when there was no longer material enough to sell. Her hair was caught in a loose bun at the nape of her sunburned neck and seemed always about to fall loosely about her shoulders in untended strands. She was barefooted, ankles dust-darkened, and she carried a whimpering child slung against her hip. The infant appeared to be about Scandal's age.

"That there's some fancy baby carriage," one of the men said. He laughed and slapped his hip.

Ellen looked up, face taut, troubled. She had seldom even been as far away from Falconhurst at the village of Benson. She was completely unaccustomed to being the center of attention, to feeling the gazes of strangers fixed on her. The backs of her legs felt weak, and she longed in panic to run away. But this association with strangers was something that had to be faced in her new existence as a freedwoman. She managed to smile. "Hit totes her," she said.

"Surely it does," Portia Wilkes said, her voice kindly and

riding over the snickers of the loiterers. "Wishin' I had me a barrow to transport my Hester."

Ellen bent over and took Scandal up in her arms. She straightened and walked up the wide pine plank steps, smiling but tense and terrified. The idlers watched her curiously.

"You the new woman in the Deakins place, ain't you?" one man said.

Ellen hesitated on the step. She twisted her mouth into a faint smile. She nodded. "Name of Ellen Maxwell," she said.

"You *Miss* Ellen Maxwell?" A smirking man jabbed another with his elbow, snorting. Ellen was beautiful, shapely, even in her shapeless frock. Her tea-rose complexion gave her a beauty that made a man look again, think, and remember.

The other men grinned and leaned forward, awaiting Ellen's answer. She drew a deep breath and nodded. She was *Miss* Ellen. The loafers glanced at each other. They grinned, licked their lips, leered. But once of the older men who had been studying Ellen closely put a chill in the atmosphere. He said, "You a *nigger*—ain't you?"

Ellen caught her breath. She hadn't realized her race was in question. Her stomach going empty, she realized suddenly how important her answer was going to be in this community. It never occurred to her in her innocence to deny her heritage. She nodded. "Part," she said. Her head tilted slightly. "But I free . . . I a freed person."

The smirks seeped from the sun-seasoned faces. Some of them flushed to the hairlines of their red necks. They felt somehow defrauded and tricked. They'd tried to be nice to this new woman in their midst and it turned out she was a nigger. They sagged in awkward silence. They no longer grinned. Instead they now eyed Ellen with chilled prejudice—and new interest—shadowing their eyes.

Ellen moved toward the fly-studded screen door. "Come to do some shopping," she said to the Wilkeses.

"Of course you did," Portia Wilkes said. "You jes' come right on in. . . . Trout, don't stand there a-gapin'." She smiled. "Folks'll think you never saw a customer before. . . . Come see what we can sell to Miss Maxwell."

"Shore, Ellen." Trout Wilkes bore down heavily on the black girl's Christian name. Later, he would speak sharply to Portia about calling a black woman by her surname. She knew better. And God help him, the way Portia had called the nigger gal "Miss." It was enough to clean your shovel, all right. Was

Portia trying to run off self-respecting white customers? Was the woman trying to get him ostracized?

They entered the store. A few of the loungers inched in and leaned silently against the shadowed shelves. For a long time that taut silence hung over the stoop where the villagers loitered. From the first there had been the rumor spread that the woman in the Deakins' place was black, but now the fact was established. A black freedwoman. A black woman lived in a white man's house, among white people, as if she were as good as any of them. It was a sobering development. It was as if something that had been good in the village was endangered—blacks got into a place, they spread, like a cancerous growth, everybody knew that.

Ellen brought candles, a coal-oil-burning lamp, a bottle of crude coal oil. She selected a wedge of cheese, sweet vanilla crackers and some vegetables preserved in jars. Obviously she knew nothing about store-buying, or laying in food supplies. Mostly, she just stared about helplessly, holding that pink-white baby slung on her hip.

"You'll be needin' a cow—fresh milk for that baby," Portia Wilkes said. "Ain't she just a lovely pink little thing, Trout?"

"Looks pert," Trout said. He scrubbed at his stubbled beard. "Might be I could locate you a good milk cow what's come in fresh an' all—if'n you can pay for it. Might cost you though—as much as—as a gold eagle."

Ellen smiled and nodded. "I would be very grateful, suh. Very grateful. . . . An' you could teach me to *milk* the cow—I would gladly pay you."

Snickers wafted from the shadows at the shelves.

Trout stared at her, shaking his head in disbelief. "You a nigger wench an' don't know how to milk a cow?"

Ellen spread her hands. She felt her face color hotly in shame. "I never did it," she said. "But I know I could learn, Masta, suh."

"Of course you could," Portia said. "I had to learn after I came here—I was a schoolteacher before. Well, when Trout has the cow sent to your place, me and Hester would be happy to come over and teach you how to milk."

"Portia." Ill-suppressed rage shook Trout Wilkes' voice. He tried to ease off because the mulatto woman had suggested that she could afford to pay cash for a milk cow. His commission as broker in such a transaction would be worthwhile. "You got all you can do around here, Portia."

"I understand," Ellen said. "I do understand."

"Sure you do," Wilkes said. "We'll find a cow for you. But we got a lot to do to run this here store. Can't be teachin' nigger wenches what they ought to be borned knowin'."

"Well, I'll learn," Ellen said.

'I'll just teach you." Portia's defiant tone was meek, but persistent. She stared directly into her husband's weather-browned face. "What are neighbors for?"

Trout bit back whatever he was about to say. Ellen chose cloth from a new bolt of printed cotton. The mills in England and New England were putting lovely hues in the cotton fabrics now. Portia exclaimed over it, and Ellen offered to make her a dress.

"You mean that you know how to cut, sew and hemstitch—by hand?" Portia said. "Maybe you can teach me."

Trout's face turned beet red but he remained silent. The black woman's purchases were considerable. No sense chasing away a cash customer in these times, no matter the color of her skin.

When Ellen handed Trout Wilkes a gold eagle in payment for her purchases, the merchant's face paled slightly and his ferret's eyes darted frantically as if afraid of being caught. He placed the merchandise in a croker sack and dropped the gold eagle in his cash drawer, smiling, the transaction ended.

Ellen accepted the action as normal. She smiled and bobbed her head politely. But Portia Wilkes' face grew taut, pallid. Her eyes glittered and her voice shook with suppressed rage. "Ain't you forgot the customer's change, Trout?"

Trout glared at his wife, but managed a false smile. He took a few coppers from the cash drawer and let them bounce on the use-slick counter. Ellen reached out to gather the coins up, but Portia shook her head. Ellen paused, hand extended, puzzled and troubled. Portia stepped closer to her husband, caught his bicep above his pink arm garter and pinched fiercely.

Trout Wilkes winced and cursed under his breath. Then he reluctantly placed a paper dollar on the counter. Portia gouged him again, her face set. Trout swore aloud now and counted out what must have been the correct change because Portia released her crablike grip on his arm and smiled at Ellen, nodding. Then Ellen took up the money.

"You can't cipher, can you, Ellen?" Portia Wilkes said over her shoulder. She sat on a milking stool in the lean-to where the Guernsey cow was secured and calmly munching grain. Portia's fingers stripped the cow's teats, the milk squirting into the bucket on the ground, whistling and foaming hotly.

"Cipher?" Ellen frowned. "What's that?"

"Count. Know what something costs in a store. Know when you're getting correct change." She laughed. "You make me a new dress—and I'll teach you numbers and letters and how to write them."

Ellen laughed, excited. "I'll make you a dozen dresses. Just as soon as I learn how to milk this old cow."

When the pail was brimming with milk, Portia led the cow out to the rich pasture behind the barn and secured her to a stake at the end of a long hemp rope.

Laughing and pleased with their achievement, they went into the house, where Scandal and Hester lay together on the floor. Portia discovered the stacks of quilting, needlework and crocheting Ellen had done. She stood, exclaiming over its intricate workmanship, incredulous. "You do this kind of work, Ellen?"

Ellen nodded. "Just something to pass the time."

Portia held the work up before her. "Why, we have customers coming in the store who'd buy your quilts. They'd pay dear for them, too. And your fancy work! My, I never saw anything prettier."

They were like chattering young girls, transporting the colorful quilts and needlework, with the babies, along the road in the wheelbarrow. They were aware of chilled glances from people on stoops of the houses they passed, faces set and eyes fixed on some distant specks. They laughed together, too filled with plans to care what people thought of them.

Trout Wilkes put the village's attitude in words when Ellen and Portia came laughing and excited into the general store, carrying their babies. They could hear fragmented dialogues of men at the bar in the adjoining tavern. Trout said, "Where the hell you been, Portia Wilkes? I need you round here. I tole you. I need you round here. Hadn't needed you to help me round here, I'd've never married you. You gone crazy—traipsing around with a black woman—like she is your equal?"

"Wait till you see what we brought, Trout." Pride made Portia's voice vibrant. She ignored the savagery in his tone.

But Trout knew what people were saying, that white men had heard him denounce his wife, and that many townsmen were listening to find what would happen next. A man had to rule his own nest, or he was nothing, less than nothing. "Damn you, woman," Trout said. "You listen here to me, Portia Wilkes. I run a business in this town . . . got a reputation to consider . . . got the feelings and the opinions of good Christian white folks to mind. And here you take up with a black woman—you run off all our trade, what becomes of my store then?"

"Oh, Trout, don't." Portia went on smiling, but her eyes shadowed, troubled. "Look at these things. Ellen does such beautiful work. Look at it. Just look at it, Trout! Just the sort of thing we could sell to folks right over our counter—people traveling through."

Trout's righteous anger subsided slightly. He was first of all a merchant, wanting to make a dollar. He lifted the spread, gazing at it. Finally he nodded and glanced toward Ellen. He managed even to smile toward her. "Might give you a dollar for this."

Portia caught her breath sharply. "You know you can give her two dollars for such lovely work, Trout—and still make yourself three or four dollars."

"I know you are asking for trouble, woman," Trout said. "Telling me how to run my business. You asking for trouble, purely. I know that."

Ellen had dreaded her loneliness and having to live alone with no one to depend on after having been waited on by Falconhurst servants most of her life. She didn't know how to *do* anything. Every task was a new lesson to be learned—the hard way. And she had been afraid time would hang heavily on her in this isolated community among strangers, so far from the people she knew. She had lived in the big house at Falconhurst almost as long as she could remember. It was a busy place; one was seldom alone; there was always somebody underfoot, always someone to chat with. Now, for days at a time she saw no one. She had never worked, cooked, kept house or tended to the needs of an infant. But she learned slowly, and she was absorbed in her lessons. She was not as lonely as she'd feared. She was kept so busy learning to live free there was not time to accomplish all she wanted to do.

At first she'd awaken early every morning, having gone to sleep only at last, afraid of the dark and terrified by strange and unknown sounds. But when she opened her eyes and saw the neat respectability of her own house, and saw Scandal playing with her toes in her crib, heard the new cow lowing in the stable, she was suffused with a wonderful sense of being free, and she lay yawning, no longer afraid, convinced her freedom was worth any price it cost her.

The villagers remained cold, remote and aloof. Though Ellen lived quietly, nodded her head and spoke respectfully when she encountered any of her neighbors on the roadway, they resented her. "Damn white Negress," they said. "Owns a house good as ours. Thinks she's good as humans. And she owns more land than any of us. We ought to run her out, that's what we ought to do. We ought to run her out."

But though they talked savagely among themselves, they did nothing overtly to harm her. The arrival of the freed black wench gave them conversation when they gathered outside the Baptist Church after Sunday services, as they loitered on the stoop at Wilkes' store, or when they met on the road.

Portia Wilkes came regularly to visit Ellen. She escaped the store in the quiet early afternoon when the town lay sunstruck in the heat and business was at a standstill. She and Ellen traded information, crafts and knowledge. Portia saw a drawing in a seed catalogue of a "satisfied lady customer of Selma, Alabama" —a woman with her hair brushed, rolled and pinned neatly, bowl-like about her head. It gave the woman a look of elegance, and Portia was entranced. Ellen washed Portia's hair, trimmed and brushed it, then pinned it in an almost exact replica of the pictured satisfied customer. Portia stood before the wavy mirror, speechless with pleasure.

Painfully, Ellen learned to read. From the primer books Portia had used in her former classrooms, Ellen learned the alphabet, learned to combine letters into words, the words into simple written sentences awkwardly spelled out on cheap ruled paper.

Learning numbers was the most exciting and most rewarding of Ellen's achievements. Suddenly—it was a long time actually—Ellen could read the prices marked on goods and materials in Trout Wilkes' store. She was no longer afraid of being cheated unless Portia hovered, protectingly, like an avenging and watchful angel, at her husband's elbow.

Trout could not accept Ellen any more than the other white villagers could. But he was in conflict. Her bright quilting and intricate needlework sold excellently, as fast as he displayed it, and at good prices. He encouraged Ellen to work faster, to set aside regular hours in the afternoon to accomplish her craft, to produce more. He even entered into a limited partnership with Ellen in which he furnished materials and Ellen furnished the labor.

But every time the bell jingled at his screen door announcing a new customer, it seemed somebody was cursing the uppity white-nigger woman at the Deakins' place. He could only nod his head and agree silently. He couldn't chase away his white trade. And he was reminded in no uncertain terms, many times a week, how his neighbors felt about his wife's friendship with the "freed nigger woman."

"First time there's the least hint of sinful behavior, we'll run her out," the Baptist minister told Trout. "You know how niggers are. They rut like animals. Ain't none of 'em no different. And she ain't no different."

"Ain't seen the slightest sign of nothing like that, Reverend." Trout winced and shook his balding head.

"It'll come. It'll come. A young high-yeller living alone like that. . . . You know the devil's at work there . . . in her black heart . . . in her nigger head. No. We ain't seen nuthin' sinful and dirty yet. But the minute we do, we run her out—we won't tolerate some black slut ruinin' the morals of good decent Christians." The reverend's eyelid batted frantically and uncontrollably. "Her carryin' on immoral right in front of our children."

Several farmers warned Trout that they'd likely drive across the new wood bridge spanning the Tombigbee to Bannion's store if they had to rub elbows with that uppity "high-yeller" freed Negress in his place. "You ain't doin' yo'self no favors servin' that nigger—treatin' her like she's white and good as us humans," they warned him.

Once harassed by his regular customers, Trout suggested to Ellen that rather than her coming inside the store to shop, she might stand out on the roadway in front of his building, beside her wheelbarrow, and call out her order to him. "Ain't the way I want it, Ellen," he said. "But you is black. You run off my white trade that I depend on, what's to become of my store?"

Portia caught her breath raspingly and shook her head, her hairdo shaking violently. "If Ellen has to stand out front of our store, I stand out there with her. If Ellen can't come in my store, then she can't send in her quilts, or her crochetin' or her needlepoint, or her hand-stitched dresses and linen kerchiefs—they black as she is."

Trout threw up his hands, retreating. "All right. All right." Trout gazed around helplessly. "You come on in, Ellen, same as always—but don't stand round visitin'—you and Miz Portia. That ain't right. Don't no way look seemly. Don't look seemly at all."

Ellen nodded. She found living free and on her own very difficult. And yet she knew one thing true—she would never go back. She would die before she would go in bondage again. She had no place in the village life. The devout Christians would not permit her in their church on Sunday where they sang and preached about the Golden Rule. The white people passed her on the roadway without speaking, as if they did not see her. At night she barred her doors and lay rigid with fright and loneliness until she fell asleep at last from sheer exhaustion.

Still, she would not trade her new life of freedom for anything. Master Ham Maxwell had said he would send money to her if she asked for help through Miss Dovie Verder of Dovecote Plantation. But she never went near Dovecote. She'd never been on the big farm but knew it to be, like Falconhurst, dedicated to breeding, raising and selling herds of slaves. She did not want to go there.

She did not need to. She understood that Master Ham would send money to her—anything to keep her forever away from Falconhurst. But she felt exulting pride in the fact that she never had to ask him for anything.

She had had only one visit from the people of Falconhurst. One day, Mem and Jingo Jim arrived with three other husky young slaves who unloaded furniture for her house, silverware, pots and pans, all the items Miz Lucretia Borgia felt a woman would need to keep house for herself. Ellen had cried, standing on her front step, sobbing helplessly as Mem and the others rode away in the flatbed wagon, but she had not wanted to go with them. She missed them. Their coming brought back all the familiar sounds and sights and memories of home at Falconhurst, but she cried in loneliness, not in yearning.

She had lived at first in terror of that time when her hidden pouch would be empty of gold eagles. Sometimes, in the beginning, she had taken the pouch from under the loose hearth brick and held it, fearful. How would she live, alone and without money, among hostile strangers? But the sales of her quilts and frocks and fancy work replenished the pouch. She had more money than Master Hammond had left with her. Her small hoard of savings grew, and with it her pride and sense of accomplishment.

One morning she awaited Miz Portia, sitting with Scandal on the sunlit front stoop. But time passed and Portia did not come.

Ellen went into the house, fixed a light lunch. She was not hungry. She was troubled, afraid something had happened to Miz Portia. It was not like Miz Portia Wilkes to stay away from her arithmetic lessons. Besides, Miz Wilkes was almost finished with her first hand-stitched dress under Ellen's direction.

By sundown, Portia still had not come along that sun-dappled clay road from the village and the store. Troubled, Ellen wrapped Scandal in a light coverlet, put her on a pillow in the wheelbarrow and set off on the quarter-mile walk to Wilkes' store.

Trout Wilkes stood alone on his front stoop. Late-afternoon shadows sprawled gray and shapeless across the rutted roadway. "You come to trade, Ellen?" Trout said.

Ellen paused at the foot of the wide steps. She squinted up at the grocer. "Come to ask about Miz Portia, Masta suh," Ellen said. "I worried. She didn't come to see me."

"She ain't comin' to youah place no more, she ain't," Trout said. He cleared his throat and shifted his weight from one foot to the other. He wiped at the crown of his sweated bald head with the flat of his palm. "And I ax you kindly, Ellen, that you don't come here no more less'n you deliverin' some of your fancy work to sell, or you buyin' supplies."

"Is Miz Portia sick?"

"No. She ain't sick. Now, you don't want nuthin', Ellen, you go on back home. . . . Don't want no trouble with you, gal. Just can't have you hanging round my store. Now, go on."

"Can't I just see Miz Portia for a minute?"

"I tole you, gal. No."

"What you want, Ellen?" Portia's voice, oddly subdued and timid, came through the fly-matted screen door.

Ellen squinted past Trout Wilkes, trying to see within the cavern-dark store. "You all right, Miz Portia?"

"I'm all right, Ellen. . . .Trout just won't allow us bein' friendly no more. . . . I'm sorry, Ellen, I'm truly sorry."

Ellen nodded. "I finish your new dress for you . . . I bring it along in a day or two."

"Yes. Thank you. That will be nice.' Portia remained half-obscured in the shadowed doorway.

Ellen started to bend over to take up the handles of the wheelbarrow. She changed her mind, straightened, and drew a deep breath. She looked up at Trout Wilkes with a timid smile.

"Maybe I buy me a spool of sixty-white thread," Ellen said. She left Scandal in the wheelbarrow and came hesitantly up the steps.

Trout Wilkes tried to bar her way, but Portia spoke in a low, dead voice from the shadows behind him. "Let her come in, Trout."

Ellen stepped around the grocer and opened the door. Flies clouded upward, buzzing. She stepped inside the door, let it close behind her. She stopped as if she'd walked into a fist. She stared at Portia's bruised and battered face, her purpled eye, her hair loose about her shoulders. "I—fell," Portia said in a thin voice. "I hurt myself."

"An' she'll keep on fallin'—and keep on hurtin' herself—till you stay away from here—or she learns to keep her place—a white woman's place," Trout said. There was anger in his voice, but there was torment, too. "That's the way it be, Ellen . . . that's the way it be."

6

The days and nights were long and empty at the Deakin place without Portia to share and brighten them. Sometimes it seemed the loneliness and the unbroken silences were more than Ellen could stand. She'd never been alone before, never out of the reach of babbling voices, the sounds and presence of other people at Falconhurst. She felt isolated, as if she were on an island, or a leper, damned and in exile.

She continued with her reading and arithmetic, but it was desperately slow trying to progress without her teacher. She grew confused over words she had never seen before; she needed help with the sound of a little-used letter. She tired quickly and sat pressing her fingers against her reddened eyes, feeling hopeless and defeated. She remembered the way she and Portia had worked and laughed together, and she sighed and spent each day filled with an empty sense of sadness and loss.

She tried to stay busy. There was so much to do around the place—so many things she was forced to do for the first time. It seemed every problem she faced, no matter how trivial and inconsequential, was huge and insoluble, and without precedent in her life. She had never cooked at Falconhurst. She had no idea how long a leg of lamb should cook or when a ham was safe to eat. She had never planned or prepared meals. She had never even tended an infant.

Every task had to be learned, slowly, by trial and error. Some of the trials were ordeals, and the errors painful. She burned her arm when she baked; the cow kicked the milk pail over when it was finally brimmed full; she left Scandal lying in the sun on the stoop and red ants got on her blanket. But she learned, and seldom made the same mistake twice. She didn't need to. There were so many mistakes she hardly had time to make them all once! But she learned, making painful or costly mistakes, and always trying to recall what Miz Lucretia Borgia had done at Falconhurst under similar circumstances.

She remembered the kitchen garden which had been Miz

Lucretia Borgia's particular pride and joy. There were always fresh vegetables from that garden for Miz Lucretia Borgia's table. Of course, Miz Lucretia Borgia had as many slaves as she wished to call upon to hoe and weed and fertilize and water her garden. Ellen had only herself, but she determined she would plant her own garden. She found a heavy hoe, rusted and dull, abandoned in the old barn. She sat on the back porch steps sharpening the hoe with flintstones as well as she could. Scandal played happily in the warm sand at her feet.

Wearing overalls turned up about her bare feet, a tow linen shirt and floppy-brimmed straw sun hat, Ellen chopped out the weeds in a half-acre plot beside the barn. The ground was friable here, the weeds less tough, as if this might once have been cleared soil.

Half an acre seemed an impossible amount of land to cultivate, plant and tend. But she didn't think about that. Sweat running down into her eyes from under her hat brim, she chopped out long, straight rows as she remembered the earth had been prepared at Falconhurst.

From Wilkes' store she bought seeds and seedlings, politely seeking Trout Wilkes' advice on what vegetables were best to buy and plant this time of the year. Portia stood silently, withdrawn, watching, smiling faintly when Ellen glanced toward her. Ellen tried to share the news of her newest project with Portia, but Trout stood between them scowling until Ellen's voice trailed off and she retreated from the store with her purchases.

Her garden flowered and produced beyond her wildest expectations. Each morning soon after dawn and long before Scandal wakened, she was out with her hoe, digging, weeding, loosening the earth, carrying water from the pump in buckets. She'd planted one long row in cabbage seedlings. Within weeks a few heads of cabbage sprouted, grew daily larger and matured.

She stood slump-shouldered and stared helplessly at her overabundance of cabbage. She delivered a wheelbarrow piled high with cabbages to Wilkes' store. Trout bought the entire load for two bits. Ellen did not protest. At least, this was more than she'd paid him for the seedlings. She carried the money home in her fist and hoarded it in her pouch.

By the next morning it seemed she had more cabbages than ever. Loading her wheelbarrow again, she went from house to house in the village. At first, the householders shook their heads. They weren't buying.

"Not selling," Ellen said. She smiled and nodded. "Giving."

"Don't want gifts from you, nigger," the minister's wife said.

"Won't help you none trying to give things to folks, making up to them like that."

"If you don't take them, ma'am," Ellen said, "they spoil." She spread her hands and shook her head. "I purely hate to see that, ma'am."

The minister's wife considered this, staring along her nose. At last, she nodded. "Well, if you're sure it's a help to you, and you not expecting to truckle up to folks, I'll take six or eight heads. The reverend is most partial to boiled cabbage."

Everyone in the village accepted Ellen's cabbage, but they did so grudgingly and without warmth. The gift did not improve Ellen's lot among them. They resented a Negress having things better than they did, farm produce in such abundance that she could give it away. It didn't seem right.

Ellen was thankful for one thing. Her arduous labors—in the house, her garden, with her cow and small flock of laying hens, her sewing—left her exhausted. By nightfall she was so tired she was ready to drop, with just strength enough to bathe Scandal in a washtub and topple across her own bed. She had little trouble falling asleep at night, even though shadows crowded in after dark, and the world seemed a haunted place with disembodied and unexplained noises and she went to bed troubled and apprehensive and lonely.

By morning the fears dissipated with the last gray wisps of night and she looked forward to her work. Whether she wanted to or not, she watched the clay road out front each day for Portia, but the merchant's wife did not come. Trout Wilkes had effectively destroyed the friendship.

Sometimes, she lay at night and remembered Herman. She recalled moments of happiness at Falconhurst. She *had* been happy there. She'd been a slave, a bed wench, but existence had been far easier, far more secure and less frightening than her life as a freed woman of color.

One night, she drifted finally off to sleep and then wakened suddenly to a barrage of thunder. Her first waking thought was of a storm. She must get up and close the windows. But the night was palely purple, warm, cloudless. Then she realized someone was pounding on her front door.

She sat up in the darkness, enveloped in terror. She checked first to see that Scandal was all right. The baby slept peacefully in its crib.

Someone was calling her name, over and over, in panic.

As if in a nightmare, Ellen recognized Portia's voice. She threw off the cover and sprang up from the bed. With a long sulfur match, she lit a candle and called out, "All right, Miz Portia. All right. I'm coming."

Portia Wilkes stood at her front door with her baby in her arms. Portia's mouse-brown hair fell loose about her face and shoulders. She wore a man's heavy overcoat loose and unbuttoned over her nightgown. Her bare feet were caked with mud. She was shivering, but Ellen saw at once that it was from panic and not caused by chill or dampness.

She's fought with Trout Wilkes, Ellen thought, staring at Portia, disheveled, face terror-stricken, and he's thrown her out.

Holding the candle high, Ellen said, "Come in."

Portia's teeth chattered and she hesitated. "Better wait till you hear—you may not want us in your house."

"Come in," Ellen said. Her quiet voice had a calming effect on the distrait woman, but still Portia hesitated.

"It's Hester," Portia said. "Hester is sick. Bad sick. I think surely she's dyin'. . . . Minister's wife said Hester's sickness is contagious—nobody will take us in."

Ellen stared beyond Portia into the darkness. "Where's Masta Trout?"

"Trout? Pore Trout's half out of his mind. Just as I am. He's ridden all the way to Benson to find a doctor who'll come see the baby. . . . I waited but I couldn't stand waitin' alone. I couldn't stay at the store alone any more. . . . The minister and his wife—they wouldn't take me in. Nobody will—there's only you, Ellen. Only you."

"Come in," Ellen said. Her voice wavered, weaker, in her own ears. No matter how firm or brave she sounded, she was terrified inside. If Portia's baby was ill with an infectious disease, what about Scandal? Might not Scandal contract the illness? Her stomach empty and her heart pounding oddly, Ellen nodded again, her voice firmer than ever to hide her fear from both of them. "Come in out of the night."

Portia came hesitantly into the living room. She placed Hester on a blanket on the floor and knelt on her knees over the child, as if praying.

Ellen lit lamps from the candlewick. She made a fire on the hearth, pouring coal oil on the dried wood to hurry the blaze. All the time she was searching her mind, trying to think what Miz Lucretia Borgia might do in a situation like this. Only Miz Lucretia Borgia was so full of knowledge, so strong and sure of herself. Ellen felt more helpless than ever.

She knelt on the floor across the writhing baby from Portia.

The child's face and body were flushed with fever; she stank. Watery, greenish stools oozed from her diaper.

"One minute she burns with fever," Portia said, face pallid. "Next, she has chills. . . . If she isn't exhausting her poor little self with vomiting, she's running off at the bowels."

Ellen placed her hands on the infant's swollen, fevered abdomen. Hester wailed in anguish at Ellen's gentle touch.

In panic, Ellen sought back in her mind for some kind of helpful answer. It was as if she tried to call Miz Lucretia Borgia into this room, to bring her from Falconhurst with all the uncommon wisdom this woman had accumulated. Ellen stared at the crying child. She had seen this sickness before. She concentrated intensely, closing her eyes. After a moment she spoke, almost from rote, as if repeating something painfully recalled. "Chile got bowel fever—that's what Miz Lucretia Borgia calls it. Doc Redfield—the vet—he say it's called typhoid fever. Say it comes when heavy rains cause the outhouses to overflow and get into the drinkin' water or the streams . . . say it cause the fever and then the stomach and the bowels git awful tender and inflamed. . . . People—" Ellen stopped talking abruptly and bit hard on her under lip. She'd almost said aloud what experience had proved: people died from bowel fever. The few who did recover got well only slowly and over a long time. She drew a deep breath and finished lamely, "People what do gits bowel fever—they gits it no matter how careful we be."

Portia rocked back and forth over her baby. "Can't stay here. Can't expose you—and poor little Scandal—"

"Where you think to go?"

"Back home. To wait. For Trout. The doctor."

Ellen made a sharp slashing downward gesture of disdain with her arm. "Onliest doctor in Benson a white man what stay drunk mos' of the time. Carries the clap, Miz Lucretia Borgia say. Neither Miz Lucretia Borgia nor Masta Hammond Maxwell ever let that trashy no-good white man on the premises at Falconhurst."

Portia burst into helpless tears. "Oh God, Ellen, what will I do?"

Ellen spoke with a confidence she didn't feel. "We do the best we can," she said. "That's all we can do."

While Portia remained on her knees praying frantically and helplessly under her breath, Ellen got up and went into the kitchen.

She walked as if she were in a trance. Her concentration was more intense than ever. She had never willingly remained near an ill person at Falconhurst. She had always run from sickness, superstitious, fearful of it. But now, in her mental images, visions of Miz Lucretia Borgia materialized, moving confidently as Ellen had always known her, not even afraid of death itself.

"I got to be like that," Ellen said. "I gots to be like Miz Lucretia Borgia. Not afraid of death. I can't let pore Miz Portia see how scared I is inside . . . it may be all I can do for her." She reminded herself from ugly memory how infectious, how deadly, bowel fever was, and added emptily inside her mind, "All I can do for any of us."

Without truly understanding why, Ellen placed a large pot on the stove. She lit fire under it, moving as if silently directed outside herself. Never had she once watched Miz Lucretia Borgia nurse the ill at Falconhurst, but she must have stored unconscious memories and carried them away with her.

"Gawd, how I wish Miz Lucretia Borgia was here right now," she said aloud. She pumped a jar of fresh water, poured it in the pot to boil. Then she stood a long time, staring into the waiting vessel. "They's your remedy, Miz Lucretia Borgia," Ellen whispered tensely. "I needs it. For Gawd's sake, help me recalls it."

Moving slowly, but with an air of confidence, she poured a cup of vinegar into the bubbling water. The pungent odor rose and filled the room. Then she added honey, broke a raw egg, added dry mustard and stirred the mixture as it heated.

She heard Portia's scream of terror from the front room. "Oh God, Ellen. Come quick. Hester's gone into convulsions. Oh Jesus God, help me."

"I tryin' to help you," Ellen called. Inside she was trembling violently, weak and frightened. She continued heating the mixture. When it had boiled, she set it aside to cool. When it had cooled enough that she could touch it to her tongue without scalding herself, she added a liquid licorice extract.

She walked into the parlor with a cup of the steaming mixture. At the sight of the child, now lying in a grayish puddle of watery defecation, she bit back vomitus that came hotly up into her throat. She wanted to turn and run away. She remained where she was though it took every ounce of discipline in her to do it. Hester's fevered arms and legs twitched wildly in convulsions. The child's face was darkly blue—almost black—and its eyes were glassy, staring, and yet not focusing on anything.

"She's going to die," Portia whispered. "I know she's going to die."

"Bowel fever is mighty terrible," Ellen admitted. "We got to look straight at that. No good to lie to ourselves about that. But I do recall Doc Redfield sayin'—he say them that lives through bowel fever—they never have it ag'in in they lifetime."

She knelt beside Hester. But there was no point in attempting to force the fevered child to drink anything. Ellen brought a bucket of fresh well water and clean towels. "We tries to cool down her fever, then we washes her up," she aid.

Portia's voice broke. "Why? It'll only pour right out of her again."

Ellen nodded. "It does and we clean it up again."

Finally, when they had brought Hester's fever down a few degrees, the fearful convulsions subsided, the blankness faded from her eyes; she lost the staring, glazed look.

By now, Ellen had cleaned the child, replaced the sodden diapers, which she touched only with the tips of her fingers. Fighting back nausea, she held her breath and dropped the wet, stinking blanket and clothing into a bucket which she set outside the kitchen door. "Come morning," she said, "we burn them sick things."

Portia only nodded. "I've seen this fever," she whispered at last, as if speaking to herself, to her gods. "I never saw anyone survive."

"I have," Ellen said, with far more confidence than she felt. "I seen Miz Lucretia Borgia nurse folks back to health when they much sicker than pore little Hester."

Ellen brought the heated potion and set it on the floor beside the child's fresh blanket pallet.

"What's that licorice smell?" Portia said, looking up.

Ellen shrugged. "Probably jus' to make it smell good—to hide the taste—until after you is already swallowin' and it's too late to moan."

The baby refused to drink the mixture. Hester pressed her lips together until they whitened and she rolled her head back and forth, crying piteously. Feeling helpless, Ellen pinched the child's nostrils together. Hester's mouth popped open as she gasped for breath and Ellen poured the mixture into her mouth and held her nose closed until she swallowed, then lay gasping for breath.

Portia and Ellen exchanged pleased smiles.

At almost this precise instant, Hester began to vomit and defecate simultaneously. Weak with inner sickness, Ellen cleaned up the greenish slime, bathed and redressed the child. She fed her another dose of the mixture and repeated the whole routine again.

By now, Ellen had settled into a quiet, unhurried patience she hadn't even suspected she possessed.

They sat up all night, alternately cooling Hester's fevers, changing and discarding her clothing and covers. By morning, the fevered child slept fitfully.

Trout Wilkes arrived at midmorning. He trembled, unshaven, distracted, exhausted. He shook his head, his voice hoarse with outrage and helplessness. "The doctor won't come. For no amount of money. Says there's nothing he can do for typhoid fever . . . nothing." Trout shuddered visibly, his red-rimmed eyes filling with tears, his mouth quivering. "Nothing nobody can do."

Ellen watched the grocer, awaiting the outburst she anticipated from Trout Wilkes at finding his wife in this house in direct disobedience of his orders. But the distraught man merely touched his fingers gently against his fevered child's face, her swollen abdomen, and shook his head, whispering, disconsolate, "She going to die. She's going to die."

Hester's fever remained high, for chills set in and left her shaken. But at last the greenish, watery stools diminished, her bowel movements stabilized. Neither Ellen nor Portia mentioned this fact. They recognized a miracle, but they were afraid to hope, afraid to call this slight change to the attention of the gods.

After the first week, Hester's fever lowered several degrees and and she slept less fitfully. There had been no further convulsions after that first terrible and endless night. "Rose spots" appeared during the second week on the baby's trunk, upper abdomen, lower chest. But gradually the distended abdomen deflated and was less tender to the touch.

"What was that medicine what worked like a miracle?" Portia asked.

Ellen shook her head. "Something I recalled Miz Lucretia Borgia fixed at Falconhurst for folks when they come down with bowel fever. Miz Lucretia Borgia say it b'iled out the liver . . . the liver is where the poisons mass up, Miz Lucretia Borgia say. . . ."

"I think it helped Hester," Portia said timidly, as if still afraid, after two eternal weeks, of angering the gods.

"She do seem some better," Ellen agreed.

They boiled all the water they drank, all they fed to Scandal and to the abnormally thirsty Hester. They boiled wash water. They boiled milk. "Why do you suppose we should boil things like this?" Portia asked.

"Don't know." Ellen shook her head. "Must be some reason. Anyhow, it what Miz Lucretia Borgia do."

They fed Hester and Scandal boiled milk and boiled egg custards.

At last the rose spots on Hester's body faded and disappeared. Hester looked like a wraith, but she was alive. She slept all night and most of the day now.

Portia continued to teach Ellen her lessons as they ministered to the sick child. Lessons passed the time quicker, took their minds off their fears that they would find Hester dead and cold on the pallet when they went back to her. Portia taught Ellen to read every word of her manumission papers. For Ellen, this was her finest achievement.

Sometimes, when Portia had sunk into sleep, overwhelmed by exhaustion and concern, Ellen would sit near Hester's small mattress, reading her manumission papers over and over. She never got tired of the beautiful sound of the word "freedom," to her, and to her children and to her children's children. . . . My, that did sound elegant and secure and promising.

Trout Wilkes came to the front door in the quiet midafternoons. He approached reluctantly, as if holding his breath, tense and fearful, afraid each day that he would hear the final report on his daughter. He came every day expecting to hear that Hester was dead.

He delivered the groceries and items from the list Portia gave him each day as he left. At first, he had grumbled. He no longer complained or protested. Superstitiously, he believed he was witnessing a miracle so frangible that any sound might destroy it.

Portia stood beside Ellen in the shadowed doorway and watched the stocky, balding man walk away across the yard. "Trout's a good man," Portia said.

"Despite hisself," Ellen said.

They laughed together. "One thing I know that I never would've known if Hester wasn't deathly ill . . . I'm Trout Wilkes' second wife . . . he's got older children that he never sees or never speaks of to me . . . I know now how much he loves our Hester."

Scandal cried out from the bedroom. Ellen felt her heart sink, going weak with a premonition of wrong. Scandal was so good, she seldom whimpered. And Ellen admitted she had lived in secret agony that Scandal would contract Hester's contagious disease.

She pressed her hand against her heart now. She heeled around from the front door and ran across the room. Scandal stood up in her crib. Her body burned, flushed rose red, her teeth chattered with chill.

Portia ran into the room, stood close at Ellen's side. She

whispered, agonized, "This is the way it started with Hester, Ellen . . . gradual . . . ill . . . feverish and chilled at the same time. Oh God, Ellen, I'll never forgive myself if anything happens to Scandal."

Ellen caught Scandal up in her arms, as if she would physically protect her with her own body. "Nothing going to happen to her," she said. Her jaw tightened, a savage line. "Nothing . . . no . . . . Gawd knows . . . I won't let nothing happen to her."

Portia heeled around and ran into the kitchen. She boiled the potion she'd learned to mix from Ellen. She cooled it, added licorice and brought it into the bedroom.

Ellen sat immobile, holding Scandal tightly against her chest. Ellen looked up, distracted. "She all fevered," Ellen whispered. "Her stomach is swole up. Sore to the touch. Oh Gawd, Portia, she's got the bowel fever." She held up her hand and stared at it, covered with greenish, watery excretion. "Oh my Gawd."

"Let me have her," Portia said. She held Scandal as Ellen had, forced the heated liquid into the child's mouth and down its throat by holding its nose tightly closed. The child gasped, wailing at the top of her lungs and then vomiting and defecating at once.

"I didn't let her near Hester," Ellen said. "Kept her way off in here—she never touched nothing of hern."

"*We* touched her," Portia said. "You've got to stop blaming yourself. . . . We have no idea what all carries this fever—on our hands, maybe, in food, in milk or water, or the air itself. That's why none of those people would take me and Hester in."

Ellen brushed that aside. "I got to clean her up," she said. She nodded. "I got to stay busy. Or I go crazy."

"We'll take care of her, Ellen," Portia said. "We won't sleep a minute—till Scandal's well."

And so began a new and desperate vigil over Scandal. Hester improved, her appetite returned. Her color brightened and she crawled about the front room. When Trout heard that Scandal was ill, he came striding down the hard road from his store. He stood outside Ellen's house in the sun, his flat-crowned hat shading his face, and yelled for Portia.

"You bring our baby. I come for you, Miz Portia. I want you should come home with me at once."

Portia and Ellen walked out to the shaded porch, blinking against the blinding glare of sunlight reflecting from the bare sand yard. Trout repeated his command, his voice quavering.

Portia only stared at him from the porch. He came to the foot of the pine-plank steps and gazed up at her, squinting, his whiskered face set. Portia shook her head. "I can't leave, Trout," she said. "I can't leave now."

"Why cain't you, woman? When I tells you."

"No matter what you say to me, Trout. I can't leave Ellen until her baby is well—recovered. Fully."

"Ain't Hester well?" he demanded.

"Praise God, and thank Ellen," Portia said. "Hester is well."

"She cain't stay in this house of pestilence—"

"Don't say things we'll regret, Trout. Things you'll wish you never said. Things you don't really mean inside. You know in your heart you don't want me to leave Ellen alone."

"All I know is her chile is sick—dyin'. . . ." He shook his head and swallowed as the bile gorged up through his throat. "An' you keep my baby here—an' my baby dies, I never forgive you, woman." Trout swung his arm and gazed about the sunstruck yard in anguish.

"Forgiveness I'm not worryin' about now," Portia said.

He stood at the foot of the plank steps for a long time. He stared up at her, his eyes showing his inner sickness. Portia tried to smile but she remained unmoving on the shadowed porch. Ellen leaned against the wall, silent, watching. She heard Scandal's labored breathing, the clucking of hens at the kitchen door, the scream of yellowhammers in the pine thicket.

At last, Trout exhaled heavily. He gazed up at Portia one last time but did not say anything more. Then he turned and walked away, shoulders slumped.

Neither Portia nor Ellen spoke. They remained unmoving until Trout was out of sight around a curve in the hard road, then, still unspeaking, they returned to the silent house, to their unyielding vigil against death.

7

Miz Lucretia Borgia prowled the streets of New Orleans from the Vieux Carré to Canal, searching.

Dressed in a black silk dress which had been a gift from Master Ham Maxwell the day after their arrival in the city, in high-topped black button shoes and shaded from the sun by a red parasol, she moved with the outward majesty of an Amazon queen, but the inner uncertainty of a lost child.

Miz Lucretia Borgia had never searched for a white man downtown in a strange city. She wandered, helpless, yet determined. Sometimes when she was tired, she hailed a horse-drawn hack and rode in the tonneau, an imperious black queen. People stared at her, but there was not the resentment white people usually felt to see blacks riding in style. Somehow, Miz Lucretia Borgia looked as if she belonged in a carriage. It was only in her heart and mind where she was distressed and uneasy.

She meant to find Master Herman Hengst if he was still in New Orleans, if he was still alive. The notion of finding him began as a whim, but settled and hardened into a determined crusade. She would find him. She began by questioning the black employees at the grand St. Louis Hotel where Master Ham had engaged a room for her next to his own suite. She described Herman Hengst. He was not a man one easily forgot once beheld. He was a blond young giant in a world of pygmies.

No one could help her. A few thought perhaps they might have seen such a man, but not for a long time. Others offered to find Hengst for her, for a "fee." These freed blacks she stared down in contempt. "Because I from the country, boy," she said. "I ain't no fool. Nobody gwine take my money and run with it."

She walked the busy streets. Avenues shaded by giant willows and water oaks. She walked carefully, avoiding puddles. It seemed to her it was forever raining or just about to rain in the bayou country. Someone told her that rainfall had been measured fifty-eight inches yearly in the town. She believed little she was told. She believed this. The huge drainage ditches hacked like canals to make human occupancy possible in a place five to fifteen feet below sea level either rushed like swollen rivers or stood green and stagnant and stinking in the blazing sun.

The smell of the ditches, the damp odors from the countryards she passed where crepe myrtle, yucca, spanish dagger and sterile banana trees grew profusely against ancient walls, were all somehow obscene, reminding her of the wealthy humpback named Roche. She had hated white men in her life, but none with the passion with which she recalled that slave buyer. Once, Roche had owned her. For a while he had taken her, along with her twins Alpha and Meg, from Falconhurst. Roche had brought them with him here to New Orleans and his mansion on St. Charles Avenue. He had made playthings of her boys, spoiling and perverting and ruining them. She had stood it until she could endure it no longer. She had run away, walking all the way across two states to Falconhurst. When she came back home neither

Master Warren nor Master Ham mentioned her sale to Roche. Not only had they realized she would die rather than return to her misshapen master, but the Maxwells needed her desperately at Falconhurst.

She shook these ugly thoughts from her mind. Remembering Roche aroused her, depressed her, made her cold with rage. It was all a long time ago. A lot of swill down these murky canals. She had something else on her mind. She had to find Herman Hengst. It became the most important drive of her life. It had begun as a notion. It became an obsession.

Luckily, Master Hammond was too busy to need her or to notice that she was gone almost every day from the St. Louis Hotel. Master Ham was involved in renewing old friendships over hot toddies in the bar at the St. Louis and in arranging sale of the herd of the Falconhurst fancy slaves. The very publication of the news of the first public auction of Falconhurst blacks had created a sensation in the streets, the newspapers, across the state. People were crowding in for the big event. Master Ham was too busy to take any notice of her. For this she was thankful. It seemed to her that God had brought her to New Orleans in His wisdom and to serve His purpose. This purpose, as near as she could understand it, was to inform Herman Hengst that he was the father of a lovely little girl. Nothing else could claim Miz Lucretia Borgia's attention for more than a few minutes at a time.

A freedman Lucretia Borgia met soon after her arrival at the St. Louis Hotel invited her to visit Congo Square. When Sunday afternoon and her beau arrived to walk with her to the center of black activity in the French Quarter, Lucretia Borgia stared at her newfound friend in disbelief. He was incredible in a purple broadcloth coat with matching plum-colored waistcoat. His lavender trousers had creases sewn in and fit so tightly, there was nothing about him left to the viewer's imagination.

They paraded together in the bright Sunday-afternoon sunlight, a magnificent pair. People turned to look at them, he in ruffled white shirt and brilliant green cravat, she sporting a picture hat with ostrich plumes. Until they reached the perimeter of Congo Square they bedazzled the eyes, turned all heads. But once among the other brilliant plumage, they were swallowed up in amazing displays of color and elegance.

Sunday was the day of the week that the blacks of New Orleans lived for and dreamed toward, whether they were freed or servants for life. This was the one day when they were free in their own domain. For one brief afternoon and evening they were aristocrats among their own fellows. There was laughter and excitement and beauty everywhere. Booths, spread with tatterdemalion patchworks of bright awnings, fringed the crowded banquettes. Refreshments of every kind were offered by smiling purveyors—and most everything could be bought for a copper penny. Smells wafted from pig knuckles, hamhocks, spare ribs, crackling, chitterlings, boilers of rice and red beans, from pots of clams and oysters, shrimp and caldrons of gumbo. People strode along chewing stalks of peeled cane, the juices dripping sweetly down their chins. There were other booths of jewelry, most of it cheap and worthless, some stolen and priceless, all priced the same. Conjure men's and fortune-tellers' booths lined the walkways. Bands played and people danced. And yet, in all this laughter and raging after pleasure, Lucretia Borgia found herself thinking about Herman Hengst, looking for him in the crowds, even when she knew she would never find him down here. Herman Hengst had escaped the yoke of being black in a white man's world. He was never going to slip back, or be caught again. He would never come near a place like Congo Square, even though for a little while it encompassed all the pleasures known to the imaginations of men.

She prowled the streets, asking about Herman Hengst, describing him. As time passed, the grits-white faces blurred and she felt she was hunting a boll lost in a cotton sack. She become unable to describe those differences which might make Brass Door stand out among his doughy-featured fellows; in her mind he faded, a wraith, featureless and unreal. All white people looked exactly alike, and she was no longer even sure she would recognize Herman if she did find him.

It never occurred to her to give up her quest, to stop looking for him, even when she could not learn if the mustee was still in the crescent city, or still alive.

Her being in New Orleans was providential. Master Hammond Maxwell was in the city to dispose of a herd of black slaves at auction and to solidify his plans to marry Miss Augusta. He had brought Lucretia Borgia along in the unlikely event that Miss Augusta decided to return to Falconhurst with them and needed the services of a personal maid.

For weeks now Falconhurst's immense acres had rung and echoed with the joyous spirit of rejoicing, as well as with a bustling of activity unknown to Lucretia Borgia. Masons, carpenters, laborers worked from sunup to dark erecting the lovely new mansion for the bride. Also, at the same time, slaves were being prepared for the coffle that would see over one hundred prime and fancy black animals delivered to vendue at New Orleans. New clothing had to be provided, sewn and fitted for the slaves being sold. Each slave had to be inspected closely by the veterinarian to be certain he was in excellent health; Hammond Maxwell never knowingly sold an inferior or ailing animal.

The big kitchen at Falconhurst writhed with activity and hurrying blacks. Candies, cakes and condiments were produced in mountainous quantities. Slaves, made skittish by whispers of their being sold away from Falconhurst at auction, could be calmed and soothed and diverted by gifts of sweets and by the busy routine of inspections, curryings and fittings.

"Best herd of fancies we ever had to offer, Lucretia Borgia." Ham Maxwell smiled and nodded. "Got to give you a passel of the credit, even if you is black and all, the way you kept this place runnin' and the animals healthy and all, even with Pa sick and being kilt." For a moment, Master Ham's eyes saddened and the smile seeped from his sun-leathered face. "Wish only that Pa could be with us in New Orleans to see our bucks and wenches being sold off at the highest prices we ever got. He'd bust a button with pride, I can tell you. Poor Pa. He never missed a sellin' of Falconhurst servants—any more than he'd make any trade without he got coin to boot, no matter what."

"We all of us learnt *that* lesson from ole Masta Warren—got coin to boot in every blessed trade." Lucretia Borgia watched the clerk Master Ham had brought in to copy out the pedigree of each slave onto bills of sale. These papers would be filled in at the New Orleans auction with the buyer's name after the animals were purchased. It promised to be a magnificent transaction, both in quantity and quality of black animals placed on vendue. Falconhurst's fame and reputation would be further enhanced and there would be new boiler pots of gold to bury in the yard when they came home.

Miz Lucretia Borgia felt a mounting excitement as the moment approached for the long march to begin southwest to Louisiana. She hated New Orleans but she thrived on excitement, change, action.

It would be thrilling—seeing white folks bidding wildly for black slaves that she had raised for market. Falconhurst slaves, although strong, healthy and always of fancy to elegant quality, were seldom bought for labor in cotton or cane fields. They were far too expensive to be thus misused. Most spent their lives as studs, with light yard or house work to keep them occupied. Each was a "prime" specimen. Often they led pampered existences in rich plantations, brought out and stripped down so guests could admire their beauty and the owners could boast that this was a Falconhurst fancy. Just as blooded bulls or sleek stallions might be acquired for looks, prestige and stud value, so went a Falconhurst buck on the auction vendue. Plantation owners vied savagely among themselves to buy a Falconhurst thoroughbred.

"We could sell off a herd twenty times this size," Master Ham said. "Falconhurst quality is what buyers are lookin' for today. And they want 'em in quantity, too. Seems like they just cain't get enough of them."

Lucretia Borgia smiled. She'd learned how true this was in the years Master Ham was away across the Texies and she sold the animals to buyers who came from as far away as the Carolinas to buy her stock. Once, a plantation owner bragged of the acres he had under cultivation. Now that same man boasted how many blacks he owned, how many of them were of Falconhurst quality. A man who owned a hundred slaves rated higher on the social scale than a man who owned only fifty. A man who held to Falconhurst quality was highly placed indeed. And so, prices for the black animals rose steeply and swiftly. There were not enough to supply the demand. Possession of Negro slaves represented wealth in the South as nothing else could.

On almost every plantation, Falconhurst slaves received preferential treatment. A big investment, they were treated carefully. Falconhurst bucks and wenches were showpieces of the finest plantations, along with fine horses and registered cattle. And so Hammond Maxwell had become the acknowledged best judge of nigger flesh in the South. He was sought after for advice, for counsel, for the glory reflected in his company.

The morning came for the coffle to leave the plantation. The slaves were lined up nude for a last check by Doc Redfield and Hammond Maxwell. One by one the blacks were called up and put through a close scrutiny, forced to kneel, bend and part the cheeks of the buttocks, to peel back the foreskin of the penis. As the vet and the master inspected the stock for the last time before they reached the slave barracoons in New Orleans, they chatted quietly between themselves, remarking on the quality of each specimen. A handsome buck would bring the biggest price. A prime slave should not be too African-black in color, too thick in the lips, too heavy-browed, or with receding short forehead. The strong-thewed, mahogany-brown stud with muscled arms, narrow hips and deep chest sold best.

Finally, the coffle moved out along the trace. The slaves remaining behind watched silently as Hammond and Doc Redfield, riding horses, followed by a light buggy in which Miz Lucretia Borgia rode with two servant girls, and supply wagons, led the long parade of black animals on their way to auction, to new lives in strange places. It was a solemn moment.

They followed the same route south and west that Hammond had traveled so many times since he first made the trip with his father when he was only ten years old. The pace was slow because of the coffle.

The caravan could move only as fast as the spanceled slaves, those bucks who could not be trusted without fetters. They ate and slept in the open, beside large fires. Still, management of the huge coffle of slaves over such long distances, and on foot, was, Miz Lucretia Borgia learned, a complicated undertaking. Thank God she'd stayed at Falconhurst all these years and let the buyers come to her. She admired Master Ham more than ever. It required all his vast knowledge and hard-won experience to bring the troop safely into New Orleans and to the slave barracoons. They arrived without losing an animal, exhausted, taut, edgy, but triumphant.

Miz Lucretia Borgia could never say when she first struck upon the idea of looking for Master Herman Hengst in New Orleans. But once she set out, she did not falter. She covered the town, she left messages, she described him over and over. She did not find him.

She sprawled exhausted, barefooted, her black silk dress open to catch the faint breeze in the wide French windows, in a club chair. Someone knocked on her door. She managed to push herself up to her feet and to a half-stagger across the carpeting to open the door.

She stared, stunned with shock. Master Herman stood there grinning at her. His Nordic blue eyes were troubled and he appeared taut, ill at ease, but he was smiling, as always. And as always Miz Lucretia Borgia was exalted at the male strength, cleanliness and beauty of him. Her eyes fixed on Brass Door's shiny boots and moved admiringly upward until she met his eyes. In all her life, only the magnificent Mandingo Mede had been a more perfect male specimen than this mustee. Mede, a giant, standing well over six feet and weighing two hundred muscular pounds stripped and barefooted, was scarcely taller or more godlike in sculpted appearance than this blond Germanic mulatto.

Brass Door showed all the strength and masculine beauty of his Nordic ancestry, blended and enhanced with the grace and sheen of his black forebears. His hair glowed the color of field oats and clenched in the tight curl from African ancestry. His head was close-cropped—she supposed to conceal its Negroid kinkiness. He wore long sideboards and a trimmed saffron mustache. Pale flesh, suffused with the bronze patina from the sun, exaggerated the Nordic blue of his eyes and the brilliant whiteness of his teeth. His aquiline nose, straight forehead, full-lipped mouth and strong, cleft chin held the fascinating beauty of rare old coins. His wide shoulders and thick chest tapered to flat belly, narrow hips and long, sturdy Viking legs.

Miz Lucretia Borgia exulted. No wonder Scandal was such a beautiful baby—with this god of a father and flowerlike Ellen for her dam! And there was not the least doubt in her mind that Scandal would grow to breathtaking young womanhood—whether it happened in penury and slavery or in protected freedom was all that mattered to Miz Lucretia Borgia now.

She stared at Herman, drinking him in. She saw him wince, the blood flushing upward to the roots of his cropped hair. Her ethnic sensitivity, keenly honed by long servitude under quicksilver white masters, told her Brass Door thought she looked at him critically. This was not true—nothing could be further from fact. She felt a deeply held devotion and admiration for him, which he missed because of his own dense inner guilts.

Rather than disapproving in any way, Miz Lucretia Borgia saw in Herman those exceptional character strengths and virtues—the excellent bloodline—which reinforced her faith in little Scandal's personal worth and inner quality.

Miz Lucretia Borgia recalled her first meeting with Brass Door and, recalling, felt reassured about the quiet strength, dignity and courage against incredible odds which he'd displayed—all qualities she believed he'd passed along in his blood to his daughter.

Brass Door—the mustee slave—came to Falconhurst as the sole asset, possession and ill-used servant of Cousin Charlie Woodford.

How she despised and detested Cousin Charlie, from his flashy clothing and varnished boots to his tall white beaver hat flaunting its cockade of polished brown feathers. She especially mistrusted his thin weasely face with a receding chin that not even a coarse beard could conceal and cheeks badly mottled with an adolescent acne. More than anything else, she feared almost superstitiously his badly crossed pale-blue eyes, peering oddly from beneath light sandy brows. Miss Blanche had had crossed eyes, and had passed them on to Miss Sophie, Master Ham's daughter. Cousin Charlie's appearance declared him a sneak, but his stealing money and a Falconhurst slave on his last visit branded him forever worthless and vile in Miss Lucretia Borgia's estimation. He was a white man and she could not speak aloud against Cousin Charlie, but no one could deny her thoughts.

Although Cousin Charlie had stolen money and a slave from Falconhurst, he came and went as though nothing had happened. He haunted Falconhurst as an unwelcomed guest for months at a time since his sister—the late Miss Blanche Woodford—had married Hammond Maxwell and been slain by him because of her adulterous alliance with Hammond's slave Mede. Miss Blanche had been dead these eight or nine years, but this did not deter Cousin Charlie from using Falconhurst as retreat, way-station and second home all this time.

On Cousin Charlie's last visit he'd brought along a young blond giant whom Miz Lucretia Borgia mistook for a friend and companion.

"Brass Door ain't no white man," Charlie had told her. "He nuthin' but a goddam mustee. Clear white far's you can see, but he's a nigger just the same. Brass Door—that's French meanin' *gold arm*. Some say hit mean *gold leg*—and damn if it ain't. That nigger boy has shore got it! Heaviest-hung Nigra in the whole world. Man name of Roche in N'Awleans had him, but got sick of him so I swapped Roche a pretty Spanish Morisco boy for him."

Beside Cousin Charlie, the slave was especially impressive to Miz Lucretia Borgia—like a strong and dignified being from another world, despite the shabby, threadbare clothing he wore. One's first impression was of scrubbed and gleaming cleanliness—his skin shone, his flesh appeared freshly washed, his eyes open and clear. Though clad in castoffs of Charlie's which were much too small and constricting, he carried himself with dignity, though there was a look of shame and disenchantment about him, as if he were unwillingly resigned to a life of slavery, but not defeated by it.

When, from the first night, Miz Lucretia Borgia learned of the way Cousin Charlie used Brass Door behind the locked door of an upstairs bedroom, her hatred for Charlie intensified. Her distaste did not extend to Brass Door. His very cleanliness absolved him. Instinctively, she saw he submitted unwillingly to his master's perversions, that he was forced to do his master's bidding no matter how repellent it might be. Her heart went out to Brass Door. He was enslaved in a land where a black could be hung for striking a white master, whipped—perhaps to death, depending on the whipper and the number of lashes ordered—for refusing to obey that master's least whim.

Cousin Charlie delighted in abasing and degrading his slave in public. "Nigras love to git whopped. It makes 'em wild and passionate inside to be whopped good—with bullwhip or chains. You Nigras like to get whopped, don't you, Brass Door?"

Eyes lowered, the slave nodded. "If you say so, Masta."

"Ah do say so, damn you. An' you likes gittin' whopped, don't you, Brass Door? Really loves it better'n anything, don't you?"

Brass Door hesitated, with nothing but innate dignity left to him. "Yes, Masta Charles, I like to be whipped."

"And the harder I pours it on, the better you likes it?"

Brass Door nodded, his eyes on the floor until Charlie raged at him. "Answer me, you Nigra bastard!"

"Yes, Masta Charles, the harder you whip me, the better I like it."

Miz Lucretia Borgia stared at the master and his slave, incredulous. She knew one thing. She would die before she would be tormented and mistreated as Cousin Charlie mishandled Brass Door. She stared in contempt at the white man, thinking, *Whips and chains and cross-eyed Cousin Charlie.*

She and Mem heard Cousin Charlie whipping Brass Door and then using the young giant as if he were a pliant woman at night in that locked bedroom. They could hear the buggy whip cutting across Brass Door's buttocks. "That Cousin Charlie," Miz Lucretia Borgia moaned. "He a bad 'un."

"Glad I ain't Brass Door," Mem whispered, taut. "Me, I couldn't no way do them things for no white man."

"You do it—or you git really whupped—not jus' love taps to redden yore skin. Bull whips to make you bleed. You fights back 'gainst any white masta and you gits hung or burnt to death."

Mem shuddered, but shook his head. "Not me. If'n I Brass Door, I'd kill that white booger even if he be my masta."

"You talk big, Mem." Miz Lucretia Borgia shook her head, overwhelmed with sorrow for what Brass Door silently endured each night. "They'd hang you to a tupelo tree if'n you laid a hand on a white man in anger. No matter what a white man tell you to do, you does it. Pleasurin' a white man bad, but ain't so bad as being burnt alive."

Brass Door's suffering at Cousin Charlie's filthy hands was an old, sad story to Lucretia Borgia. She'd seen her own twin sons suborned to Roche's perverted tastes. But despite all Brass Door was forced to endure, he retained his calm courage, his dignity, and she admired him as she had never admired any man before. She wondered how Brass Door had sunk so low—and from where.

Then Cousin Charlie had killed Master Warren Maxwell, trying to force the helpless old man to reveal the hiding place of his money pots. In turn, Brass Door had risen up and slain Cousin Charlie. Falconhurst had teetered on the brink of jeopardy. Brass Door had been forced to "pass" as white in order to save Falconhurst plantation for Master Hammond Maxwell, who was far across the Texies.

During those long months, sitting in Master Ham's own deep chair in the Falconhurst parlor, Brass Door had told Lucretia Borgia about himself, the strange story of his life—and for the first time Lucretia Borgia understood the inner beauty and strength of this new master of Falconhurst, the man who had sired little Scandal.

Brass Door's mother had been one of the celebrated octoroons of New Orleans. Her presentation at the annual Octoroon Ball had created a sensation. She had caught the fancy of a young German, Otto von Stolz, who had come to New Orleans to learn the cotton brokerage business. Von Stolz had purchased the young beauty and had set her up in her own house on Rampart Street, where Brass Door had been born.

An only child, he'd been adored and pampered by both his parents and their Negro servants. Educated by a private tutor, he read, spoke and wrote English, French and German. Until he was eighteen, he had not even realized he possessed a drop of black blood or that he was not a free man.

In his supremely happy home, Brass Door had been called either Herman or Armand, depending upon whether he was being addressed by his German father or his Creole mother. His father had taken both his mother and him back to Germany. Here Herman had gone to school at the same gymnasium as the other boys. On their return to New Orleans from Hamburg, Herman's father had died. He had never manumitted either Herman or his mother. In settlement of the estate, both Herman and his mother had been sold—as blacks. She became a lady's maid and he had been sent to serve the exotic tastes of Roche.

Conditions in the Roche menage had been beyond his ability

to survive, but he had persisted. He showed Lucretia Borgia the pierced holes in his ears where he had worn diamond earrings—otherwise buff naked—to please his master.

His servitude to Roche had been unbearable, but it was paradise compared to what he endured with Charles Woodford. Charles had only funds he could borrow, cadge, steal or pick up in crooked poker games. He lived in a run-down house in the Vieux Carré. Often, Brass Door—as Roche had named him—had nothing to eat for days at a time when Charlie's luck at cards or theft ebbed. Mostly, they existed on corn pone and black coffee.

As master of Falconhurst, Brass Door had proved himself a brilliant leader, organizer, administrator and slave dealer. He and Lucretia Borgia made more money for the stud farm than had ever been amassed before. Brass Door's traits all were admirable. For all these reasons, Lucretia Borgia believed Scandal blessed to be his offspring, and that she had only to locate Herman to ensure his daughter's secure future.

All these thoughts fled through Lucretia Borgia's mind in the seconds she stood in that hotel room gazing up at him.

She exhaled heavily. He was beautiful—inside and out. His body was as sparkingly clean as his generous heart—and this was all that mattered.

Now, unable to speak for the moment, Lucretia Borgia continued to gaze unabashed up at the blond and magnificent young giant. He looked well, strong and as she remembered him—unconquerable.

She smiled, thanking the ancient gods of her people that Brass Door was still free—living as a white man, as Herman Hengst, his ugly past as the slave forever behind him.

Her eyes brimmed with tears, and she smiled up at him and nodded. She was so glad to see him, so pleased he was well and safe. Maybe, though she hadn't even suspected it, this was another reason for her searching so obsessively for him. He *had* saved Falconhurst. She had come to love and admire him above all men. She could not simply let him go away without knowing he was all right. And, too, Scandal needed him. He had to know he was the father of a breathtakingly lovely little girl.

His own smile was shy, reticent, uncertain, but certainly genuine. He loved her, too. One could not be deceived about this.

"Well, you *have* been looking for me, haven't you, Lucretia Borgia?" Herman laughed. "Can't I come in?"

Lucretia Borgia laughed with him and reached out her heavy yet shapely arms to him. Laughing deep in his chest, he swung her up into his own arms as easily as if she were a child. He swung her around and around, half-carrying her across the room.

They talked for hours. Lucretia Borgia waited politely for Herman to mention Ellen's name. It would be less than seemly for her to broach the subject of the octoroon bedwench and her git. After all, Herman had slept with Ellen gathered into his arms all those nights at Falconhurst. He must care what happened to her. He'd known Ellen to be pregnant long before he'd departed the plantation for the last time. But Herman did not ask about Ellen. He sprawled in a chair, his long legs stretched before him, and conversed easily, but he did not mention Ellen's name.

Finally, Lucretia Borgia could contain herself no longer. She refused to dally further with etiquette, ceremony or protocol. After all, he had come because he'd learned she was looking for him. He was a smart man. Surely, he didn't believe she'd searched so long and so painfully just to discuss the weather and the crops and the way New Orleans had grown. She drew a deep breath during a lull in the conversation and said. "Miss Ellen had her baby."

She watched Herman blanch slightly, going gray to the roots of his tight blond hair. He winced and bit down on his tautened lips. It was difficult for Herman to sort out his feelings about Ellen. During those long nights at Falconhurst he had believed himself madly in love with her. Almost every night she came to his bed, and he welcomed her heatedly. He admitted he'd longed for the early hour of bedtime on the old plantation which sent him bounding up the stairs and striding into his bedroom, inwardly praying she would be there. The caress of her lips on his mouth and along his body set him afire. Her soft, slender fingers on his bare skin inflamed him with a fiery passion that threatened to consume them both. He had never wanted anyone as he had wanted Ellen in those dark nights.

Yet, he had to admit, a sense of release and relief had flooded through him when he departed Falconhurst. He had felt he was escaping something and gradually came to admit that his escape was from the cloying, clinging arms of the lovely mustee girl. He had not missed her. He admitted, too, that she no longer held any appeal for him. He supposed he owed her something—a great deal. But it would not solve her problems to compound his own. If he pretended he cared anything about Ellen, he would be lying to her, and he could no longer lie to himself. She belonged to a part of his life that was past, over, behind him.

He sighed and said with a faint, twisted smile, "How is Ellen?"

"She tol'able." Lucretia Borgia watched him with those deep, undeceived black eyes. Wincing, he looked away, staring through the windows to the dusk-clouded street.

He tried to put concern in his voice, knew he did not deceive Lucretia Borgia any more than he fooled himself. "And—the baby? How is the baby?"

"She a beautiful little chile. A li'l gal baby. With your pale rosy skin. We calls it Scandal." Lucretia Borgia smiled, nodding. "It plumb a scandal how pretty that baby is."

Herman smiled tautly. "But not a *scandal* that I violated *Master* Hammond Maxwell's personal bed wench?"

Lucretia Borgia laughed, nonplussed. "That too."

He exhaled heavily again. "Will—they be all right, Lucretia Borgia? Ellen? Her baby?"

"*Her* baby? How they is might be up to you."

Herman winced again, finding facing the truth far less easy than Lucretia Borgia did. Facing the truth meant facing all of it for him, including the truth about himself. "Me? Up to me?"

"Masta Ham done sent Ellen and her git away from Falconhurst."

He sat straighter, his heart slugging. "Where? Did he sell her?"

"He done give her her manumission. First slave in all his life that he done ever set free. He set Ellen free."

"Thank God."

"Yes. Thank God."

He tried to speak with conviction. "She should be all right, then. She is freed."

"Yes. She done been set free. But Ellen still a black woman. Even if she is freed. Even if she is most white as you. She got to live among white people what knows she's black and what don't want her round."

He clenched his fists, his jaw squaring into a hard line. "Where is she?"

Lucretia Borgia told him. She retailed the story of Ellen's new home, her new start. Then she gazed at him, unblinking. "You expectin' maybe to go to her?"

He shook his head. He had no such expectation. The thought was more a nightmare. Going to her? He couldn't go to Ellen. That would ruin everything. "I can't go to her, Lucretia Borgia. . . . I'm getting married. I'm leaving the country. The young woman I'm marrying—she—she's a lovely girl. But she doesn't know about Ellen—"

"An' she a white lady, I 'spect?"

He nodded. "She is white. She and I can be happy—in Europe. We'll live in Europe. We'll never come back here."

"Yas, suh. Cain't nobody fault you fo' leavin' this place where you been so mistreated, hurt and all, and goin' someplace where you can live better."

"I'm sorry—about Ellen."

"Yassuh."

"I really am, Lucretia Borgia. I made a mistake. An unforgivable mistake. But I cared for Ellen. Truly. Deeply. I did. But not —not as I love Emeraude."

"Emeraude?"

"Lucretia Borgia, I'm not a bad man—"

"No suh."

"Not an evil man."

"No suh. You ain't evil. Not a evil bone in your body."

He winced, unable to face her. "If there were anything I could do for Ellen . . ."

Lucretia Borgia shook her head. "I don't rightfully 'spect Ellen looks for you to do nothin' for her no moah. She cried and carried on something terrible at first, waitin' fo' you to come back to Falconhurst—"

"I *am* sorry."

"Yassuh."

"My God, Lucretia Borgia. You're like my conscience. Worse. Because you don't even blame me or censure me. You just look at me."

"Don't mean to be disrespectful—"

"You must know if I could do *anything* for Ellen, I would do it. . . . I know I am the cause of whatever has happened to her. I walked out on her. It's my fault. I'll have to live with that for the rest of my life. But I would not be doing Ellen any favor by pretending now that I love her or by taking her away with me. . . . That would not work, Lucretia Borgia. We would both be in hell." He breathed deeply, almost painfully. "It is a price I cannot pay."

Lucretia Borgia gave him a wan smile. "Like I say, Ellen hardly 'spects anything from you no moah."

He stared at the backs of his clenched fists. He glanced up, laughing at himself in self-hatred. "But *you*—you expect something of me. You looked for me to tell me about Ellen—"

"No, suh. Mostly I wanted to tell you 'bout Ellen's baby—little Scandal. I reckoned you should know that she well and healthy. Little Scandal. She such a beautiful chile . . . gon' grow up here in the South—as a black girl. No matter the color of her skin. A drap of black blood means she black. That the law. No matter that she freed. No matter how free she is—in the eyes of the law, in the minds of all the white people she gone meet, she black."

"You don't have to remind me of that kind of hell, Lucretia Borgia."

"No, suh. You wuz in hell first time I saw you, being used by that evil Masta Charley."

"I went through every degradation known to man, Lucretia Borgia. I know what hell is." He shuddered. "And I know what it will be for my daughter."

"You got your own life."

He prowled the room as if caged. "What do you want of me?"

She smiled and shook her head. "I don't want nuthin' of you. I just come to tell you—'bout Scandal."

He stood over her, clenching his big hands into fists to conceal their trembling. His eyes were reddened with tears and his voice was hoarse with inner agony. "Listen to me. I've got *one* chance to live like a man. A real man. A human being. Free. That's in Europe. I want to go there. I love Emeraude. As I've never loved anyone else. Without Emeraude, freedom in Europe would be another hell for me. Life without her would be hell. I can't envision my life without her. If I don't marry Emeraude and take her away from here with me, I lose this one last chance of happiness. Can't you see that, Lucretia Borgia?"

"I want nuthin' but happiness for you."

He seemed not even to hear her, so entangled in agony was he. "I've been through the deepest pits of hell here in the South, Lucretia Borgia. You know that. You saw what happened to me at Falconhurst. I can tell you I endured much worse before I got there. . . . And what can I do for Ellen—or for her baby? All right, damn it, *my* baby. Our baby. What can I do for them? As thanks for saving this evil stud farm, your wonderful Master Ham has threatened to hang me if I ever return anywhere near Falconhurst."

"Masta Ham what he is. What he was borned and raised up to be and to believe. Just as you and me are what we was raised up to be."

"That doesn't change the fact that he would kill me if I returned to Falconhurst. And I couldn't do it, even if I wanted to. And I don't want to, Lucretia Borgia. With all my heart and mind and soul all I want is to marry Emeraude and get on a ship bound for Europe. There is nothing more I could do at Falconhurst—except perhaps get myself killed. Would that help Ellen? Or our baby? . . . I can't do it, Lucretia Borgia."

"Ain't axt you to do nuthin'."

"Oh God, Lucretia Borgia. No. You haven't. Not a word of reproach. No demands. Not reminding me of duty, obligation, responsibility. . . . I wish to God I were as good and strong and decent inside as you, Lucretia Borgia. But I'm not. I'm scared in my gut to go on trying to exist in this evil place. I'm not brave or strong. I'm a man who's been beaten, who's lived in hell—a hell not even you have ever suffered, Lucretia Borgia." He laughed coldly. "I did one selfless act for a white man—for your sainted Master Hammond Maxwell—and to repay me for that one selfless act, Maxwell called me a *nigger* masquerading as a white man and threatens to hang me if ever he sees me again. . . . I can't do any more, Lucretia Borgia. For anybody else. Even a helpless baby. I've got to think about myself now."

"Yassuh."

He swung around, stretching his muscular arms toward the high ceilings and the vaults of heaven beyond. "Oh God . . . I can go to Europe. I can marry Emeraude and board the first outbound ship. I'll escape slavery forever. I'll get away from the stigma and horror of being a black man in the white South. . . . But I'll never escape you, will I, Lucretia Borgia? Your gentle face, your deep eyes fixed on me, asking me only to do the right thing—as you see the right—"

"Ain't axt—"

"Ain't had to." He taunted her by mocking her tone and her voice. He paced the room again. "It's all so simple in your mind, isn't it? I can tell Emeraude about Ellen and my bastard child. I can lose Emeraude. I can lose my one chance at freedom and happiness. And for what? For what, Lucretia Borgia? What could I do—for Ellen—or for the baby?"

Lucretia Borgia spoke absently, almost to herself. "Long as that baby stay with Ellen, she a black chile. She live black. A kitchen slut, somebody's bed wench, or maybe cane-cuttin' in fields somewhere."

Herman burst into sudden helpless tears. Lucretia Borgia went to him and took him gently into her arms, soothing him.

8

The feeble flame of tallow candles provided only wan yellow illumination that did little to dispel the abysmal gloom of the dark night or to lighten the mood of despair that gripped Ellen and Portia. They could hear Scandal's agonized wheezing, her fevered writhing on her crib mattress, her whimpering even in her disturbed sleep. They could hear nothing else, think of nothing else. Portia made coffee and set a cup before Ellen, but the mustee woman was barely aware of it. She was lost in grief deep inside her own mind. Portia sat down on the straight chair beside Ellen's rocker. She took Ellen's hand in her own and for a long time they sat in silence.

"I'm being punished," Ellen whispered.

"What?"

"I am. It's God's will. I know it. I'm being punished."

"You? Punished for what?"

Ellen drew a deep breath. She gripped Portia's hand tightly. She nodded, her voice oddly empty-timbred. "I—didn't—want Scandal. . . . You know? . . . It's true. I never wanted her—"

"Of course you wanted her."

"No." Ellen's head came up and she gazed, unblinking, into the shadowed corners of the room where her own personal demons lurked. "No. I didn't want her. I really didn't. Maybe there was something wrong with me."

"You were just young. Afraid. We all feel that way sometimes. At first."

"No. It was more than that. I prayed something would happen—that she would be dead when she was born. . . . I was selfish . . . I reckon I still am selfish. She only meant trouble to me, and I was afraid of trouble, and afraid of her."

"It's all right. I understand."

Ellen turned her head, her eyes brimmed with tears. "But I have learned to love her, Miz Portia. I have. I ain't learnt yet to love all children—any children except her—but I did learn to love little Scandal."

"Of course you did."

"I can't imagine my life, or my house, without her in it. . . . If anything happens to her, I don't see how I can go on living, because I won't have any reason left for living. . . ."

"We'll save her, Ellen." Portia realized how flat her voice sounded, how lacking in any conviction. She added, "We'll do all we can. We won't give up."

Ellen seemed not to hear her. She smiled oddly, staring down at her hands. "I guess all babies are sweet and full of love and you have to love them because they are so helpless and because they love you." She shook her head, recalling Falconhurst. "Miz Lucretia Borgia, she say each child brings it own love. I didn't know then what she meant. I know now. . . ."

Portia nodded, squeezing Ellen's hand in her fingers. But the lovely young woman seemed only vaguely aware of her, of where she was. Troubled, Portia watched Ellen lift her eyes toward the ceilingless roof, as if in supplication.

Ellen whispered, pleading, "God, please God, do what you will with me—pain or cold or hunger . . ." She shuddered. "Or even death, God, if you will it . . . I can stand anything You will it . . . but Scandal, she just a baby. And I need her, God. Need to hold her in my arms, I do, to love her and care for her tenderly. . . . I'll spend the rest of my life looking after her, seeing she has good things—so much better than I ever had. . . . Help me, God . . . I'm strong. Stronger than I ever knowed I could be. And I'll take care of her—if God will only let me keep her and love her . . . please, God."

The long empty night dragged itself out. Ellen slept at last, from sheer exhaustion, her head lolling awkwardly against the backrest of the old wicker rocking chair. Portia slipped from the straight chair and lay curled on a rug, her head resting on her arm.

When first sun rays wakened them, early morning dankness chilled the room, the house, the world; the gray fields glistened and dripped with dew and waking birds shrilled in the hammocks.

Ellen's first thought was for Scandal. She lunged up and ran into the bedroom. Scandal lay helpless and wan with fever, but alive. Ellen sagged against the crib and whispered, "Thank God."

Scandal's fever rose and burned hotly through the morning. Fearing that the child was dying, Ellen stood helpless beside the crib until Portia drew her away.

They sat together in the front room. While they huddled, each drawing strength from the other in their constant vigil, Portia saw Ellen change, withdrawing from reality.

Frightened, Portia stared at Ellen. It was as if the mustee woman could no longer face the thought of her baby's imminent death and so she shut the idea from her mind. Ellen began to talk in a low, muffled tone—at first hesitantly and ramblingly—about her plans for little Scandal's schooling and life as a young woman. Looking into the nebulosity of the future afforded her hope she could not find in the ugly, threatening and dangerous present. Ellen raced ahead of time, escaping its unbearable burdens, finding sanctuary in the only place where she could not be hurt—the unborn tides.

"This here's no place for a black child to grow up—even if her skin is white, her hair is red-gold as sunlight and she is freed."

Portia kept her voice level, trying to bring Ellen calmly back to this moment. "You're right about one thing. This village is no place for any child to have to grow up—regardless of color."

Ellen seemed not even to hear her. She smiled crookedly. "I want my Scandal to have good things—all the good things—"

"We all want that for our children."

She saw that this desire was not a general matter with Ellen. Everyone did want the best for his child, this was a natural wish, but for Ellen it was far more: it was an obsession. "I wants her to have good of life. I want it something terrible. So I hurt inside with wanting. Maybe other people *wants* good for they chile—but from this day I ain't gone think hardly about nuthin' else—day or night."

"You just make yourself ill, Ellen. There's some things we can't change. We can only break our hearts."

"No." Ellen shook her head. "I ain't thinkin' round and round on some impossible thing I can't change. . . . I can change everything for Scandal. I can and I shall. . . . You'll see."

"I know you'll want to. I know you'll try. I just don't want to see you hurt fighting against things nobody can't change."

Ellen tilted her head as if seeing beyond the distant horizon. "One of these days—when I can read a mite better and know my times tables clearer—I take Scandal and we go away from here." She nodded emphatically, smiling wanly.

"I'll miss you." Portia sighed heavily. Time ahead without Ellen in her narrow deprived life disturbed Portia. "I will miss you."

Ellen seemed not to have heard her. "I gon' take my baby away from this place to a land where nobody knows neither one of us. . . . I gon' say Scandal, she white. No matter what I have to say of me. . . . I gon' declare and vow Scandal—she white." She nodded, seeing how it would be. "She gone live *white*. . . ."

"I live white," Portia said in an empty voice.

Ellen did not hear this, either. "She live white. . . . Ain't hardly no other way to live in this here world. This world purely belongs to the white people. Us folks got no chance . . . and Scandal she gon' be one of *them*. She gon' to *belong* among 'em. She *be* one of them."

Portia exhaled heavily, grieving. Ellen had set out on a path—uphill, filled with barriers, impossible, and yet Portia saw the mustee woman would not be deterred or turned away, because Ellen was not thinking of herself. She would go through hell for Scandal—if God let the child survive. "Where will you go?"

Ellen glanced at her friend and smiled faintly. "Don't rightly know yet. I'm thinkin' and studying on it. There must be some place where Scandal can live good."

"People are pretty much alike, wherever they are," Portia said. "Their faces are different, their names, but—"

"I sell this place, get me money so I can go north—or maybe I take Scandal to New Orleans. I often hear my old Masta Hammond and his daddy at Falconhurst talking about the *white* ladies in New Orleans with their fine silks and sleek horses and shiny carriages—and some of *them* with skin the color of tea roses. . . . Scandal already whiter than that."

Portia saw it all as accomplished fact. She said emptily, "What will you do? How will you live?"

"How I live here? I strong. I young. I can work. Don't care what work I have to do—long as I free and Scandal white. . . ." She nodded again, emphatically. Something else was determined inside her mind. "I can put Scandal in one of those private church schools—"

"A convent?"

"A convent. Where rich white folks send they chillun. Where them nuns and all teach fancy white girls to grow to be ladies. . . . Scandal be a lady. A great lady. She learn how . . . and she have everything good . . . and she marry a man with tote bags full of gold eagles and she never want for *nuthin'* to the longest day she lives. . . . And she know nuthin' 'bout being *black*—or bein' some man's bed wench to hurt and use any way he likes—or his kitchen slut or his maid, carryin' slop jars for his ugly cross-eyed *white* daughters."

Portia's eyes filled with tears. How wonderful it must be to believe in something—even something in the intangible, unknowable future, even something as impossible as Ellen's plans. How she envied her! How beautiful to have sublime, unquestioning faith in your ability to change this world, even a little bit. And how much more beautiful to believe the fevered, restless, dehydrated baby would live—even through one more night—to grow up to become a great lady, like a princess in some fairy story. But she saw that Ellen *did* believe. She believed that Scandal would survive this deadly illness, that she would take her away from this place to a distant land of milk and honey where she would wrest the milk and honey for Scandal with her own two bare hands and where Scandal at least would live happily ever after.

Blinking back her tears, Portia reached out and gently closed her hand over Ellen's fevered fingers. . . .

By some miracle, or through the unknown properties of the boiled mixture Ellen had learned at Falconhurst, Scandal slowly recovered. Her fever burned incredibly high and burned out quickly. At the end of the first week, the chills abated.

After midnight, Ellen walked into the bedroom, dimly yellow with candlelight. Scandal lay sprawled, face down across her crib. She slept soundly; her forehead felt cool to the touch; her stomach no longer stretched taut and distended. Ellen stood beside the crib, crying silently in exhausted release. . . .

Portia gathered her belongings, ready to leave the next afternoon when Trout walked over from the store. By some mental telepathy, Trout seemed to divine that the long siege was ended. He arrived with a bottle of wine. He came up the steps smiling.

They welcomed him excitedly. They sat together at Ellen's dining table. They laughed mindlessly and drank to the sunlight, to the bees, to leaves on the trees, to the inexplicable joy of being alive. They laughed at nothing. They looked at each other and smiled warmly, filled with genuine mutual love and affection and esteem and gratitude. Each had done his best, made unbelievable sacrifices, learned new ways to exist.

Trout said, "Ain't no way me and Portia can repay you, Ellen. . . . Can't pay *nobody* for savin' a baby's life. . . . But we *know* . . . we fully know . . . your nursin' did it."

"I done only what . . ." Ellen began and then paused.

What had she done? Certainly she had not acted from knowledge or from experience. She had found unsuspected images in her mind and had clung tenaciously to them while she put them into action. It was as if Miz Lucretia Borgia had stood at her side, cautioning her, prompting her, teaching her, refusing to let her waver or retreat or give up to the fear and anguish that tormented her every second. She shook her head. There was no rational explanation for what she had done.

"Whatever you done, it worked." Trout lifted his glass in a tribute. "I been bad toward you, Ellen. I been evil. In my heart. But no more. I'll never forget what you done for me, Ellen. . . . If you'd been human or white, you couldn't've done more. From here on, you our *friend* first above all other folks—"

"Friend?" Portia shook her head vehemently. "Why, Ellen is closer to me than ever any of my own sisters was."

"—and anybody what don't like it," Trout went on and put his head back laughing, "they can answer to me . . . or they can just go straight to hell."

9

Ellen was laughing and talking with Portia and Trout Wilkes when the stranger entered the store. Somehow an unreasoning sense of chill flooded through her as the man appeared, and all laughter ebbed and died. She fell silent and the three of them stood watching the outsider.

He came through the batwings, his stride arrogant and self-important. The screen door screamed on its hinges, slammed shut, flushing coveys of flies.

Though they'd never seen the youth before he gave them an overfriendly and familiar greeting that was somehow condescending. His thin-lipped mouth smiled, but his faded eyes remained flat and watchful. He looked like a man accustomed to glancing often, warily, across his shoulder. He appeared at first glance to be in his midteens. Closer scrutiny showed him to be actually in his twenties. His sunburned face was smooth and immature, but he wore the thickening blond face hairs in patches on his cheeks and chin. Looking at the fellow, Trout reckoned the youth's mind had stopped developing some years earlier; the boy was as mature mentally as he would ever be.

Trade was slow in the early afternoon like this. Most of Wilkes Corners lay in sun-stunned lethargy.

"Howdy, folks." The youth's glance darted around the cavernously shadowed store as if counting heads. He grinned widely, but that strange smile never reached his eyes. "Ridin' through trailin' a runaway nigger. Ain't seed no black buck lurkin' round here, have you?"

Trout tried to laugh warmly. No matter that there was something aggressive, threatening and unwholesome about the young stranger; business was slow and a dollar was a dollar. You didn't run trade away because you disliked the cut of his jib. "We see mighty few slaves round these parts, mister. Nobody within hollerin' distance is wealthy enough to own slaves." He laughed. "We'uns do all our own work. Onliest slaves we got is our wives."

"We'uns got passels of slaves on our place," the youth said

with pride. He waited to let the impact of his statement impress itself upon them. He nodded and smiled that empty smile again, waiting.

"That a fact," Trout said. Though the youth looked like a hundred other shiftless rednecks who eked out a subsistence existence from the red-clay backcountry, obviously this one was set apart, or lied to bolster his own inadequacy.

"Name's Lightfoot." The boy shifted his proud gaze from one face to the next. "Ransom Lightfoot. Own a plantation called The Patch where we breed and raise niggers to sell. Also own the Dovecote Plantation."

"Know Dovecote Plantation well. Lovely old place. Owned by the Verders," Trout said.

The boy shook his head and laughed vacantly. "Ain't no more. Owned by me. Lock. Stock. Barrel. I married Miss Dovie, I did, an' I'm runnin' her farms and her business for her now. As her husband, I reckon I don't exaggerate to say it's all mine." The youth swaggered in self-importance and quivering self-esteem along the aisles, touching at various goods and pretending to read the labels, squinting seriously and pursing his dehydrated lips.

Ellen caught her breath. She recognized the name of Dovecote Plantation and of Miss Dovie Verder. It was she to whom Ellen was to go if she wished to send a message to Master Hammond Maxwell at Falconhurst. Well, she had never gone to Dovecote, never needed to, hoped she never would. All of that was behind her. Falconhurst. The Maxwells. All of it. And she did not mention the fact that she knew Miss Dovie by name for reasons hard for her to analyze. For some reason she had no wish to become involved with this white man, even casually. Something about him troubled and disturbed her. She was afraid of him, even when this made no sense and she could not explain it. She felt as if a chill had entered the store with him and lay across her like a dank shadow. She pressed back against the use-slicked counter into deeper shadows.

"The nigger what runned," Ransom Lightfoot announced loudly, "is a buck. Name of Cairo. They should have nutted the animal when he was a colt and wouldn't have this frettin' with him now."

"There is ladies present," Trout reminded him in a mild tone. He had no wish to offend any potential customer and he felt no particular premonition of wrong or evil about the youth. There existed in his mind only the ordinary prejudice and suspicion every villager felt initially toward a stranger. Anything or anyone unknown to us somehow stirs doubt and traces, at least, of fear. He felt nothing more chary than this toward the visitor. Travelers composed most of Trout's business, people stopping as if at an oasis for sweet drinks, rat cheese and soda crackers. He figured this was likely the extent of any sale he'd make here to the renowned Mr. Ransom Lightfoot of Dovecote Plantation—but a dime was a dime.

"No offense intended, ladies." Ransom looked up and laughed.

"None taken. It's just they ain't as used to discussing the brutal facts way men are," Trout said.

"Sorry. When I talks about niggers, it's just like airy other animal to me. A pig. Or horse. Or cow. 'Ceptin' they talks and grunts, blacks and other beasts are all alike."

"They're not." Portia spoke suddenly and angrily in a firm, low tone.

The young stranger emitted a hoot of derisive laughter. "Now will you listen to that? A nice Southern gentle lady what thinks niggers is not animals?" Lightfoot shook his head, incredulous. "This here lady your wife, suh?" He stared, unblinking, at Trout.

"She is." Unaccountably, Trout felt his face flush with embarrassment. He felt apologetic and hated himself for it.

Lightfoot's mouth twisted with contempt. "You ought to teach her. I kin tell you. Women git to thinkin' of blacks as human. That's when trouble starts. First thing you know they git to thinkin' about them heavy-hung bucks as studs, then them studs as human men. And then you got passels of trouble—a white woman gittin' herself pestered by a nigger buck. Ain't nuthin' lower on this earth."

"No call for you to talk like this, mister," Trout said.

"I'm jus' tryin' to tell you the truth, brother. You know it in your heart. A white woman gittin' herself covered by a black buck is an abomination before the Lord. An' I know niggers. You don't keep a nigger in his place, you got big trouble. I know niggers. Maybe better'n any white man livin' 'ceptin' maybe Mr. Hammond Maxwell of Falconhurst Plantation." His eyes narrowed and he nodded. "Given time I means to make Dovecote Plantation a nigger-breedin' stud farm that will be greater than Falconhurst. Truth is, I've had a lot of experience past few years with them black animals. I serviced black dams for a while. Collected a fee for goin' round and studdin' them black wenches that was in heat—puttin' a little white blood in their gits. . . . Cain't tell me nuthin' 'bout niggers. I know niggers on sight." He laughed. "I can *smell* a nigger, half a mile away."

"What would you like to buy, suh?" Trout prompted. He had developed an intense antipathy for this man and felt he might momentarily catch himself ordering the stranger from his store. This was no way to build a trade or make a profit. And perhaps the youth was not lying. As unlikely as it seemed, perhaps Ransom Lightfoot had married into the aristocratic and respected Verder family. This was a family a merchant was careful not to antagonize.

The front screen door squealed open and slammed shut in a frantic cloud of blue flies. Trout jerked his head around, almost relieved to see the Baptist minister entering the store.

Ransom Lightfoot appraised the minister with interest, sure he'd found an ally. "Howdy, preacher," he said. "Name of Lightfoot. Mr. Ransom Lightfoot, Esquire, of Dovecote Plantation, suh."

The minister smiled in his obsequious way and extended his frail pink hand. "Yes, Mr. Lightfoot. I did indeed hear that Miss Dovie Verder had remarried. Well. Well. Congratulations."

Ransom nodded but waived this topic, his mind involved as it was with his favorite subject, the superiority of the white race over black animals. "Don't truly envy you your work with your flock here in this parish, Reverend," Lightfoot said.

"Why is that, suh?" The minister's smile remained unflappable.

"Well, you got folks right here what see no difference between white and black. Surely, Reverend, you'll verify what I say that the Bible declares plain and undisputed—the sons of Ham, the blacks, is beasts of burden, animals of the fields and borned to slavery."

The minister nodded, his smile gone, replaced by a look of deep sincerity and some dismay. "That is indeed God's word, suh. As the beasts of the fields. Born to slavery. This is the lot of the sons of Ham."

Lightfoot laughed deprecatingly. "These here folks don't seem to agree with you—or with your Bible, Reverend."

The minister smiled in chilled disdain. "I don't doubt that, sir. They that consort with blacks. On equal terms. Take them right into their house. Drink from the same utensils. I don't doubt it."

Ransom Lightfoot peered at them narrowly. "What kind of folks are you?"

"Good Christian folk," Portia answered. "Who believe what Jesus taught."

Lightfoot put his head back laughing, but it was laughter not to be shared, sound without mirth. "Jesus never taught no pesterin' with black bucks, ma'am," he told her, his voice clawing with contempt.

"Did He preach the right for white men to defile black women?" Portia said, her face pale.

Trout looked ill. He lifted his hand but let it fall to his side ineffectually.

Ransom's voice rasped. "He didn't say 'bout that, either way, ma'am. That's just business. Good business. Put some human blood in your black herd. That don't hurt 'em none. Makes 'em look more *human*—even if'n they ain't. Makes 'em sell better on the auction stand. Brings a better price, ma'am. . . . No, ma'am, it ain't the same at all."

"How nice that must make it for you and the minister. Believin' that part of the Bible that pleases you—and shuttin' your minds to the rest," Portia said.

"Portia. Now please." Trout's voice quavered.

Offended, the minister straightened, his back going ramrod straight, his face flushing, his body tensed, set against her and anything she had to say. "And what part of the Bible do I—a holy man—shut my mind to, Mrs. Wilkes?"

"She didn't mean nuthin' offensive, Reverend," Trout said.

The Reverend waved Trout aside. "No. I must insist that she answer me. She's made very grave charges against a man of the cloth. I feel that the church itself has been desecrated."

"Can't be that serious," Trout whispered.

Portia stared across the counter at the taut standing minister. "I don't mind answering you. Don't mind telling you." Her eyes filled with tears and she clenched her hands into fists to hide their trembling, to conceal even from herself her inner terror at a verbal attack upon the preacher. "I'll tell you what part you don't even believe in—the part that says do unto others—do unto others as you'd have them do unto you."

The minister's lips grayed and his bleak eyes glittered, ignited by the fires of his inner rages. He opened his mouth to reply, but before he could speak, Ransom Lightfoot cried out in the horror of discovery, staring down into Ellen's face. "Why you—you is a nigger wench, ain't you?"

Ellen said nothing. She was afraid to trust herself to speak. Her legs felt weak, as if they could not support her weight. The minister was pleased to answer for her. "She's a Negress, all right. A freed black person of color, if you will. Living biggety as you please in a house right among white folks."

"My Gawd." Ransom shook his head, his dull eyes fixed on Ellen's face. "They's one thing on this earth I cain't no-way tolerate—hit's a biggety nigger."

"Amen," the minister said.

"Sashaying round, pushing white folks out'n their way," Ransom said, trembling at the very idea.

"There's no call to take on this way," Trout said. "Ellen is a customer. Same as you folks. She's welcome here to trade—same as anybody else."

"More welcome than some." Portia stared coldly at Lightfoot.

"And why not?" The minister's voice grated and bristled with righteous indignation. "She owns her own house. Free and clear. More land than any of the rest of us. Gold eagles to spend. Where does she get this money? I tell you, I feel the devil himself has come among us."

Ransom Lightfoot paced back and forth, staring at Ellen, licking at his downy-whiskered mouth.

"What was it you wished to buy, Mr. Lightfoot?" Trout's voice started strong and determined but faded, despairing.

Lightfoot didn't seem even to hear him. "Cain't believe that self-respectin' white folks would trade in a store alongside a nigger. Not even a so-called freed black."

"We're being sorely tried by the good lord," the minister said, shaking his head, his voice pious and unctuous.

"And her with gold eagles to spend." Lightfoot shook his head, gazing around him. "Likely she gits them whorin'."

"Get out," Portia told him.

Both Lightfoot and the minister ignored Portia. "My very words," the minister said. "Where else would she get money except selling her body in lascivious sinful ways? We can't prove her evil. Not yet. But I say to you this. When we do have our proof, we'll stone her from our midst—as the Bible says."

"The Bible says *forgive*! Turn the other cheek! Love thy neighbor as thyself," Portia cried, trembling.

"That don't mean niggers," Lightfoot said. "Niggers ain't your neighbors. They your animals. Your slaves. I can tell you folks this right plain out. Mr. Bannion at his store across the river, he don't 'low biggety niggers hang around his store. Inside. Or out. They come to his front stoop. They stand on the ground at the foot of the steps. They calls out their order and Bannion brings it out and sets it on the steps. Like any self-respectin' white man ought."

"Why don't you go across the river to Bannion's store to trade?" Portia said. Ellen wanted to calm her friend, but knew that her touching the white woman would incite the minister and Mr. Lightfoot to fury. She did not move.

"I'm white," Lightfoot told her in towering anger. "A white gentleman. I goes where I wish. But I won't come back in this place as long as you serve niggers same as if they was human."

Trout cleared his throat. "Maybe you best get along now, Mr. Lightfoot, suh."

"You tellin' me to git out?" Lightfoot's voice quivered.

Trout nodded, his face twisted in misery. "Yes, suh. I'm sorry. We don't need your trade."

Lightfoot looked around, wounded in his pride, pained and enraged. He had never before encountered such injustice and discrimination. "You'll regret this, Mistah Wilkes."

"Likely." Trout glanced about, agonized. "Still I'm askin' you polite to leave. Now."

Lightfoot glanced toward the minister, raked his gaze across Portia's face, looked for some moments at Wilkes as if burning the image of the storekeeper on his mind. He took one long stride toward the doorway and the brilliant sunlight beyond. Then he turned and stared directly at Ellen. "A biggety nigger, eh? Livin' in her own house? Passin' gold eagles round like copper pennies —reckon my brother Jonas be mighty interested in a black wench like that."

10

The next weeks were the happiest in Ellen's life. True, once in a while some ugly occurrence, such as that brief, disturbing scene in Trout Wilkes' store with the stranger, Mr. Ransom Lightfoot of Dovecote Plantation, troubled and terrified her, magnified her sense of loneliness. But she realized she must anticipate and accept this kind of fearful confrontation as long as she existed in the white man's world. This threat was something she just had to live with, something she would always hate and fear, but which she was learning to live with. She bent like a reed in the wind; she compromised, she bowed and scraped before her white neighbors. She did everything she could think to ease the tensions. If they did not welcome her in their midst, they left her alone.

She was learning how to live alone, too. She became daily more independent and self-reliant. She found she could use a saw if she had to; she could drive nails and wring necks of chickens for Sunday dinner. Sometimes, with a feeling of exultant accomplishment, she felt there was nothing she could not do, as long as she was working for her own freedom and for Scandal's security. The baby's desperate illness had demonstrated to her how valuable, precious, sweet and fragile human life was. She now found pleasures in small things she'd never even noticed before.

Every morning she woke with the crowing of her dominique rooster out on the split-rail fence of the pigpens. She found Scandal standing in her crib, smiling, ready to begin the new day with her. She lifted the baby in her arms and held her tightly. "It's all worth it, Scandal," she whispered. "You make it all worth it."

She looked forward with eager anticipation to each fresh morning with its chores and routines and puzzles and trials and challenges. Making her own way in the world brought her the exultance of achievement she'd never experienced before. She was free! She had Scandal, her own home, her own garden. This was sufficient for her.

In the daylight hours she was far too busy and preoccupied to think about woes or depressing threats or anxieties. Night, at first and for a long time after she moved into this lonely house, was a hell for her. But now, with all this physical exertion, she was too exhausted by nightfall to lie awake in fear. She slowly forgot to be afraid. . . .

Something wakened her.

Ellen could not say what it was, a sound, a whisper of noise, a mouse in the rafters, night wind trailing a hibiscus limb against the house. Usually, she slept as if stunned from eight at night until dawn the next morning.

She sat up in bed, her heart pounding. The night was thickly black with gloom which covered the room like a shroud. She could not see anything. She sat, feeling her blood pulse achingly at the base of her throat. This unreasoning panic didn't make sense. She didn't even know why she was frightened. But fear possessed her as it had not since her first nights alone in this house.

The night world was breathlessly still. The countryside was so quiet she was conscious of her own ragged breathing. She supposed it must be some time after midnight. The village lay silent. No raucous yells of laughter rose from Wilkes' Tavern next door to the general store. Sounds carried in the village night. So, she learned, did silences.

She longed for a sound, even the rustling tread of a prowler, or a night animal, anything that would explain what had wakened her. Even the barking of a distant dog would be reassuring. The idea raced through her mind that tomorrow morning she would get a dog of her own, first thing.

She exhaled heavily, told herself to lie down and go back to sleep. She was letting her imagination drive her over the brink into panic. After all, perhaps the fragment of some bad dream had wakened her.

She decided she had been too inactive these past weeks. She hadn't worked hard enough in the garden to send herself to bed exhausted and ready to sleep.

She sighed. The long pleasant summer days had boiled into a spell of dank inclement weather when there was little for her and Scandal to do but stay inside and watch rain stretch slow, syrupy patterns along darkened panes of the windows. Days followed nights of bitter chill, rain and drizzle. Each morning the yard stood mired in black puddles and the road was cut and rutted by small torrents. There were few chances to get outside to work, to visit Portia at the store. It was a wet, cold unpleasant time.

She heard a whisper of sound from the yard. Thinking it might be a weasel after her chickens, Ellen got up and ran to the window.

The night was overcast and clabbered with low-hanging black clouds which seemed to smoke close across the dark scalloped tree tops.

She saw something move in the yard. She stared, certain it was the lean shadow of a skulking man in the deeper shadows of the trees. Frozen in inarticulate terror, Ellen stared out the window trying to find that fleeting shadow.

She swallowed hard at the lump in her throat. Someone was out there. She backed away from the window, knocked over a chair. The sound was thunder-loud in the stillness. She gasped and stood immobile for a moment, frantic.

The falling chair wakened Scandal. The baby pulled herself up in her crib, crying lustily.

"Oh my God, Scandal," Ellen whispered in an agony of fear. "Be quiet. Please be quiet."

Icy cold and stiff with fright, Ellen padded to the crib and took Scandal up in her arms, whispering, petting, quieting and soothing her.

Standing there with Scandal caught against her breast, she heard footsteps on the porch. Then a man's whispered voice, cautious: "Don't reckon there be a dog, be there?"

Scathing whispered laughter answered him. "Since when has a dog scairt you, Jonas?"

Now certain there were prowlers—at least two—and that there was immediate danger, Ellen could think only one thing: flight. She had to get out of here to her nearest neighbor. Even if they refused to take her in, she would be safe from assault.

She caught up a flannel robe and worked her arms into it. She'd heard the whispers from the front porch. Carrying Scandal, she ran toward the back door.

In her panic and anxiety to escape, she did not hear the squeal of the door hinges. The kitchen door was thrown open. She stopped, numbed with terror, and stared up into the deeply shadowed face of a man in a flop-brim beaver hat.

"Who are you?" Terror made her whimper.

Instead of answering her, the man yelled, "Jonas! Round here. I got the bitch."

Clutching Scandal against her, Ellen heeled and ran toward the front of the house. Heavy boots pounded in pursuit. Scandal screamed in mindless terror. Ellen pressed her closer.

The front door was broken at the lock and swung back on its hinges like a broken wing.

A man strode through the doorway. Like a trapped rabbit, Ellen stood, looking about wildly, paralyzed with fear.

The man behind her caught her about the waist and jerked her body roughly back against his. She felt the hardness of his muscles, the rough fabric of his clothing, smelled the nauseating musk of his sweating, the stink of chewing tobacco on his breath.

"Heah she be, Jonas. Jest like I tole you. Black woman livin' lonesome all by herself and jest pinning for some good pesterin'."

"How 'bout we light a lamp and see what we got heah, Ransom?" Jonas laughed, his voice fluting in anticipation. "Likes to see the wench what's goin' to be pleasurin' me, I do."

"Don't need no light," Ransom said. His hands crawled like vermin over Ellen's body. "Light 'tracts attention. "Sides, all cats is gray in the dark, you know that. Takes my word. She's some gyascutus-lookin' little baggage—for a nigger gal. Looks almost human—damn near white she is—and built like a picnic."

Scandal's screams rose to a wail of terror. Ransom cursed. He released Ellen and caught the child in both his hands. Ellen fought furiously and silently, but she was helpless against Lightfoot. He jerked the baby from Ellen's arms. Casually, as if it were a tote bag of beans, he tossed the infant to Jonas. "Git rid of this yellin' brat," he said.

Jonas caught the baby. "Hell, I don't want it." He threw the child across the room.

Scandal struck the floor and baseboard in the darkness. The sound was sickening, like a ripe watermelon dropped on an unyielding surface.

"My baby!" Ellen screamed. Lightfoot caught her wrists, but she fought savagely.

"Shut your mouth, you black slut." Ransom backhanded her across the mouth. "You can git yo'self plenty more bastard drops, but you never find 'nother pleasurin' like you gon' git here tonight."

"Amen." Jonas came closer, massaging Ellen's body with his hands, his whiskey-hot breath ugly and nauseous in her face.

"What do you want?" Ellen begged. "You want money? I'll give you my money—all I got."

"We'll take the money, too." Ransom laughed. "When we gits round to it. But first things first. And first, I means to have me a good ole time with this pretty little body."

"Come on, wench," Jonas said. "Git out of them clothes. Le's see them goodies you got for us."

"Let me alone. Get out of here," Ellen wailed.

Raging, Ransom caught her throat in his fists and closed his fingers until she could no longer breathe, until she no longer was able to cry out, or even to whimper.

"You don't tell us what to do, slut. We white. Ain't none of your goddam business what we do with you. That's up to us. But I tell you this much. Oh, I will. I mean to have me some fun . . . Now we can have it with you helpin'—or you fighting'—don't make no never-mind to me, long as I gits it."

"Amen," Jonas said. "I like a fightin' woman myself," he panted. "I like some scrap in my rides."

Jonas stepped closer and ran his hands over Ellen's body as Ransom held her pinned against him. His breath burned, liquor-hot and sickening; his hands seared her, hard and callused and cruel.

For one moment Ellen sagged against the hardness of Ransom. He was lulled into momentary torment of promised delights. He worked her upon his stiffness. As Jonas caught the bodice of her cotton gown, ripping downward, Ellen brought her knee upward with all her force into his crotch.

Jonas fell away, wretching and gasping for breath. He bent over, staggering, and clutched at his belly.

"Damn black slut," Ransom said. "Goin' fix you good for that."

He caught her throat in the crook of his arm and applied terrible pressure. She felt as if her neck would burst like squeezed fruit. She fought, at first furiously, then frantically, and finally weakly and despairingly. The fierce arm tightened like thick coils of wire, strangling her. She could no longer breathe. Her mind spun, her mouth parted as she tried to gasp in one breath of air and could not. She fainted.

She wakened once. She was barely conscious. She was naked and sprawled across her bed. One of the soured, malodorous men thrust himself upon her cruelly, gasping for breath, wild with passion.

From some incredible distance she could hear Ransom Lightfoot's ranting voice. It was as if he sucked sensual pleasure from verbally abusing her as he physically ravaged her body. "Think to live among decent, God-fearin' Christian white folks, do you, Ellen? Wench? You a nigger, ain't you? Ain't you, damn you? No matter you got paper what say you freed, you jus' a nigger. Say it, damn you . . . you jus' a nigger—like beasts of the field. Live like you white, eh? Think us Christian white people goin' to allow that, black slut?"

The raging voice faded and she plunged into unconsciousness as if to escape the unbearable torture being meted to her without pause, without mercy.

Once more, after a dark eternity, she wakened. She opened her eyes, her body wracked with pain as if she were afire inside. A wan light flared, painful against her eyes.

Ransom Lightfoot stood over her, a candle held aloft. Ellen tried to move, but could not. From that incredible distance, she heard Ransom's voice: "Look at the high and mighty black slut now. Bloody mess, ain't she? Looks like your big ole tool just 'bout whopped her to death, Jonas boy."

From somewhere, outside the narrow focus of her blood-occluded gaze, Ellen vaguely heard Jonas' cold laughter. "Well, I shore 'nough whopped on it—ever' blessed way I knowed."

"You had 'nough?"

"Gawd yes. Le's get out of here."

"Yeah. Yeah. Soon as I take care of this here biggety black slut."

"What you gon' do 'bout her?"

Ransom laughed. "Jus' what we meant to do, all along. Kill the uppity black bitch—teach them other freed niggers they cain't come livin' big and mighty 'mong decent white folks."

"Gun make lot of noise this time of night."

"Use a knife. Jus' as quick. Jus' as deadly. Hell, she already nearer dead than alive, no-how."

Jonas shook his head. "I cain't do it."

"Why not? Hell, it's just a nigger. You slaughter hogs, don't you?"

Jonas sounded ill. "You do it, Ransom. Hell, I'm tired talkin' 'bout it. I cain't find no money hid nowhere. Let's torch the goddam house and git out of here."

Ellen tried to raise herself, searching for Scandal in the wanly lighted room. She saw Ransom Lightfoot bending over her. Helpless, she fought to ward off the arm and the four-inch knife blade glittering in lamplight. His guttural laughter spewed like bile over her. The knife was driven upward to the hilt into her vagina and ripped upward. She sagged back on the bed and did not move again. Blood gorged up in her throat and bubbled across her lips as she died. She whispered, "Herman." It was the last word she spoke on this earth.

11

Emeraude slumped tiredly on the buggy seat. She clung to Herman's arm, bumped, battered and shaken with every turn of the iron-rimmed wheels on the potholed, ill-marked trace.

"You all right?" Herman asked for the uncounted time since they had droven out of New Orleans three days ago.

Emeraude nodded, too exhausted to speak. How lovely she was! When he'd first known her—in the long-lost years of her childhood—she'd been a leggy little cherub who had adored him. She had turned into a startling beauty. She was tall, with a heavy coif of smooth black hair that seemed too heavy for her slender neck. Her skin was the texture and old-ivory whiteness of magnolia petals, with a faint tint of rose in her cheeks. Black brows, slender wings over emerald-green eyes that were lost under incredibly long curling lashes. Her lips were full, moist and inviting, her teeth gleaming and white. Her perfectly formed full breasts and pointed nipples rose against the gauze of her blouse. He could have spanned her slender waist with both his hands. Her hips were slender yet rounded to long, beautifully formed legs concealed beneath her flowing pastel skirt.

Emeraude stared at the slowly passing woodlands, bay trees,

oaks, tupelos. This was like entering a world unknown, unknowable. This was territory she'd never seen in her life before, an existence unlike anything she'd ever experienced. The farther they traveled from New Orleans the more it was as if they abandoned civilization and entered a strange, wild region of flies, gnats, enervating heat, suspicious innkeepers and flat-eyed farmers, and always with fearful, skulking wild beasts in the underbrush close beside the trail. Their stops in the ordinaries and inns along the way were the worst times of all: they slept—as much as they could—in vermin-infested beds, ate greasy, ill-cooked food in cracked dishes.

"Are you sure you want to do this?" Herman said.

"I only want this torture to end," Emeraude said in flat honesty. "This trip from New Orleans to Alabama must be a survival test —if you live through it, you can endure anything." She shook her head, glancing around nervously at the menace of encroaching forest and tangled swamplands. Sometimes, for hours at a time, they seemed to have the world to themselves, only it was not a world she wanted. Even God seemed to have forgotten and forsaken this steaming wilderness. "No. Really, I just worry about Ellen. What she will say. What she will do. Will she want to let her baby go—even if it is best for the child?"

"I'll talk to Ellen. I'll make her understand. She knows—almost as well as I do—what hell it is for a black child to grow up in a world like this down here in this redneck country."

Emeraude sighed. "I don't know which one I pity most—Ellen if she lets her baby go with us, or the poor child if Ellen won't let her go."

"Ellen will let her go," Herman said. He spoke with an assurance he did not feel. "She'll have to see what is best for Scandal. . . . No matter what else, she'll have to see that you and I can give her baby—" He winced. "—our baby—everything in Europe. We can give her things she could never have here. I'll make Ellen see that. . . ."

Herman clapped the reins hard across the sweated rump of the horse, staring ahead almost as if he could see Ellen's gentle, tea-rose face in the blue-misted distance. . . .

Herman followed precisely the directions given him by Lucretia Borgia. He could not still a sense of panic fluttering deeply in his belly like disturbed wasps as they neared the village of Benson. Falconhurst was only a few miles beyond the town. He did not want to meet Hammond Maxwell. He and Maxwell had had their confrontation in New Orleans. The master of Falconhurst was not a man given to idle threat: Maxwell had said he would kill him if he ever again came near the plantation. Maxwell might well attempt to assault him if he discovered Herman Hengst in the environs of the stud farm.

Herman sighed out heavily, feeling a sense of relief and release when they turned away from Benson on the narrow, poorly marked trace to an even smaller settlement, Wilkes Corners.

When he drove the chariotee into the village, Emeraude was somehow asleep, exhausted and physically battered, slumped against his side.

Herman grinned gently, glancing at her lovely young face. She had been more understanding—about his liaison with Ellen, about the baby—than he had dared hope. He could see the faint hurt in her eyes as he confessed the truth about his affair with the mustee girl at Falconhurst. She may have wished things different, but she realized Herman had had a life away from her—an often cruel and anguished existence. She tried to keep it all in perspective. Herman loved no one but her now, and this was important. She tried to think what was best for Herman's daughter. She had laughed ruefully. No matter how she felt, no decent person could deny a child—any child—a God-given opportunity to escape this evil, narrow, deprived and depriving backwater land. . . .

Though Herman observed Lucretia Borgia's directions to the letter, he did not at once find the house where Lucretia Borgia had said Ellen now lived as a "freed person of color."

Herman pulled on the reins, halting beside a village shack. A weathered white man sat in the shade of a chinaberry tree repairing aged leather straps. Emeraude awoke and sat up, looking around, disoriented, blinking, faintly troubled.

The man stared at Herman oddly at first when he asked for the house of a woman named Ellen. Then, after a faint delay, the aging man shrugged and inclined his head along the narrow, hard-packed clay road. "Yonder," he said. "Second place. You cain't miss it."

The white man sat idly watching as Herman turned the buggy on the narrow roadway. He slumped on the broken chair with the rotted leather harness gripped in gnarled fists, squinting after them until the vehicle was out of sight beyond a ragged hedge of pines.

Herman drew the carriage to a halt in the charred yard.

"The house," Emeraude whispered, hoarse with horror. "It isn't here. The house has been burned down."

Herman could only nod. He sat as if struck numb, like Lot's

wife, for daring to look back, and stared at the blackened remains of the razed shack. A chimney and fireplace reared, the only remaining structure in the flames-wasted ruins.

"Can this be the right place?" Emeraude whispered, shaking her head. "Can it be?"

Sick, Herman sat immobile. Somehow, he knew this was all that remained of Ellen's home. He recalled the odd look in the face of the white man under the chinaberry tree. Herman's eyes brimmed with tears. He blinked them away. Rage moiled deeply in his belly as his gaze trailed slowly, horrified, across this senseless destruction, the ravaged house, incinerated barns and outbuildings. Nothing remained but the blackened chimney. He shivered, deeply shaken.

Emeraude spoke again, numb. "Maybe this isn't Ellen's place."

Herman only shook his head. Nauseated with agony and outrage, he knew: this had been the small farm Hammond Maxwell had bought for his exiled concubine, the place to which Ellen had come to live as a freed woman of color.

Emeraude's voice shook. "We've got to find her, Herman. She must have lost everything in the fire."

His voice rasped savagely over hers. "They burned her out."

Emeraude closed her fingers on his wrist. "She and the baby. They must be somewhere near. Somebody would have taken her and the baby in after this terrible tragedy—"

"No. No white would take in a black. . . . They burned her out. Goddam them, they burned her out."

The weathered white man remained sitting on the broken chair shaded by the wide-reaching chinaberry tree. When he saw Herman pull the carriage in before his rickety gate, the man sprang up and walked stiffly toward his front door.

"Mister." Herman's voice rang like gunfire. It stopped the man like a pistol mouth against his spine. "Just a minute, mister."

"What you want?" The man turned slowly, sun-hardened face chilled.

"You didn't tell us they'd burned her house."

"You didn't ast me that."

"I'm asking you now. Where is she?"

The man shrugged. "Don't know. . . . Didn't have no truck with her before the fire. . . . Maybe you could ask the preacher." He jerked his head toward the church and its small frame parsonage next door.

Both the Baptist minister and his stout wife answered the front door when Herman knocked on it. Emeraude stood at Herman's shoulder. The preacher smiled warmly. "Howdy, folks. Welcome to Wilkes Corners. Won't you come in and set?"

"We just want to ask you some questions." Herman forced his voice to remain calm.

"Of course."

"About Miss Ellen. The freed woman who lived down the road."

Smiles died on both the faces beyond the screened door. A sense of tension bubbled and smoked out around them.

"We don't know anything about her," the woman said. "We didn't know her. . . . She was black—a nigger, you know."

"Yes." Herman's hands clenched at his sides but he forced himself to keep his voice level, neutral. "Yes. I know she's black. . . . We'd like to find her. It's very important. Could you tell us where we can find her? That man—there along the road—sent us here. He said you would know where we could find the freed woman."

The preacher's smile stretched, unctuous. "Caleb knew better . . . he just didn't want to talk about her—to strangers. That's all. This is a very strange business. Very sad. Ellen—the freed black woman—and her child. They came here to live. Well, we're God-fearing people, but we believe the races each have their place—as I'm sure you believe—"

"Not a sermon, sir. Just tell me where she is."

The minister's voice chilled, hardened. "She's dead. . . . She was—consumed in the fire."

Herman staggered. It was as if the preacher had struck him in the face. He managed to ask, his throat tightening on the words, "And—her baby?"

The minister shrugged. "The baby's dead, too. Far as we know. . . . As I say, we didn't want Ellen here. Living among us. But none of us—no one in this village—would have burned her house. I know that. I would swear that."

"Somebody did."

The preacher nodded. "Somebody did. We're sorry. Deeply sorry. It's cast a pall over our town. . . . But that's all I can tell you. . . . You might ask at Wilkes' store."

Herman smiled coldly. "Pushing us on—like Caleb did, eh?"

The minister spread his hands. "You asked, mister. That's all I can tell you. All I know."

"It's all we *want* to know," the minister's wife said.

12

Darkness smoked in over the village from the timberlands, lancing bleak shadows across street and buildings. Wilkes Corners, like most backcountry settlements, fell into stunned inactivity at nightfall, inhabitants retreating for the night into wanly lit houses where beams creaked and mice scrurried in the walls, moths battered mindlessly at lamps. A cacophony of frogs shattered the silence and became a part of it; crickets squealed in thickets; a frightened dog barked, a barn owl hooted, and lost in the black swamplands, a panther screamed.

A thin, seedy man and a tired-looking woman in shapeless cotton shift were closing Wilkes' general store for the day when Herman drove to its front stoop in the two-seater buggy.

The man paused, straightening up from the sacks of dried beans which he was removing from the stoop. He stretched tall, supporting the small of his back with the heels of both his hands. The woman continued to move merchandise inside the store, letting the screen door slam loudly behind her. Three small boys, in tattered and faded blue overalls, lounged barefooted, near the door. They gazed with dull eyes at the strangers.

The storekeeper was already shaking his head. "Closing for the night, mister," he said as Herman swung down from the carriage. "You have to come back in the morning. We open bright and early in the morning. Six o'clock sharp."

"I'm looking for Mr. Wilkes." Herman smiled, exhausted. "Are you Mr. Trout Wilkes?"

The dull-eyed children giggled and nudged each other. The man shook his head. "Not likely. My name's Peavey, mister. Herschel Peavey. I own this store."

Herman kept his tone as friendly as possible, but firm. He would not be put off any more by these xenophobic rednecks. "I was told I could find him here."

"Well, I don't see how you can." The man winked at his giggling brood. "He ain't here."

"But I was told Mr. Trout Wilkes owns this store."

The man shrugged. "Maybe folks think he still owns it. His name is on it and all. He did own it. He sold out. Turned it over to me. Months past." As if ending the interview, he bent over to take up one of the heavy bags of beans.

"Can you tell me—please—were you here when the freedwoman's house burned?"

The grocer seemed relieved to delay the moment when he must heft the seventy-pound croker sack of dried beans. He straightened again. He peered down at Herman at the foot of the steps. "Don't know nuthin' 'bout that, mister."

The screen door slammed again and the slump-shouldered woman emerged from the lighted store. She glanced toward Herman and then at Emeraude in the carriage, but shuffled toward a rack of shovels which had to be taken inside for the night. The grocer spoke to her. "You know anythin' about some nigger woman's house burnin' down, Miz Peavey?"

The woman hesitated, shrugged. "No more'n you do, Herschel. Only what I heered. Nigra woman lived here. Biggety Negress, they say. Nobody wanted her here. Her place was burnt down. Happened before we come here. We never knowed her."

Herman sighed heavily. "But the Wilkeses were here? They knew her?"

"Reckon."

"Maybe if I could talk to them."

"Told you, mister. They ain't here no more." The grocer shook his head. "Turned this here store over to us and moved out."

Herman glanced toward Emeraude, feeling lost, overwhelmed with fatigue. He wondered if he could ask Emeraude to endure further search in this torturous backcountry where every stranger was an unwanted alien, suspected, despised, feared and mistrusted. He exhaled heavily. "Could you folks be kind enough to tell us where the Wilkeses moved?"

"Nowhere close round here, mister."

Herman nodded. "If you could just tell me what town?"

"No town. Farm near the Chattahoochee River."

"Portia and Trout, they tooken over our farm," the woman said. "They come to us and said they would run our farm and let us take over the store here."

Herman frowned, mystified. "Did they say why they would do that?"

"They wanted to, mister," the grocer said.

"A farm would have to be worth a great deal to equal the value of this store—and this tavern," Herman said.

Herschel Peavey shrugged. "It was what they wanted."

"But why would they want that?"

Herschel Peavey laughed. "Beats me, friend. Cousin Trout never was no farmer. Hated plowing. Chores made him sick. He left off farmin' when he was just a tad. His wife Portia, she was a schoolteacher. Always acted uppity towards us. Both of them.

Like they was better than us dirt farmers 'cause they owned this here general store. They offered it to me and it was a good deal and I grabbed it, mister. No questions axt."

"They wanted to get away from here," Mrs. Peavey said. "For some reason, they was real anxious to git away from here."

"That's for sure." Herschel Peavey nodded, grinning and slapping his leg.

They slept that night in a rented room at the Baptist Church parish house. The minister charged more for the facility than they'd paid in any inn or ordinary on the trail east from New Orleans. He prayed lengthily over the supper of pork, sweet potatoes, navy beans and corn pone, praying for the safety of the travelers, for that day when they would find God in the one true church, for the dedication and funding of God's work, and he charged extra for the meal. Before Emeraude and Herman were permitted to go to bed, they had to join the minister and his wife on their knees in the parlor for evening prayers. That voice droned interminably. Herman's knees ached and he fought back the urge to savage laughter. The minister prayed over them again at breakfast—the cost added—and suggested that a financial contribution from the travelers might incline God's heart warmly toward them in their mission. Herman started to tell him to go to hell, but superstitiously decided he wanted even this man's deity on his side in his search for Scandal. He contributed and escaped the place, feeling a sense of taut freedom that dissolved finally, miles long the trail, in amazed laughter.

"Someday we'll look back on this and laugh," he said.

"Yes." Emeraude touched his hand. "The three of us."

Herman winced slightly, discouraged and fatigued. "You really think we'll find her?"

Emeraude nodded emphatically, "I know how terribly you want to. I know God will help you."

Herman laughed, self-mockingly. "I'm afraid the God who approves of that minister back there wouldn't recognize me."

"Yes. But how do you know God approves of him?"

The twenty-five-mile journey ended at last. Twenty-five miles removed Trout and Portia Wilkes two and a half days across execrable roads from their old home and former friends at Wilkes Corners.

If, for whatever reason, the grocer wished to be removed from anyone he'd known in Wilkes Corners, this farm accomplished his purpose, put him apart from them. It was as if he and Portia lived in another world. Few people traveled the dangerous country paths and lanes and traces by horse, or carriage, as far as twenty-five miles from their own homesteads. On the subsistence farm near the rim of the Chattahoochee River swamps, Portia and Trout Wilkes lived now among strangers.

Herman guided his horse into the bare farmyard almost to the sagging front stoop of the unpainted shack. A dog lunged up from the washwater-wet ground around the sun-petrified plank steps; it barked tentatively and then loped under the pinewood porch, tail between its legs.

Holding his breath, without knowing why he did, Herman swung down from the carriage, went up the steps and knocked on the door. "Mr Wilkes?" he called. "Anybody home?"

Late-evening silence hung oppressively for some moments and then the door was pulled slightly ajar. A balding man with large head, thin shoulders and short bandy legs stared out at them. His hands were blistered, callused, torn by unaccustomed farm labor. His lean face was pocked with purpling sun sores.

He hesitated a long breath, studying them, suspicious and wary. Herman saw he held a gun concealed against his right leg. "Who you looking for?"

Mr. Trout Wilkes," Herman said. He smiled, hoping to reassure the man, allay his ill-controlled panic.

The balding man frowned. "I'm Trout Wilkes. What you folks want of me? We got no money. No food to sell. No room to rent. I'm sorry."

He looked as if he would close the door. Herman touched its facing, holding it tentatively. "We'd like to talk to you, Mr. Trout." He nodded toward Emeraude, who sagged with weariness on the boot of the carriage.

"What about?" The man looked ready to force the door closed.

"We came to Wilkes Corners. To your store. Looking for a freedwoman. A Negress—named Ellen." Herman tried to smile. "Folks at your store sent us here to you. They said you knew Ellen, might know what happened to her—and her baby."

Trout Wilkes sighed out heavily. He hesitated a long beat and then he opened the door and stood in it gazing at Herman. He held the gun in plain sight now. His sun-paled eyes were bleak and watchful. His thin-lipped mouth pulled down at the corners. He looked like a man driven to the brink, a man who had forgotten how to laugh. His thin hair hung in lifeless strings down the sides of his head. "Might've knowed such a woman. Why?"

"We came looking for her," Emeraude said. "All the way from New Orleans. We'd appreciate anything you could tell us about her."

"And her baby," Herman said.

The bald man's unhappy eyes lightened faintly under Emeraude's persuasive smile. He relaxed slightly and nodded. "I knowed Ellen."

"We found her house burned."

Trout Wilkes nodded. "Burnt to the ground."

"Is Ellen dead?" Herman asked.

Trout Wilkes nodded. He hesitated, then: "Maybe you folks would care to come in. Got no idea why fine white folks like you would be looking for Ellen. But hope you might be friends of hers."

"Oh, we are," Emeraude said. Herman came down the steps and helped her from the carriage. Wilkes watched them come across the narrow pine-floored porch.

"Nothing very fancy here," Wilkes said. "We don't have much company these days. So far from any town and all . . . things have been pretty rough for us . . . getting started on a farm and all. . . . But take out and set. We can't talk about Miss Ellen out here."

Trout held the door open. Herman and Emeraude entered the sparsely furnished parlor and followed Wilkes into the lighted kitchen. This room looked to be the heart of the house, boasting a wood-burning stove, a pinewood table holding remains of a meager evening meal, a few kitchen chairs, and two cribs in the shadowed corner most distant from the old iron stove.

All windows were opened to the humid evening, but the heat inside the room was enervating. A woman sat on a kitchen chair at the cluttered table. She appeared to be in her early thirties, much younger than her husband, but already graying, her eyes lined and somehow inexplicably frantic. Her skin was dry and coffee-dark. Mingled odors of damp diapers, coffee, soured milk and spoiled foodstuffs pervaded the room, but the woman appeared oblivious to it.

"My wife, Miz Portia," Wilkes said, nodding toward the distracted woman. "Portia, these here people have come all the way from N'Awleans looking for Miss Ellen."

Portia nodded listlessly. Her eyes brimmed with tears and she shook her head, without speaking, as if she dared not speak.

Wilkes' faded eyes touched at his wife. He said, "Miz Portia, she ain't been well—not since Miss Ellen died. Miz Portia, she taken it pretty hard. . . . We was first ones at Miss Ellen's place that night. We found it burning."

Portia looked up and nodded absently. "Ellen was a fine woman. Couldn't have been no better if'n she'd been purentee white. . . . I was the only one who ever visited her in her house . . . and she come to visit me at our store. . . . We was close, Ellen and me. . . . She kept my baby alive. She taken me and my sick baby in when nobody else would—when my baby was dying and stricken with bowel fever. . . . Ellen was a wonderful person." Her voice trailed off and she lapsed into vague silence, staring at her work-blistered hands.

"What happened?" Herman said. "How did her house burn?"

"Was set afire. Vicious set. Malicious." Portia nodded, her mouth quivering. "Set a-purpose . . . they burned her out."

Her husband spread his callused, broken hands. "Folks round that village—white folks—they got no more'n me and Portia have. Less, most of them. Prideful. They didn't cotton to a Negro woman owning her own house right there in our town—and it some better than most with twenty acres of friable land—and her with a kitchen garden like none of them white folks had the energy or the gumption to make."

"And her house—Miss Ellen kept her whole house scrubbed and dusted and polished. Spotless." Portia glanced around the littered kitchen helplessly. "Them white people hated Ellen and they wanted her out. They treated her bad, hoping she would leave. She was feelin' bad about the way they acted toward her. She asked me if I thought she should try to stay on there in that house of her own when plainly the neighbors thereabouts resented her and didn't want her living amongst them. . . ." She shuddered and sighed deeply. "I told her nobody had the right to run her off her own land if she didn't want to go. She had good, clear title. Just as she had legal papers declaring her a freedwoman. . . . I told her to stay in Wilkes Corners." Portia trembled and looked as if she might weep in agony. "I reckon all that happened to her is my fault."

Trout Wilkes shook his head. "Now, I don't believe that. No-way. I don't believe any our own townspeople had anything to do with—that tragic business. . . . I ain't proud of them. Nor of the way they acted toward Ellen. And I was little better—until after Miss Ellen worked so hard to save our baby's life—and almost lost her own baby in the bargain. . . . Our folks back at Wilkes Corners got nothing to be proud of. They didn't want Ellen there. And they was cruel, the way they let her know it. But I know in my heart they didn't burn her out."

"Somebody burned her out." Herman whispered it, but the words rang loud in the silent room.

Wilkes nodded. "Happened late one night. After the tavern was closed. Town dead asleep. Men from outside. I feel that, I believe it. I can't name you no names—because I can't prove nothing—"

"I can name you names." Portia's voice shook with chilled vehemence.

"No, Portia. No, you can't." Trout's voice was low, sad, but firm. "You got no more proof than I have. These fellows. Strangers. Two of them. Likkered up. Drank late in my place. Talkin' loud against uppity niggers. Must've decided to run Ellen off her place, the two of them. Raped her and knifed her. Never saw anything so vicious. Left her dead in the burning house. They rode away yelling. Right by my place. Realize it had to be them. They threw a brick through my store window. Woke us up."

"We saw the fire," Portia said.

"We run down there as fast as we could." Wilkes stood silent a moment, sickened by his vivid memories. "Burnin' too bad by the time we got there. House was raging with flames when I got there. Got Miss Ellen out. But she was terrible burnt, horribly knifed by some maniac. Tore. Bleeding. Mercifully, she was dead. I buried her—and then Portia and me—we went on back home. A sorrowful night."

Emeraude trembled visibly. Herman put his arms about her protectively. She said, voice empty, "And the baby—Ellen's little girl?"

"Scandal," Herman whispered, ill.

Wilkes drew a deep breath. His sallow face grayed. "They must of kilt the baby, too." He stared at his wife. Their gazes locked for a long moment. He shook his head. "I didn't find the baby . . . the fire—raging out of control—I couldn't go back in. . . . I'm sorry."

Emeraude and Herman stood immobile, stunned with grief that went too deep for words. The silence deepened in the overheated, malodorous room.

"Ellen had some money," Herman said. "Did they steal that, too?"

Trout Wilkes peered at him. "We found nuthin' after the fire, mister. Nuthin'. . . . Ellen didn't have any money. Nuthin' to speak of. A few gold eagles to live on. That's all. . . . If them men thought to rob her, they was bad deceived—"

A baby cried suddenly in one of the cribs across the room, and the balding man stopped talking abruptly. He and his wife started anxiously, glancing at each other tautly. They would have ignored the sound, but the infant's wailing grew louder, lustier. "It's Hester," Portia said. "Pore little tyke is hungry."

Wilkes gestured toward the cribs. "Might as well take her up; she won't stop yellin' till she's had a bate of food."

Portia nodded. She got up tiredly and padded across the room, her sandals slapping against her heels. She took the baby up in her arms and brought it back to the chair beside the table. She sat down, cradling the infant in her arms. She rocked her body in the chair, the baby half-covered by a shabby quilt in the sweatily hot room.

"May I see her?" Emeraude asked.

Portia glanced up at her husband and after a slight hesitation, smiled and nodded. She turned back the ragged edge of the blanket. "Hester's just over a year old," Wilkes said, his voice proud. "She's a good baby—an' she ain't wet or hungry, that is."

The baby was fair-skinned, with wheat-colored fringes of hair over its forehead and large round blue eyes, well formed, though somewhat underweight. Herman pitied the child, wondering what chance it had in this life, reared in an environment like this, in soured air, in debilitating heat, with poor food and inadequate clothing. He shuddered.

Emeraude smiled at the baby, touched its cheek with the backs of her fingers. Watching her, Herman felt a rush of sadness. Emeraude would have made a perfect mother for Scandal. They could have taken her to Europe, given her everything.

He winced, remembering that Miz Lucretia Borgia had had to send him here to carry out his obligation—and he had delayed too long. Scandal was dead. He could not help but think she was better off dead than spending her life in this evil backwoods existence.

Emeraude straightened. "I'm sick inside—about Ellen—and her baby." Her eyes clouded, she glanced toward Herman. "We really should go. It's a long ride back to New Orleans." She shuddered slightly in dread, contemplating the rugged journey.

Herman nodded, but as he turned, a second child, in the other crib near the far windows, suddenly wailed. Neither the balding farmer nor his wife moved. They remained locked in place, staring at each other.

"Your baby is crying," Herman said.

"It's Rachel," the farmer said. "Just leave her be. She ain't rightly had out her nap yet."

The baby went on screaming lustily. Herman gazed at Wilkes

and his wife for a beat, then crossed the room. He stared down at the baby kicking and crying in its crib.

Something lurched in his chest. It was as if his heart slipped its moorings. The child Hester was an ordinary baby, neither beautiful nor arresting, while this lovely brown-eyed baby, with incredibly perfect features, soft lips, tea-rose complexion, fragile profile—her beauty grabbed at you, clutched you and wouldn't let go.

He went on gazing at the beautiful baby, unable to turn away. Even with one cheek swollen and discolored, clad only in ragged diapers, the child was extraordinarily lovely. She pulled herself up in the crib. She stopped crying, peering up at Herman.

"Rachel is all right where-at she is," Wilkes said from behind him. "Leave her be."

Herman nodded, gazing at the child, enchanted. God knew the Wilkes were blessed, rich with the beauty of their children. Someone had said beauty was the wealth of the poor family. Wilkes was a rich man. Herman felt his throat tighten; his eyes burned, certain than if Scandal had survived the fire, she would have been so lovely.

For a brief moment, he looked ahead to the life he could have given Scandal if she had lived, if he had reached Ellen in time. She would never have to suffer as he had. He would have taken her to Europe with him, devoted his life to her happiness, knowing suddenly that her being with him would have been his own source of happiness. She would have had all she ever could want in life. All he could have given her. He saw now that Miz Lucretia Borgia had been right to send him here—he owed that to Ellen, he owed it to their child. But now there was nothing he could do and he must live forever with the guilt eating at him.

The lovely cherub smiled and put out her arms. Herman bent over the crib and took her up. The baby smiled and touched his cheek, stroking it with tiny fingers.

"I'd like you to put her down," Wilkes said from behind him.

Herman nodded but continued to hold the baby. Her feedsack diapers were sopping wet, but neither he nor the child noticed. Rachel gazed up at Herman, cooing unintelligibly, but quite happily.

"We'd better go," Emeraude said. "It's a long drive back to New Orleans."

Herman nodded, but for the moment he did not move. He clung to the child and she pressed close to him. His mind spun with a sense of terrible wrong that he was unable to sort out inside himself.

Trout Wilkes took the child from him. She cried out in protest, and Herman winced as Wilkes walked away. "My God, she's wet again," Trout said. "That little thing of hers is a fountain, I tell you."

Herman watched Trout cross the room, holding the baby gently. Near the stove, Trout paused, silent, remote and withdrawn, waiting for them to leave.

Herman shook his head, gazing around the ugly, odorous kitchen. It couldn't end like this—they had come so far, with such growing hope. God in heaven, it must not.

Emeraude touched his arm, calm but unyielding. He nodded again and followed her through the darkened house to the damp, night-blue yard. Trout Wilkes followed them to the screen door. "We'd ast you folks to stay the night. But like you can see, we just got no place for you."

Herman gazed at him, empty-bellied. He said, hesitantly, "I'm sorry if we intruded—bothered you. . . . Thank you for all you've told us. . . . I hope—your children—will be all right." He gazed about, feeling helpless, futile. How could they be all right, growing up in this place? And why should he envy this haggard man because he wished that child in there were his?

Trout Wilkes inclined his head. "Why shouldn't they be all right, mister? We don't have much. I can see what you think. Clear in your face. But we love 'em and care for 'em—enough to give up everything for 'em. . . . You don't have to worry about either of my girls, mister. We're dirt-pore, but they'll be all right. They'll be fine. You'll see. . . ."

Shaking his head from side to side, as if to free it from the clamoring thoughts raging inside it, Herman forced himself to smile and went down the steps to the carriage. . . .

part two

Trace to New Orleans, 1860

13

Anyone of the land gentry sensed instantly that despite a certain regal bearing, Wade Cameroon wasn't a gentleman because he didn't travel with at least one or two black male slaves in attendance.

Everybody south of the Mason-Dixon knew that no plantation aristocrat ever ventured from his estate for any reason without black servants-for-life at instant beck and call. A landed grandee may be less than physically or mentally imposing—often much less—but one reckoned his status in Southern society by his elegance of manner, his foppish appearance and his slaves at heel like obedient and well-trained collies.

Except that he traveled unattended, Wade Cameroon presented every outward aspect of the true aristocrat. He stood two or three inches over six feet tall—depending upon his wildly fluctuating moods from exuberant euphoria to slumping melancholy—long-legged, slender in the thighs, flat-bellied, thin as a winter coyote and with shoulders too wide for the casket everyone predicted he'd soon and eternally occupy unless he changed his violent and and reckless ways.

He swung down from his chestnut stallion, carelessly stroked his hand through the gold mane before he secured the reins about the use-slicked hitching rail. The big horse snorted and tossed its head.

Cameroon grinned. Troilus was a fancy—like many of the best horses, on the track, the chase or the show, out of an old mare by an aging stud. Troilus had been sired by Voltaire at twenty-two, out of Octavia, at twenty. Sometimes, the first foal of a mare is the best horse she ever produces. This is not always true, however—some improve with age like old wine, and Troilus' was a noble lineage. Voltaire still stalked and pranced like a monarch and both he and Octavia were almost thoroughbreds, with just enough of the mixed blood for stamina. Like me, Wade thought, smiling.

He crossed the wooden walk and strode into the brilliantly illumined tavern. The room rang with noise, crowded, but people paused and turned to glance at Wade Cameroon—to speculate, admire briefly, a few to stare. He moved with that fluid devil-may-care grace of a young aristocrat, a young panther or a young hellion yet to be broken or tamed by the rigors of existence. As I never will be, he assured himself.

His crop of thick yellow hair and his fair skin exaggerated the fearful blackness of his wide-set eyes. He attracted and held attention anywhere he went, a man who stood out in any company. He was used to being stared at. It meant nothing, and he ignored it. His was a Scottish legacy from his father, with just enough mixed blood from his mother, God rest her soul, to give him stamina.

He elbowed his way through the chatting, yelling, laughing men to the bar. Few of the patrons were plantation or landed gentry. They smelled of sweat. Their clothes hung carelessly, of cheap materials. Those not yet broken by life were bent, or bending. They retreated to this place. It was an escape for most of them.

The bartender, a happy man earning a good living in evil and uncertain times, grinned across the damp surface of the bar at Wade. He jerked his head toward customers lined arguing along the bar. "War talk. Makes a man thirsty." He shouted to make himself heard. "I encourage it. Bring up the subject when nobody else does." He laughed. "What's your pleasure, suh?"

"Ale," Wade said.

The barkeep nodded. Idly, Wade watched their distorted reflections refracted in the wet bar. As he filled a mug from a keg, the tavern owner said, "New around here, ain't you?"

Wade nodded, licking at the road dust coating his lips. When the ale was set before him, suds leaking over the brim, he drank thirstily. The bartender watched him admiringly. "Must have come a fur, dry piece. You've worked up a man-sized thirst."

"I carry one. Built in."

"Where'd you say you were from?"

Wade drank again, shaking his head. The bartender retrieved the empty mug and turned the bung faucet for fresh lager. "Where you headed, where you traveling?"

"From here to there. Tonight I reversed myself. Traveled from there to here."

The barkeep laughed. "Looking for somebody, mister, or *something*?"

"Looking for action," Cameroon said. "In some quiet place where nothing ever happens. Looking for a beautiful girl with the disposition of a saint. Looking for a place where everybody is rich—but honest. Healthy, but uglier than me. Looking for peace and tranquility, where so much is happening, I'll never be bored. In short, my genial host, I'm looking for heaven in hell, hell in heaven—and finding something of both everywhere I look."

The tavernkeep's smiled widened, his mouth gaped. "Have another beer, friend. On the house. You have come a long way." He put his head back laughing. "And I can tell you. From this place, you got a long way to go."

He saw her, a saucy hussy whose large eyes were an open invitation, meeting her gaze minutes after he sat down in a loser's vacated chair at the poker table. The men around the table growled a sour welcome, warning him that this was a man's game, five card stud, no wild cards, nothing fancy. A man earned what he took from this table.

He barely heard them, staring at the hot-eyed barmaid serving this table, refreshing drinks, stroking heads forward to bring luck. He met her eyes across the green-topped table. She glanced away and then looked back quickly, finding something she must have been searching for. She smiled faintly, tentatively.

Wincing, he realized his mistake. He'd wanted action but saw clearly that gambling would never satisfy his longings. The apple-cheeked, melon-breasted barmaid alone in this place could do that. Her wheat-gold hair was caught in a careless ponytail. A touch of red illumined her lips. Her throat looked warm and shapely above a low-cut bodice. He saw what he wanted in this girl's challenging green eyes.

"You're a heavenly-looking succubus," he said across the table to her.

"I don't know what that means, but it sounds exciting," the girl said, her eyes holding his.

"Play cards," the man beside Wade growled.

"Wasn't talking to you," Wade said. "You're even uglier than I am."

"You look pretty heavenly to me." The girl laughed. "I'll bet you taste good."

"What does a man do to amuse himself round here?" Wade held the girl's smiling gaze.

"He plays cards or cuts bait," the man beside him said.

The girl removed a Spanish olive from a tumbler on her serving tray and reached across the table, pressing the olive between Wade's lips. "Depends on who he's with and how friendly he is."

"Oh, I can be powerful friendly," Wade said. "And on short notice. Hard fast friends. I make fast friends fast—but not too fast, y'know. Just fast enough. Just slow enough."

The girl writhed, shivering with delight: "Sounds wonderful."

The card game was temporarily suspended, all attention fixed on the byplay between the barmaid and the stranger. This suspension was an incredible event and one of the first times a game had ever been even tentatively delayed on a friendly basis in the memory of the oldest native. The players sat, grinning tautly, faintly flushed, sweated, watching the excitement flicker in the charged atmosphere between the rake and the hussy.

"When can you get away?" Wade asked.

"How soon can you put down those cards?"

"That long, eh?"

"How long is up to you. It may be long. But not too long. You know." She laughed and licked her tongue across her murrey lips, "Just long enough."

One of the gamblers swore, laughing. "I never saw such swift arrangements made in my life."

Wade dropped his cards on the table. "Gentlemen, my apologies. You'll just have to count me out."

The man beside Wade gripped his arm warningly as Cameroon moved to rise from the chair. For an instant his fingers closed, viselike. "Mister, I don't know why I bother. No skin off my rump. But you better make one more arrangement before you leave with Missy here—with your next of kin."

"Oh?" Wade did not take his gaze from the girl's dancing eyes.

"That's right, stranger. If you knew what I know—or any of these boys know—you wouldn't touch Missy with a ten-foot pole."

The men around the table laughed raucously and nudged each other. Wade recognized the odd tenor of the laughter—it was not meant to be shared by him. A middle-aged man across the table said, "And I got one ten-foot pole you wouldn't touch Missy with."

The girl's gaze didn't falter but she stopped smiling. "Don't listen to these old maids, honey."

Wade grinned. "I listen only to my heart."

"A purentee wonder you've lived this long, come this far," the man beside him said. "As a friendly gesture and in an effort to get this here card game back on track, I'll tell you in three words the good reason to keep your paws off Missy."

"I'm listening," Wade told the man, then assured Missy, "but not with my heart." She smiled tentatively.

"Henri Le Blanc," the man said.

"What's that?"

"That's the three words I promised you, Mister. Now let's ante up and place your bets."

Wade scowled. "What's a Henri Le Blanc?"

"For you, he's a poison," another gambler said.

The man beside Wade cursed urgently. "All right. I'll lay it on the line for you. Henri Le Blanc is the youngest of the Le Blancs. The Le Blancs own French Pines Plantation. Sugar cane. Showplace of this part of the country. They're rich. Strong. Mean.They take what they want. They keep what they take. For more'n a year now, Missy here's been the personal property of young Henri Le Blanc."

"And God help the trespassers."

"So far there ain't been none."

"None that's around breathing and talking about it."

Wade tilted his brow and pretended to survey Missy with mock minuteness. "Don't see any brand on her. She looks like a stray to me."

"That's because the Le Blancs don't brand their possessions. Figure they don't have to—everybody knows the Le Blancs has got sense enough to stay off their preserve."

"Thank God I don't know the Le Blancs," Wade said.

The girl loved his reckless and headstrong daring. Her smile returned, bright and eager and heated. She drew the tip of her tongue across her lips and curtsied before him across the table. "I bow to your manhood and your courage," she said. "Something very rare in this pit."

"What you're really doing," Wade said, gazing raptly into the opened top of her bodice, "is giving me an irresistible view of your breastworks."

"That too," she said, and laughed.

Grinning, feeling excitement stirring and churning in his loins, Wade pushed back his chair and stood up. "Gentlemen." He bowed. "May we meet again."

"The six of us will serve as your pallbearers," the man beside him said sourly.

"You're a damned fool, young fellow," another player said.

"Maybe." Wade inclined his blond head. "But you're all so convinced that M'sieu Henri Le Blanc—whoever and whatever he is—is going to kill me . . . and you wouldn't want me to die with a hard-on, would you?"

Shivering with delight and anticipation, the barmaid came around the table to Wade. He was so tall her face was level with his pectorals. She buried her face against the corded thews of his chest. Laughing, Wade put his arm around her. They turned and walked toward the narrow dark stairway to the upper floor.

Silence washed out across the room behind them. There were

as many expressions registered as there were faces to contain them. Envy. Shared lust. Hatred. Concern. Contempt. Admiration. Dread. Some there were who licked their mouths anticipating what young Henri Le Blanc would do when he learned that his Missy had flagrantly put the horns to him before the whole town.

For moments the approaching war between the South and the bloodthirsty Yankees was forgotten. Arguments died and planning was set aside, bets suspended, judgments deferred, prophecies postponed.

The amiable bartender stopped smiling, stopped mentally counting the house and toting his receipts. He even indulged a quick, regretful inventory, estimating the cost of wreckage in case of an altercation—and an altercation was dead ahead. As surely as God made cotton-boll weevils.

Wade and Missy had just worked their way through the crowd to the stairwell when tension hissed in at the doorway and across the room like steam under pressure. The batwings were shoved open and a slender, fashionably attired young man entered imperiously. He wore polished boots, riding trousers and tailored jacket set off with full scarf caught with a glittering diamond stickpin. Two Negro servants decked out in black, highly glossed uniforms padded at his heels.

Wade would have ignored the commotion stirred by the new arrival except his instincts warned him this was no ordinary patron. The youth was in his earliest twenties, with the pinched, unsmiling face acquired by the very selfish, the self-centered, self-idolizing, self-indulgent. His eyes were narrow, his nostrils thin, his tight lips pinched. Wade would have gambled that the fellow was constipated. But more important, the youth swaggered in as if this were a corner of his suzerainty, as if he held first mortgage on this patch of the universe by some special dispensation of accommodating gods created in his own image.

"Oh God," Missy whispered. She faltered, trembled violently and pressed against Wade as if trying to suck strength from his rock-hard body.

"Henri?" Wade asked.

"Henri."

"Come on." Wade tightened his arm about the girl's waist and propelled her up the stairs.

The silence was fragmented by the sharp intake of mob breath.

Wade glanced over his shoulder in time to see strong men lunging for the floor and whatever safety it afforded. Just inside the batwings, Henri Le Blanc had paused, stared, calculated the situation, reacted and cursed in frustrated agony. But the youth moved swiftly. He whipped a long-barreled gun from a holster concealed deceptively under the elegant cut of his tailored jacket.

"Duck," Wade said to the girl. He shoved her forward on the steps. She fell to her knees, then prostrated herself on the stairs. She pressed into the wall as if trying somehow to melt into its rough sanctuary.

The youth fired the pistol. The bullet slapped past Wade's head, a lethal wasp. Son of a bitch, he thought, doesn't even wait to ask questions . . . so I won't bother thinking up answers he doesn't want to hear.

Crouching as low to the stairs as he could, Wade duck-walked up the stairwell. Behind him, men yelled, chairs overturned, tables were upset. The bartender bellowed for order, but no one heeded. He yelled louder and louder, if only to make himself heard in the bedlam, by himself.

Gun extended, Henri Le Blanc ran across the room to the stairwell. At the doorway, his two black servants stood immobile, eyes white-rimmed with fear.

Henri paused at the foot of the stairwell only long enough to grip the girl by her hair. He dragged her to her knees. "You bitch," he said. He spun her backward behind him and propelled himself upward in the same motion.

At the head of the stairs, Le Blanc strode off the step, running.

Wade stepped from the shadowed wall directly into Le Blanc's path. Wade's voice bristled. This bastard had shot at him without even bothering to exchange cards, insults or evidence. "You were looking for me, m'sieu?"

Le Blanc stopped in midstep, crying out in shock as he caught his balance. He staggered, astonished to find himself nose to nose with his adversary. "I'm going to kill you," Le Blanc said.

"Then you'll hardly object if I do everything in my poor power to keep you from doing something both of us may regret eternally?"

Le Blanc snorted with righteous outrage. While Henri still reacted with contemptuous, disdainful choler, Wade snagged the youth's wrist, viselike, in his fist. He twisted until he felt the gun hand relax.

"I'll just take that." Wade removed the pistol from the paralyzed fingers. Wrenching the weapon free, Wade backhandedly tossed it as far as he could along the uncarpeted corridor. The gun bounced and rattled along the thick oak flooring.

Le Blanc reacted almost as swiftly. He brought his free hand hard across the side of Wade's neck. If the chop had caught his Adam's apple, it would have smashed his larynx. This was certainly Le Blanc's intent.

His black rage flaring, Wade released Le Blanc's wrist and drove his fists, one-two, into the youth's temples. For an instant, Henri wavered, helpless, his nerve centers short-circuited, stomach walls crumbling, bladder relaxing. He shoved Wade, buying a moment of recovery time.

Wade caught his balance. He brought his left fist upward. He glimpsed the flash and glitter of a three-inch knife blade in Le Blanc's grip. All thought of reasonable defense dispensed with, Wade fought for the only reason he ever battled seriously—to stay alive.

He drove his boot into Le Blanc's crotch as the youth lunged toward him, ripping upward with the knife.

Le Blanc retched, gasping. He dropped the knife and doubled over. As he toppled forward, Wade hit him twice, with a left to the solar plexus and with a right cross to the side of the head.

Le Blanc straightened. His pinched face was gray with shock, taut with agony, wild with outrage that he should be treated so vulgarly. He staggered forward, reached out wildly for support. Finding none, he half-turned, lost his footing and pitched face-forward down the long stairwell.

Le Blanc rolled and bumped downward in a terrible slow motion. Missy remained half-crouched at the foot of the steps. Le Blanc plunged beyond her and lay with his boots pointed upward, his handsome head twisted at an unlikely angle on his shoulder.

Breathing through his parted mouth, his long legs planted apart, Wade stood at the head of the stairs, staring down at the crowded room.

At first, no one in the stunned crowd moved. They waited for Henri Le Blanc to get up, to make his next assault in the attack.

Le Blanc did not move. Missy crouched nearest him. She saw death in his glassy, staring eyes fixed on her, the gape of his mouth, the broken angle of his head against his shoulder. She screamed. She opened her mouth as wide as she could. Screams spewed like vomitus out of her.

Patrons sidled forward reluctantly. One man knelt beside the prostrate body and confirmed Le Blanc's death. "Deader'n a mackerel. Poor son of a bitch. Neck's broke. Clean as a chicken."

The two black servant boys wailed. They cried helplessly, like children. Missy went on screaming, trying to press herself into the wall to escape the accusing gaze of her paramour.

Wade waited to see no more. He heeled around and ran along the corridor to a rear window. He shoved it up, levered himself through to the courtesy roofing. He slid along the aged cypress shingles and leaped out to the ground. He ran around the building, jerked the lines free of the hitching rail. Troilus tossed his head, turning, already trotting as Wade swung up into the saddle.

Damn, he thought savagely. Story of my goddam life. Go looking for a little heaven—and find more hell.

14

Cameroon halted his stallion in the shade of a black tupelo. The lathered horse quivered with exhaustion, but Cameroon knew the animal had just that extra reserve of stamina if he had to call upon it. This reassured him, as did his own extra ounce of strength and will that had kept him alive this long.

He glanced in some apprehension over his shoulder and admitted he was a fugitive. He had killed in self-defense, but this would offer little in the coin of preservation. He'd slain the youngest scion of the first family of this backwater region. There were no extenuating circumstances in such crimes.

He shivered with inner chill and fatigue. He had taken a human life.

He tried to laugh himself out of this black mood of depression and could not do it.

The only real tragedy, Cameroon, he told himself, is that you killed on an empty stomach. A gnawing hunger left unfulfilled—Urges that drove him just after the need for breath and just ahead of the requirement of food and drink.

But he could not smile. The tragedy was murder, even death in self-defense. His family tree was blighted with hang-rope scars, with savage men pursuing their own unholy grails recklessly. Well, now he was one with them. He had tried to deny his heritage, but in one swift and terrible moment, two days backtrail, he'd proved he was a son of his violent-mooded father, of all his fathers—and that the fruit doesn't fall far from the tree.

Growing up at Heather Hill, he'd watched his father and brothers slaughter animals for sport, leaving carcasses by the score for vultures, seen them whip slaves to see the wretches jump comically and yell in amusing terror. He saw blacks lashed up and whipped until they bled and hung unconscious. He was sickened by it all. It was a way of life he could not stomach. He was his mother's son—most of the time, except for the wild rages. There was some question about her ancestry, if not her gentle and overwhelming beauty and kindliness. At Heather Hill that beauty faded, she retreated into herself and died, sickened by inhumanity and casual cruelty.

Because of some terrible intrafamily battle, his father and three brothers fought furiously and unforgivingly. When his father died suddenly, of heart failure while beating a recalcitrant horse with a lead-filled whip crop, Wade found himself the sole heir to Heather Hill.

His brothers descended on him like vultures, hawks, eagles, like falcons diving for the jugular. He laughed at them. The three thousand acres, almost all the fine horses, the herds of purebred Guernsey cattle—everything went on auction. The three hundred slaves he deeded land and provided manumission.

His family and his peers stared at him in shocked disbelief. His brothers didn't have to tell him—but they did, vociferously and unyieldingly—that he had not inherited Heather Hill because of his father's devotion. "Father hated you. He hated you because like your mother, you refused to fight with him. He loved us and admired us because we did fight with him."

"But he willed me Heather Hill and all his worldly goods."

"Only to get even with us. He expected you to do what is right—divide it all."

Wade shrugged. "Looks like you bastards will finally have to work for a living, doesn't it?"

They encroached upon him, scowling blackly, raging. "Bastards? If any of us are bastards, it's probably you. You're the only one totally unlike the rest of us—the git of that Martinique woman."

"I'm the bastard with all the money, too."

"Setting free our slaves. That proves you're an insane bastard. That will break the will in any court—insanity."

Wade only laughed. "It only proves I don't believe any man of any color has the right to enslave another human being. . . . I remind you, brothers, Thomas Jefferson believed as I do. The only difference is that Jefferson didn't have the intestinal fortitude to free his slaves while he lived. I do. I don't want them."

"Did it ever occur to you *we* might want them?"

"Didn't give a damn. You want horns but you're going to die

butt-headed. Our loving, unlamented father left those slaves to *me*."

"But not to set free! Just when the country is about to fight a war over our right to own slaves. We're going to fight for the right to keep slaves."

Wade met their gazes levelly. "Just as I'm willing to fight for my right to get rid of them. My right to do with them as I wish. I set them free."

"We're going to fight you, you mindless bastard. On the street. Every time we meet, one of us will beat hell out of you. In the courts. You won't get away with this robbery."

When the auction finally was completed, the old manor house and acreage sold to the highest bidders, Wade called his brothers together for what he fervently hoped would be the final gathering of the Cameroon clan.

He had the money stacked in three piles. "There it is," he said. "Our father's accumulated harvest. Gold. I hated the way he got it, hated what it stood for. I don't want it. Take it. It is divided equally between you three jackals. And may I never see any of you again this side of hell."

He had ridden away from the family plantation on Troilus, with a few golden eagles in his saddle pouch and the clothes on his back, feeling truly alive and free and clean for the first time in his life.

He stared over his shoulder, listening for sounds on the back-trail. Well, his freedom had been good if of brief duration. That quick glimpse of paradise was abruptly ended—by more hated violence. He'd hoped to start a new life, and here he was, on the outskirts of some unknown, unnamed, godforsaken village, on the run, a fugitive.

He slapped at a robber fly and urged the stallion forward on the rut-pocked trace. He rode into the town with as much dignity as he could muster, stinking with sweat, weak with exhaustion and ravenously hungry. The grime of two days' fast riding caked his face, smeared his hands, discolored his clothing.

He rode into the yard of a tavern. Chickens, guineas and turkeys screamed and fluttered into shadows. A black youth leaped up from a haystack and ran out to meet him, shapeless felt hat gripped in both hands. "Mawnin', young Masta suh." The boy caught the reins, smiling and bowing.

Wade tossed the boy a silver dollar. "Give my horse water and a feed bag of oats and grain mixture, and rub him down." He exhaled and warned, "And watch him. He bites the hand that feeds him." Troilus was a bona fide, bloodline Cameroon, Wade told himself with a tired and bitter smile.

He walked into the darkened tavern. He stopped as if struck in the face, bat-blind in the deeply shadowed room after the brilliant sunlight.

He caught his breath, warning himself that he had to be smarter than this to stay alive. He had been heading east and north toward Alabama, thinking he might throw off pursuit—fugitives typically headed for the anonymous West—but he could hardly be certain he had left no trail. At least until Le Blanc's vengeful family abandoned the chase, he had to see well and clearly every time he entered a strange room.

He stepped away from the doorway, standing for a long beat against a wall draped in rectangular shadow until his eyes accustomed themselves to the darkened atmosphere. Figures moved as if through occluding red smoke before him.

"Welcome, stranger," the bartender said. "Take out and set."

Wade nodded tiredly and tried to smile. He sat at a table against a rear wall, removed from the busy bar and near a closed exit door.

The innkeeper came to his table carrying a mug of beer. He wiped up the pinewood surface and set the ale down with a flourish. "Begin with that, young friend. It'll whet your appetite."

"For what?" Wade inquired.

The tavern owner smiled. "Why not a bowl of steaming seafood gumbo for a start? Then we serve wild rice and hot red beans. Add a dash of cayenne sauce and you'll remember this place warmly for three days at least. A slab of baked ham to pry your ribs apart, and you couldn't eat better in New Orleans' finest."

Wade nodded, yawning helplessly. "Sounds great for a start." He'd downed the beer before his host returned to the bar. He called after him. "And a couple more mugs of beer."

The innkeeper smiled over his shoulder. "Like my beer, eh?"

"Don't know yet. Drank too fast to taste it."

In minutes, the tavern owner returned with fresh beer, gumbo and steaming dishes of red beans, rice and ham. He set the vessels before Wade. "Eat hearty. Gonna cost you two bits. But you can eat as much as you can hold."

Wade ate hearty. He began to feel better. He drank the second beer more slowly, but gulped down the spicy seafood gumbo ravenously.

When he'd finished the thick soup, he forced himself to devour the red beans and rice more sedately. The food was tasty, highly spiced and well prepared. Less tense, not as overwhelmed by fatigue, Wade glanced up from beneath the shapeless wide-brimmed hat he had not bothered to remove.

His vision was clear now. Several other men occupied tables or lounged at the bar, talking without heat, about the approaching war. The issues and the rage all seemed remote to this place. They did not yet see how it could touch them in this pigtrack village. A few of them felt they should enlist if the criminal Yankees invaded their county. "One of them thievin' bastards so much as steals one of my chickens," one man said, "I grab my gun shore."

"Pow," another man laughed. "Blow his bluebelly head off."

"Them Yankees ain't got guts enough to come down here and fight us."

"Be the shortest fight they ever got in."

"And the worst."

"Them sons of bitches. I hate them sons of bitches. Tryin' to tell us how we got to live."

Wade bent over his food. He'd heard talk like this for years whenever his father and brothers gathered together of an evening. Wade used a large spoon, ladling the beans and rice into his mouth hungrily. He forced himself to chew slowly and then washed it all down with a long draft of beer.

"—tall, lean man. Never seed him myself. . . . Have found out that his name is Cameroon, Cameron, something like that. He killed my brother and I mean to kill him."

Feeling as if he were abruptly and inextricably entangled in the steel strands and webbings of recurring nightmare, Wade jerked his head up at the sound of that voice across the room at the bar. He held his loaded spoon poised before his mouth.

His eyes widened and his heart seemed to miss a beat. It *was* a nightmare. He was staring at Henri Le Blanc—the man he'd accidentally slain a hundred miles away two days ago. Even the two attendant blacks were the same!

Forcing himself to remain calm, Cameroon realized the Le Blanc standing at the bar, though physically much like Henri, was far more formidable, older, heavier, with a look of seasoned arrogance twisting his features where Henri's face showed only self-indulgence.

Obviously the Le Blancs were headstrong men who killed in haste and repented at leisure, if ever.

He set the spoon untouched upon his plate. His stomach churned. There was no way to stop Henri Le Blanc's vengeful brother except with force. If he didn't kill Le Blanc, he would be killed by him. If he did not stop Le Blanc here and now, in this place, he would find him forever on his backtrail.

He stared at the thick-shouldered planter standing half-turned from him at the bar, speaking coldly and loudly to the tavern-keeper.

Wade felt his guts tighten. For a moment he was afraid he would be sick. The hot spiced food gorged, with bile, into his throat, at the thought of killing again. One death was one too many. He had been unable to forget the horror of taking Henri Le Blanc's life even if he'd slain in self-defense. One killing was too much. Maybe it got easier for others—like getting the first olive from a bottle mouth—but not for him. He hated senseless violence, senseless killing.

If he went on sitting here, he must face Le Blanc. Confrontation could end only in death—and he didn't mean to die yet. Still, he had no stomach for another killing—the death of another stranger. Buying his own freedom wasn't worth it. Nothing was worth murder. Yet, if he ran, it would be merely resuming the chase. Le Blanc would come upon him again, somewhere, perhaps in far less auspicious conditions.

In that lightning flicker of time, Wade considered the options and made his decisions. Quietly removing money from his pocket, he slipped it onto the table beside his plate. Then he stood up, holding his breath. Slouched over, hat pulled down shielding his face, he sidled to the rear door, opened it slowly, quietly, slid through it and ran across the yard.

15

Sweet Jesus, but she was beautiful. . . .

She looked ethereal, unreal in the smoky lantern light. He whistled under his breath. What she looked like was that someone had started pouring on the beauty and forgotten to say when. She wasn't buxom; far from it. She was slender, reedlike, willowy, almost boyish, but she was no boy! She was only very young; she simply wasn't finished yet. Her uptilted breasts were not matured but God knew they were blossoming like fragile fruit under the miserly cotton fabric of her stingy blouse.

She was armed to destroy him.

Wade sprawled, prostrate, fatigued where she'd discovered

him in the haymow. He was aroused by her fantastic beauty as he'd never suspected he could be by any breathtaking but underage beauty. Dammit, Cameroon, he reminded himself, she's a *child*. Perhaps if he'd not been left repressed, denied and frustrated by his experience with the barmaid Missy three nights ago, he'd be less vulnerable to this girl's immature appeal.

He exhaled heavily. He knew better. He'd never encountered such exquisite, fragile beauty before, even on the dusky verandas of the finest old plantation manor house, certainly not in such unlikely surroundings as a musty-smelling barn. Perhaps, he admitted in deep sadness, he never would see such breathtaking pulchritude again—an angelic gamine in cotton blouse and checked skirt which looked as if it might once have served as someone's second-best kitchen tablecloth. Cheap tow linen at best.

She poised, legs apart, with smoke-streaked lantern hoisted well above her head. Her upraised arm pulled her taut breasts tauter, the high undercurve stretched higher. Sensational. She held a pitchfork at the ready in her right hand, but both of them had forgotten the tined weapon as she gazed avidly, even greedily down at him.

The lantern glow poked gently among the soft tendrils of her raven-black hair. Small curls twisted and crinkled impishly across her forehead, along the sculpted lines of her high, fragile cheekbones, spilling thickly about her shoulders. Her eyes were large and black and liquid in her tea-rose face, her nose exquisitely dainty, her lips full and rounded over even teeth. Her face was heart-shaped and her throat long and slender. In the lamplight she shone, a faint tan, her smooth skin glowing with pale-gold undertones. If it was true that beauty is a poor family's wealth, this girl's father—no matter his status or condition—was a Midas.

"Who are you?" she said. Her voice was as soft as Southern cotton, silky, smooth as damask.

"Who are you?"

"Rachel."

"What place is this?"

"Wilkes Corners. And this is our barn, and we rent rooms and horse stalls, we sell food for a man and his animals, and we don't cotton to tramps. You catfooted around pretty cautious, all right. But you'll never be able to sneak in here. There are too many of us in this family."

"Oh? How many are there?"

"Seven. Pa Peavey. Ma Peavey. Their three boys. And my

half-sister Hester. And me. Do you expect to pay for the grain you fed to your horse? I saw you feed and water him first before you sneaked in here. He's a pretty animal, but he looks as if you've near rode him to death."

"Never wanted to. And I'll pay. I'll pay for sleeping here in this hay, too."

"You certainly will." Her voice hardened oddly.

"Only, do you mind, Rachel, if we keep it quiet? About my being here in the barn? About my being here at all." He had continued traveling north and east, hoping to outsmart his pursuer by staying away from towns and inns where people would remember his passage, and now he must depend on this girl and her family.

"Somebody looking for you?"

"Let's say I don't relish company."

"Did you kill somebody?"

He bit his lip, his eyes darkening. "I kill only if I have to."

"That means you did kill somebody." She sighed. "Did you escape from prison?"

"No. I've just tried to avoid meeting up with a few unfriendly people lately. How'd you know I was here?"

"I saw you ride in. Saw you put your horse out in the lean-to, saw you rub him down. Saw you take a leak out by the post. Oh, you're not the first man I ever saw relieving himself. . . . You are built elegant, though."

His mouth pulled into a grin. "The only heritage of my clan. Armed thus with this single weapon alone, they sent me out to seek my fortune."

She almost smiled. "You ought to amass quite a fortune." Her manner chilled. "I asked you. What's your name?"

"I told you I'd pay. Why is that important, my name? Must you know the name of every poor traveler who sleeps one night in your hay?"

"Yes, I must—if I'm going to sleep with him."

Wade gazed up at Rachel across a taut charged buffer of silence in stunned disbelief. He shook his head to clear it, deciding fatigue was playing tricks on him. He was so exhausted he was hearing what he wanted to hear.

But even as he thought this, the lovely girl-child had set the pitchfork against the rough plank wall. Solemnly, she turned down the wick in the lattern. Then she kicked a place clean on the flooring and set the lantern in the middle of it.

He still did not believe her, and yet he felt a deep anticipatory stirring in his loins. She tilted her face and smiled shyly at him.

He tried to answer her smile, but his mind spun. One thing she'd accomplished. He was no longer tired. He no longer worried about the vengeful man on his trail. He felt suddenly young and vibrant with life.

He cleared his throat, watching her. "You mean this? You're not teasing?"

"Even when I'm teasing I'm serious," she said, her rich-timbred voice taut with suggestion.

She padded forward slowly and sank to her knees in the hay beside him. This was unreal, the stuff of fantasy. A man wished for something like this—a young, fresh and fragile angel crawling into the hay with him—but a reasonable man stored such vagaries high in the cabinets of his mind along with other unlikely fancies.

His heart slugged faster. Though she was underage, though she was probably playing some game in which he was the joker, though he should know better, he watched the lovely vision crawl closer. The warmth and sweetly intoxicating musk of her body washed through his mind, overwhelming all his senses. Her slender long-fingered hand touched his chest shyly but firmly, moved on the muscles corded about his paps. He waited, holding his breath. She did not move away. She did not dissolve like some evanescent image. Her lips parted slightly, and she sighed, breathless.

"Don't you want me to do this?" she said in a husky whisper.

He closed his hand over her fingers which squeezed at his paps. "Not if you're playing a game."

"Do you think I am?"

"I think you may be getting in over your head. You're fooling with danger."

"I'm not afraid."

"That's 'cause you're a baby that hasn't developed instincts about danger. . . . You don't know me. You could get hurt, pulling tricks like this."

Her hand unbuttoned his shirt, slipped inside, her fingers icy but the palm of her hand fiery hot. She caressed his chest and downward on the flat plane of his belly.

"You're hairy," she whispered in that husky, breathless tone.

"So I'm not what you want after all. You can still get out of here."

"Do you want me to?" Her nails dug at his navel.

He bit his lip, yelping. "Damn you."

She laughed softly. "That's better."

"Better?"

"Yes. You know now. I'm not teasing." She pulled herself up so her heated thighs parted over his. She worked her trim little hips, settling herself upon him. Her deep-black eyes swam so close her face was out of focus. He saw naked hunger in those ebony pools. But this was crazy! She was a child. She didn't know anything about hunger, naked or otherwise.

Good God! A few nights ago he'd killed a man in a brawl over a faithless barmaid. Now, in the middle of nowhere, he was adding to his crimes by raping a girl-child. He was fighting it, but he was fighting a losing battle.

He lay under her faintly writhing body. Breath burned in his throat and pulses throbbed in his temples. He could hear distantly the nearby shuffling of animals in their stalls, skittering mice mindless in the rafters, rustle of errant wind in tupelo trees, and from some other planet where ordinary beings existed, raucous laughter borne from the tavern up front. The real world spun and careened on its axis while he lay lost in some eddy of insubstantial fantasy with a young girl who probably thought the climax of all this petting would be a chaste kiss on the lips. God help us all.

"If you think I don't know what I'm doing," she said as if following the complicated skein of his thoughts, "I had a real nice uncle who taught me everything I should know and some things that Hester says no lady should ever even suspect."

"Good Lord."

"Why do you talk so much? Why don't you kiss me?"

"Because I keep waiting for you to laugh—and run away."

"You fool. You're wasting time." She clung to him and pressed her soft baby-smooth mouth over his. Her lips parted, wide as any succubus. He tasted a heated sweetness he'd never even anticipated in this existence. A shudder of exultance and wonder wracked through him like a wildly banking pool ball. He closed his arms about her, one hand at the small of her back, working her faster and harder upon his stiffening crotch, the other bringing her sweet-tasting face closer upon his.

His hands moved on her. God help me. If this be a dream, then let me never waken. He caught her blouse, pulled it over her head and tossed it aside. Then he lifted her so that one small globe, its pink nipple marble-hard, was poised over his mouth. He drew her down then, suckling thirstily. She whimpered in sweet agony, her body shivering and working convulsively upon him.

She reached down, jerked his belt buckle loose and unbuttoned his trousers. He did not move, either to aid or delay her. He continued to caress one bared breast and to nurse the other. No matter that she may have begun this business as a charade, she was hurtled far beyond the point of return now. She freed him from the fetters of his clothing, clutching his rigidity greedily. He felt himself pulsing against her caressing palm.

"I can't wait any more," she whispered, frantic. "I can't stand it any more. . . . Do it . . . oh, please, do it to me . . . now . . . hurry."

"Yes." He released her bruised, blood-reddened breasts and slipped her skirt down below her knees. She kicked it away. She wore no underthings. Her dainty form pressed prone upon him. She opened her legs wide.

Holding her against him, Wade turned their bodies as one in the hay and thrust himself to her. She gasped, breathless, and drove herself upon him. As he closed his arms about her delicate body, she put her head back and screamed.

Shaken by her frantic screaming, Wade fought to break away from her. As he'd known it must, suddenly the fantasy boiled into nightmare.

In this new nightmare, he was unable to break free from her embrace. Her slender arms were like steel cords. Her legs locked fiercely about him, knotted at the ankles. She dug her nails into the flesh of his back, all this time screaming at the top of her lungs.

He heard sounds of running feet close by. He reached up, chipped her on the chin. She sagged. He caught her in his arms and leaped up.

He stood, legs apart, trousers half down his calves, holding the naked girl, dead weight, her head back, her hair trailing thickly toward the hay-littered floor.

Helplessly, he stared at the wall of people reared abruptly before him—a middle-aged man and woman, a girl who appeared about Rachel's age but who bulged awkwardly, bulkily pregnant, and three hard-faced young men—all of them armed.

No one spoke. Raging inwardly, Wade saw it had been a game the girl played with him, a deadly game, and he *was* the joker, after all.

16

Wade instinctively kept checking the backtrail over his shoulder. The first pink ribs of false dawn shattered the darkness and intensified the shadows along the narrow wilderness trace.

"What did you say?" His voice rasped. He tried to remain cool and unruffled on this first morning of his marriage, but he knew now how a plucked goose felt resting in the oven. His bride looked delicate, but he knew better, hers was the deceptive strength of steel wire and duplicity. She looked fresh and even virginal, but she was as brassy as Lilith. She looked soft and chaste, but inwardly she was tougher than the grandmother of all whores.

"I said—Mrs. Wade Cameroon." Rachel's voice, as deceptively sweet as pecan divinity warm from some plantation kitchen, mocked him. "It's a beautiful name . . . Mrs. Wade Cameroon . . . most beautiful name I ever heard."

"And you've as much right to it as to anything else you've stolen in your fraudulent existence."

She purposely misunderstood him. "Yes. You're right. I have had a cheated life. But that's over now."

He laughed at her bitterly, coldly. "Don't be too sure. We're married. As legal as any shotgun wedding, I suppose. But it won't last, my scheming little sweetheart." He glanced over his shoulder. "Thanks to your delaying me through your devilish trickery, you may become my widow any minute."

She shrugged, unconcerned. "I'll still be Mrs. Wade Cameroon. I'll still get to New Orleans."

He'd agreed to head back to Louisiana, since that was where she wanted to go and he didn't care where he went. The Peaveys had agreed to tell anyone who asked that he had headed out for Atlanta—though he suspected Le Blanc was not going to be misled so easily.

He slapped the reins, trying to hurry the dray horse pulling the open wagon he'd *managed* to buy from Herschel Peavey back at the tavern in Wilkes Corners. In the flatbed behind them an aged carpetbag held Rachel's entire earthly possessions. Troilus stalked, secured to the tailgate. And thus began their married life. Rachel sat almost primly beside him, wearing her Sunday-go-to-meeting dress, her one decent frock. The only thing that had delayed the wedding last night was the time it took her to don this outfit. By the time she was dressed one of the Peavey boys had returned with the Baptist minister, who simpered and smiled and prayed over everybody.

He glanced at her from the corner of his eye. God, she was beautiful. The little fraud. Her cheap little straw bonnet perched at an angle on her breeze-tipped black hair, its bow caught under the fragile point of her chin.

He tried not to look at her at all. It was hard to hate her when you came head-on upon her delicate beauty, her fresh youthfulness. She was heartbreakingly lovely, even if her heart was as black as her hair.

"You couldn't care about anybody," he said. "Except yourself. You have to have a heart to feel emotions—"

"I've got a heart—"

"If you have it's as hard as these iron-rimmed wheels—"

"It's just that it's been broken so much. Maybe it doesn't work like yours any more."

He laughed. "At your age, you don't know what a broken heart is."

She straightened, defiant, her face graying. "Damn you. Don't you laugh at me."

He turned and stared at her. "My God! You tricked me into marriage. You slow me down. You saddle me with an evil little child bride. You'll probably get me killed. And now I'm not even supposed to laugh."

"Laugh," she said between taut teeth. "Go on and laugh like a jackass. Just don't laugh at me."

He peered at her, brow tilted. "You better hope I *do* laugh at you, honey. The minute I stop laughing at this miserable comedy, I'll probably beat hell out of you and throw you in a ditch."

She smiled, complacent. "No you won't."

"Oh? Won't I? You know me damned little, miss. How can you be sure what I'll do?"

She moved her shoulders in a faint shrug. "I know you well enough to know one thing. You hope to get me naked again. Until you do, I've nothing to fear from you."

He growled, savage. "Just something missing inside you, eh?"

"What do you care?"

"I do care."

Abruptly, he wheeled the horse off the trace into a thick-growing copse of loblolly pines. The wagon rattled, bumped, jostling her. She had to grab his arm to keep from being thrown from the wagon boot or battered senseless by low-hanging limbs. "Are you crazy?" she raged.

He spoke with cold laughter edging his tone. "If I am, you can take total credit, Mrs. Cameroon. It's just that I've decided we've gone far enough until we get one thing settled. And that is, who wears the pants in this family."

She taunted him. "Just as I said. You can't wait."

"That's right. It's time for our honeymoon to begin."

"Don't be a fool."

"Don't you be a fool. You didn't think you got a beautiful name like Mrs. Wade Cameroon for nothing, did you? It may be the costliest bargain of your life."

"You are being a fool."

"We've a little unfinished business. Something you started in that hay loft last night." He stopped the wagon, where a low-drooping curtain of pines and underbrush shielded them from the roadway.

Wade wrapped the lines about the whip socket, taking his time. He swung down. She remained immobile, staring straight ahead. For the moment he ignored her. He found a blanket under the seat. He shook it out and spread it, wrinkle-free, over the pine-needled ground. Then he turned and came back to the wagon. He held out his arms to her and inclined his head toward the blanket. "Our honeymoon suite."

She sat rigid, refusing even to look at him. Her face flushed pinkly to the roots of her black hair and her lips parted, but she clasped her chilled trembling fingers in her lap.

"No armed family waiting this time," he taunted her.

"Maybe your friend will get here in time to kill you."

"Then, at least, I'll have died happy. Few are so fortunate in this vale of tears. Come on."

"You come to your senses."

"Get down, little bride, or by God, I'll pull you down."

She stared at him. "You would, wouldn't you?"

"That's right. We've played getting married your way until now. We're going to play house now. My way. You can scream your conniving little head off out here. Nobody'll hear you but the birds and God. . . . You tricked me into this marriage, but by heaven, I mean to claim the rights that ceremony gave me."

She sat a moment longer, but as he stepped closer to the side of the wagon, she stood up and leaped lithely to the ground. She caught her balance and stared up at him defiantly.

"Take it off," he said.

"I will not. If you're going to rape me, it'll be rape all the way—I won't help you."

He shrugged. "As you wish, little hellion." He snagged the front of her dress and ripped it downward, tearing the fabric as easily as if it were aged and dry papyrus.

Now she screamed in rage. The woods rang with her cry and

disturbed yellowhammers chattered at her echoes. "Damn you." Her eyes brimmed with tears. "That's the only decent dress I own."

He laughed, yet somehow his savagery was softened at the sight of exquisite skin tones, symmetry of breast and belly and thighs, and the shapely beauty of her naked body. "I'll buy you a dozen dresses—if you please me."

"And if I don't?"

"You can buy your own dress." His hands caressed her nakedness. "Or walk around like this. I won't give a damn. I know what I want and I mean to have it."

Her head tilted. "Rapist. I'll kill you if I can, but I'll never try to please you."

"If that's the way you want it." He swung her up in his arms. Once more he closed his sucking mouth over her unguarded breast. She shivered in exquisite agony. She fought, but only weakly. Gently, he laid her down on the rough, itchy blanket, but she was unconscious of its prickling discomfort, the smell of old sweat. Despite herself, her whole body reacted to his lips on her breast, pleasure radiating outward, and she sagged, feeling as if she were being transported out of time and space on a soft and vaporous cloud.

Her emotions wheeled and skidded, confused and wild. Her thoughts spun as he touched her. Nothing was clear except the heat and rigidity of his body. She tried to remain aloof but found herself submitting, submissive, enslaved.

Holding her hips in one hand as if she were a child, he brought her parted thighs savagely upward to him. He drew her to him in an embrace that forced her arms and legs to open to him and close upon him, outside her own will. When he drove downward, she felt as if she were drowning in a burning mist of boiling fountains. She went weak. His hot lips pressed down, forcing her mouth open to his kisses and the probing of his tongue. Her mind warned her to hold herself in hatred and loathing, but she was betrayed by her own body, being hurtled outward into a delicious excitement, the like of which Rachel had never known, dreamed or suspected before, in her wildest fantasies.

She struggled, driving herself closer into his arms, the increasing intensity of their passions overwhelming her. Nothing had ever been like this. She felt she was fainting, her consciousness ebbing and then flaring sharper than ever. She felt stronger than a goddess, wilder than a winter storm.

Her eyes brimmed with unshed tears. She hated herself and her weakness. She was helpless when she touched him. In his arms she felt as if she had been born for this, for what was happening to her in this magnificent stranger's arms.

Her senses reeling as if short-circuited, she clung to him. The forest wheeled and skidded when she opened her eyes. The only patch of sky she could see between the spreading trees looked lime-green. The primeval Eden loomed cool and serene when she closed her eyes.

Rachel felt no pain, only the exquisite torment of unbearable pleasure. Hester had told her it would be like this, and she had believed that Hester lied. Now, she recognized that Hester knew only a trace of the incredible truth! There was no joy, no pleasure, no dream or no reality vouchsafed to human beings on this sad planet to compare with this God-given delight. She bucked and tossed mindlessly, unable to control herself, transported by ecstasy. She moaned aloud, weeping, "Oh my God, my wonderful God."

She bit him, sinking her teeth into his shoulder, as unable to control this action as she was to direct and command any other area of her body. He had lifted her out of herself, exalted her, carried her to heights beyond the reach of reason.

They sagged and lay locked together. She breathed helplessly, spent. She wanted nothing more than to stay knotted to him like this forever. She was brought rudely back to earth by his cold, angered voice. "All right, let's go, Mrs. Cameroon. It's a long way to your New Orleans. But at least you've earned a couple of new dresses."

17

Cameroon leaned against the wagon and watched Rachel dress in a faded calico dress taken from her half-empty carpetbag. A wave of tenderness flooded over him. He warned himself this wasn't love, only compassion. This was the reaction of warm pity roused by the sight of any helpless puppy which feels itself unfairly abused.

When Rachel was dressed, Wade folded the blanket and tossed it into the bed of the wagon. She remained standing where she was, her eyes glittering with tears.

Grinning, he swung her up in his arms. He lifted her toward the wagon seat, then hesitated, closing his hand over the warm and supple rise of her breast. He bent his head and tried to kiss her, but she clamped her teeth savagely upon his lip until he set her down inside the wagon.

He retreated, still grinning, but probing gingerly at his lips. He pulled himself in beside her and took up the lines. "You got what you wanted," she told him. "You raped me. You don't have to kiss me."

"I wanted to thank you for raping so cooperatively."

"Go to hell."

"You seem to forget, Mrs. Cameroon. You *are* Mrs. Wade Cameroon. I told you that name didn't come free of encumbrances. One of them is that you are my wife and you'll act like it."

She shrugged. "I'm your wife until we get to New Orleans."

"Whatever." He smiled and turned the horse back toward the roadbed. They passed through the low-hanging limbs, across the light and shadow of overhanging trees to the rutted trace. Rachel found she glanced back, stung with an unexplained pang of regret toward that quiet bower she'd never see again. His voice brought her head around sharply. "What do you expect to find in New Orleans?"

"Heaven." She stared straight ahead. When he laughed cuttingly, her curt voice lashed at him. "You just get me there. You'll be free of me and it won't matter what I want—or what I do."

He glanced at her, musing. "Why do you think you'll find heaven in New Orleans? There's an old saying—a person carries his own hell with him. Or don't you know that one?"

She yawned raggedly. "I told you. Don't worry about me. My getting to New Orleans was what my mother wanted for me. She died wanting that."

"I thought Ma Peavey was your mother."

She yawned again. "Just don't worry about it."

He glanced at her. She tried to sit rigidly straight but could not. She slumped in the seat, yawning and sagging inwardly, her head nodding forward. Accidentally, she sagged against him. She tried to straighten, could not and then relaxed there, her head on his shoulder. Her head slipped along his arm. Soon, she had moved so she lay with her head in his lap. In minutes she was fast asleep, her perfect lips parted, her breathing deep and regular and exhausted.

Cameroon grinned tautly. Then his grin melted and widened into a smile. Then he laughed. He put his head back laughing.

*

She awoke after two hours, hungry. "Sorry," he told her. "There's nothing to eat. Maybe we'll come to a village soon."

"There are birds. Game. Rabbits. Can't you kill something?" She stared down at herself and her voice sharpened. "Or are you no good for anything but tearing up a person's only dress?"

"Don't worry about the dress. I'll buy you a new dress. Ten, if you like."

"Oh?" Her tone mocked them both. "I pleased you then—back there?"

He pushed his tongue into his cheek. "Your uncle really taught you."

She cursed him fluidly, fluently, without repeating herself. "Nobody taught me. . . . You taught me, damn you. You . . . I didn't know . . . what it was . . . until you . . ." Her voice trailed off, grim with self-loathing, and she stared across the thick swamp growth encroaching upon the trace.

"How kind of you," he teased. "And such an about-face. And likely as true as anything else you've said so far."

"I'm not proud of it, damn you. But it is true."

He laughed. "Any time. At your service."

"Oh, no. I'm not going to do that again. Not with you. Not willingly." Her head tilted and her sculpted jaw tightened.

"Thought you liked it."

She raked him with a strange, cold glance. "Liking has nothing to do with it. . . . I know what I've got to do. Don't worry, Mr. Cameroon, I'll *never* fall in love with you."

He laughed at her. "You already have, my dear."

"I'll never fall in love with you because I won't let myself." Her black eyes clawed him like talons. "I know what I have to do and it has nothing to do with you. . . . Nothing personal, husband dear. . . . I hate *all* white men. Equally."

Shocked, he turned and stared at her.

Her eyes met his defiantly, and she laughed at him. "That's right. I hate you. Because you are a white man. . . . I'm a Negress. According to white man's law a trace of black blood makes one a Negro. Well, I've got *more* than a trace. My mother was an octoroon and my father had part black blood—I don't know how much. I never saw him. Anyhow, proud and mighty Mr. Wade Cameroon, the girl who tricked you into marriage is not only a little backwoods hussy, she's *black*. And if you think I regret what I've done to you, you're wrong. Nothing could please me more."

He stared at her a moment, then laughed.

"Damn you." Her eyes blazed. "What are you laughing at?"

"Told you. I like to laugh, Mrs. Cameroon. You'll just have to get used to it. Especially if you're going on telling me such fairy stories. And on an empty stomach, too."

They rode almost a mile in taut silence. She had moved away from him on the seat. It was as if she had never surrendered to fatigue and slept trustingly with her head in his lap. He smiled, studying her from the corner of his eye. She was a headstrong, self-disciplined little jezebel. She had some sort of plan mapped out in her mind and she meant to follow it as long and as colsely as she could.

He wanted to reach out and enclose her in his arms—partly to reassure and protect her. He knew better. She would resist. She was sufficient unto herself. She didn't want him to touch her. He said, musing, "So you tricked me into marriage just to get away from that town back there. If not me, it could have been anybody."

She nodded coldly. "Any white man. Yes."

He grinned tautly. "Why don't you stop that black-and-white talk? You wanted to get away from your parents and your pregnant sister. I'll buy that. You don't have to decorate it all up with lies for me."

"I don't lie." She exhaled heavily. "Unless I have to. And there's no reason for me to lie to you. I don't care what you think."

"You've built quite a real hatred for white skin, all right."

"If you knew why, you'd understand. If you knew what white men did to my mother—"

"Mrs. Peavey looked fine to me when last I saw her. Crying over the new bride and begging you to take care of yourself."

"Mrs. Peavey is not my mother. And those louts were not my brothers. And Mr. Peavey is not my father—"

"I know. And pregnant Hester is not your sister." He laughed.

"That's right. For a long time, people thought we were sisters. But my mother—"

"The octoroon?" He shook his head, laughing.

"That's right." The girl spoke with terrible inner dignity. "The octoroon. She was born on a slave-breeding farm in Alabama. Her name was Ellen. They say she was lovely. Far prettier than I'll ever be."

He laughed and she impaled him with a glance of such fierce rage in her eyes that he lifted his hand in a placating, conciliatory gesture. "Go ahead. Do go ahead. I'm listening."

"Well, my mother was the mistress of the white owner of this plantation."

" 'Course she was. Every plantation owner has at least one."

"Well, this one did. He was going to marry—a white woman. He didn't want my mother any more. And he didn't want her around to embarrass him and make his new wife uncomfortable. But he had cared for her—once—deeply. He couldn't forget that. She was lovely. And so he set her free. He bought her a house and land and gave her money. I was just born. Before I was a year old, some white men—they think two of them—raped and killed my mother and burned down our house. They left me inside to burn. But some white people saved me."

"Oh my God."

"What's the matter?"

"Honey, even the rubes along the frontiers quit believing stories like that on the cheapest tent-show stages."

"It's the truth, damn you. It is the truth. My mother—Ellen—had helped to save Mrs. Wilkes' baby's life when the baby had typhoid fever. Hester was that baby. Mr. and Mrs. Wilkes ran that store and tavern at Wilkes Corners then. They took me in and pretended I was their child—Hester's sister.

"Miz Portia—that's Mrs. Wilkes—always told me my real mother was a wonderful and beautiful person. And she told me how my real mother had talked about her plans for me. My real mother wanted me to have nice things, pretty clothes and shoes and a good education so I could read and write. She wanted me to get out of those backwoods to some place where I could be somebody . . . like in New Orleans . . . and I *will* be somebody. I've got to be somebody—for my mother. She died trying to make a *free* life for me—and I can't waste what she died trying to do. I've got to be worthy of her . . . and I will."

He bit back his incredulous laughter and managed to inquire in a restrained tone, "What about this saintly Miz Portia and her selfless husband—Hester's real parents? What happened to them?"

"Do you care? Or do you just want to laugh some more?"

"Oh, I care. I can't wait for the next act of this melodrama. Believe me, it has everything—arson, rape, murder, incest, slavery."

For a long time she refused to speak at all. Finally, she said in a low, firm tone, "When Hester and I were about ten—"

"Last year?"

"Seven years ago, damn you. One summer, seven years ago, we had a yellow-fever epidemic. Hester and I survived. Miz

Portia and Mr. Wilkes died that summer. Cousins of Mr. Wilkes'—Herschel and Ma Peavey and those boys you saw back at the stable—they came back and took over the store and tavern again. They'd run it for a few years for Mr. Wilkes. He and Mrs. Wilkes moved away for a while when Hester and I were babies. When we were about five or six, Mr. Wilkes came back and took his store over because the Peaveys had just about bankrupted it. The Peaveys ran it as best they could. They worked Hester and me like slaveys. Hester got pregnant by one of the Peavey boys. I wouldn't let them touch me—"

"Saving yourself for New Orleans?"

"I hated them. They were white, I hated them for that. They were poor white trash. I hated them for that. You're right—I saved myself. I knew that someday I was going to get away. And no matter what you think—or how much you laugh—I *will* get to New Orleans and I will live like a lady—like a white lady."

"Sure you will." He chewed on his underlip to restrain the laughter boiling up inside him. "You get to be a great lady—and you'll get revenge against the white men who raped, killed and incinerated your true mother."

She exhaled heavily. "No. I can never find the white pigs who raped and killed my mother. But one thing I know for sure about them. They were white."

"And so you'll hate all white men—because of them."

"I do. All." She stared straight into his eyes. "All."

"Why?"

"Somebody has got to pay."

"That doesn't make sense."

"Maybe not to you."

"But I will say this. You're one hell of a storyteller. But I wouldn't tell that story too often in New Orleans. They've all seen it on the stage a dozen times."

"Damn you. I'm telling the truth."

He laughed, nodding. "Sure you are. My dearest little hellion, don't you know that every child believes her real parents are not her real parents? They're so vulgar and trashy. They couldn't be. Every child believes gypsies left her on her parents' doorsteps."

"Go to hell."

Laughing, he said, "I will say, you added some creative touches. Most kids believe they're nobility. At least, you insist you're a mulatto's child—and that takes real bravery in this part of the world. A mulatto child by the fine white owner of a great plantation, of course—"

"Go straight to hell."

"I'm sorry, Rachel . . . I can't help laughing." Laughter boiled up inside him and he put his head back.

She stared at him in impotent hatred, looking as if she might slay him. She even looked around for a weapon, found none. Suddenly, she leaped up, braced herself on her knees and brought the carpetbag up over the seat rest. She sat down again, the bag on her knees, shuffled through its meager contents, finally came up with a tattered, aged sheet of legal foolscap.

"Read that," she raged in a savage whisper. "That proves I'm not lying. That proves my mother *was* a slave. She was black and she was freed, just as I said. That paper was all that was saved after the fire—that and a little poke of money my mother kept hidden with it in the brick hearth of the fireplace. Miss Portia found it and saved it for me—and you can just go to hell, you laughing hyena."

He read the aged-crisp paper, then returned it to her. Carefully, she refolded it and returned it to the carpetbag. He bit his lip to conceal his laughter and kept his head fixed on the road ahead. Waning sunlight dappled the trace with engorged shadows and broken shards of yellow.

"When are you going to get me something to eat?" she said.

"As soon as I can." He waved his arm, indicating the deserted forest. "I'm no magician."

"What are you, besides a fugitive from justice?"

"Not much. I'm a Cameroon. Of the Cameroons of Heather Hill."

"A plantation?"

"Yes."

Now Rachel threw her head back and laughed as savagely and mockingly as he had. "Why are you running around now, sleeping in haymows?"

"You're not going to believe this. But I did own a plantation—my father did. He willed it to me. He disinherited my three half brothers. I sold everything. I set the slaves free."

"And you gave all the money to your half brothers?" She laughed wickedly.

"That's right." He laughed, too.

"That's the stupidest, dumbest story I ever heard in my life."

"I admit it's not as good as yours. But I didn't have as much time to think it all up. If I wanted to go to New Orleans, I'd just go, without making up a lot of hogwash about rape and arson and living with white trash." He laughed.

"You'd just free all your slaves, give away all your money and go." She laughed with that same savage intensity.

They looked at each other, smiled, then laughed. They had only to look at each other and they went into paroxysms of laughter, putting their heads back, laughing. . . .

18

It was such a long hard drive—such a wearying journey, plodding over rutted roads that faded at times to weedgrown paths winding randomly through silent, forbidding forest land. Cameroon stayed off the main trail, when he could, knowing that Le Blanc could well have guessed his direction and could be covering the roads in his fast carriage. There was no relief, only mile after tiresome mile of merciless sun, gray dust and steamy humidity. Rachel's skin felt sweaty and sticky to her own touch. She gazed ahead, seeking even a poverty-stricken, slab-sided farmhouse where they might beg water and buy clabber and sidemeat. Anything. She was famished. The trace ahead stretched onward into empty eternity, arid woods and sun-struck countryside drifting past, all sickeningly familiar and yet foreboding and depressing. Rachel despaired of ever finding that village Wade promised her "must be just around that next bend, a little ways more up the trail." The farther they plodded in the open wagon behind the despairing horse, the more every sign of civilization seemed to recede into the unreachable distance.

"There," Wade finally said. "A town."

Late-afternoon sunlight rimlighted a few unpainted, decrepit houses and a tavern. The place was little more than a settlement tossed down on the long trace to New Orleans, but at least it would provide food, rest, a change from the monotony of this slowly moving caravan.

All life in the saffron-tinted settlement seemed concentrated in the shaded forecourt of the rustic tavern. A small barouche caught the eye at once, shiny with varnish, bright with paint and impressive with its liveried black servant-for-life attending. Other horses and buggies were hitched at the railing. Suddenly, Wade slowed his horse and the wagon creaked to a stop in the middle of the sun-hazed roadway.

"What's the matter?" Rachel said.

Wade inclined his head toward the barouche. "That carriage. There near the corner of the tavern. I've seen it before. And those two black slaves sitting in the rear. I've seen them before too. I'd know them anywhere. And that coach. That's that damned Le Blanc's rig. He beaten us here."

"I'm hungry."

He didn't appear even to hear her. He was scarcely aware of her. He'd grown taut, watchful. His eyes were only for that elaborate carriage with its two high-stepping horses, fringed roofing and narrow-rimmed wheels. "Practically cut down for racing. That's Le Blanc's rig, all right. Le Blanc's probably sitting in there waiting for me to walk in."

"Bring me three sandwiches," she said.

He laughed coldly. "Sorry, my love. I'm not going to risk getting killed just to feed you."

"What are you going to do?"

"I don't know." He turned the horses away from the tavern yard, going past toward the rutted trace south out of town.

Angrily, Rachel caught the reins. "I'm hungry."

"I'm aware of that."

"Then do something."

He considered a moment. When he suggested it was likely no more than ten miles to the next town, she cursed him so cuttingly that he grinned. He reached into his pocket, gave her a silver dollar. "Go in there. Don't answer any questions. Buy what you can. I'll be pulled off the road in the hammock just beyond that last house."

"Hiding as usual."

"If you like Brother Le Blanc's looks better, stay with him." He glared at her. "If you're not back in twenty minutes, I'll go without you."

She strolled toward the wagon unhurriedly, sauntering along the dusty road like a native of the place. She hungrily devoured a poor-boy sandwich and carried food in a paper sack at her side. She seemed totally without a care in the world. He supposed she had none. After all, it was only *his* life at stake. She couldn't care less.

"Damn you," he greeted her. "Can't you hurry it up? We can't hope to outrun Le Blanc in this rig. Our only hope is to outsmart him—and we're not doing so well in that department."

She shrugged and climbed into the wagon and plopped down on the seat. She placed the bag between them. "Want a sandwich?"

After a moment he exhaled, laughed, and took one of the foot-long sandwiches made of French bread, beef, pork, lettuce,

Swiss cheese and pickle slivers. His mouth watered. He hadn't realized how hungry he was.

As he took a bite of sandwich, Rachel said in an unconcerned tone, "Your Mr. Le Blanc really looked me over."

He stopped, sandwich poised before his mouth. "How'd you know which one was Le Blanc?"

She moved her shoulders in a careless shrug. "I figured it out. He looked bigger. Richer than the others. Arrogant. He was the only man who looked as if he was seething with rage. Also, I heard someone call his name."

"I hope you're as calm when he overtakes us, shoots me and leaves you unprotected on this trail. We're still one hell of a long ways from New Orleans."

"Eat your sandwich. I'll do all I can to protect you—until we get to New Orleans."

He laughed coldly and took a savage bite of the sandwich. "I'm truly grateful," he said, chewing. He shook his head, angered at her casualness. "You feel pretty good, don't you?"

"Yes. Now that I've eaten. It's hard to be charming on an empty stomach."

"Why didn't you just stay with Le Blanc? Believe me, you'd have been safer—"

"And he *was* eating lobster and steak—not poor-boy sandwiches on the run."

He chewed angrily. "You say he looked you over. Didn't he like what he saw?"

"I don't know. I only know he'll remember me next time he sees me."

"I'm sure he will."

"As I'll remember him."

"But you didn't like him enough to stay with him—comfortable coach, black servants, steak, lobster, wine?"

She shrugged. "He has a certain mean, pinched look. Cruel. Besides, he's white."

"So am I."

"But you're prettier. If you just had a dimple in your chin you'd be positively beautiful—for a white man."

He put his head back, laughing. "I'll swear—you're a scandal, that's what you are. A scandal."

She stared at him, wide-eyed. "How'd you know?"

At a crossroad, he chose the narrowest, least-traveled trace, turning the wagon on it. "You know this isn't the road to New Orleans," she said.

"I never said I'd take the straightest path. You want to get there, and I'd like to make it alive. You mind?"

He did not stop for the night at dusk. He reasoned that Le Blanc might spend the night in whatever comfort the tavern afforded. He wanted to put as many miles as possible between him and that village. It was terribly slow going with the horse picking its way along the stony path. They crossed a creek where, in the last shafts of sunset, he watered the horses.

Rachel stood at the edge of the blood-red creek watching the snuffling horses drink at the reflected cerise and crimson clouds. They heard something rustle in the dry underbush and both went tense, straightening, listening.

Rachel recovered first. She knelt quickly and took up a water-smooth creek rock.

Wade half turned as the rabbit emerged, nose twitching, from a clump of wiregrass. Sensing their presence, the animal leaped high and raced along the creekbed.

Rachel led the animal for a moment, drew back her arm like a boy and threw the river rock. The stone struck the rabbit in the head. It lunged upward and pitched out, dead.

Laughing delightedly, Rachel ran along the creek and took up the rabbit proudly. She returned, holding it by the ears. "Build a fire," she told him. "We'll feast on roast rabbit for supper. Give me your knife. I'll skin him. I'm starved."

"Where'd you learn to kill a rabbit like that?"

"At Wilkes Corners. After the Peaveys came, there wasn't always ammunition, but there was always somebody hungry enough to kill a rabbit."

"You."

"Me. I'd never have stayed alive without knowing the *important* facts of life."

He laughed. "Like killing a rabbit on the run. That trick should stand you in great stead in New Orleans."

"I can forget," she said. "I can forget anything I have to."

They drove along the dim trail until well past midnight. They moved slowly, pushing through deep shadows into deeper shadows. Rachel wavered with fatigue when at last he made camp in a hidden copse where he found grass for the horses.

He spread one blanket over pine boughs and loosely piled leaves, with a second quilt for them to share as cover. She watched him silently. He lay down and held out his arms to her. "We'll have to lie close to keep warm. Gets mighty cold and damp before daybreak."

She shrugged and to his surprise lay down closely beside him. She snuggled closer, shivering slightly. He shook his head, laughing. "You *are* a scandal."

She said nothing. He reached over under the quilt and placed his cupped hand over her breast. Her heart pounded crazily against his palm. He sighed out expansively. "My God, you are a *scandal.*"

He pulled her closer to him, loosening her clothes, pushing his hands inside the fabric to caress her bared flesh. Suddenly, he felt something prick the soft underside of his chin.

He winced. She pressed the point of his own knife—the one she'd used to skin the rabbit—against his throat.

He tilted his head but that sharp blade pursued him relentlessly. "Don't be a fool," he managed to whisper.

"You're the fool if you don't let me go."

"I want to love you. I know damned well you want me to."

The knife pressure increased. He gasped, afraid even to grab her wrist. He lay immobile. "I told you," she said. "No more. If you wanted pay for marrying me, you've had it."

He tried to laugh her out of it. "I was thinking of this more for old times' sake—for practice—just for the hell of it."

"Make your jokes. But take your hands off me, or I'll rip. I swear it. . . . I'll give myself. As I wish. When I wish. But I won't be taken by force again, ever. . . . Now, if you're smart you'll roll over—and go to sleep."

"Are you crazy? How can I sleep now?"

"Think about something else."

"With you pressed against me? What else is there?"

"Nothing's ever easy."

Carefully, he released her, reluctantly withdrawing his heated hand from her soft and pliant breast. Cautiously, he turned his back on her. He felt the knife removed. He lay still. He stared out across the dark and silent forest. He felt sick with frustration.

He heard the horses snuffling as they foraged out in the darkness. An owl wept; a distant panther wailed; a wolf bayed at the moon. He watched distant stars glitter, lost as he, in the black void beyond the thick foliage of the trees. He could really think of nothing except the pain in his groin, the engorgement of blood at his fly, the need that flooded his entire body, and the enchanting beauty of the girl beside him. He ached with thwarted desire.

My God, God, he thought. What in hell have you got against me and my sex life? I don't ask that it be *sane*, but couldn't it be fulfilled, just once in a while? So, I'm oversexed. So I need more than ordinary men. But who made me like that? Is terrible need and terrible frustration part of some infinite scheme I can't understand? Because I can tell you, God, I sure as hell can't understand it.

He felt Rachel—Scandal—press in closer against his back. For warmth, he thought in rage. God knows, she should get warmth—I'm burning like a furnace inside.

He heard her breathing deepen, going regular and unbroken. The little minx could go right off to sleep. He told himself to take her now. He might hate himself in the morning, but meantime he'd get some sleep—and he'd get to hold that excruciatingly lovely body against him one more time.

He did not move. He had one scruple, he supposed. One. One too many. It was great to want a woman with every fiber of your body. But it was perfect only when she wanted you. . . . To hell with her.

That was easy to say. Still, the night hours dragged slowly and he could not sleep. His eyes burned with weariness and a sense of incredible loss, but he was unable to forget her heated body outlined against his. Unlike her, he could not forget so quickly the incredible God-given delight of the first time he had her. He was never meant to live on memories! Having her body only whetted his appetite for her body, as it always would. He would want this scandalous little creature above everything else, as long as he lived. But he could not *force* her to want him. In God's fouled-up cosmos, if ever two people were meant to meet and love, meant one for the other, she was intended for him alone. No matter what God's plan was, it couldn't be otherwise. He had had her and he believed that she was made for him. Now only three things stood between him and mortal fulfilment—her ambition, his knife in her hand and God's indecipherable will. . . .

He slept at last, as a refuge, sanctuary, an escape from his tormented waking dreams of her.

He never afterward knew what wakened him—a sheer drop in the temperature, Scandal's pulling the last wisp of blanket from his shoulder, the stirring of his horses, the lingering shard of nightmare.

He opened his eyes, aware of a fearful tension in the night. He rolled over on his back. His mouth sagged open. His eyes widened.

Le Blanc stood over him. He held a rifle slung in the crook of his arm, making a close-range handgun of the weapon. He crooked his finger, ready to press the trigger, and pointed the ugly barrel mouth at the space between Wade's eyes.

19

A sense of total exhaustion clamped down over Wade. He felt entirely helpless. Though the stygian black of late night shrouded the glen, he could see Le Blanc's contorted face clearly, the hatred and greed for vengeance burning there like some holy fanaticism.

Le Blanc kicked Rachel with his boot, never taking his eyes from Wade. "Get up. Get over there. Out of the way. . . . I'm going to kill this vermin. . . . I want him to live just long enough to know that I, Albert Le Blanc, am killing him to avenge the death of my brother Henri."

Holding his breath, Wade watched Le Blanc, trying to anticipate his next move. Beside him, Rachel cried out when Le Blanc booted her. When, sleep-drugged, she did not move swiftly enough to please him, he kicked her again, more savagely. "I told you. Get over there. Out of the way."

Keeping the quilt about her shoulders, Rachel crawled away from Wade on the bed of leaves and boughs. He felt the urge to ironic laughter, the way she clung to the quilt. After all, he wasn't going to need it where he was going. For one brief instant, he let his gaze trail after her in the cavelike darkness under the low-hanging trees. And so ends the wedded bliss of the young Cameroons, he thought. And no great loss at that, though he did feel a terrible sense of loss, deep inside. A fugitive husband and a prudish wife.

"You have prayers, say them." Le Blanc spoke down at him, almost as if each word were spat upon his prostrate form.

"I have no prayers."

"Before witnesses, I accuse you of the willful murder of Henri Le Blanc of French Pines, Louisiana. None can say I have not trailed you from the scene of the crime and found you guilty—"

"If you ever go on trial, your black witnesses won't help you much. They can't testify in court against a white man."

"True." Le Blanc's voice bristled with self-commendation. His voice lashed down over Wade, like bile. "Blacks can't testify *against* a white man in court. But their testimony *for* him is quite in order."

"Looks like you've got it all on your side. Unless my wife decides to tell the truth—that you killed an unarmed man in cold blood."

Le Blanc's answer was deadly chilling. "The woman will have a choice as to her testimony—before she leaves this place tonight."

Le Blanc's body tautened and he extended the gun slightly in his hand. Suddenly everything moved in exaggerated slow motion. In the deep forest quiet, Wade could hear the two blacks gasp. They too sensed the crisis moment. Only Rachel did not move. She remained crouched on her knees under the quilt, watching Le Blanc in the mesmerized way a bird watches a snake.

The signal that Le Blanc was about to press the trigger was his sharp intake of breath. He neither blinked nor hesitated. As the gun moved out in his hand and his fingers clutched tighter at the trigger guard, Rachel moved suddenly, throwing off the quilt.

She did not even disturb or turn Le Blanc. His nerves were like taut wires. She did not startle or deter him. He didn't glance her way, but he should have.

It all happened so swiftly Wade was never afterward sure he even saw the glitter of the hurtling knife. What he did hear was the impact and the slash of the knife through jacket sleeve and taut flesh of Le Blanc's biceps.

Le Blanc howled in astonished agony. The impact of the thrown knife almost knocked him off his feet.

Wade levered himself upward, coming off his back from a prone position, his knees bent, his boots digging into the blanket, limbs and earth beneath him.

Le Blanc caught his balance, half turned, bracing himself. The knife hilt stuck up from his biceps. Pain paralyzed his left arm. He held the gun in his right hand and he heeled back around to face Wade, bracing his weight on his widespread legs like tree trunks.

This was his second mistake. Wade lunged upward, striking at the gun with his left arm to deflect it, sending his right fist toward Le Blanc's face. But both these moves were hastily conceived diversionary action, and Le Blanc reacted, his senses dulled by the icy prongs of pain numbing his arm, his shoulder and his nerve centers. He ducked away from Wade's fist, tried to protect the rifle. And Wade got him where he was vulnerable.

Wade drove forward, bringing his bent knee up between Le Blanc's wide-set legs. Too late, Le Blanc realized he was not opposing a gentleman who would observe rules of fair conduct, but a man fighting for his life.

Wade's driving knee caught Le Blanc in the crotch, half-lifting the big man from the ground. When Cameroon's knee battered into Le Blanc's gonads, everything inside Le Blanc's mind and body instantly short-circuited. He lost control of his bodily functions. Bile and vomitus gorged upward from his belly. His own knees buckled, weak as whey. His body caved in upon itself. He grabbed at his testes with his numbed left hand. He bent forward, retching. His right hand and finger muscles went lax. He dropped the rifle.

Wade shoved Le Blanc away and leaped for the rifle, but Rachel beat him to it. She scrambled toward Le Blanc, already clutching at the gun before it struck the ground. She set herself on her knees and brought the gun up in her arm, fixed on Le Blanc. She had killed rabbits with rocks but she'd learned to use a rifle too with deadly accuracy.

Wade saw her hand close on the guard and her fingers reach for the trigger. His voice rasped at her. "No, Scandal."

She hesitated, but her face was taut. "He'll be after you. As long as you live." Her voice, low and savage, raged at him.

Wade swung his arm. "Get in the wagon. Hold the gun on him. We're getting out of here."

Her rigid face was set and cold with disdain and violent disagreement, but wordlessly she retreated a few steps. She kept the gun fixed on Le Blanc as if praying the big man would provide her the slight provocation she needed to press that trigger.

Wade glanced toward the two black servants in the carriage. They shivered with terror. "You. You Negroes. Bring rope. Step on it—or I'll cut your hearts out."

"Yas suh. We comin'." One of the black youths, sniffling loudly, caught up a coiled line. The two of them ran across the clearing, anxious to obey any white man's commands. With their master writhing like a toad on the ground they were lost.

Wade formed a noose, slipped it over Le Blanc's head. Using the rope as a snubbing line, he jerked the big man off his feet. He tied Le Blanc's arms behind his back, bent the man's knees and tied off his ankles. Every time Le Blanc moved either his arms or his ankles, the noose tightened on his throat, choking him.

"Those boys will loosen him as soon as we're out of here," Scandal taunted Wade.

He shrugged. "Every five minutes we buy is time on our side, Mrs. Cameroon."

As he spoke, he led his own horses to the rear of Le Blanc's carriage and secured them.

The blacks watched him in growing terror. "Masta." One of the boys wept, falling to his knees. "Please, kindly Masta. You ain't gwine fixing' to leave us out chere in these dark woods with no horses and our pore masta ableedin' to death?"

"Maybe if you're lucky he will bleed to death." Wade glared

at them, unblinkingly. "Either of you boys got guns?"

Both blacks shook their heads, eyes wide, mouths agape. But when Wade continued to stare at them, the bigger youth nodded, his teeth chattering. "I do believe I has this one little ole gun, Masta, suh."

"I'll take it." Wade shoved the handgun under his belt. Casually, he yanked his knife from Le Blanc's upper arm and wiped the blood on Le Blanc's jacket. Le Blanc sobbed in agony.

"Don't weep, Le Blanc," Wade stalked to the wagon and took out Scandal's carpetbag and his own gear, which he transferred to the rear of Le Blanc's polished rig. "You're lucky you're alive. I've seen her throw. If she had wanted to hit you in the heart with that knife, she could have."

"I wanted to," Scandal said from behind him. "But he moved."

The Tennessee carriage horses moved briskly. The light-mounted, narrow-rimmed wheels spun gracefully across the ground on thickly greased bearings. The carriage rolled swiftly along the trace in the predawn darkness. For a long time Scandal had sat unmoving beside Wade, tense, the rifle across her knees, frequently checking the backtrail.

Cameroon glanced at his child bride, overwhelmed by a sense of tenderness, of admiration, of a deep emotion he'd never felt toward anyone else and for which he had no name. He kept his voice casual, though he was anything but confident and sanguine inside. "I want to thank you for saving my life."

"I'm sure you do. You'd like to take me right to bed to prove how grateful you are."

He laughed. "Wondered why you bothered."

Her voice was cool. "You're my husband."

"Until New Orleans do us part." He touched her hand. She did not move away. "I was surprised . . . me being white and all." When she remained unmoving, her hand under his, and did not speak, he said. "And bloodthirsty! You're a bloodthirsty little Scandal. Why were you so anxious to kill a man you didn't even know?"

She shrugged. "Because until you finally stop him, he'll hound you." Her laugh raked him. "And maybe next time I won't be around to pull your chestnuts out of the fire. . . . Besides, he's white. That's reason enough for me."

He sighed. "Killing looks easy, Scandal. It's like shooting a deer. Or a rabbit—"

"Or a snake—"

"—only it's not. . . . It's *after* you've taken a human life that the hell sets in—and it's not like killing a squirrel for food at all. . . . I've got one murder on my conscience. So help me God, that's one too many."

She stared at him, without compassion. "Don't be a fool. You killed accidentally. You killed in self-defence—to stay alive. You haven't *murdered* anybody."

"It still makes me sick inside."

"It was your life or his."

"Try telling Le Blanc that."

"No." She shook her head and her voice was cold. "I won't try to. You let Le Blanc live . . . you see where it gets you."

She did not speak again and they drove for a long time in silence. The first pink shafts of dawn split the sky along the horizon. At last Scandal placed the rifle on the box of the carriage and sat back, exhaling heavily.

The towns, villages and settlements were no lovelier, no more inviting, but they were more frequent along the trace as they approached New Orleans. They followed the long trail skirting north of Lake Pontchartrain. Wade saw the excitement and anticipation building in Scandal, her eyes brightening and her cheeks flushing with blood as the miles rolled away and they entered the fringes of the bayou country.

They stopped for dinner in a settlement of under three hundred people. When the tavernkeeper told Scandal they could make New Orleans town limits by sundown, Scandal was almost too excited to eat. She hurried Wade, wanting to be on the road again.

The local hostler entered the tavern for lunch. He stood at the bar, a red-faced man, and asked who owned the two fine Tennessee-bred carriage animals outside. Wade touched Scandal's arm warningly, motioning her to silence, but she said, "We do."

The man grinned and crossed the room to them. "I'm from Tennessee horse country myself, ma'am. Just had to stop and admire that horseflesh. Beautiful animals . . . might pay you up to a couple hundred—in gold—for the pair."

"They're not for sale," Wade said. He shook his head at Scandal, ordering her to keep quiet.

Scandal refused to be silenced. She glared at Wade. Her voice lowered, tense. "Are you so rich we can't use two hundred extra dollars in New Orleans?" she demanded.

His black eyes struck against hers. "You going to pull that coach on into town?" he inquired. "Troilus is a saddle horse. He'd be as helpless in those traces as I would."

"No problem. No problem," the hostler said, smiling expansively. "I can throw in a couple of good strong dray horses that you could sell in New Orleans—plus the two hundred. Why, I'd do it just to sweeten the deal."

"Sold," Scandal said.

20

They approached the town limits of New Orleans. Cameroon suddenly looked back on the long and dangerous odyssey, with Scandal at his side, with relish and a sense of regret and loss. It had been an experience unlike any other in his existence. He had met many females, white and black, slave and free, but never one quite like Scandal—the willowy fragility of the daintiest infanta, but she could throw rocks like a boy, and he suspected she could shoot a rifle with the deadly accuracy of a man. He sighed. No matter where life led him now, he would never forget the nights they had spent together out under the stars. They had eaten before an open fire and then curled up together in their blanket and quilt. Always, by sunrise, she had appropriated the quilt, rolled tightly in it. But he had his revenge. She would not willingly permit him to love her, even to touch her. She did sleep close against him in the chilled wet night for the warmth his body afforded. After she was asleep he lifted her gently, placed her body on his and held her there, fondling and caressing her for long and breathless hours of forbidden delight. There was no satisfaction. But God, there was pleasure.

Now that the hectic journey was almost over, Cameroon regretted its end. New Orleans lay just ahead of them, and he was apprehensive, not for himself but for Scandal and her dreams. He saw nothing ahead for her but heartbreak. Whatever happened, the brief rapturous intimacy between them was gone. It could never be again as it had been in this carriage on the trace. Despite her shrewish tongue, she had seemed almost content with him—as content as a driven and ambitious young female like Scandal could ever be. She was pleased to be with him alone. They passed mansions and comfortable farmhouses where they could have stayed overnight and been welcomed. She was satisfied to stop only for fresh milk. She never suggested spending a night in the taverns or ordinaries they passed along the trail. She bought food in the inns and general stores, and they ate beside creeks or on grassy knolls. She lay back and slept, unself-consciously, and he leaned against a tree bole and drank in her exquisite beauty, his eyes hooded, his lips dry with unquenchable thirst.

He wished he could delay the moment of parting a little while longer, but he knew better. Scandal seemed already to have hastened beyond him into a place made real by her fantasies where he could not even follow. She seemed only vaguely aware of him. No. It couldn't be delayed. Whatever small fraction of heaven he'd found on that trace with her, it too had passed and could never be recovered.

He laid the whip across the sweated backs of the dray horses. Not even the brilliantly varnished vehicle looked elegant any more. With the fine carriage animals gone, the splashboard thick with dung, the sides streaked with red clay and orange mud, the rig had lost all its old majesty.

"We should be there soon," he said.

She nodded and licked her tongue across her lips, her eyes brightening, but she did not speak.

Though Scandal had always dreamed ahead to her arrival in New Orleans in quivering anticipation and empty-bellied excitement, she was not prepared for her first actual discovery of the crescent city spawled along the river in bayou lowlands. The town burst suddenly into view, and she gasped, enchanted, and leaned forward in the carriage. She gripped Wade's arm to steady herself, not realizing how deeply she dug her nails into his flesh. She stared, her heart pounding and goose bumps standing along her arm and on the nape of her neck, at her first panoramic glimpse of the ancient town. Two cities really, and still sharply marked by the Esplanade, the French Quarter and the American, and over all of it the flavor of the departed Spanish. The badly paved streets were not lined with gold after all, but they did not have to be—Scandal's imagination so encrusted them. The avenues were crowded, busy with people: hurrying, exciting beings in a worldly melting pot. All roads seemed to lead to the levees, the wide snaking river, the water craft of every description and registry, all promising a strange, mysterious region stretching beyond the bayous.

Dusk smoked in across the town, and the gas lamps, many imported from Paris, glowed in saffron ineffectuality against the deepening night. The piers lay stacked high with commerce from all crannies of the earth. Vessels of all rigs, shapes and tonnage were moored, sometimes three abreast in the sluggish river. Some were oceangoing ships, sails furled, gangplanks dropped, flying flags of dozens of nations, cabin lights like yellow peepholes to unknown existences. Upriver, at the docks of the American town, conglomerations of keelboats, paddle-wheelers and every variety of river boat gathered like tramps. From everywhere rose pungent odors of rum and molasses, coffee, naval stores, newly milled pine, cedar and cypress. Every nationality swarmed over the quays and cobblestones and banquettes, a modern Babylon of tongues—Spanish, Cuban, Sweden, French and raw, backcountry American. A babel of languages assaulted her ears—English cockneys yapping querously, Portuguese rattling against Spanish and Italian, and the Cubans clearly understanding none of the dialects and nuances. Tennesseans talked of fine horses, Carolinians of beautiful women, Georgians of corn whiskey, and everywhere men shouted about the invading Yankees and the hovering cloudbanks of war. Everyone hurried and yet no one seemed in a hurry. They stopped to talk and laugh together, to argue and kiss and fight. Negroes laughed and shouted in the streets in a way unknown anywhere else south of the Mason-Dixon. Freed blacks strode as if they owned the cobbled streets: hawkers, peddlers, pickpockets, pimps, whores, flower sellers, children dancing for pennies. And everywhere the grog houses loomed like huge fiery hearths of welcome. Old black men staggered along selling boiled peanuts and hot crab legs. In rickety curbside shanties black men and women shucked oysters and gulped them down raw, splashed with blood-red cayenne pepper sauce.

Cameroon threaded his carriage slowly through the tangle of traffic and unheeding pedestrians. Wide-eyed, Scandal swiveled her head, trying to see everything at once. All movement paused when a brightly varnished Creole coach rolled through, bearing women so lovely and so brilliantly attired that the very vehicle seemed to glow with refracted elegance.

"I'm here," Scandal whispered. "I'm truly, really here."

With some difficulty, Wade maneuvered the horses and coach around a sharp-edged corner and along the narrow walled street of the Vieux Carré. Scandal caught her breath; her heart slugged in her rib cage, her swimming mind unable to credit all it saw. Creative and fragile wrought-iron latticework decorated the upper floors of every building. Because of the wet, unstable soil, no building rose over three stories high. Residences were built remote from the streets, protected behind gates and served by open courtyards where grew every species of subtropical plant—crepe myrtle, Spanish dagger, sterile ornamental banana shrubs, and jacaranda. Willows wept over high concrete enclosures, and the night grew redolent with smells of jasmine, roses and magnolia.

Raucous cries of vendors echoed along the shaded colonnade of the French Market. Aromas of freshly ground coffee, ripening fruit, vegetables, caldrons of bubbling gumbo, fresh-baked bread and the sweet bainy—which proved to be a doughnut without the hole. They passed furriers displaying sleek mink, sable and sealskin, silversmiths, jewelers, and huge arenas where every exotic item collected and imported around the world was hawked.

Wade stopped the wagon before a walled court and closed gate. He left Scandal sitting alone in the carriage. Men, black and white, loitered along the banquettes on both sides of the shell-paved avenue, ogling her. Some called boldly, some whispered loving obscenities as they passed. She ignored them all. They dispersed like cockroaches in lamplight when Wade reappeared, wide-shouldered, tall, muscular. She smiled, delighted with him.

The gate was opened timidly and he drove the carriage into a sheltered courtyard. The gates were closed quickly and barred. Scandal followed Wade up the outside stairway shaded by oleander. They entered a small apartment which shone neat and clean and was brightly lit with gas lamps. An old iron four-poster bed dominated one wall under a golden-plated crucifix. French windows, draped, opened on a balcony overlooking Dauphine Street.

"Only temporary, of course," Wade teased. "Until you move into a Charles Street mansion with your doddering old millionaire."

She stood uncertainly in the middle of the room. Remote sounds of this strange city assaulted her, caressed her, seduced and lured her. The gala town seemed to whisper to her—its own loving obscenities: wealthy men, beautiful gowns, bright dresses, brilliant diamonds, champagne and all the impractical little slippers she could ever hope to wear.

"Like it?" he said.

"I feel as if I'm in heaven. In paradise. It's not real yet. I can't believe I'm really here at last. I keep waiting for Hester to kick me in the back and wake me up."

He yawned exaggeratedly. "Tomorrow's a big day. We've had a hellish trip. Why don't we go to bed?"

Scandal laughed at him. "If you were really tired, my great stallion, you wouldn't be trying to get me in that bed."

Wade gazed down at her for a long taut beat. His black eyes glittered. His fine mouth tightened into a gray line. Then abruptly he shook off the mood of rage, shrugged, put his head back and laughed. "To hell with you, Mrs. Cameroon."

He heeled around and caught up his slouch-brimmed hat and clapped it on his blond head. He grinned at her coldly. "I'll see you in the morning." He strode toward the door.

"Where are you going?" The lash of her voice arrested him in midstride.

He paused, glanced over his shoulder. "Out."

"Out where?"

"What do you care? As long as I don't force myself upon you."

"I don't want you to leave me alone—my first night in this strange town."

"Get used to it. It's got to get used to you. It's going to be *your* oyster, remember."

She bit her lip. "Please don't go."

"The hell with you. You can live like a nun if you wish, but by heaven I don't intend to live like a monk." The door slammed behind him.

On the street, he slowed. He wanted something all right, wanted it desperately, but unfortunately what he truly desired was behind him, upstairs in that little room. Damn her. He wasn't going to let her inhibit and frustrate him. She wasn't going to dictate his life the way some milksops let their women rule them. No woman would ever castrate him, even symbolically. If she hadn't sense to know that what God gave a man and a woman was the nearest to paradise they'd ever have on this earth, the hell with her.

Plenty of prostitutes cruised the narrow streets of the French Quarter. They wore evening gowns, tired and bedraggled garments from better times and better places. Their pimps monitored from dark crannies, attired in brilliant plumes, tight-fitting pants, colorful jackets and wide-brimmed feathered hats.

Dispirited ladies of the streets ornamented every shadow. Ever since old Andrew Jackson had subdued, ravaged and destroyed the Indian tribes of Florida and then insisted upon disbanding his forces in New Orleans, the town had been the capital city for whores. They came first lured by the millions in army discharge pay; they stayed to establish a red-light district larger than many towns.

He looked them over but could not force himself into liaison with streetwalkers. There was always something wrong—too much mascara, a broken tooth, whiskey breath, terminal weariness.

He entered a tavern and stood alone at the bar drinking Scotch whisky and branch water. The men around him shouted, but there was little laughter. Arguments raged. The Louisiana convention had met in Baton Rouge in January 1861. These representatives proposed that Louisiana follow the five Southern states which had already seceded from the Union. Yet nobody really wanted to break away from the republic. Even now, only the most radical favored secession. Most still hoped against hope that somehow the Union might be preserved. Yet they were caught in a tide and carried along inevitably to the fatal break. The whole business depressed Cameroon. He set down his empty glass and walked out onto the night street again.

He recalled a visit long ago to New Orleans with his three older brothers. They had visited the Academy of Music, that superb spa of lovely women dedicated to the sensual pleasures of men. It was here, under the ministrations of a lovely Creole, that he had been initiated into the wonders of sex. He had been young, callow, shy and frightened. His brothers had laughed at him. Even the lovely girls in the parlor had snickered behind their fans. Well, damn them, they wouldn't laugh at him now. He had built up a need that was going to be explosive.

He laughed aloud. Not the loveliest, freshest *demi-mondaine* in Madame Alix's incredible organization could ever drive Scandal from his mind, but by God she would help! He would select the most ravishing creature in the house and he would spend the night entangled in her perfumed embrace, burning Scandal from his mind. He would be free of her. By God, he would. He paused outside the sedate old stone house and then took the wide marble steps up to the front door two at a time.

Albert Le Blanc could barely think straight, obsessed as he was with rage. He drove the decrepit wagon behind a sway-backed mule he'd bought from a farmer for more money than the rascal had seen at one time in all his life.

The sun blazed down on his unprotected back. In the bed of the wagon the two black servants alternately slept and whimpered. He'd warned them that the next one to protest would be castrated along with the hogs when they got back to French Pines.

He drew his hand across his sweated forehead. The mule plodded along the streets of another unnamed settlement on the road to New Orleans. Le Blanc swore. They were gone, evaporated ahead of him, lost in time and space. Perhaps they'd turned off the New Orleans trail—no one in the past day's travel had remembered seeing his high-stepping pair and carriage. But he would find them. Damn them, he would find them.

His left arm throbbed, fevered and painful. He'd stopped in

some Godforsaken settlement where a saddlebag sawbones had washed his wound and doused it with iodine.

The boys whined in the bed of the wagon. There was a tavern ahead. Couldn't Masta stop and buy food there for them, even if he was not hungry?

Raging, Le Blanc turned on to the seat to castigate the slaves. Something snagged at his attention, and for a second he did not know what it was. It was as if a humming-bird had flitted across his line of vision. Yet it was not that. He slowed the mule and tilted his head, looking around him in the blaze of sunlight.

The town was slab-sided, unpainted, ugly and much like all the others he had passed through. There was nothing to attract his interest. Then his gaze touched on a corral behind a livery stable, and his mouth sagged open. For a long beat he stared at his lovely carriage animals in that enclosure.

Holding his breath, he turned the wagon into the livery. A huge-shouldered, red-faced man came out of the shadows, squinting against the lances of the sun. "Yes, neighbor. What can I do for you?"

"Where'd you get those Tennessee horses—in that corral back there?"

The hostler grinned. "Biggest bargain of my life, mister. Bought them off a young fellow and his bride."

"What'd he look like? Tall? Blond? Muscular? And the girl, petite, reedlike, with black eyes?"

"That's the pair, mister. You know 'em?"

Le Blanc drew a deep breath and spoke with studied calm. "You might say I'm looking for them. Did he mention his name?"

"Don't recollect that he did."

"Cameroon?"

"He didn't say."

"Did he say where he was going?" Almost certainly New Orleans, he knew—but Cameroon was slippery, and might have sold the horses just a few hours from the city in order to suggest a direction he had not taken.

The red-faced man laughed. "That's how I bought the horses. He didn't want to sell. But the little lady, she insisted they'd need the money—when they got into New Orleans."

Wade smiled all the way to his new apartment on Dauphine Street. He felt exultant, renewed in body and spirit. Refreshed. He'd had his shovel scraped, his coals raked, his bucket filled, his ashes hauled. Oh God, it had been *good*! No arguments, no coy refusals, no hypocrisy, just heated cooperation and breath-taking creativity.

Madame Alix had welcomed him warmly. An aging, perfumed, beringed, curled and corseted madame, Alix could not possibly have remembered him but she pretended she did, which was almost as satisfactory. He was so youthful, rugged, virile and handsome that all the ladies eyed him hungrily.

He made his choice—a red-haired Cuban girl who spoke little English yet somehow reminded him of Scandal. Perhaps it was nothing more than the liquid blackness of her eyes.

Madame Alix shook her head and waved the Cuban beauty away.

"No, no, m'sieu, not her," Madame Alix whispered behind her perfumed fan of ostrich feathers. "An ordinary performer. One might say she blows an instrument well enough, but for you, a sensitive artist to pluck heaven from the strings—eh? Eh, *chérie*?"

Madame Alix clapped her ringed hands and the black youth, bared to the waist, chest muscles like bronzed hawsers, wearing bright-green cotton pajama pants over orange slippers, escorted in a young blond girl from another room. The girl looked fragile, yet her breasts protruded, ripe young melons under the transparent negligee.

"Diane will serve you well—whether you wish it once or extended through the night. . . . She is new to us, but experienced in her way. She came to us after an uncle of hers had violated her—used her in every way he could imagine, got her pregnant, disgraced in her village. Her family denied her. She came to me. She's been very happy here—for the first time."

Feeling it ironic that Diane's uncle—like Scandal's—had taught her the convoluted truths of sexual intercourse, Wade walked with her to a second-floor cubicle furnished only with a freshly made bed.

Hours later he was still there, exhausted, sated, weak at the backs of his knees, but exhilarated. He held her for a long time, memorizing the poetry of her body. She was wistful when she kissed him goodbye. Her lips skimmed across his chest, over the planes of his belly and down to his thighs, where she nursed and nuzzled, clinging to him, burning herself, she hoped, into his mind. "Come back again to me," she whispered, licking at him with the fiery tip of her tongue. "I'll always be special for you. . ."

He paid his bill at the parlor on his way out. Jesus! It had cost a small fortune to spend the evening at the Academy of Music. He did not regret the money, though he was almost broke. He'd left the two hundred in gold in a poke with Scandal. Tomorrow, when he was rested and revived, he would sell Le Blanc's carriage. Polished and cleaned, it would bring a good price. And he had to start thinking about a job, an income. The hell of it was, he wasn't good for anything except overseeing a cotton-economy plantation. Not a hell of a lot of calls for such skills in the New Orleans job market, likely.

Scandal was awake when he came into the apartment. The bed looked unrumpled, untouched. She huddled in a chair near the balcony doorway, wrapped in the old quilt. Her face was bleak, rigid, her eyes black and chilled and hurt. A wave of tenderness rushed through him. He smiled and bent over her.

She drew back, raging. "Don't touch me," she said. "Don't you ever touch me again."

21

Cameroon awakened early, restless in spite of the fatigue of their journey and his energetic sport at the Academy of Music. He swung his legs off the bed and sat looking at his bride. Scandal lay as far as possible from him, crouched on the edge of the mattress, almost lost under her smelly old quilt.

He sat for a long time gazing at her, or at the lump she made under that cover. He wanted to touch her, to caress those fiery globes, to suckle her sweet-tasting nipples, to kiss her until she clung to him as he wanted to cling to her. But he did not reach out his hand. She did not want him. He would not force himself upon her, not upon any woman. Never—even though, at times like this, it seemed less than a reprehensible notion.

He watched the first stria of dawn light up the room with strange pink tints. He admitted that he loved Scandal with every nerve and fiber of his body, yet all the while his mind, ruling his heart, warned him that it was no good unless she loved and wanted him. And she never would. She was too ambitious. Driven. Obsessed with money and social status. Compelled by dreams of pomp and elegance which would have been ridiculous except for the trusting innocence that informed them.

Exhaling heavily, he got up, dressed quietly and prowled the early-morning streets for a long time, walking along the river. A black man hunched on pilings and stared at the swirling water, sobbing. Troubled, Cameroon paused beside him. It was his friend, the youth said, a man like his brother, closer than kin. They'd been out drinking together last night and had wandered down here with a couple of bottles of cheap red wine. They'd fought. He could not even recall the cause of the battle. Nothing. Nothing worth a penny. They exchanged blows, even laughing when they swung and missed, but still fighting in earnest. His friend fell into the river. "Tides. Riptides. Undercurrents. Undertow. That damn river got 'em all. He fell in. He was gone. That quick. Drowned." He had slumped there all night, unable to leave. He could only crouch on these pilings and stare at the water where he'd last seen his friend. "It's like I'm lost. I'm all lost."

Wade nodded. "I know how you feel." All lost.

He walked away. The town was coming sluggishly to life, the routines of living, struggling, dying—by design, by accident, by violence—with people hurrying faster and faster toward that unknown, unknowable destiny.

He stood in the rising sunlight and watched crews drive horses from a barge to a special corral built near the pier. The animals were terrified, wild-eyed, fractious, dung-smeared.

A man struck a high-strung filly with a lead-weighted rope. The animal squealed, terrified, slashing at the drover with her teeth. Enraged, the man beat the horse wildly.

Wade caught his arm, yanking it down and gripping his wrist. "That's not going to help anything."

The drover heeled around ready to fight. He surveyed Cameroon's size and heft and changed his mind. "I got my job," was all he said.

A slender man, in a gray, lightweight suit, pearl-gray vest, panama planter's hat and dung-streaked boots, touched Wade's arm. He removed the expensive cheroot from his mustached mouth and smiled sourly. He was as tall as Wade, at least twenty-five years older, graying at the temples but standing ramrod straight. "You trying to make trouble, suh?"

Wade grinned back at him, as coolly and unruffled. "You need some made?"

"Then you are a troublemaker by profession?"

"No. Only by inclination. You don't handle horses that way. Horses are stupid sometimes, but you can't be stupider than they are."

"Some of my men can. They're the best I can hire. They get the work done. Not always as I'd wish, but always on time. My trouble is with you bleeding hearts, you prevention-of-cruelty people. Usually it's some old biddy, her vagina gone to vinegar and nothing left but to enforce her ideas on others."

"I started early."

"We've got an auction here tomorrow. Got to get these animals in the corral, washed and glossed up. They got to look good. By tomorrow. We don't have any time for prima donnas who decide to go their own way."

"You've got some beautiful horses, but they won't be worth a damn to anybody, half-broken, scared shitless."

"You a horse breeder, or just a busybody?"

"We used to breed horses. At a place called Heather Hill. We auctioned them off, too. But we never drove them into frenzies first."

"Lucky you. I told you. We're working against time."

"And against good sense."

The man smiled faintly. "So you will allow that I have a line of pretty good horseflesh here?"

Wade didn't answer at once. He walked to the rail fence enclosing the busy corral. He watched the animals for some minutes without speaking. "Looks like you've got some good thoroughbreds in there. Enough to give your operation class, but nothing more. Trouble is, you've been trying to improve the breeds instead of preserving the purity."

"Farmers want animals breeded up. They want them with size and stamina."

"They think they do. They buy fat horses thinking they'll stay fat under working conditions. They think a fat horse is a healthy horse. They'll buy your frenzied animals as unbroken, or half-broken, thinking they can train them. And all the time you and I know better."

The man scowled, staring at Wade's face. At last, his mouth pulled into a crooked smile. "You anticipate being round here at my auction tomorrow?"

Wade shrugged. "Why?"

"Well, I tell you, suh. Like the cut of your jib. Also, I know horses. And better than that, I know men that know horses. Truly know 'em. You happen to fall in that class. You around here talking down my animals might cost me several thousand dollars."

"Why would I do that?"

"How in hell do I know? Why did you stop Lambakis from beating on that filly? Tell you what. My name's Guille Desmare.

Tantallon Horse Farms. How would you like to work for me tomorrow? On a commission basis. But you could make yourself a few hundred dollars—if you worked it right. I'd give you ten percent on every sale you helped me put through."

Wade laughed. "What you really mean is, you'd rather pay me to work for you than take a chance on my talking against you."

"Exactly. More than that, you know horseflesh. You might induce many to buy who'd otherwise hesitate."

"How do you know I won't tell them what I believe to be the truth?"

Guille Desmare laughed. "The truth has a way of looking different at ten percent, old son."

Wade walked into the lodgings a little before noon. The place seemed different. The smell was pungent. Scandal had bought three pounds of the huge Louisiana shrimp, boiled them for three minutes, peeled them and served them on the small table heaped in a bowl. She'd warmed French bread and made coffee.

"First day in our new home," Wade teased. He tried to kiss her but she eluded him. "What brought this on?"

"Knew you'd be hungry after your big night out."

He winced, then grinned. "As long as I'm not giving away anything you want, what do you care?"

"That's right. What do I care?" But she did not smile.

"I got a job," he said. "Temporary. But it might pay well—if I can keep my mouth shut, and speak only when I'm spoken to. Do you think I could lie convincingly for ten percent of five hundred dollars?"

"I hope so." She sat down and dipped one of the large pink shrimp in cocktail sauce and carried it dripping to her mouth. She stared at him across the table, chewing. "You're going to hate me."

"Any special reason?"

"I went out shopping."

He munched on shrimp. "I see you did."

"I bought more than shrimp." She got up from the table and brought a flowing white eyelet lace gown in its tissue-paper wrapper and stood before him. "Isn't it beautiful? Hold it. Only don't touch the dress with your stinking fingers . . . See how light it is. Like down. Gossamer, the saleswoman over on Royal said. Oh, Wade, isn't it the loveliest thing you ever saw?"

She held it up against her. It flowed down over her feet, cut low at the bodice with narrow straplike shoulders. The gown was unadorned, but he knew instinctively that it was simple elegance, the truly expensive kind. "You look ravishing," he said. "Take it off and we'll go to bed."

"Think about something else once in a while."

"Maybe I will . . . How much did that thing cost?"

"Except for what I spent on shrimp and bread and coffee, it cost everything."

"Everything?"

"All the money in your saddle pouch."

He whistled between his teeth, his appetite suddenly gone. "Including what we got for Le Blanc's horses?"

"Isn't it beautiful?"

"We're too broke to go anywhere. Where in hell are you going to wear it?"

"Out." She spun around, the gown fluttering, even restricted in the tissue paper.

"Out where?"

Names tripped off her tongue. One might believe she had been born a native in the Vieux Carré and not arrived only last night. Pascal's. Creole Mansion. Maxim's. Court of Two Sisters. The St. Louis dining room. The Old Absinthe House. She rattled off the places. Scandal had spent a busy morning. She met his eyes levelly. "Either you will take me, or I'll go alone. . . . I came to New Orleans to see—and to be seen. I shall do that."

"Still going to be the belle of New Orleans, eh?"

"You can't stop me."

"God knows I wouldn't try."

Scandal did lovely things to the lovely lace gown. It was fragile, weightless, almost gossamer. She'd bought almost transparent petticoats and crinolines to support it. Her silk stockings felt sensual on the flesh of her legs and thighs. The slippers looked too fragile to carry her across the room, to say nothing of serving her for an evening on some ballroom floor. She spent the entire afternoon getting ready to go out on the town. Wade, who had gone out to sell the carriage and Le Blanc's weapons, returned at six, and by seven-thirty they were on the banquette outside their apartment hailing a hack.

The creaking hansom cab, driven by a cottony-haired black man in ornamented derby and rusty frock coat, set Scandal and Wade down at the glittering entrance of the most popular address in town, the St. Louis Hotel at the intersection of Royal and St. Louis streets.

Scandal caught her breath, awed.

The famous structure was already twenty years old by the time Scandal first beheld it that early spring night in 1861.

Her throat ached with the sudden acceleration of her heart. Her wildest fantasies were realized. She gaped, open-mouthed, as formally attired men and fashionably accoutered women alighted from fine landaus and sedans and promenaded in regal splendor under the brilliant gaslights.

The building held beauty, charm and majesty—especially for a young girl from Wilkes Corners. Its balloonlike central dome reared high, reached towards the sky; behind its walls ornamental banana trees spread profusely. The place still retained its aura of wealth, its magnificence, as the finest expression of the town's prosperous and golden years.

First built in 1835—at the mind-staggering cost of one and a half million dollars, at a time when skilled craftsmen commanded a dollar a day in wages—it was the unequaled gathering center for the wealthy sugar planters and slave owners.

The building housed the city auction exchange, magnificent ballrooms, dining salons and extravagant suites of ten and twelve rooms where entire plantation families came with their retinues in season. On the Royal Street side, a slave block was part of the hotel.

A fire in 1841 had gutted the original hotel. An even more elegant structure had replaced the first—taking up the whole block of St. Louis Street from Royal to Chartres. Not even the splendor of the ancient Maison Seignoret next door on Royal could detract from the hotel's compelling grandeur.

The beauty and excitement surrounding the canopied entrance engendered a rush of conflicting delight and fear in Scandal, and she hesitated, retreating slightly.

"Come on," Wade teased. "Hold your head up. If you're going to be the belle of this town, you've got to look the part."

Warily, Scandal padded beside Wade up the wide steps. His suit was far from fashionable—it looked almost disreputable beside the elegance of the men around them. But he was younger, taller, handsomer, and his rakish go-to-hell attitude got him admiring scrutiny and some deference.

Scandal was warmly aware that they presented a striking couple and attracted favorable attention. Her face flushed, blood tingling against her taut cheeks. She had never walked on such deep carpeting, nor had anyone bowed to her as the doorman and other attendants did as they made their way into the plush hotel lobby.

At the entrance to a brilliant dining salon, they were halted by the smiling but smugly snobbish maître d'. Scandal stared longingly beyond the officious, haughty employee. The white linen-covered tables glowed, peopled by the most glamorous-looking human beings Scandal had ever beheld. A few gray uniforms of the newly forming Conferederate militia dotted the evening suits, but the approaching war seemed as remote as the farthest evening star in this room of laughing, elegant people. "Do you have a reservation, sir?" the maître d' asked Wade.

"I'm sorry." Wade shook his head. A brief pregnant pause ensued. Wade saw Scandal's face mirror her sick disappointment. He placed a folded bill unobtrusively into the maître d's palm. A moment later, they were seated at a tiny table near the dance floor where a small ensemble of violins and piano played the popular music of the night.

Scandal sighed. She felt as if all the lights in the room were fixed on her. Wade laughed. "Well, you've got them looking at you, at least."

"I feel like Cinderella."

"Don't be silly. Those slippers will never last till midnight."

Wade ordered for both of them from a menu which was unintelligible to Scandal. He seemed at ease, unruffled either by the languages or the prices. His coolness astonished her but suffused her with pride, too. He was by far the handsomest man in the salon; the eyes of other women in sables and diamonds confirmed this for her.

When the waiter brought their clear broth in delicate Dresden cups, he placed a card beside Wade's plate. The waiter nodded towards an aging man who sat alone half across the room. The man bowed and smiled faintly. He looked to be at least sixty, a dissipated, worn-out, unprincipled sixty. His hair and face were gray. He wore a small diamond-and-gold earring in his left ear.

Wade glanced at the card, handed it to Scandal. According to the *carte de visite*, the man's name was Julien-Jacques Gischairn. This meant nothing to Scandal, less than nothing. The scribbled note—in elegantly etched Spencerian—asked that he be allowed to join them briefly at their table. "Want to meet the old goat?" Wade asked. "He looks like one of those millionaires you're after—but from here, he doesn't look the type who is interested in girls."

Scandal looked up. She met the aging man's disenchanted eyes across the tables. Involuntarily, she found herself smiling and nodding. Gischairn came bouncing between the tables at once, carrying his linen napkin, smiling and greeting them as if they were acquaintances of long standing.

The old man lisped slightly and punctuated every dramatic revelation with a flick of his limp wrist. He chattered continously, like a magpie, a parakeet, an old maid. He refused to be headed, interrupted or detoured. He had a great deal to say and he intended to say it all. He swung his lorgnette, making points with it, the refracted light it hurled in every direction attracting the atention he obviously relished.

He assured them he was *the* social arbiter of the two cities of New Orleans—the French and the American. Actually of the six cities which composed the metropolitan area of the most glamorous city of the world—Paris not excepted. What pleased Julien-Jacques Gischairn pleased Creole and Southern aristocracy, which hung on his choices, waited for his smile or frown. He could make or break reputations in society with no more than the tilt of his brow, the sweep of his lorgnette, the way he smiled. He had been doing this, to his own inner delight, for more than thirty years. Now that he was in his dotage, this persisted as his single pleasure. Tomorrow, for example, he was buying the best carriage horse on auction for a social dowager whom he despised and who hated him as cordially. "We need each other in our bitchiness. She gave me an extravagant gift. Now, I must do something more foolish and extravagant. I have decided on the best horse I can buy her. It's one of the games we play in our twilight years. The horse must be—the best, you know."

Wade managed to suggest that he knew horseflesh. Perhaps he might be of assistance. Gischairn almost wept in gratitude. "My gift must be *faultless*. God knows, the old bitch will have it appraised! If you were to guarantee excellence, I'd be forever indebted. Just forever." He swung the lorgnette. He studied Scandal and smiled. "I know you two babes are strangers in New Orleans. When you've been here longer you'll understand just how invaluable it can be to have Julien-Jacques Gischairn indebted to you. . . . But tell me, what do you want? What may I do for *you?*"

"Why should you want to do anything?" Wade inquired.

Gischairn gestured limply. "I told you. It's all life offers any more for an old person. To do something outrageous. Unheard-of. On a whim, I could make you two the most socially sought-after couple in New Orleans. Would you like that?"

Wade laughed. "That wouldn't do anything for me. But it might please Scandal. . . . She aspires to be the belle of this town —all of its six cities."

Gischairn studied Scandal, silent for a long beat. The music swelled behind them and dancing couples watched them, fascinated.

"Yes. What an intriguing idea! Yes, Yes. I might do it. . . . A lot of work. Polish. But every diamond has to be painstakingly polished, eh? I could do it. . . . You are a diamond, my sweet, a diamond in the rough."

Before Gischairn finally left their table, he said, smiling and twirling his lorgnette, "You'll see. Because I've spent twenty minutes at your table with you, not a soul in this room will dare snub you. Many will grovel—at once—like toads. . . . But remember, those that grovel like toads are toads. I shall enjoy watching it immensely." He stood up. "Shall we meet for dinner tomorrow night? At Maxim's. As my guests, of course. I realize what it must have cost you in money and courage to come here tonight. I admire you deeply. Really. You and I, Mr. Cameroon, shall buy a purebred carriage horse and meet your lovely little wife for dinner, eh?"

Wade shrugged, deferring the decision to Scandal. She astonished him and stunned Julien-Jacques Gischairn by refusing his invitation. "I'm most grateful. Truly." She smiled, oddly pale and rigid of cheek. "But I could not. Not possibly."

22

The chubby pink fingers of dawn smeared the wall of the sky when Wade and Scandal returned to their tiny apartment. For Scandal, it was like coming back down to chilled reality after a brief glimpse of some fairyland. But she did not regret returning to this place with Wade. She was happy, content, exhausted, her mind teeming with excitement, coinage of memories she could hoard forever. No matter what befell her now, she'd tasted the beautiful life she'd dreamed of for so long. There *was* such an enchanted existence, even if she never touched it again, even fleetingly.

She sagged against Wade's shoulder, clinging to his hand as a child might. They walked the silent banquette along Dauphine Street. "What's the matter?" he asked.

"I'm happy. Truly happy for the first time in my life." He did not answer, and she sank into a pleasant reverie, the evening spinning in bright colors behind her eyes. She and Wade had danced, at first awkwardly. They drank champagne and wine, and they danced. She found men writing notes to the table, or appearing formally, bowing and introducing themselves, pleading with m'sieu to allow them one dance with his *charmante* lady. She glimpsed Julien-Jacques Gischairn at his table, enjoying the little playlet as if it were all arranged for his evening's amusement. She played a silent little game with the aging Gischairn. Whatever presented itself—an offer of rare champagne sent to her table, an invitation to a gavotte, a proffered introduction—she glanced quickly toward Gischairn. She set him up at once as *her* social arbiter for the evening. He seemed to read her thoughts. He either smiled, nodding unobtrusively, or stuck out his lower lip and scowled. If Gischairn smiled, she said yes—whatever it was. If he pouted in that faintly petulant way, she refused—however badly she wanted to say yes. It worked perfectly.

When at last they left the hotel, people gave them warm smiles, bowed slightly. She had not made any mistakes; she had entranced a few, she seemed not to have outraged any.

She yawned helplessly. Wade laughed and swung her up in his arms. He carried her easily up the steps. The early morning was redolent with an alloyage of jasmine, honeysuckle and wet reeds.

Wade laid her down on the bed in the pink misty half-light. He knelt and removed her slippers. The soles were worn through, though she'd walked home on the cobbles barefooted and uncomplaining. "They wore out hours ago," she said sleepily. Her wistful voice became self-accusatory. "Oh, if you knew how much they cost. . . . You have every right to hate me."

"I don't hate you."

"I've been a selfish little fool. Spending all your money on this foolish dress. On one evening I forced you to spend more money than I've ever even seen before."

"We all deserve the right to behave foolishly at least once."

"Well, I won't do it again. Ever."

He stayed where he was on one knee beside the bed. He massaged her fevered, swollen feet. The gossamer silk stockings were torn away. "How will you be the belle of the town? You have to do this every night to really be the talk of the city."

"I've been such a fool. The stupid dreams I had. I thought I was so pretty—"

"You are pretty. Beautiful. Fragile. Petite. Unusual—"

"I saw a hundred girls prettier than I. I guess I was pretty enough for Wilkes Corners. A thousand girls in this town prettier than I am. . . . I'm nothing. I'm glad about tonight. It was wonderful. Exciting. I'll never forget one minute of it. . . . I'll never stop being grateful to you. But it showed me what I am."

"What are you?"

She writhed on the bed crying out, "Don't try to be kind to me!

You know what I am. You've known all along. I'm just a little backcountry tramp from a backwoods town."

"Your friend Julien-Jacques Gischairn didn't think so."

She moaned. "You heard what he said. I was a diamond—a diamond in the rough."

"He said he could make you the sensation of New Orleans."

"What he really meant was that it would be the impossible kind of challenge that intrigued him. That's what he was really saying. I went there thinking I looked so lovely—so chic. Those women in that boutique let me think so. How they must have been laughing behind their hands! Like a stupid fool I spent all your money."

"You looked lovely. It was worth it. I don't regret a penny."

"That's because you're so good inside you can't hurt me—"

"I don't want to *see* you hurt." He slid his hands up the sensual silky stockings and removed them. She seemed unaware of his touch, wrapped in her own inner agonies. "But you *were* the prettiest woman there—you looked like a fresh flower among a lot of faded old pot plants."

She laughed in spite of herself. "That's what I mean. I looked *fresh.* I looked like what I am—a scullery maid out on the town, for one night, in fine feathers. Do you see *my* hands? Did you see the soft, manicured, feathersoft hands of those other women? They could look at my *hands* and know what I was."

He sat on the side of the bed and turned her over, loosening the dozen of tiny pearl buttons along her spine. He slipped her dress over her shoulders. He said, "Is that why you refused Gischairn's invitation to dinner?"

"No."

"Why, then?"

She exhaled heavily. "I couldn't wear this same old dress. Not again. Even to a different place. It would spoil everything. Even before it started, it would be over. You think that wouldn't be the first thing a man like Gischairn would notice?"

He worked her dress down over her slender hips, along her legs. He pulled it free and tossed it behind him on the floor. "I can tell you truthfully that Gischairn understands about you. I don't think he expects you to own a closetful of Paris originals—yet."

"Just the same, I won't do it."

"What are you going to do?"

She writhed fretfully on the bed. He removed her crinolines. "What do you care? I've cost you enough. You don't have to stay with me any more. You got me here to New Orleans. That was what I wanted from you. You helped me meet my first rich old man. Gischairn. That's more than I expected from you. We're quits. You can get free of me before I cost you everything."

He smiled and removed the last petticoat and undergarment, surprised that she did not protest. He supposed she was so involved in her unhappiness, so wrapped up in imagined woes, she was scarcely aware of him. He spoke gently. "What have you cost me? A few dollars I had with me. I give them to you gladly. You owe me nothing. The rest? Money we got for Le Blanc's horses, and his carriage and his rifle."

"Money you could have eaten on—for weeks."

"I told you. I'm going to work in a little while. You're still my wife. I'll give you what I can—as long as I can. Then we'll talk about it."

"No. I've played this evil game long enough."

"What evil game is that?"

"I was never your wife. Not really. Unless you want to be arrested—along with me—for miscegenation."

"If you do have black blood, it sure as hell doesn't matter to me. And it's our little secret."

"No. I've cheated you. And it's all based on trickery. I am black. You are white. You didn't marry me because you loved me, but because I tricked you."

"It was a legal ceremony."

"You married me to keep my brothers from killing you."

"Only they wouldn't have killed me—"

"You didn't know that. I didn't love you. Or care about you. Or even think about you. Whether you were good or evil. It didn't matter to me. I married you to get out of hell. You deserve better. . . . It's over, Wade. We're quits."

"Not quite," he whispered. He bent his head over hers and covered her lips with his mouth. She resisted for a moment, struggling, then her arms went up around his back, her long fingers closing on his shoulders and pulling him down to her. He shivered, realizing how deeply he wanted her, how much he loved her. For all the brief time he'd known her he'd been saying little prayers that she would reach out to him, always hopeful that she would come to him like this. And now her nearness enflamed him. The touch of her lips set him on fire. The movements of her hands consumed him. The secret parts of her body opened to him with a passion he'd never even fantasized. Each response of her hands and mouth and body was an exalting experience unlike anything that had ever happened to him before, and he reached new heights of sensation and plumbed new depths of feeling.

They lay together like that, close, for a long time. The room glowed, strangely, pinkly lit, the sun like a lone candle on a far candlestand so the corners of the apartment lay shadowed in the feeble light. He gazed in agonized delight at the arabesque of black hair on the pillow, the soft curve of her cheek and the pale shoulders against the white sheet.

She spoke in a muffled whisper, barely audible. "Hold me. Love me. Please hold me."

He grinned, pleased to comply. He too experienced a flooding of desire. Only his own clothing lay between them now, and he acted to remove that final barrier. Tugging at his boots, he slipped them off, shedding his clothes in a heap on the floor and stepping out of them. He was aware of the throbbing prominence displayed before him. He lay down beside her, the white sheets gleaming a lighter pool in the wan darkness. Gently, he eased his body against her, pressing his pulsing staff into the warmth at her thighs and feeling the chill of the undersheet against his naked skin. Much to his surprise, he found he was trembling. Whether it was from the chill of the early morning or the excitement pulsing in his blood, he did not know.

His hands moved on her, encountering new warmth, new planes of pleasure. He closed a hand on her breast, feeling the frantic throbbing of her heart. He waited, still unable to believe she was submitting willingly, anxiously. He halted, listening to the pounding of his own heart. Then he closed his fingers on her nipple, kneading it, delighting in the supple roundness of her lustrous flesh. His fingers moved into the heated triangle at her thighs, the tips of his fingers finding fevered, bubbling warmth. Again he halted, waiting for her to protest, but she remained quiet. He moved his fingers on her smooth flesh, making slow, tiny circles at first. Her breathing accelerated and he felt her legs relax. Emboldened, he moved his hand downward, finding her fiery and wet. Her mouth was parted and she breathed raggedly through her lips, sighing, writhing as if involuntarily, under his hand.

He opened her slowly and imperceptibly to him, pressing the throbbing rigidity into the burning caldron at her thighs. He closed his mouth over hers, bringing her so close that his cheeks were brushed and caressed by the strands of her hair. She moaned aloud and moved, shoving her hips upward to him, her arms again encircling his shoulders and pulling him down to her. He heard her deep and exultant sigh and she pressed herself closer, driving suddenly wildly.

He forgot everything except the pistonlike pulsing of her body upon him. Their mutual climax came swiftly, a kind of madness that was overwhelming, blinding, deafening and numbing them for long sweet moments.

When it was over, they remained pressed close as if now sharing the same thoughts. He was for the moment stunned, but unwilling to release her. His hand covered those soft, rounded breasts and he marveled at their resilient softness, the marble rigidity of her nipples. While he fondled her breasts, she continued to sigh in unintelligible little murmurs, pressing his hands to her and moving her own fingers on his body. He did not know how long they caressed and loved each other, only that gradually her sighs grew to the murmur of moans and she clutched him to her, working her hips frantically.

Now in his exigency, it was his turn to moan and chew at his lips in unbearable ecstasy. He tugged at her, forcing her to shift her position to accommodate and pleasure him, with the sudden selfish ruthlessness that is sheer joy to share—the giver and the taker. She was giving now, with all her passion, her lips locked against his, her breasts pressed flat upon the corded muscles of his chest. As he had moved his hands upon her, now she moved her hands over his hips, stroking and caressing his testes and then grasping them in sudden vehemence.

"No," he whispered in anguish. "No. Not yet. Please not yet." She withdrew her hand and for a moment they lay unmoving, enjoying the unbearable bliss, the self-inflicted torture of delay. She began to whip her hips again and he caught her pelvis. "Slowly," he whispered, and she obeyed his command. She opened her lips wider and he thrust his tongue deep inside, exploring the smoothness of her teeth, the heat of her own darting tongue. They moved faster and faster, carried upward and out of themselves and beyond their power to control.

He sagged into the bed, his heart slugging and then fluttering strangely. She pressed close upon him, her hand closing on him, stroking, fondling, caressing, adoring. Despite his satiated exhaustion, he felt himself responding to her, and when she moved her head down to his chest, his blood pumped more wildly than ever. He felt her lips stroking his paps, her tongue tracing the hardness of his musculature, moving downward. He caught at her head, but she wrested free, kissing and nursing him to a terrible violence. He could stand no more and he caught her head, holding her fiercely to him, with all his strength. She could not breathe, but it did not matter, to either of them.

She crept back into his arms and pressed closer to him. He

wanted her to speak to him but was afraid that if he spoke he might break a spell he did not even understand. He did not want to understand, he wanted only for this sense of shared oneness that he had never experienced before to last forever. The old restraints between them completely vanished. There were no longer any barriers. They loved a long time in a calm and gentle way, exploring, probing, fondling, caressing, kissing. And when they rose one more time to inexpressibly agonizing heights, their bodies behaved as if directed by one mind, one desire, one being. Her fragile body arched to him fiercely and she gasped, "Oh God, now. Do it now." She pressed his face between her breasts, her hips battering him wildly, torturing him with aching delights. He could wait no longer and drove himself to her in madness and without mercy.

She cried out, a helpless, murmuring cry, and he went taut, fearful that he had hurt her, but the frantic driving of her thighs told him the only pain she felt was sweet, and the agony of her body was pleasure in her mind. She worked faster, thrusting with vigor he did not believe could still be left to her. Nothing could stop them now, and even when she cried out, "No, no, no," they both knew the word had no meaning, as nothing had meaning except the fusion of their bodies and hearts and desire.

He tried to delay the fiery pressures rising within him and could not do it. He dreaded the moment of the aching spasm of delight, knowing it might be more than he could bear, and yet there was no way to control its eruption. His calves ached, the backs of his legs were drawn in muscle spasms, his mind spun.

He was actually conscious only of the anguished writhings of her body against him, as if somehow the final tip of flame could not be extinguished and until it was, she could not rest. She could only whimper, cry out and thrust herself to him. He felt fevered, his heart pounding as if it would burst, a dizziness overwhelming him, but he knew he could not rest until the sweet agony inside her was quelled. He plunged and withdrew and plunged, and the room wheeled in an orange ball of fire.

From some great distance he heard her cries, her murmurs of pleasure, and felt the softness of her body supporting his sagging weight. She pressed her mouth to his ear, whispering her delight with him, and in the middle of a sentence she sagged into drugged sleep, total unconsciousness. She slumped against the white covers, her lips parted, her body lax. He fell beside her, and little by little his gasping subsided and he could breathe almost normally.

In her sleep she moved to him and her arms encircled his face. He was burning, fevered, and her body clung to his, but he did not move her because he did not want to disturb her. He lay a few moments wishing for ice-cold water, a cool breeze, a chilled place on the rumpled, over-heated bed. Then he too fell asleep, holding her, clinging to her until dreamless oblivion erased the last traces of reality and they slept, content.

23

The blaze of the ascending sun slashed in through filmy window curtains and burned into Cameroon's eyes, waking him. He lay a moment, disoriented, troubled without knowing why, caught between utter exhaustion and a compelling sense of wrong demanding immediate action.

He sat up, taut. Half the day was gone, that was the wrong! An auction of horses offering him an opportunity to earn sorely needed cash, and he lay sleeping, stunned. This was the dereliction demanding prompt redress.

He glanced down at Scandal, curled naked where she'd plunged into sleep, pressed slowly against him. He smiled, suffused with tenderness, warmth and a sudden unholy need to possess her body once more, now, to ravish it, to drive from her mind even the most enthralling sublimity of their early-morning love-making.

As if to warn him, a river breeze fluttered the curtains and the sun flared in a brassy hard yellow rectangle at his feet. He could submit to his passionate desire for her, as he wanted to with every sinew of his body, every impulse of his mind, and she'd go hungry tonight. If he was going to start supporting her, he had to get out of here—and damned quickly.

He shaved and dressed hurriedly, taking up from the floor the clothing he'd worn last night and trying to shake out the wrinkles before he put it on. Eating a hunk of leftover French bread, he let himself out of the apartment and ran at a half-trot down the stairs.

The auction was in full swing when Wade reached the temporary corrals at the piers along the river. He hesitated, catching his breath and cursing himself at the same time. Never in his experience of selling horseflesh had he seen such a crowd. Expensive coaches, landaus, sedans and richly saddled horses occupied every foot of the open lots, the approach streets and even the cleared spaces of the merchandise-laden docks. Hundreds of Negro servants, grooms and slaveys gathered in groups near the carriages, seeking refuge from the blaze of the sun, which didn't even trouble their preoccupied white masters.

"Damn it, Cameroon," he muttered, "you've played the fool this time."

He'd had no inkling that Guille Desmare had so publicized this auction, or that a sale of Tantallon horses attracted such an overwhelming response. No wonder the St. Louis Hotel had been brimmed to capacity last night with the aristocrats, landed gentry and horse fanciers. Every planter who cared about horseflesh, breeding or bloodlines was packed in the mobs milling and shouting over these muddy flats. Inside the corrals, as Desmare had told Wade they would be, the horses were showered, brushed, curried and groomed until they glistened in the pitiless noon sunlight. On a raised pinewood dais near the corral gate where horses could be briefly promenaded in a small circle for prospective bidders, a professional auctioneer harangued the crowd.

Edging his way through the multitude of abstracted, jostling men, Wade sought Desmare. He and the horsebreeder were at least a head taller than most of the assembled buyers. Wade tilted his head, searching, but when he spied Desmare, he instantly sensed the man's righteous annoyance. The auction was already four hours old. Perhaps Desmare had awaited him expectantly before eight o'clock this morning. Now he let his annoyed glance touch at Cameroon's face and fall coldly away, recognition flickering with disinterest.

Cameroon halted, dismayed but not blaming Desmare for the chilled nonreception. Desmare's business was selling horses. Anything which interfered with that industry displeased him.

Wade looked around, seeking a likely sales prospect, but without much hope. Perhaps if he located a quick buyer, helped him choose an animal and brought it to auction, he might yet return to Desmare's good graces.

Many men still inspected the stock, inching along the snake-rail fences, but most of the advance selection had been made. The majority of the assembly stood, gazes fixed on the chanting auctioneer.

Wade's gaze touched at an aging man examining a fat mare which had been roped and led from the corral for his personal inspection. Something familiar struck Ware about the tired, even depraved gray of the face, the petulant pull of the mouth, the sallow wrinkles of the cheeks, the superb tailoring of his pearl-gray outfit. Whom did he know among these Louisiana Creole grandees? Then the sun caught itself and glittered, refracted, in the gold-and-diamond earring in the man's left ear.

Wade pushed his way through the throng. Julien-Jacques Gischairn was being quietly but firmly and persistently harangued by a sweated stout man in brown derby, mud-splattered brown boots and checked twill suit far too heavy for this steamy atmosphere. He looked as if he were drowning in his own sweat, consumed by prickly heat.

As if instinctively aware of his presence, Gischairn pulled his head around and waved a limp wrist, his cheeks crinkling into a warm smile. "Well, hello there." Gischairn lisped, smiling. "My gorgeous young friend. You did get here after all, didn't you?" He caught Wade's arm and propelled him close to the sweating salesman and the placid horse. "Look at this mare, Wade. Isn't she just beautiful? This gentleman . . . Earl . . . Earl warrants her to be the single finest selection of horseflesh Desmare is offering today."

Earl sweated, dark rivulets coursing along his bulging forehead and padded jowls from the band of his derby. His suet-socketed eyes watched Wade narrowly. Wade gave the horse only a cursory glance. He shrugged. "She's fine horseflesh." Earl exhaled with relief, then tautened abruptly as Wade added, "Depending on what you want her for."

"I told you last night, *chéri.*" Gischairn spoke with some impatience. "I want her as a gift—a gift nonpareil . . . What's wrong with her, then?"

"Yeah." Earl's tone hardened, menacing, as if Wade had somehow disparaged the man himself. "What's wrong with her?"

"For some uses, nothing. But she certainly isn't the finest horseflesh Desmare has for sale."

"What the hell you know about it?" Earl said.

"I know she's an *improved* breed." Wade made something less than admirable of the word.

"Improved?" Gischairn said. "What does that mean?"

"It means, Mr. Gischairn, this here mare's been bred up to git just the qualities you're looking for in an excellent carriage horse—no matter what your know-it-all young friend here says." Earl bit off each sweated word.

Gischairn glanced at Wade, smiling wickedly. Nothing he loved more than being catalyst in a good conflict between opinionated adversaries. "What do *you* mean by improved, Mr. Cameroon?"

"It's upbreeding all right, as Earl says. But what it really means is a bloodline impurity. She's not a thoroughbred. She's been bred from a heavier breed mixed with thoroughbred stock. Maybe her dam or sire *was* purebred English blood. But she's a mixture of heavy draft stock. That's why she's fat. She's fat and she'll be clumsy and awkward as a carriage horse. And, since we're on the subject of *improved* breeds, I can tell you that purebreds—in a wild state, at least—are almost totally free from disorders of every kind."

"Go out and lasso one," Earl suggested, enraged.

Wade shrugged. "In the pure state horses live as long as sixty years, disease-free. Hell, if they weren't starved or killed off or didn't die of thirst, they had no problems. But when they are forced to live among civilized men"—he grinned wolfishly toward Earl—"and made a beast of burden, with *improved* breeding, they can become subject to hellish diseases and premature death and outright failure. Unless the best breeds are preserved in their purity, they fall—through well-intentioned men's attempts to *improve* them—into all kinds of disorders and failures."

Gischairn smiled. "You really love horses, don't you?"

Wade drew his hand along the sleek fat neck of the mare. "Yep. Even beauties like this. She's a good horse, as I'm sure Earl has told you. But not for show. Not for carriage work. Not to be considered a gift nonpareil."

"What's it git you, bub, comin' round here foulin' up a sale for me?"

"Oh, don't you worry, Mr. Earl. I'm going to buy a horse. From you. But you won't mind if my dear young friend helps me make that selection, will you?" Gischairn gave the salesman a disarming smile.

"Looks like it won't matter much, don't it?" Earl said, and with a sour wave of his arm he signaled a black handler to remove the mare. "I just say you're making a big mistake."

"I'm sure you're a good and honest man, Mr. Earl." Gischairn said with a disarming smile. "And we shall never blame you if my purchase is less than—perfect, eh? You've offered me every bit of your professional skill."

"Yeah. Let's see what your *dear* young friend turns up. What I need in this sun is a good laugh about now."

They walked to the high rails of the corral. Gischairn held a scented cachet against his nose as he minced along between Wade and the stout salesman, and as Wade studied the animals remaining in the corral. "For your purposes you want a purebred.

At least they call the English carriage horses purebred—which I guess they were before they were brought to England. A horse that won't be gross or clumsy in the shafts of a landau or buggy. You can never really know the defects of a fat horse in advance. You don't buy him just because he's big and healthy-looking—unless you want a slow and heavy draft animal. Eleven hundred pounds is plenty heavy for ordinary driving. Usually he's much better than a heavier one." He pointed out a stallion, talked for a moment about its good features. Gischairn excitedly asked Earl to have the stallion cut from the herd.

Earl obeyed, but complained, "Hell, Mr. Gischairn, I could have touted you on that self-same animal myself. But good God, that purebred's going to cost you a thousand dollars, sure."

"But that's what you said the mare would cost," Gischairn reminded him.

Earl flushed faintly. "And she will. I was trying to get you a bargain, that's all."

"No cheap horse is a bargain," Wade said. "My old grandfather always told me that."

They had wine while they awaited the stallion's being placed on auction. The wine lessened Earl's thirst not at all and appeared almost instantly as droplets of sweat on his stout cheeks. When the stallion was brought to the examining enclosure, Wade checked his teeth. "Still got foal incisors," Wade assured Gischairn. "Not half as long as his horse teeth and nippers will be when he gets them. He doesn't even have his hook teeth, so I figure he's around three years old. Unless the bidding goes crazy, you'll get a good buy here."

There was spirited bidding at first. Gischairn signaled his bids by fluttering his scented kerchief. He remained totally unconscious of the snickers of the rabble; they were beneath his notice, not in his class and therefore not even worth a glance. Gischairn moved in a world removed from them.

He bid in the stallion for eleven hundred. "Not bad," he said. "About a dollar a pound." He was pleased with his purchase and signaled two black handlers to remove it to his St. Charles Avenue mansion. Earl thanked him profusely and assured him he was going to be happy with this great horse. "We got you the best, Mr. Gischairn."

But the transaction was complete and Gischairn was barely cognizant of the salesperson's presence. He thanked him absently and turned his back on him. He spoke warmly to Wade. "Let's repair to the cool of the St. Louis Hotel dining room. Any activity as strenuous as this makes me ravishingly hungry. I hope you'll be my guest."

Wade smiled and nodded. "Excuse me a moment, sir," he said.

"Surely. I'll meet you at my coach. It is there, the varnished one, with the blown-glass vases and blue curtains."

Wade grinned. "I couldn't miss it."

He hurried through the crowd to where Guille Desmare stood near the auctioneer's stand. "I hope you saw, Mr. Desmare. Because of me, Mr. Gischairn bought the purebred—for eleven hundred dollars."

"Go to hell," Desmare said. "That was Earl Fellame's sale in the first place. You horned in."

"He was pitching a mare. I sold a purebred stallion."

"Yeah. My best horse."

"Eleven hundred dollars."

"Look, friend. I don't need you. If you'd kept your mealy mouth shut, I could have got eleven hundred—for the mare."

Wade gazed at Desmare a moment, his black eyes clashing against the pale blue of the horsebreeder's. Wade exhaled, nodded, turned away, feeling Desmare's gaze on his back.

Gischairn awaited him in the cool of his coach. A small black boy sat on a jump seat steadily waving a large palmetto fan to stir the dung-laden breezes inside the cab. Gischairn half-reclined, the cachet pressed under his nostrils. He smiled. "You look upset, Mr. Cameroon."

Wade shook his head. When he sat beside Gischairn, the footman closed the door, the driver slapped his whip and the horses moved the carriage away from the docks. "No. Everything's fine," Wade said. "You learn something every day. It's just that some days you don't get up early enough for what you learn to do you any good."

"Interesting. But involved." Gischairn pressed a folded hundred-dollar bill into Wade's hand. "A token of my appreciation for your splendid assistance. I was totally at the mercy of that horsethief until you arrived. . . . You'll find me a very grateful friend, Mr. Cameroon."

"It's my wife who needs your friendship," Wade said. "She is driven by a need to be a celebrity in New Orleans society."

"I know. I wish it were worth what she thinks it is. I wish it were worth what it would cost her. I am so sorry she refused my invitation to dinner tonight."

Wade smiled faintly. "I think you know why."

"Nothing to wear?" Gischairn laughed and waved his handkerchief. "I think Eve was the first woman to make that complaint. . . . I'm sorry she feels that way. Perhaps you can prevail upon her to change her mind."

Wade laughed. "Perhaps. If I buy her a new dress."

The driver pulled the coach into the curb before the canopied entrance of the St. Louis Hotel. As Gischairn moved toward the coach door being opened by the footman who haughtily brushed the uniformed hotel doorman aside, Wade caught Gischairn's arm, delaying the older man.

Wade stared from the coach toward the doorway of the hotel. His gaze focused on Albert Le Blanc. Wade winced and his heart sank. He exhaled heavily as if he'd been holding his breath for an incredible time. "I'm sorry," he said. "A man I prefer not to see."

Gischairn smiled across his shoulder. "Point him out to me. I'll have him removed from the premises."

Wade grinned. "I wish it were that easy. Thanks for everything, M'sieu Gischairn."

"Keep in touch, *mon cher*."

Wade nodded. Quietly, he opened the other door of the coach just far enough to step through. He waited until Le Blanc had turned his back and entered the hotel foyer, then he stepped into the busy street, sidling between moving carriages, and kept walking.

The dresses in the boutiques along Royal Street were lovely, but extremely expensive. He needed underthings and slippers as well as a gown for Scandal. Buying her something that would set her off among the wealthy Creole women was costly.

A beautiful young quadroon was departing the dress shop as he was. He held the door open for her to precede him to the street. She smiled, but he was too preoccupied to be aware that she'd expressed her gratitude.

"M'sieu?"

Still involved in his own thoughts, Wade paused on the narrow banquette and glanced at the quadroon. She was incredibly lovely, petite, sensual about the full red lips and the liquid purple eyes. Her features were delicately hewn, but her breasts were startling full against the symmetry of narrow waist and tapering hips. Wade shook his head. He was not interested in any woman just now except Scandal, even one as radiantly charming as the quadroon. Easy to understand that the Quadroon Ball was the highlight of the Vieux Carré season and that young Creole dandies fought duels behind the cathedral over these lovely women. Still he had nothing on his mind except finding suitable evening dresses for Scandal. "I'm sorry," he said. "Thanks just the same. You are truly lovely."

Her laughter was musical. "Why do you think I stopped you?" She bit her lip and shook her head. "It is my fault, for daring to speak to you so boldly on the street like this. . . . I am not soliciting, m'sieu, I assure you. . . . Though I might choose such a prospect as you, if I were."

Wade managed to smile and to give her his attention. "It's the old fellows who have the money," he advised her.

She gazed at him admiringly. "Sometimes money she is not everything, eh, m'sieu?" She sighed and brushed the topic away with a gesture of her lovely hand, which looked as if it had never done one minute of manual labor. No wonder poor little Scandal had been miserable about last night.

"I spoke to you, m'sieu, because it became evident to me in the boutique that you and I share the same problem."

"And what is that, ma'mselle?"

"High prices," the girl answered, smiling. "Exorbitant prices. You want something extraordinary and yet—like me—you find money limited, *n'est-ce pas?* There is a place. I am going there now. I dislike going alone, but I must go. There they sell dresses far lovelier than anything in these high-priced salons. Some have been worn once, none more than twice. Some were given to servants of rich families for charity, others were stolen by servants of rich families. For profit. Whatever reason, they are like new. Often better than one can find this side of Paris itself."

"I'd like to see this place."

"I thought you would, m'sieu. And I would appreciate your escorting me. It is—shall we say—not the best part of town?"

"A thieves' market?"

"Almost."

The lovely quadroon and Wade set out together in the searing sunlight. The girl did not mind the heat and seemed to relish walking through her beloved Old Square. She'd been born here, she said, but was still enthralled with the narrow streets and the iron lacework balconies and the excitement, totally unlike any other city on this hemisphere. As they strode along the narrow sidewalks—Isabel informed him they were called banquettes—she pointed out the barely visible tropical greenery—azaleas, camellias, great red hibiscus beyond the doorways they passed. She wondered what more fascinating sights might be hidden from the eyes of passersby.

It was a long walk to Congo Square, and it was midafternoon when they got there. The square was crowded with ramshackle slab-sided temporary booths erected around it. Several moments elapsed before Wade realized he was the only white person in the huge arena. The square swarmed with blacks, most of them freed persons of color. They promenaded up and down the banquettes, eating rice and red beans, bananas, gumbo, fried shrimp, raw oysters, all the superabundant bounties of this paradise of the bayous.

"I think this is the very best place we'll find—for what we want." Isabel paused before an unpromising-looking shack displaying various articles of clothing such as one might see at a church rummage sale. The enterprise was presided over by a stout, laughing-eyed woman with graying hair caught in a red bandanna. She balanced her copious breasts on the makeshift counter and grinned at them, chewing a matchstick dipped in snuff. "This is Belle-Mère Antoinette, M'sieu Cameroon. To be trusted no more than anyone else in Congo Square. But no less, either. If she likes you, you may even get an honest deal and the correct change, eh Belle-Mère?"

The corpulent woman only smiled. "I got the best clothes in all N'Awleans. All the rich folks send their clothes to me—some of them even come and want a percent of the money I get. So you can see, I get the best."

Isabel said, "He wants something elegant, Belle-Mère. It is for his wife—young and petite. Do you have anything like that?"

The huge woman waddled around the counter. She looked Wade over admiringly. Then she nudged the girl in the ribs. "If he's got a wife, what is he doing with the likes of you, Isabel? Are you trying to lose the rich M'sieu Oberle, head of the Cotton Exchange? Or has he thrown you back in the gutter where you belong and will undoubtedly end up?"

The girl gazed at her coldly. "Just get the dresses, old crone. Unless you have nothing fine enough. There are other places, you know."

Belle-Mère Antoinette gestured. "There are other places. Where you can be cheated. But you will find nothing like this." She returned behind the counter and reappeared with a bundle carefully wrapped in a sheet. "Where do you think your fine young gentleman will find something as elegant as this, eh? Got jus' what he lookin' for. Not like you. What he git from you maybe ain't what he lookin' for. . . . Looky this, young Masta, suh! Jus' got it myself this morning. Belongin' to young Missy Tressville, it did. One of our grandest Creole families. So grand they wouldn't speak to this Isabel if she appeared at their door wearing the jewels of Spain. . . . Poor Missy. She died of a broken heart only yestiddy morning. Sudden. Her lover sailed for France and she jus' took to bed and died. So I right on hand, soon's ever I hear from her own dressin'-maid that she dead, I right there to git her clothes. Her folks sayin'—'twixt they tears—some of these beautiful gowns ain't never even been wore."

Her sausagelike fingers deftly undid the cloth and disclosed dresses of white Chantilly lace, barège, green muslin, transparent textures of chine fabrics, watered silks and satin. It all appeared, as the big woman said, to be untouched, new. Probably stolen. Carefully, Belle-Mère held them up for Wade's scrutiny. He heard the lovely quadroon catch her breath and knew Scandal would be entranced. The dresses were far more lovely than any he had seen in tramping among the best stores of the Vieux Carrè.

The beauty of the dresses troubled him, because Wade wanted them all for Scandal. He wanted them desperately. He was prepared to offer the woman a hundred-dollar bill and, hat in hand, get on his knees and plead for mercy. He would even come back later and make other payments. He would swear it on the life of his beloved. But as he thought what best to say, Belle-Mère Antoinette quoted a price for the entire package. Before he could agree, Isabel coldly rejected the amount, saying it was much too high. Wade stood speechless as the two women wrangled loudly. Finally, the fat woman placed the loveliest of the dresses on the counter and invited Wade to stroke the material. He ran his hand over the cloth, feeling an almost sensual thrill looking ahead to how lovely Scandal would look in the gown. "Is seventy-five dollars too much to ask for these matchless dresses, m'sieu? If you were my own son, I could not give you a better price."

Wade glanced at Isabel. She shrugged, winked and made a little moue with her full red lips. He handed the woman the hundred-dollar bill. He found underthings and slippers. Finally, Belle-Mère Antoinette pushed the crumpled money between her breasts and kissed her fingers.

"I promise you this, young Masta suh. You will have the prettiest wife in this city in these dresses. And at such a price! Almost, you have stolen them from me."

"Why not? Will you swear you did not steal them last night, old woman?" Isabel put her hands on her hips, laughing.

Belle-Mère Antoinette did not answer Isabel directly. Instead, she gazed at Wade and smiled. "I say this to you, young masta. If you have a good wife at home, cling to her, and shake free of the likes of this beauty. Someone said, a beautiful woman is a jewel, but a good woman—ah! she is a treasure."

Wade told Isabel to select any dress she wanted from those he had bought. She didn't hesitate, clutching the green muslin and holding it up against her. "You are a sweet man, *chéri,*" she said laughing. "Maybe we will meet again."

"Not," Belle-Mère Antoinette observed, "if he is also a lucky man."

Carrying the carefully wrapped cloth package, Wade strode out of the square and walked swiftly toward Dauphine Street. He was broke again, but he was certain Scandal would not care—or even notice—once she glimpsed the incredible contents of this bundle. He laughed in anticipation. He could tell her they would go without supper unless they dined in splendor at Maxim's with Julien-Jacques Gischairn. He would get more money, but there would never be a moment more rewarding than when he saw Scandal's face light up with pleasure at the sight of these beautiful gowns. No matter her expectations, she could hardly anticipate anything as wonderful as this. He hurried his steps.

He entered the courtyard on Dauphine Street, letting the wooden gate slam shut behind him. He bounded up the stairs, taking them two at a time. He opened the door to their apartment to an ominous and disturbing stillness. The room was swept; it was clean, dusted; but it was empty. Of Scandal's meager belongings only the lace dress she'd worn last night remained, tossed over the back of a chair. Her carpetbag was gone; Scandal was gone. He stood in the center of the room, holding the package. He stared around him, lost, bereft, unable to think clearly. Only one thought plodded back and forth across the empty chasm of his mind. He spoke her name, but there was no answer. He walked out into the court and asked if anyone had seen Scandal. They shook their heads. They had not seen her. They had not spoken with her. After he spoke to all of them he walked slowly back upstairs and resumed prowling in the abandoned room.

24

Almost without knowing how he got there, Wade found himself standing out front of Julien-Jacques Gischairn's mansion on St. Charles Avenue. On a street of imposing edifices, this iron-grillework-fenced home stood out in breathtaking magnificence. Wade had not believed he would ever impose upon Gischairn on so short an acquaintance, and yet there was nowhere else to turn. He knew no one else in this city. Few, anyhow, who would have the influence of Gischairn. All he could really think was that he could not leave any opportunity for finding Scandal left unexploited.

He rang the doorbell, and though the house was obviously occupied, candles and gas lamps glowing against the late-afternoon mists, he was surprised that he was permitted to wait almost ten minutes cooling his heels on the welcome mat. But he did not turn away. He could not. He kept pulling the bell chain that announced his presence.

When the young black butler finally appeared, he seemed to be hastily and haphazardly dressed. He opened the door only a slit. When Cameroon gave his name and claimed a matter of great urgency, the young butler nodded and said, "Yas suh, young masta. I see. You waits."

A few moments later the door was pulled wide open and Gischairn himself stood there, wearing only an opulent lounging robe of black silk and silk slippers. He obviously had been preoccupied, but he greeted Wade warmly and affectionately.

"Come in, come in, my dear young friend. How gauche of me to allow you to stand so long out here." He possessed himself of Wade's elbow and propelled him across a brilliantly illumined lobby to a sunroom where the scent of exotic incense was strong. The damask drapes had been drawn at the windows. A few gas lamps burned low, almost guttering, and tall candles burned in candlesticks.

Shocked, Wade saw the two young black boys lying naked on a Persian carpeting before a low, pillow-covered divan and a small altar where a long-stemmed opium pipe glowed. Wade kept his face blank, knowing Gischairn would be checking his reaction. Gischairn himself appeared totally unself-conscious about the scene.

Gischairn flung himself back on the divan and took up the flexible stem and bowl of the basket-shaped narghile, but did not bring it to his lips. Instead he held it in both hands as if warming himself from it. He jerked his head, ordering the naked boys to resume their lewd games. The gold chains, bright with opals, garnets and moonstones, rattled when they moved. Necklaces of priceless diamonds, emeralds and sapphires writhed, serpentlike, about their necks and shoulders, glittering against their dark skin, sweated and satiny in the candlelight. Gischairn's faded eyes hooded over under their dewlap lids. He sank back in the pillows in sensuous reverie.

Though Gischairn must have surmised Cameroon came to him

in an extreme emergency, Wade thought the old roué was going to force him to sit through the entire performance before he would suffer him to speak.

To his surprise, Gischairn spoke to him, quietly and without taking his eyes from the two boys entangled and writhing on the expensive carpeting at their feet. "I hope you will forgive an old person his vices, dear boy," Gischairn said. "I'm too old and too cold to be aroused by the ordinary acts which arouse ordinary men. Sometimes I wish I were more like them." He gazed at Wade with those hooded eyes. "Other times"—he smiled faintly—"like now, I thank my gods I am not. Are they not beaitiful young animals? And look at them, look at how they go at each other. You'd think they truly meant to devour one the other, eh?"

"They're quite expert."

"But you didn't come here to be amused by one of my *petits ballets*, eh?"

Despite his exigency, the urgency he felt when every moment chilled whatever trail Scandal left behind her, Wade forced himself to say, "I can wait."

"Why don't you talk about it? I can listen."

For a moment the room was quiet except for the clatter of precious jewels and golden bracelets, the ragged breathing of the boys on the floor. Finally, Wade said, "I know I have no right to break in on you like this. To presume on such brief acquaintance. Yet, I had nowhere else to go."

"My dear boy. Apologies are so—bourgeois. Beneath us. You are my true friend. I am deeply indebted to you. There is nothing you could ask of me I would not grant if it were in my poor power . . . Oh, look at that, the little devil. Ymir, do that again, you little imp. Come, Aditi, lie still . . ."

Wade waited while Ymir repeated his gulping of Aditi's gonads and his nipping down on them, this time more savagely, until Aditi yelped in pleasurable anguish. Gischairn sighed and sank back in the pillows, face flushed, something racing his tired heart, at least briefly. Wade said, "Scandal's gone."

"I thought it was that."

"How did you know?"

"By your face."

"I am heartbroken."

"Of course you are. And of course I understand. I too have lost a lover now and again. Not female perhaps—since that is not my taste—but I assure you agony of loss is no less."

"I have no right to ask you. But I hoped you might . . . use your influence, your knowledge of this town, to help me find her."

Gischairn kept his hooded gaze on the boys on the floor, but his voice was quite sincere. "Of course I shall. I told you I am eternally indebted to you. You need never doubt my friendship. I am a sated, blasé old person who no longer speaks anything except the truth."

"I do thank you. . . . There's little I can tell you. She was gone when I returned today from the auction. No one appears to have seen her. Unless she was taken away forcibly, it is as if she simply disappeared from the face of the earth."

"You magnify everything, dear boy. All lovers do. That's why they are so pitiable and amusing at the same time. I will put detectives out tracing her immediately. I retain the outstanding firm of sleuths in New Orleans. At least my law firm does. I shall be in touch with them at once."

"Thank you."

"Somehow, I believe she is playing a game with you and will return when she feels you have suffered enough."

"God knows I wish I believed that."

"I suggest you not sit around and stew. Employ your time looking for her. If you will meet me at eight in the bar of the St. Louis Hotel, I promise and warrant I shall have Scandal there in the flesh, or word of Scandal and her whereabouts, or a full reading on every step she has taken since she departed your ménage."

Wade returned to the Vieux Carré. He trusted Gischairn, believed that the aging man would indeed set talented sleuths on Scandal's trail, but he was afraid to believe she would be found and returned to him. He wanted her too much.

Walking the narrow streets, he admitted he was heartbroken. He had never even realized anyone could mean so much to him. He had to force himself to accept the obvious truth that she had walked out on him. How could she, after what they had meant to each other this morning? Not money, social status, driving ambition, clothes, jewels or riches had been in her mind. She was completely and totally his. He would swear that. Yet, a few hours later she was gone, not even leaving a word of farewell.

He winced. It had been proved over and over to be a realistic and unpleasant fact of life that a woman could walk away from a love affair unscathed. He had never understood it; never would understand it. How could a woman give herself so completely—

as Scandal had last night, naked and struggling, mindless with passion in his arms—and today make decisions coldly and irrevocably which were entirely unrelated to her infatuation with him, as if he had touched her everywhere, except in her heart?

He returned to the empty apartment which he had shared with Scandal. It was forlorn and deserted, as if she had never been here. He spoke her name and there was no answer, and yet her presence haunted this room, as it would forever for him.

He could not stay here. He wavered between agony of loss and bitter rage that she had run away from him without a word. Damn her! She had used him, tricked him from the first, conscienceless, and now she had discarded him. She didn't give a damn about last night, she cared nothing about their love, less than nothing. She didn't want him. He was in her way now.

Sweated, he could not stay inside the apartment any longer. He strode out and went down the stairs. He entered every rental unit and *pension* in the five blocks of the Old Square to the river. None had seen her. Or if they had, none admitted it. The manager in one *logement* leered at Wade when he described Scandal. "I wish you luck in finding her, m'sieu—and if you find one like her, save her for me, eh?" He was still laughing as Wade turned and strode back to the street.

It grew dark, the night smoking up from the river and sluicing in at the corners and crannies of the narrow streets, throwing shadows into deeper shadows. Wade admitted it finally. He could not find Scandal. It was true. One could never find a missing girl in this Vieux Carré if she truly wished not to be found.

Agonized, he walked along Royal toward the St. Louis Hotel. Unless Gischairn's detectives turned up some trace of her, he was lost. His sense of helplessness enraged him. For the first time in his life he was in a position in which he was impotent to help himself.

He warned himself that panic was not going to buy him anything. He had to think clearly, wait for the report from Gischairn.

It was quiet in the bar of the St. Louis Hotel. This was the supper hour, and only those most devoted to Bacchus remained in the saloon. Evidently the long day's sale of Tantallon horses had provided enough diversion for the men of the city and the region, and they'd all repaired to their homes or their women, for dinner. Only two men, well dressed and affluent-looking, stood at the long bar. They drank quietly and spoke infrequently. Wade ordered a Sazerac cocktail and walked along the buffet table, where elaborate and free hors d'oeuvre were temptingly displayed. He had not eaten all day, but he was not hungry. He did not touch the food. He finished off the cocktail and ordered a second brought to him at a remote table in a shadowed corner of the room. Subdued sounds from the dining salons and the lobby drifted in around him. The large Seth Thomas grandfather clock showed seven o'clock. The longest hour of his life loomed ahead of him, and he faced the prospect with dread. Each long minute stretched out taut to its fullest extent, the way time dragged when you wished it to hurry. He sipped at the cocktail, aware of a terrible emptiness in his belly unrelated to hunger for food.

He had just finished off the last sip of the cocktail and was debating whether he would order a third when a man entered the saloon from the lobby and ordered a Scotch and water. The voice was faintly familiar. Wade glanced up to find Guille Desmare staring across the room at him. The horse breeder looked sun-blistered, sweated, but affluent and self-satisfied. He smiled and nodded toward Wade. He spoke to the bartender, and then came across the room carrying his own Scotch and a Sazarac for Wade. "May I sit down?"

Wade nodded. He couldn't help watching the entrance of the bar, though it was almost an hour before Gischairn was due.

"Wondered where you got to," Desmare said.

"No sense touting your horses for ten percent of horseshit," Wade said. He had not touched the Sazerac cocktail Desmare had placed before him. "Which is what you gave me."

"So I was mad. It was not entirely my fault. I like to be able to depend on my people. But it's as Earl Fellame was saying to me before I came up here. He never met a man—including me, for hell's sake, Earl said—that knows and loves horseflesh as you do."

"Too bad it doesn't pay off."

"Come on. Forget and forgive."

"It's easy to forget and forgive when your bank account is running over. I too could be gracious as hell under those conditions."

"Listen to me. I'm rushed. Got to meet with some important horse buyers from the North. Want to close a big sale before this goddam war throws up a blockade we can't ship through. Stupid bastards! Who needs another war? Goddam 'em. Only good thing I can say for a war is that it uses up a lot of horses. A hell of a lot of horses. I want to sell as many as I can to both sides before they run out of money and start conscripting my property. Figure I can make a few million. That's where you come in. I'd like to hire you. Take you back up to Tantallon with me. You can get rich." He finished off his drink and stood up. "Well? What do you say?"

Wade exhaled heavily. "I can't give you my answer now."

Desmare laughed in mocking sympathy. "Woman trouble, eh?"

"That obvious, am I?"

Desmare shrugged. "What the hell? Every man with balls gets thrown by a woman if he lives long enough. It's hard to keep hurt out of your face."

"Your offer is generous."

"You goddam right it is. Tell you what. I'll be in town the rest of the week—counting my money." He laughed. "Let me know. Like to have you with me up at Tantallon. Always good to have another man around who knows and loves horseflesh. I got dozens of the other kind."

Guille Desmare gave him a cavalier little salute and strode away, hurrying. Wade watched the tall man go through the wide doors into the hotel lobby. After a moment, he exhaled heavily and took up the cocktail. He glanced at the clock. Still an eternal thirty minutes to eight o'clock.

When he brought his gaze down, his eyes widened in shock. Three men stood before him, watching him silently. He could not even say how or when they had entered the room. They had simply materialized.

There was nothing too prepossessing about their appearances. Their clothes were cheap and ill-fitting. One man was almost as tall as Wade, the second was squat and thick-shouldered, the third thin and sallow.

"Cameroon?" the tall man said. "Wade Cameroon?"

Wade nodded. The tall man's voice was low, almost apologetic, but it was firm and without weakness. "You'll have to come with us, Cameroon."

"Go to hell. Why should I?"

"We're police officers, Cameroon. We don't want no trouble. But you are under arrest."

"On what charge?"

"Fugitive slave."

Wade stared at him, incredulous, and then he laughed. "What kind of stupid joke is this?"

"It's no joke, Cameroon. We advise you to come quietly."

"I'm not going anywhere. You want me to go with you, you'd better decide right now which one of you pays for the wreckage."

"What wreckage is this, Cameroon?"

"I don't believe this. And even if I believed it, I'm not going anywhere. Quietly. Or any other way. You three clowns are outnumbered. I'll break your faces before I'll leave here."

The three men glanced at each other. The tall man said. "Don't make trouble, Cameroon."

"No trouble, unless you make it. You take your insane charge and get out of here, I'll forget I ever saw you. Fugitive slave, for Christ's sake. I'm as white as any of you. Whiter than fatty here. Cleaner than the gray ghost. And if there's trouble, I'll take you apart first. Now, get out of here."

They did not move. The tall man said, "Wait, Cameroon. We are police." He produced his badge naming him a plainclothes detective. "We are only doing the duty that's been assigned to us. Only our duty. You got no fight with us. Come along. If the charges are false, you'll be free in an hour."

"I don't have an hour to waste."

"There are charges, Cameroon. You are going to have to face them. We didn't bring them. We got no beef with you. No stake in this but our jobs. The man's yonder who made the charge against you. Fugitive slave. He's got papers to prove you're a fugitive slave. His papers were signed in the courthouse at Heather Hill. They describe you. They name you fugitive slave."

"They've got to be forged," Wade said. Then he looked beyond the plainclothes detective where the tall man indicated with a nod of his balding head.

"They're legal. Legal and ready to serve against you." the detective said, but Wade didn't even hear him clearly.

Blood throbbed in his temples. His heart felt as if it had slipped its moorings. He stared at Le Blanc poised in the lobby doorway, the gaslights bright behind him, his face faintly shadowed. Le Blanc fixed his gaze on Wade, face rigid and cold, implacable with hatred. The big man's mouth twisted into a savage smile and he bowed slightly, and mockingly.

part three

New Orleans—Black Years

25

Some hotheaded Carolinian, incensed to excessive patriotism, almost three hundred miles east of New Orleans, fired on Fort Sumter early in April that year and brought the world tumbling down. The half-finished fort stood in the harbor at Charleston, a hated symbol of Yankee arrogance.

From the first, Northern leaders knew that one of the most important strategic points to take and hold in this struggle was New Orleans. The crescent city was a sheltered Confederate port and it commanded entrance to the Mississippi River, the great roadway of the South. Conscript armies were being hastily uniformed, disciplined and handed new rifles amid inspiring traffics of military bands, fiery oratory and patriotic tears.

But Wade Cameroon, arrested and held without bond, heard nothing of Fort Sumter, nothing of the war fever in New Orleans and throughout the south.

Wet, sore and shivering from long hours left spanceled and in chains in an open pit, Wade Cameroon sprawled forgotten in a Royal Street barracoon. For reasons nobody bothered to explain to him, he spent his first days in an excavation, isolated from the other inmates of the slave corral. Though he'd been arrested by city police, he had not been placed in the city stockade.

"Nobody says you're a criminal," one of the bailiffs told him. "What you done was criminal—running away. But you're a fugitive slave. That means first, you're a Nigra. That means we keep you with the other nigger runaways."

"Lookin' white don't make you white," another bailiff told him as they shackled him to wall chains. His arrest warrant called him a fugitive slave, and this plainly manifested him Negro. The law was clear about this, quite specific: a trace of Negroid blood in a person explicitly defined him as black before all courts of justice and all officers of those courts.

He slumped, a knot of simmering rage, in the stagnant water in the sump of the pit. Sometimes shadows fell across him when guards came to the brink of the hole and peered down at him.

"Get me out of here," he raged, standing ankle-deep in sour water.

The guards either laughed at him or, to amuse themselves, threw clods of mud at him. "You'll get out when we tell you, Nigra."

He staggered back against the rough side of the pit, staring upward. "Get me out of here! Get me out of here!" He yelled the words over and over until the guards either threw clumps of dirt at him, or tiring of him, laughed at him and walked away.

Nights, he huddled, arms wrapped across his chest, pressed against the coarse earth of the pit. He decided he was in hell; nothing could be uglier, colder, hotter, without a moment of release. When two guards slid down the incline, removed his chains and led him from the pit, his belly shook, his hands trembled and he wept and laughed with the relief he felt.

The pit had been only the outskirts of hell. The barracoon was a high-walled enclosure with barred cells built against the wall facings and opening upon an open yard. At the rear of the cells, iron-faced doors with small barred windows opened on a narrow, lantern-lit corridor.

The open barracoon stank of urine, the musk of unwashed black bodies, of vomitus and whey-thin defecation left to harden and decay where spewed in the sun, of sweat and fear. Even after the stagnant and malodorous pit, the smell of the open barracoon was sickening, unbearable.

Wade stood, quivering, unable to draw a full breath. The guards shunted him ahead of them, past black men slumped against the walls, eyes dulled.

"Got a real lovely suite for you, Nigra," a guard said. "You'll jest think you've died and headed to heaven after that pit."

One of the guards opened a barred door. The other thrust his gunbutt into the small of Wade's back, sending him sprawling inside. The door slammed shut behind him.

Wade fell against the rear wall and caught his balance. He stared across the darkness toward the guards grinning at him through the bars. "How long you going to keep me here?"

One of the guards shrugged. "They'll git round to you, Nigra. Don't you sweat about it."

"If I'm charged with something, why don't they take me to trial?"

The two guards glanced at each other and grinned coldly. "Here's a Nigra don't know when he's well off," one of them said.

"You can't hold me here."

"Well, I'll be damned. If we can't hold you, Nigra, leave." They laughed, gripping the bars.

"I've a right to a trial!"

"Hell, nigger. The law is delayed—even for rich white people."

"How long will I be here?"

The guards shrugged. "Shit. We've had blacks like you forgot in here for months and years at a time. But don't sweat about it. Somebody will come along and want to buy you. You'll get out then."

The laughter of the guards spewed over him. He stared at their contorted faces. Buy him. Somebody would come to buy him. He would be held, unable even to get word outside this barracoon. He sucked in a breath, shuddering, the decay and rot of the place stifling him. And the worst odor of all was the musk of fear. He smelled it on himself.

He trembled, and the trembling radiated outward until he was shaking uncontrollably. He put his head back, howling. He heard the iron door unlocked and yanked open. He went on yelling, his head back. The guards pounded across the cell. They beat him with their gunbutts until he lay bloody and silent on the stone floor.

They stood over him, staring down at him. 'Hell, Nigra," one of them said, panting slightly from exertion. "You're goin' to look back on this here as the good old days."

Wade prowled the small cell. A flat straw pallet thrown carelessly against a wall corner and half lost in a trapezium of shadow was the only furnishing in the cell. Inmates relieved themselves on the floor and were provided buckets of hot lye water each morning to swab out their cribs. The cage was five feet across and perhaps seven feet deep. The inset corridor window let in barred lantern light and gusts of stale air. Even in the everlasting darkness one could find his mattress. It smelled of urine.

The days had passed with deadening slowness. He lost weight because he ate nothing and vomited often when the violent mixtures of foul odors, oppressive heat and inner despair roiled and spun in his stomach. Food was served once a day—a runny grits and spoiled sidemeat rejected by commercial markets, slopped together on an unwashed pan. Pans were placed along the ground as they might be for dogs. No spoons or utensils of any kind were provided. Inmates slopped their fingers through the mess on their plates and wiped it into their mouths, crouched hunching over the tinware.

During those weeks, Wade's lacerations and open sores healed. He had wakened each morning certain this would be the day when he would be taken from this place and given a trial of some kind. He did not care what happened to him as long as he was not abandoned here in this seventh ring of hell.

When he'd lain quietly in his cell without outburst for two days, the guards loosened his ankle chain and herded him out into the sunbaked compound. The black inmates stared at him coldly. When Wade approached, they turned away, refusing even to look at him.

Depleted, shaken inside, he grabbed a black man's arm. "What's the matter with you? Why won't you talk to me?"

"Nuthin' matter with me, nigger," the black man said. "We just don't cotton to white niggers."

The other men around them nodded, staring at Wade, their gazes empty. He shook his head, feeling the screaming moiling upward from deep inside him.

Then one morning when Wade woke, his cell seemed to stink less, to skid less feverishly about his head.

Troubled, he sagged against the wall and stared around him. He shook his head. Nothing had changed. He had not shaved in all the uncounted days he'd been in this place. His beard luxuriated; it grew, itched, matted, a nest for filth and insects. He no longer even thought about washing his face or his body. The only water for washing was in the same green-coated trough from which all inmates drank, on their knees and bringing water up to their mouths in cupped palms. He stopped going near the trough after he saw a man bend over to drink and then vomit helplessly, overcome by the putrid fumes rising from the slime-covered trough. He saw after that that few bothered or had the strength or will or quickness to turn their heads as they retched.

He ran his splayed hands down along his shirtfront. His clothing was stiffened with filth. At first, the smell of his own body, unwashed, greasily coated with grime, crawling with lice and body crabs, had offeneded and sickened him. His naturally blond hair had darkened, dyed with dirt and vermin.

He laughed, distracted. Nothing had changed. As he had lost weight, dehydrated, his senses merely dulled and he no longer cared that he stank.

No. Nothing had changed. Nothing would ever change. After the first week in this hole beyond hell, he saw he received better treatment—he was simply ignored most of the time—than those transients who were held here until claimed by owners from whom they fled, or were sold at public auction. Slaveholders came to this stockade when they needed cheap labor. If they could buy a slave for under one hundred dollars, they did not question such nonessentials as health, mental stability or physical impairment.

These bargain-hunting slave buyers came in and the inmates

were lined up. They were ordered to strip down, to stand on one leg at a time, to spread the cheeks of their buttocks, to pull back their foreskins. As each slave was examined his brothers watched, grinning. If there appeared to be left even a few months of work capacity in one of these captured wretches, he was bought for a few dollars and carted off to chop cane until he died in the fields.

Cameroon was kept inside his cell during these auctions. To be bought out of here was too easy for him, he soon realized. He was being reserved for some special dispensation.

No, nothing outside himself had changed. Gnats still crawled like maggots over his festered eyelids, flies loitered across his sweated thews, stinging and buzzing. The pallet on the stone floor still smelled like urine. Pitiable light still filtered from the high window and offered neither warmth nor illumination. The feeble breezes that penetrated this cage were hot and dead.

No, nothing outside himself had changed. The strange and terrible alteration was in himself. He laughed, uncontrollably. His mind and his body were adapting to this place. He was learning to live in this hell, to accept it. Laughing, he put his head back and his laughter erupted until he was howling like a ravening wolf.

Guards came running. They yanked open the door, yelling at him. He stopped wailing only long enough to gasp another breath.

"Stop it! Stop that yellin', you black bastid."

Yells and ululations rose suddenly all across the compound. A guard jerked up his gun and reversed it in his hands. He struck Wade across the face with the butt of his gunstock.

Wade slumped, fell and lay still. Blood leaked from his nose and ran salty into his mouth. He opened his broken lips and tried to yell again.

He could not yell. He could only moan, lying helplessly in a pool of agony so fierce it was almost sensual.

Gradually, the other cries subsided, the barracoon grew tensely silent.

The guards went on standing over him. One of them said, "You want more gunbutts across your mouth, Nigra, you just yell some more."

They waited, sweated, standing taut over him. When he did not move, they turned and walked out, the heavy iron-barred door clanging behind them, its sound ringing and reverberating inside Wade's skull.

*

At first, Wade thought he was looking into the face of the devil himself.

Certain that he'd finally gone around the bend into total insanity, he stared at those satanic features fixed coldly upon him through the window in the corridor door.

Shaking his head, weak with dehydration and hunger, Cameroon retreated, pressing his back against the thick bars, feeling the chilled metal cut into his back.

Nightmare. That face wasn't real. It was the incarnation of evil. It couldn't be real. The fact that he was awake, in the hot dusk, the sounds of inmates loud from the open compound behind him, made no difference. It was still a nightmare.

He gazed up at those unblinking black eyes in the dark face at the high window. The expression of hard malice did not alter.

Wade tried to laugh the ugly mirage away. It could be rationally explained—a waking hallucination. He was ill, sick with influenza, depleted physically, and his mind was affected. This was not the first manifestation of his mental illness. First, he had lost Scandal. Gradually, she had seeped from his tormented consciousness. He could no longer summon her face in his waking hours or in his dreams. It was as if she were dead to him, forever lost and gone.

At first all his thoughts had revolved about her—she needed him; she was alone in this strange city; he wanted her; he had to know she was all right. But after a few weeks in the slave compound, he felt only relief that Scandal had left him in time. He was thankful she was gone, spared this horror.

He shuddered at the thought she might have come to this place to visit him. Oh God. He would not want her to see him like this. Fevered, coughing helplessly, his head hollow with influenza, his thirst unquenchable, and unquenched because he was unable to drink from the trough.

Then came the nights when he tried to summon Scandal in imagery—and could not do it. He could no longer dream her face, recall it or reshape it in his failed memory.

There was only one face left to him—that cold mask of implacable hatred, watching him for a precise length of time in the dusk every day.

He shivered, laughing and coughing. That was not the devil standing and staring malevolently at him through that small barred window. It was Albert Le Blanc.

Hackles prickled along Wade's neck and his skeletal hands trembled. He tried to laugh and could not. He did not know how long Le Blanc had been coming in the dusk to stare at him, but at last there was only that one hated face left to him. He could see only one face, awake or dreaming. A face which came to personify evil on this earth in his mind—the twisted countenance of Albert Le Blanc at that barred window.

In the empty days and nights, he could see Albert Le Blanc at that door now whether the planter was there or not, and not only at sunset as at first, but in the mornings, at noon and when he wakened screaming deep inside his mind in the haunted night.

He crouched in his cell, waiting for Le Blanc's face to appear. He lived for that hated moment, because there was nothing else to live for. In the long days he watched the blacks herded into the sales yard for testing by buyers. The barracoon supervisors didn't even bother to wash up these blacks or to furnish them with fresh clothing as was done at the private auctions.

Wade shuddered. He pitied these blacks, but though they suffered every human indignity, at least they escaped this place when they were purchased at bargain rates. Only he persisted in this hell, waiting for that hated face to appear in the lowering dusk at his window.

Crouched against the bars, Wade looked forward in horror to the daily visit of Le Blanc. And yet, as long as Albert Le Blanc came to look at him in this filthy cell, he was not totally forgotten.

He slumped against the bars and stared unblinkingly back up at Le Blanc's squared face. This did not in the least discomfit the planter, because Le Blanc did not look on Cameroon as a human being.

Wade began to shake deep in his belly. The days had passed without number. No matter what Le Blanc's responsibilities in the outer world, he came without fail, for the same precise period, to stare in at him, to satisfy himself as to the depths of Cameroon's suffering. Wade was no longer clear in his mind about anything except his hatred for Le Blanc's ugly face.

"I want to thank you for coming," Wade yelled at that face. "I wish I could do something to repay you."

The eyes did not blink, the cold expression of malevolence did not alter.

Wade raged with laughter. "Maybe there is something I can do."

Le Blanc did not answer. He seemed not to hear.

Just before dark they turned Cameroon out of his cell for the evening meal. He tried to eat it, could not. The meat stank, sweetly sour and veined with green.

Cameroon turned his tin plate upside down, emptying it on

the stone floor. Slaves went tense. They stopped eating, hunkered over, watching him but keeping their heads lowered. A guard growled at him. "You want anything to eat tonight, you'll lick that up."

Cameroon ignored the guard and the watching inmates. He dragged his spanceled leg about the sour barracoon. Slaves and guards watched him silently.

Smiling savagely, his gaze fixed on something deep inside himself, Cameroon knelt on the ground, which was littered with human excrement.

He gathered up the offal in his hands and packed it onto his tin plate. The waste streamed through his fingers. The smell gagged him. He heard wild yells of laughter from behind him. He continued to duck-walk along the ground, piling excrement on his plate, forming it into a round cake.

The slaves, finishing their meals, followed him, fascinated. They laughed, nudging each other. Only the superstitious avoided him as insane. They were afraid to look at him, because everybody knew it was fatal to meet the eyes of a madman. They shook their heads, trembling, retreating. "Crazy white-skinned nigger," they said.

The other slaves found something to laugh at in this pit of terror. They followed him, nodding, talking to each other, but pitching their voices loudly enough that Wade had to hear them.

"Look at whitey. The shit-eater."

"You gwine eat all that sweet shit all by yo'self, whitey?"

"You ain't sharin' your shit with nobody, whitey?"

"Hey, whitey. They's a pile of green right over yonder. Flies all over hit—you'll love that pile, whitey."

They laughed so hard they staggered, shoving each other, raging with laughter.

Cameroon ignored them. He returned to his cell and placed the high-piled tin plate in a corner. He sprawled across his thin mattress on the floor. For the first night since he'd been in this purgatory, he slept soundly. Not even the night sounds of sobbing men, or the mindless howl of an inmate anguished in the alien dark, disturbed him.

He awoke with the first light that penetrated his cell. His belly felt empty with excitement and anticipation. He hunched against the bars, staring at that small window, waiting, chilled and silent, for Le Blanc to appear.

The guards entered around ten. "Outside," one of them said. "Out on the compound, nigger."

Wade shook his head, refusing to move.

"You git out there, nigger. And empty that stupid plate of shit, or you git no supper," the guard said. The burly man moved toward the corner as if to kick the pan over.

Cameroon cried out and threw himself across the corner to protect the piled dish from them.

The guards stared at him, shaking their heads. He was not the first inmate they'd seen break mentally in this place. They glanced at each other and backed out of the cell, locking the door behind them. They spoke quietly but tautly between themselves as they walked away.

They were back in less than twenty minutes, with the supervising guard in tow. They unlocked the barred door. The supervisor stepped inside. He took one look at Cameroon, at the plate of excrement, and gestured downward in a sharp cutting way. "Yeah. Christ. He's gone. A lunatic. Chain him up so he don't hurt nobody."

The supervisor walked out, nostrils flared. The guards fitted a wall chain and hammered it to the manacle at Cameroon's ankle. Then they too left the cell, the door clanging behind them.

Sick, Cameroon felt around for the chain. He yanked on it and found it embedded deeply into the stone wall. About three feet long and secured in an iron hook some three feet from the flooring and locked to the manacle welded around his ankle, the chain leashed him like an animal beside the inner corridor door. From where he was crouched he was unable to get a clear look at anyone behind that small high window in the iron-faced door beside him.

Anguished, he rocked on his haunches, straining to see through that small high-barred space where in the dusk Le Blanc's hated face always appeared.

He watched the shadows shorten and lengthen, the anxiety building within him. Alternately, he laughed and cried. Once when he laughed, his emaciated body shook and he laughed mindlessly until he cried, sobbing helplessly.

The afternoon waned, the heat intensified, and Cameroon crouched listening for sounds of footsteps in the narrow corridor.

He heard the heavy tread of boots beyond the corridor door of his cell. Breathing raggedly, he took up the tin plate of collected offal in both hands. He stood tall, hobbled by the iron shackle at his ankle. He could just reach out to that window. He laughed wildly. "For you, Le Blanc!" he raged. His voice quavered with fever, illness, exultant victory.

As that face appeared beyond the bars, Wade shoved the large mass through the small window space, half-heaving it.

Curses raged in the corridor. The iron-faced door was unlocked and yanked open. The guards rushed him, uniforms splattered and stinking, their clubs raised. They struck him to the ground, but a bailiff yelled them away. "Don't kill him, you damn fools. Don't kill him."

Wade crouched on the floor, sobbing. The pain of the clubs was nothing. His senses were too much dulled to respond to or to register physical pain any more. He wept in anguish of defeat. He had thrown his cake but not into Le Blanc's face after all. It was not Le Blanc. It was not Le Blanc....

He was taken from the barracoon, lodged in a courthouse cell for the night and presented the following day in the hall of justice. He was stripped, thrust down into a barrel of delousing liquid and then outfitted in tow-linen blouse and Osnaburg britches, several sizes too small. He was not provided shoes. Handcuffed and still spanceled, he was led into a small, disinfectant-smelling courtroom, hair dark with grime, matted and wild about his head, his beard thick.

The judge presented a most imposing and distinguished figure when he finally appeared from his chambers. His gray hair gleamed in the dull gaslights set about the walls and ceilings. His freshly pressed robes crackled, immaculate. He spent some long moments adjusting objects precisely to his liking before he permitted court business to proceed.

A few spectators slouched on varnished benches outside the railings which divided the room. Wade was placed at a polished table inside the rail enclosure. He sat alone there, the table cleared, innocent even of a sheet of paper, without counsel, uncounseled. At a like table also facing the magistrate's raised dais, two lawyers sat. They ignored Cameroon, whispering together.

His heart slugging erratically, belly empty, Wade glanced around. He found Albert Le Blanc. The planter sat, as if he were a disinterested spectator and not the instigator of this entire matter, quietly, in a sedate black suit, hands folded and eyes downcast, in the first row outside the railing.

He dropped his handcuffed wrists into his lap so he need not see his own hands tremble.

The court was called to order by a bailiff. The case against Wade Cameroon, fugitive Negro slave, was called. The judge nodded toward the lawyers' table. "Mr. Foucher, will you present the case of the Commonwealth of Louisiana against the defendant?"

"Don't I get counsel?" Wade demanded.

The judge peered at him, smile fraudulent. "We of the court will handle matters for you, Cameroon. We have been handling matters for you Nigras for twenty years. Impartial and fair. We know what's best for you darkies. Will you proceed, Mr. Foucher?"

Foucher stood up, a spindly man of middle height, hairline receding from a swollen brow, eyes squinting behind thick-lensed glasses, and read from a prepared sheet in a droning, toneless voice, devoid of all inflection.

Foucher read dates which he stated represented the inception of the black Cameroon's flight from slavery and the date when finally he was caught, masquerading as a white man in the St. Louis Hotel. "The fugitive left a clear trail for representatives of the law to follow—"

"What representatives of any law followed me anywhere?" Wade raged, his handcuffs crashing on the tabletop.

"Cease such outbursts," the judge warned.

"He's lying—"

"We will gag you if we have to, Cameroon, to preserve order and dignity in this court."

"To hell with order and dignity. This is my life they're lying away."

"Keep quiet, Cameroon, or I'll have the bailiffs restrain you. You will be permitted your moment in court. . . . Will you proceed, Mr. Foucher?"

Wade stood up, legs trembling. He braced himself against the table. "If you let him proceed like this, then you encourage him to lie against me. No police ever followed me. He knows *that* if he has any facts at all on that paper."

"Sit down, this instant. I won't have Nigras upsetting my court by acting uppity and arrogant." The judge jerked his head and two bailiffs caught Wade's shoulders, shoving him down into his chair. They remained standing behind him, police nightsticks in their fists.

"The men who followed me were detectives—hired by Le Blanc yonder," Wade said.

The judge's smile twisted his lips, oblique. "No Mr. Le Blanc has been mentioned in this indictment, Cameroon. I see no such name anywhere in the charges brought against you. I know of no Mr. Le Blanc involved in this litigation before us."

"He sits there!" Wade felt a hand dig into his shoulder. He

shook free. "He followed me. He hired detectives. He had me brought here on false charges."

The judge shook his head. "We are brought here, Cameroon, solely and entirely on a matter of the Commonwealth of Louisiana versus Wade Cameroon, fugitive slave. There is no Le Blanc on trial here—except in your own deranged mind."

"He sits there." Cameroon tried to struggle to his feet but was restrained.

"Remain silent. I warn you again against further outburst. . . . Please proceed, Mr. Foucher."

Foucher slicked the flat of his hand over his pomaded strands of hair. He conferred briefly with his associate. He conceded to error. It was not the state which had traced the fugitive Cameroon in his flight. The runaway had been arrested on the word of Mr. Le Blanc, an eminent planter, who had since then presented his evidence to the high sheriff of the parish so that the slave could be formally turned over to him, for he had bought the runaway's papers and intended to carry him back to his plantation.

"And does this gentleman have such papers here? And in order?"

"He does, your honor. We shall present them with other evidence."

"Very well. This is quite a customary procedure. A mere technicality and entirely legal. Continue."

Foucher retraced Wade's trail—the stolen carriage, the brutal knife attack on his pursuer, the selling of thoroughbred carriage horses, the town where they were sold, and the carriage recovered from a livery stable in the Vieux Carré, as were a handgun and rifle, also stolen and pawned.

"A classic statement of flight and pursuit," the judge stated. "How many times have I sat in this courtroom and heard similar delineations."

"The history of the defendant is interesting, your honor, and vital to our case against him. And in a way another classic example of a slave raised almost as a house pet and beginning to accept himself as a human being. For example, Cameroon will tell you he was raised as an equal son of his father, the squire Cameroon of Heather Hill Plantation. That he was indeed raised right in the plantation manor with his three brothers, treated as one of them, is hereby stipulated and admitted and accepted as true.

"Your honor, as sometimes happens in remote areas—though I hasten to add, rather than insult this court, that it occurs rarely

—when a man's beloved first wife dies and he is left bereaved, even mentally deranged by grief, with small children to rear alone, he often remarries with haste and not always wisely. He may sometimes—as in the case of Squire Cameroon—take a second wife from the staff of serving people in the house. A comely woman. Of mixed blood, but almost white."

"It does happen," the judge agreed.

"My mother was not a servant," Wade said. "She was a guest in our house."

"Cameroon has made my point, your honor." Foucher gave Wade a bland smile. "Cameroon just admitted to the court that he is *not* a full blood brother of the Cameroons, formerly of Heather Hill. We have here additionally, your honor, three signed depositions attesting to the fact that this man was their half brother, the son in marriage of their own father to his second wife, a woman from Martinique. These depositions are signed by his half brothers.

"We have also traced this woman's antecedents far enough to establish for the purposes of this court and to the point of law that this woman from Martinique was very probably a mulatto—with enough Negroid blood to qualify her, before the law, as black."

"A trace of Negroid blood," the judge agreed. "It is indeed the letter of the law."

"My mother was a gentlewoman of French descent." Wade leaped to his feet. "As white as you. As white as any of you—"

"But born on the isle of Martinique?" Foucher inquired before the judge could order Cameroon silenced.

"Born on the isle of Martinique. Yes. Not everyone born in the Vieux Carré is French, Creole, black or white."

"You have proof of your mother's bloodline?" the judge asked.

"I can provide it. Yes. Given time."

"Meantime, your honor, we have papers establishing his parentage. We have charges of illegal flight. We have sworn statements from his own half brothers."

"Your evidence is quite preponderous," the judge said.

"They present nothing," Wade raged. He leaped up. When the bailiffs caught his arms, he shook free. "They present only circumstantial evidence. Certainly my brothers signed papers that we had the same father and different mothers. This is a simple statement of facts—"

"We have dealt only with facts, your honor," Foucher said.

"Lies. Wild deductions! My mother was born in Martinique—ergo she was of Negroid ancestry? This is stupid. As many pure-blood whites are born on the isle of Martinique as are born in this city—"

"This court refuses to permit you to disparage our beloved city, already suffering as she is from the ravages of war—"

"She was white. White. She was white."

"Produce documentary evidence of this."

"Give me time."

"You have been under detention for months. You had time to gather whatever defenses you may have needed. The court has no patience. Mr. Foucher presents contrary evidence and the court is bound to accept this evidence since you do not or cannot produce counterproof."

"Don't you care for the truth? Do you have no interest in the truth?"

"This court seeks only the truth."

"What do they pay you in bribes, you evil, smiling, hypocritical old bastard?"

"I find you in contempt—"

"My God! My God! God Himself must stand in contempt of this court. Of this farce. Of this nightmare."

"Bailiffs, remove this Nigra from my court. I don't have to tolerate such behavior and I shall not."

The bailiffs caught Wade's arms, yanking him backward and upsetting the chair. He stared at the judge. "What are you going to do to me?"

"What disposition I make of this matter, Nigra, is none of your business. I told you, this court knows what is best for you. And this court will act in your best interests. Now get him out of here."

The bailiffs wrestled Wade from the courtroom. The judge sat in injured silence in his high-backed chair. Wade no longer saw the magistrate. He was barely aware of the bailiffs dragging him along the floor. He saw only one thing in this room: Le Blanc's face, cold and unsmiling, his eyes bleak and black and deadly.

26

Scandal awoke to a thunderous, persistent pounding of fists and cane heads on her door. She opened her eyes unwillingly. Morning sunlight splattered across the room. She knew this was not Wade; he would not knock at his own door. When the knocking ceased for a few moments, she rolled over and buried her head in her pillow.

The knocking was renewed and continued, unyielding. At last she got up, threw a robe over her shoulders and padded across the room.

The first men she saw when she opened the door were two burly strangers. One had his cane raised, ready to strike the door facing again. He tried to smile, failed. "Are you Mrs. Cameroon?"

"Yes."

"Scandal!"

Her head jerked up, her gaze flew past the thick shoulders of the strangers. She saw Julien-Jacques Gischairn standing behind the burly men. He sounded happy, joyous and relieved at the sight of her, and she smiled as if suddenly rescued by an old and trusted friend.

Gischairn dismissed the two men. They retreated down the oleander-canopied stairway and stood, motionless as palace guards, in the dappling of shadows. Gischairn ignored them. He smiled at her warmly and moved his head so his diamond-and-gold earring glittered in the sunlight. "May I come in?"

Before she could answer, Gischairn eased past her into the apartment. He smiled at her reassuringly, treating her as if she were a recalcitrant and wilful child, spoiled and unpredictable, but nevertheless beloved. "We scour the town looking for you. And find you, like the proverbial diamond, in your own yard."

"I came home."

"I see you did."

Her eyes brimmed with tears. "Wade has left me. Oh, I admit I ran away from him first. But I came back to him. He was not here—he was glad to be free of me."

"Was he? This is hardly consistent with the picture I had of him when last I saw him. He was distracted, heartbroken that you had deserted him. He begged me to find you."

She exhaled heavily. "Then you have seen him."

Gischairn winced slightly. "Not as recently as I would like. We had an appointment to meet in the St. Louis Bar. To discuss you, as a matter of fact. He did not show up. I waited two hours. Got quite drunk, but he never came."

"You see? He did decide to go away and leave me. Oh, not that I blame him! Not at all. Such a selfish little baggage."

"Why do you think he made such a sudden decision?"

She sniffled, drawing the back of her hand across her nostrils. "I know. When I came here, he had left this for me." She unwrapped the cloth package of dresses and underthings. "Aren't they lovely?"

"Quite fashionable. And in excellent taste. Why should such a generous gift, freely given, when we both know he had very little money, convince you contrarily that he has abandoned you?"

"Because. Don't you see?" She took up one of the sheer gowns and abstractedly placed it against her, feeling the soft smooth texture of the fabric. "This is his way of telling me he knew what I was like—an empty, self-centered and selfish little baggage. These clothes. He is telling me this is all I wanted of him. This is his final gift to me. He has left it and walked out—saying we are quits."

Gischairn shrugged. "You have fabricated quite a plausible argument in your mind, in the manner of troubled lovers. I don't believe it for a minute. But if you're satisfied with the explanation, we'll accept it."

"You're not even going to look for him? For me?"

He smiled. "Why should we? He has served his purpose for you. You have from him what you wanted."

She winced as though he'd struck her. She bit her underlip hard and held her breath to keep from sobbing aloud.

He was without pity. "Well, isn't it true? Why did you walk out on him, then? What was your rationale for leaving him?"

She did cry now, helplessly. He said sharply. "Come, girl. Stop that. Don't waste my time with your tears. This is a brutal world. If you are going to succeed in it, you have to be tough and brutal —under that lovely exterior, of course. . . . Come now. Stop crying and face the truth. Why did you leave him?"

"Because I was a fool." She sniffled, tilting her head.

"That is a conclusion. After the fact. It may also *be* a fact. But it is not a factor you considered in leaving him. I want the truth. Why did you leave him?"

"Because—dammit!—I was falling in love with him."

"And what was wrong with that?"

"Everything. You are wise. Worldly. You truly do know all the answers. Don't pretend with me. You know that it would not have worked. He is smart, educated, brilliant. And what am I?"

"A scullery maid?"

She flushed, her head jerking up, but when she met his teasing gaze, she smiled and nodded. "That's what I am."

"Well, you are at least facing the truth—the beginning of wisdom. But what does this prove—or what did it prove in your own involved thought processes?"

"You know what it proved. Wade wanted—wanted me—for my body."

"It's a lovely little body. You can hardly condemn him for that."

"I'm not condemning him. I'm talking facts. The way you insisted. The fact is, we have nothing in common except my body. What was to happen to me when he tired of me? And he would tire of me."

"You convinced yourself of that, did you?"

"I'm being truthful now. Far more truthful than you."

"Your being truthful is the only important issue here. Whether I speak the truth or not will not help us solve our dilemma."

"There is no way for me to solve my problem. He has left me and he is not coming back."

"Whether he is coming back or not is not your problem. What you are going to do with yourself is the only problem."

"What do you mean? I know I can't do anything. I found that out yesterday tramping the miserable streets of this heartless town."

"Found no work, eh?"

"I tried everything. I even offered to work—as a scullery maid. They took one look at me and laughed in my face."

"If one aims low and falls in a pit, he has no one to blame but himself, does he?"

"Don't lecture me." Tears welled in her eyes, spilled along her cheeks. "I'm too ill. Too sad. Too distressed."

"You're right. Forgive me. Live and let live, the best possible recipe for existence in this sad vale of tears. But I have come to help."

"Nobody can help me."

"No. You're right. Nobody can help you. Except yourself. Make up your mind to that. I can provide assistance. But you must find your own way, your own inner resources. If you don't have them, you may well not find employment even as a scullery maid."

"Oh, I had one offer of work."

"Yes?"

"A pimp. He wanted me to be his whore. He said he would make me rich."

"I hope you laughed in his face."

"No. I burst into tears. That's when I gave up. That's when I came back home. Beaten. Defeated. Tired. Lonely and knowing finally I was good for one thing. To be some man's whore."

"Perhaps that's what you are good for. But you must aim high. You must put foolish nonexistent notions such as true love out of your mind. You came here wanting to be the belle of New Orleans. Well, that is one thing I can help you achieve . . . if you are willing to pay the price."

She stared at him, sniffling. "Why would you do that?"

He laughed. "I look on you, my little diamond in the rough, as the supreme challenge of my misspent career. Without boasting—which I have nothing against doing—I have directed the lives and careers of scores of young girls like you. They have come into my house, and gone away from it as mistresses of the finest mansions on St. Charles Avenue, or the largest and gaudiest plantations in the state. I delight in creating fantasy *ladies* and then foisting them off on the clods who form our highest society. I am really an evil old person. It would take an incredible challenge to stir me to this one last effort. You can be that challenge."

"And you—what would you expect in return?"

Gischairn gazed at her in mock agony. "My dear young woman, in the terms you suggest, *nothing!* I thought you were sensitive enough to perceive that I am left totally unmoved by females—except as I appreciate art, for its perfection, for its value, on display."

"If we are being truthful, I must say, I don't believe *anybody* does anything—for nothing."

"Very good. Very promising. You are coming along well. You must learn—even when you lie with your lips, and even with your vagina, you must learn to face and accept only the truth in your mind. This sharpens your wits, expands your intelligence, increases the unfair advantage you have over men naturally."

"What do you want?"

He laughed, delighted. "From you, nothing. I would have every reward if one day you actually reigned as belle of this benighted city. I would have total revenge for all wrongs, total victory over all my enemies, supremacy over my peers. My reward would be to be near enough to bask in your victory. To see you come from scullery maid—to what? To whatever you're willing to buy—at whatever the price that is demanded."

She sat for a long time, silent. When she did speak, what she said astonished and shocked him. He had believed she would ask about that price she would be expected to pay. Instead, she said only in the forlorn wistful tone of the small child she was, "What —if Wade does come back?"

He frowned, gazing at her. "We'll cross that bridge if we ever come to it. He didn't come to me last night. Perhaps he has changed his mind. Whatever he has done, it is his decision, and he's a big boy. He can take care of himself. The question is not about him, but about you. Can you take care of yourself? Are you a big girl, able to learn to be hard inside? Able, if Wade Cameroon does not come back, to face the truth inside your mind, to live with it, to believe that it is for the best? If he was going to walk out on you sooner or later, it is better for you to face that truth now."

Exhausted, Scandal twisted her body in a pirouette, stretched tall on her toes. Suddenly, she cried out and flung herself into a heap on the floor. Her private instructor came with her cane and stood over her, a dark Russian woman with an imperious air. "What's the matter with you now, girl?"

Scandal looked up, crying. "I think I've broken my leg. I hope I have. I can't get up. I'm too tired. I can't go on."

"You will get up. You will go on. Those are my orders. I follow my orders. I am waiting."

"You're cruel. Inhuman."

"As I said, girl. I follow orders—from M'sieu Gischairn. I don't give a damn what *you* think of me as long as you do what I tell you. Clumsy as you are, I shall not permit you to force me to admit failure to your patron."

"I'm not clumsy, damn you. I'm just tired. I don't think Gischairn wants me to be a prima ballerina—ballet is only one of the tortures he's contrived for me."

Her teacher shrugged. "It is the only torture I'm involved in, or interested in. You will succeed. Because I refuse to fail. I refuse to admit failure. Now get on your feet. If you think I won't use this cane for something more than direction, my girl, you just go on lying there."

Scandal forced herself to her feet, miserable in her mind, aching in every sinew of her body. The muscles of her calves and ankles felt as if someone pressed upon them with a white-hot poker. She flung herself up to her toes, biting back her tears. To shut the Russian woman from her consciousness, she thought about Wade. She summoned him into the warm foyer of her mind. Wade would find her. He would come for her. He would take her away from this place. Oh, Wade, where are you? Where have you been all this time?

She had no idea how many weeks had passed since she had come as ward and prisoner-at-hard-labor into Julien-Jacques Gischairn's twenty-room mansion on St. Charles Avenue. She was recipient and beneficiary of none of its splendor. She was permitted one cup of hot chocolate every other day; she ate chicken with the crusty parts peeled away; she was served broiled fish until she gagged at the sight of halibut.

She divided her time between a small attic room where her bed had a board nailed in under her mattress so she could not remove it no matter how uncomfortable and discouraged she became, and this huge ceiling-lighted gymnasium where she suffered daily two hours of ballet, an hour of fencing, ballroom dancing, painful exercises designed to rearrange nature's imperfect body symmetry.

She interspersed this activity with endless lessons in etiquette—she had had no idea there were so many ways correctly to express your gratitude to a tiring hostess for a boring evening! When finally she had mastered the varied sizes and shapes of forks, they brought on the spoons, and then the knives and the serving utensils. God, why would people make eating so complex?

She was laboriously taught to cook, all the while being warned that she must never so much as lift a finger to boil water in person. It was just that, as an elegant lady, she must be able to supervise gourmet meals—for two or twenty! She thought back in longing to the days she and Wade had wolfed their sandwiches along the lonely trace. . . .

She was instructed again and again in the art of fine stitching, water-color painting, beauty culture. The only lesson she truly enjoyed was horseback riding. She could ride better than her instructor until they forced her to sit sidesaddle and *smile* while she hung on for dear life. Oh God, Wade, where are you? Why have you abandoned me?

She was rolled out of bed before seven in the morning—for a breakfast of coddled egg and dry toast. Then she began long, fourteen-hour days, of unlearning everything she'd been taught to this moment and replacing it with information as evanescent as it was irrelevant to the real world.

"What real world?" Gischairn inquired. "You gave up your *real* world months ago when you came here."

"I'm so exhausted. Wouldn't I learn better if I got just a few minutes of rest each day?"

"You're young. Strong as a horse. You don't need rest. You need to make up in a short time all that slipped past you in seventeen years."

"At least I was happy."

"You thought you were."

She winced. "No. You're right. I wasn't happy—even then. I just think I was—looking back from here."

"Good. See, you are learning to be coldly truthful, even without prompting from me. You've come such a long way."

"But I walk around in a daze. I'm just so sleepy—all the time."

"Forget it, girl. You can sleep late when you're rich. It'll be too late then—either for the luckless millionaire who wins you as his prize, or for you. But at least you can sleep . . . on down pillows and silk sheets."

She infrequently encountered even Gischairn. Mostly she saw only her instructors and the youthful black servants. All of these latter minced around like failed girls, simpering and giggling. She wondered how Gischairn endured having them around. But when she mentioned this to her ballet instructor, the Russian woman laughed sincerely and openly for the first time since Scandal had met her. "My poor dear *innocent!* How can you live right in this house and have no inkling of what goes on. How blind you are."

Puzzled, Scandal dropped the subject, feeling it was a topic she had no wish to pursue.

One Sunday afternoon, Gischairn interrupted her French lesson. He handed her a brightly patterned cotton dress which accented her youth and yet underlined her womanliness. "Put this on," he said. "You and I are going for a drive. Perhaps to Canal Street, along the Esplanade. I don't want you seen particularly. The dress is only in case of accident. I want you well dressed in case you have to be taken to the hospital."

Driving with Gischairn in the tonneau of his majestic coach was fun for Scandal, the most pleasure she'd been permitted since Gischairn had taken her into his home. She had never seen a carriage as elegant—a fine varnish that glowed rather than shone gaudily; 'etain-blue window curtains; expensive glass vases with fresh cut flowers; uniformed attendants leaping to serve them; purebred horses with silverplated harnessware gleaming in the sun, curried, brushed, stepping smartly, their tails clipped and tied with blue bows.

Gischairn was a relaxed and charming host. He knew every cranny and every closet with its own skeleton in the city. He pointed out sights to her she would have passed and never seen. The Catholic cemeteries where the remains of the beloved deceased were permitted one year to disintegrate and bleach in the aboveground vaults before they were pushed out the rear by a container holding the latest deceased. He told her how at first the citizens of the parish had buried their dead underground, only to have them rise from the grave with the first heavy rainfall. Not even huge boulders or lead weights could keep the biers underground when the water table rose. He pointed out the oddities along Grande Route St. John, the second-oldest street in the town, and told her how Chef Menteur Boulevard had been named for an Indian who led French soldiers on a seven-month march to get them from Biloxi to New Orleans. "He was a big liar, but he lives in posterity with a street named for his ability." She laughed delightedly, even when she was unsure whether to believe him or not. She was shocked at how narrow most of the ordinary houses were. These, he told her, were called shotgun houses, built so narrow because owners were taxed on the width of a house, and so named because one could stand on the front porch and shoot a chicken on the back one.

"And so this is the town over which you wish to reign as its most celebrated or notorious woman! Ah, my poor innocent. The price you will have to pay . . ."

"The price I am already paying," she said in vehemence.

"You're paying nothing yet. You think because you have lost your lover, and work hard a long day learning to better yourself, that you are paying some exorbitant price. You have not begun to pay. The only thing that troubles me is, is the game worth the price any more?"

She frowned. "I never heard you talk like that before."

"I never felt like this before. My poor, beloved city. My poor dear old town. Look at it! Look out there, Scandal. See those ugly gray uniforms—everywhere you look. And I would wager that in a matter of months the uniforms will be blue—an army of occupation. My lovely old town will be overrun with Yankees who have no feeling for beauty or age. Conquer it, salute it or fuck it. That's all they know. Uncouth Yankee boors. From coal mines. Farms. Shanty Irish. Factory workers.

"But at least, dear Scandal, this is history you're looking at. History is being made. The lovely old South is about to be destroyed all around us—and here in New Orleans, deepest city of all, we are almost already under the heel of our conqueror."

"I hate history," she said. "Worse even than I do French. I can see no place for either in my life."

"That's because your life hasn't begun yet, child. You're still in your university for one. You're still learning all I have to teach you. And you will learn! Before I'm through with you, you'll *know* history—ancient, past and present. The surest indication of a cultured human being is his knowledge of history."

"I don't give a damn what the Goths and the Visgoths did."

"You don't, my dear. But you will. History is one of the subjects you must master if you're ever to be put on display, made ready for your debut into what we imprecisely call *polite society*.

"History in itself may not help you earn a can of beans. But it provides you a depth—of character, of self, of personality. An interesting woman can converse about places and things. An irresistibly attractive woman can talk about *ideas*. And before I'm through with you, that's what you will be able to do."

Scandal sighed deeply and sank against the luxurious upholstery, feeling more tired and lost than ever. "Unless Wade comes and gets me."

Gischairn shrugged. "Whichever comes first."

Scandal slumped on her back in the uncomfortable chair, going over for the hundredth time the same sentence in idiomatic French. Her intonation was incorrect—"laughable" was what her aging male instructor called it.

"I don't care," she raged. "I'm tired of this stupid language. Don't you people *ever*, even once, pronounce a single word as it is spelled?"

"When you're through with your tantrum, we'll get back to work," the teacher said in a flat voice.

"Well, we'll never get back to it, because I'll never be through with this tantrum. Don't you know this is a form of torture? A form of mental torture? I'm a stupid backwoods girl who never even learned *English!* And now you want to impose French on top of that?"

"I don't want to. But I am paid to do it, and I shall. You may not ever know English as far as I'm concerned, but your French will be impeccable. As for your being a stupid backwoods girl, that's not my problem."

Scandal drew back the book to hurl it at him, changed her mind and reread the passage, perfectly, in a vindictive tone.

"Very good," he said in a cold voice. "Now, let's do it one more time."

Gischairn, alerted by the servants, found Scandal knotted in a ball in the exact center of the gymnasium, sobbing helplessly.

Gischairn snapped his fingers. One of the servants placed a

straight chair beside Scandal's huddled form. Gischairn sat down and looked at her. In a soft voice, he said, "What's the matter, Scandal?"

She looked up, gasping for breath. "I'm tired."

"Of course you are. None of this. Nothing we're doing would be worth a damn if you were not bone-tired."

"I don't want it."

He laughed. "As I might tell a woman in the last stages of labor, it's a bit late for that decision. You are by now, my dear, not a person, or a human being, or an individual at all. You are my project. One of my most difficult, I grant you. Sometimes, I tire. And I despair. But I don't give up on you. And you won't fail me. We've come too far together now for that."

" I want to go home. I want Wade."

"Where is your home, girl? Your home is here. It's the only home on this earth you have. That rented room is long occupied by other louts. Your former lover, Wade Cameroon? Who in hell knows where he is?"

"He's not my *former lover*. He's my husband."

"We'll talk about that when the time comes."

"I'm tired. I tell you I am so tired. I am tired to death of pretending to be a lady. I don't even want to be a lady."

"That's one wish you will get, my little one. In spades. No matter what we do to you, you'll never be a *lady*. Don't fret yourself about that. Oh, you'll look like a lady, and you'll sound like one. But you'll be what you are. A lout."

"Damn you! Why do you call me that? Just because I'm so tired and I can't walk and I cry, you call me a lout."

"No. The truth is—and we deal only in the truth—you *are* a lout. You *are* a scullery maid. If you have not the energy to make something else of yourself, not the will to pull yourself up from the slime, you will remain a lout. Or you would have. But you won't now. Because I won't let you."

"I'm too tired."

"You're tired because you have never learned in all your life to be graceful. Now you think we are trying to kill you just because we try to make you use the muscles which provide you grace and fluidity."

"I can't help what I am."

"You can't, but I can. You are a lout but you will be graceful. If it kills you. . . . When your muscles are used to moving your body gracefully, they won't hurt you any more. It's that simple. But whether they do or not, you can't stop now."

"I can stop. I want to stop. I want to go to Wade."

"Make up your mind, girl. Suddenly, I'm tired. And old. Suddenly, I don't care. I don't give a damn. I can throw you back in the gutter where I found you. Perhaps there you will find your handsome young Cameroon—whether *he'll* want you or not is a moot question. . . . As for me, I can in three hours find a dozen more girls just as pretty as you are—but with *guts*."

"Stop it."

"The choice is yours, girl. Entirely. And this is the moment when you have to make that decision. We all get tired. There are times for all of us when it doesn't seem worth it. We either start up again, or we fall back. You can be a scullery maid—because that's all you're good for. Or, you can do as I tell you—when I tell you—for as long as I tell you. And one day, you'll be mistress of the richest mansion on this street."

It was incredible. Within a week from that unhappy scene with Gischairn in the barren gymnasium on the third floor of his mansion, the house was a place of smiles. The French instructor smiled and spoke back to her rapidly, and in French. The Russian ballet mistress nodded, smiling at the least of Scandal's pirouettes.

She truly knew she was succeeding when Gischairn came to her, smiling, and kissed her hand. "It's time for us to talk," he said. "Soon, we'll go out. To the opera. Ballet. A truly outstanding stage production perhaps. Dinner at Antoine's. Nothing serious, no great steps. But it will begin. You are about to flower—to unfold like a chrysalis. It has not mattered before. We hardly knew if you'd be making a debut or running away, did we?"

She smiled, only faintly, as she'd been taught.

"I have been giving a great deal of thought to your name."

"Rachel?"

"My God, no. No one is named Rachel. But . . . Scandal . . . there is a name with a touch of mystery to it. It attracts attention. Many will be curious as to how you got it. . . . If ever I hear you explain any further than a Mona Lisa smile, I'll know that all my efforts in your behalf were wasted."

She gave him a Mona Lisa smile.

"The name I don't like is Cameroon."

She winced. The pain was still there, the memory of pain. "What should I do?"

"Get rid of it."

Scandal caught her breath. "What you're really talking about is a divorce, *n'est-ce pas?*"

"How clever you are. But not a divorce, my dear. In a Catholic territory a divorce is very messy, or even impossible. A divorce closes a hundred doors for every one it opens. No. I think a quiet annulment."

"Annulment? I'm afraid, *mon cher* Julien, no matter how devoutly we might wish it, an annulment is out of the question. My marriage to Wade was consummated." She bit her lip and then smiled again, quickly.

"Oh, no doubt. Spare me the details, I haven't had dinner yet. . . . No. The church will permit annulment on fraud."

"Fraud? Wade?"

"No, my dear, you. Not Scandal Gischairn, of course—"

"Oh? Is that who I am? Scandal Gischairn?"

"A distant cousin, my dear. My ward. No. Scandal Gischairn need never be involved in this ugly annulment I'm suggesting. We shall let my attorneys handle the matter."

"Do you mind telling me how?"

"I dislike lingering on it. I dislike Wade Cameroon. I have since the night he sent me and my detectives on a frantic wild-goose chase searching for you and then hadn't the decent courtesy to show up for our hard-earned report."

"Has it ever occurred to you that perhaps he *couldn't* get there?"

"No, my dear. It never has. And I'm sure you know, too, in your mind—if not yet in your heart—that his decision not to meet me was made of his own free will and volition."

She gestured negligently with her soft, silken hands which fluttered like useless butterflies. "Then, whatever it is, go on. Get it over with."

He bowed. "I shall. My attorneys will leave in the morning for Baton Rouge. There the annulment of the marriage of Wade Cameroon and Rachel Wilkes will be effected. For reasons of miscegenation."

"Because I'm black."

"No, my dear. You—Scandal Gischairn—are not black. Rachel Wilkes may have been. But we scarcely remember her, do we?"

"Some things about her I remember pretty well. The way she wished sometimes that she *and* Wade Cameroon were both black and nobody cared about them—except themselves."

"Like a bad dream, my dear, it will dissolve in the mists of the morning of your new life. Soon you shall be free to begin that life. A life that will take you wherever you wish to go. For a price."

27

The libidinous old city of New Orleans had seen many legendary coquettes parade through her narrow streets and licentious hearts since the first Canadians established a trading post, named in honor of the duc d' Orleans, on the banks of the Fleuve St. Louis. None ever flashed across her blasé horizon more suddenly, spectacularly, seductively or—in the end—more outrageously than the enchantress who called herself Scandal and tried forever to live beyond her name and her means, and for a brief moment dimmed even the color and brilliance of the Mardi Gras, simply by appearing in its midst.

Finding acceptance in the clannish, fissured and xenophobic social structure of the town was laughably easy for her, sponsored as she was by the despised, disdained but totally feared Julien-Jacques Gischairn. But one had to admit—even Gischairn laughed proudly—Scandal conquered their foolish hearts on her own, once provided the opportunity, her dainty foot in the door. She came among them, unbelievably, incredibly, beautiful, with a deference toward her elders which was ultra-charming in these times of impudent and disrespectful youth. Her restrained laughter, modulated voice, delicacy of manner could not be faked or learned; it defined genuineness, *pur sang*, as did her purity of beauty, her grace of form, her tactful, natural refinement. She was dark enough to captivate the Creoles, fair enough to be accepted by the Americans. When she conversed in rapid, perfectly accented, idiomatic French, she insulted neither the beautiful tongue nor her auditors—she was *cultured*, they assured each other happily, as at ease with French as with the coarser, less elegant English.

There was that ambience of mystery about her. She seemed first to materialize—in all the best places—on the arm of that aging libertine Julien-Jacques Gischairn. He introduced her with a savory pursing of his withering lips as his distant cousin, his ward. So potent was his power as a social arbiter that few of even the most exclusive Creole families dared question or exclude her. Besides, no one wanted to. They all, in fact, hastened to claim discovery. Men—and even their wives—admitted they'd never seen such a fresh, unspoiled and unaffected young lady. Her startling beauty was certainly unadorned, as natural as a flower. What was there to hate about her? She merely exercised, unaffectedly, the graces endowed her by nature! She was a lady, one could always recognize true elegance. It was in the blood!

From the first triumph—at the opera and afterward at Maxim's, where people gawked openly, whispering behind thir hands, to the delight of old Gischairn—Scandal was far less happy with her new life than she had ever dreamed possible. She had everything handed to her, and yet she was always "on stage," on display like some parading puppet, bound always to a precise, structured, unvarying behavior which vexed and irritated her. The men who surrounded her, begging to touch her exquisite hands, to brush only the backs of her delicate fingers with their thirsting lips, to claim a scented kerchief as a souvenir—they all bored her. They were not Wade Cameroon; not the best of them approached his remembered comeliness. She could never care for them. She didn't want their idolatrous devotion.

"Forget love," Gischairn advised her one night in his coach on the way home from a particularly rewarding dance where Scandal had almost disrupted all protocol and dignity, creating a minor stampede, simply by entering the splendid arena. She'd been presented to young Alex Vigneaux, whose family, Gischairn whispered, was worth uncounted millions. She'd met Louis Levesque, the Midas-rich director of the Sugar Exchange, which Gischairn assured her was not a place where they sold sugar at all, but rather gambled on sugar futures, a place where fortunes were made and lost overnight, the only man retaining his security for any length of time seemingly Louis Levesque. He certainly was not a very prepossessing man, bald except for a graying fringe, potbellied, thin-shouldered, hawk-beaked and astigmatic. Obviously, he had nothing except money—and watery, agonized eyes for Scandal Gischairn. With some reluctance, Levesque introduced his wife, Manon—a thin, aging woman who persisted in the notion she was as lovely at fifty as she had been at twenty. She gushed over Scandal. "She knows being in your orbit will attract handsome men around her," Gischairn said with some impatience. "She'll take the leavings, and be thankful." Scandal gave the bronze-red-haired woman scarcely a second thought. If she had a thought about the men at all, it was that she was unmoved by them, even their bank accounts. They were far less than she had dreamed they would be, thin or fat, bald or old, bucktoothed or sallow-faced. She hated them all. Perhaps she did not truly hate little Alex Vigneaux. Though he was twenty, there was about him the cherubic innocence and goodness of a four-year-old. She could cuddle him in her arms—protectively, as she might a small boy—totally without passion. He was so eager and sweet and self-effacing it was hard to hate him, even if he was white.

"Let me express it another way." Gischairn grinned at her in the darkened cab, infrequently touched with lights from passing streetlamps. "You are now a free woman. You can marry where you wish; the heights are totally your own option. In this city for the next few years, you will be able to choose a rich husband to please your own whims."

"What about Wade?"

"What about him? You're no longer married to him, my dear."

"You didn't tell me the annulment was accomplished."

"Well, it is." He shrugged. "It was of such minor consequence, it slipped my mind." He glanced at her. Also, he had neglected to tell her that when his solicitors returned from Baton Rouge, they reported that though the annulment was final, a check showed a Wade Cameroon had been registered as a slave. If this was true, there was no basis for the annulment, since both parties were black. Coldly, Gischairn reminded them that though the name was not usual, certainly there was no way to know if it was the same Cameroon; it was, in fact, highly unlikely, since Wade Cameroon looked like nothing except a full-blooded Scot, straight off the highlands. The attorneys agreed. Gischairn warned them that under the circumstances, they would not mention the matter to Scandal. There was no sense in burdening her with irrelevant materials, with factors she could not alter. "But, no matter, you are free. Your new life and all its new choices are before you."

Scandal sat silently staring at the backs of her hands, listening to the muffled clop of shod hooves on the deep shell pavement, and to the fractured pumping of her own heart. "I haven't seen one man I could care a fig for."

"I told you. Forget love. To paraphrase the Bard of Avon, my child, love only thyself, first and last, and it follows as the night the day, thou canst not then be hurt by any man."

He sat chuckling at the asperity of his own wit. She hardly heard him. She heard only the word *hurt*. Its associations opened a Pandora's box of stinging and painful thoughts in her mind. She winced in still raw recall of the way Wade Cameroon had hurt her, the way white men had brutally and bestially slain her mother, the way Gischairn now suggested they would selfishly and gleefully, with hypocritical fawning, misuse her if they could. His advice matched precisely her own intention—indeed, it defined it. She would protect her heart, shield her emotions. The white men who tried to use her would find themselves used instead. And as for her falling in love—there was no chance. She would never love anyone again. Ever. Love hurt too much; far too much. She was from this moment for sale. Let the buyer beware.

The glitter of a gaslight sparkled, refracted in her tears. Gischairn clucked disapprovingly. "Why are you crying, my dear?"

Scandal shrugged. "Just tired. It's been a long night."

Alex Vigneaux, encouraged by his dowager mother, called often at the Gischairn mansion. He would have been there every afternoon had Gischairn permitted it. "You must give the child room, Alex. My God, give her a chance to breathe." The old roué was sharp-tongued, bitchy with Alex, treating him more like a stable-boy than an eligible suitor.

Scandal was happy to have Alex near. When Alex visited, and they were alone, she was able to relax. He was content simply to be with her. He chatted wittily about people they both knew. He was an accomplished mimic and could express volumes in pantomime. He kept her amused, sometimes laughing aloud in the privacy of the music room, behind closed doors. He smiled when she smiled at him. He leaped to wait on her, trying to anticipate her least wish. He had tea with her, complimenting her on its piquancy, its perfect degree of warmth, the tastiness of the pecan cookies. He watched her at her water colors and praised them even when he saw they were done quickly, and inattentively. He lounged happily with her in the garden. She was not bored with him. He was like a close friend, another girl, with whom she could let down her hair, a true luxury now.

It was Alex who confirmed that there were bets being made concerning her, wagers current even in the highest social swims of the town. "Disgusting," he said. "I would call them out. But I can't duel them all." He laughed, making a face. "In fact, I'd be lucky to survive one duel."

"I don't care what they say about me. . . . What do they say?"

"Oh, they don't dare speak about you, or against you. I *would* call them out then. No, the bets are between the men. They are betting on how long it will be before someone is killed fighting over you under the suicide oaks at the old Allard Plantation."

"Just let them kill themselves. Don't you get involved. I'd miss you if you were—hurt. Truly miss you."

He smiled, and his eyes glistened. "Would you really miss me, Miss Scandal? Really?"

"As much as I could possibly care—about anyone."

"That's the nicest thing anyone has ever said to me. Perhaps the very nicest. Maybe the only nice thing . . . the only thing I believe, or care about. I do care about you, Miss Scandal, deeply."

"I know. That's why I don't want you doing something foolish . . . like fighting duels."

He sighed. "It's hard to walk the streets nowadays without being goaded into a fight. Everyone is nervous about the war—itching for trouble."

"I can't stay apart from all men forever, Alex."

"I know. I keep waiting for the day when your greedy old uncle will announce your engagement to some man rich enough to buy Louisiana and too old to carry it home."

She laughed. "Why, Alex Vigneaux, I believe you're jealous."

"Scandal, you're too fragile, too lovely and too delicate to be *auctioned* off to some old man—who meets your uncle's financial criteria."

She laughed again. "I agree. But I must marry sometime. . . . I'm getting to be an old maid, Alex."

"Don't say that. Not even in jest. You're too fine for those callus-handed, slop-booted old roughnecks. . . . Oh Scandal, I'd die—to see you married to such an old goat."

"Still, a girl must marry. And marry well."

"Oh, Scandal, don't talk about it. It makes me sick."

Against Gischairn's expressed wishes, Scandal dined with Alex Vigneaux in the loveliest of the dining salons in the St. Louis Hotel. "It won't enhance your reputation, or even pique interest in you, to be seen with a milksop like Alex, Scandal. . . . For God's sake, if you *must* be seen in public with an inappropriate escort, at least choose a *man*."

She looked at him and laughed. He met her eyes and laughed back.

She and Alex enjoyed their dinner. Despite what Gischairn had warned, she attracted all eyes, and with only Alex as her escort. There was no longer any doubt, Alex assured her. The town was overwhelmed. Not even the war caused any more talk than she. Her beauty and elegance made her famous. "I won't really be anybody," she teased, "until I'm infamous."

"Scandal, you scare me when you talk like that."

"Don't you think I'm capable of infamy?"

"Oh, Lord, I do. That's what scares me. Men worship you. They follow you around. Isn't that enough?"

"Obviously not."

Curious, attentive, hooded eyes followed her every move, the fluttering of her hands, her fingers bringing her spoon to her lips, the toss of her head when she laughed. It was as if colored and spinning spotlights played across her—though she and Alex sat apart in a small alcove near a potted palm—as if she were in the center of the room and all eyes were directed upon her.

They left the salon, walking between the tables, with hands reaching out, whispers calling, clutching. At the wide doors of the foyer, they encountered three people crossing the deep carpeting from the elevators. The man walked slightly ahead of the two women. He dragged one leg noticeably. This forced him to move awkwardly. His expensive clothing defined him as a gentleman, but his graying red-sandy hair was sun-bleached and his skin was so tanned by exposure that it appeared coarse and weather-beaten. If he was a gentleman, he was a planter, or plantation owner; he spent his life working hard, and with his hands. He didn't belong in the city. He lacked the urbanity of the Creole, either city dweller or gentleman farmer. He was about fifty, give or take a year, his face furrowed and sun-seared so his blue eyes seemed pale as washwater. Graying chin whiskers, cropped close, terminated halfway down his weathered cheeks. He was not tall but was well built, with the appearance of cruel strength under his white linen suit. He carried himself with an arrogance as if he'd been set apart by divine right and accepted his place in society with all its responsibilities, obligations and rewards. Instinctively, and from a distance, Scandal hated him because he epitomized all she abhorred in all white men.

The women walking in his wake were something else. The white woman, in her thirties, possessed a gentle beauty, a sweetness of face and manner that emanated from inner goodness. Somehow, the most imposing and interesting figure of the trio was the aged—God only knew how old she was—magnificent, heavy-breasted black woman who possessed her own dignity and strength in black silk dress and black silk scarf wrapped tightly about her cottony hair.

Scandal would have passed them without a second glance, even though the man hesitated, his eyes widening. He stared at her as if she were the ghost of someone he knew. He smiled, his lips parted, and he almost spoke to her before he realized his mistake and closed his mouth, looking away, embarrassed.

Meantime, Scandal heard Alex catch his breath at her side and exclaim joyously, "Why, Miss Augusta. Miss Augusta. How good to see you."

Alex strode forward and the white woman, recognizing him, smiled in greeting. She put out her arms and they embraced. The black woman's face broadened into a smile, showing her teeth and crinkling her eyes in pockets of fat. The man hesitated, then stopped, slouching with his game leg extended slightly, plainly impatient. And yet he could not pull his gaze from Scandal's face.

"Scandal, let me introduce you to Miss Augusta," Alex began, and the woman interrupted.

"You'd better let me introduce myself, Alex. My name and my whole life has changed since I saw you last! I'm now Mrs. Hammond Maxwell. Of Falconhurst Plantation. This is my husband, Hammond Maxwell, and our dear servant—without whom I, for one, could not operate at Falconhurst—our own Miz Lucretia Borgia."

Scandal felt weak, afraid she would faint. The familiar names rang and spun in her mind. Hammond Maxwell. Falconhurst Plantation. Miz Lucretia Borgia. Names from her own dim past, the lost time that Ellen had related to Portia and Portia had passed on to her.

Scandal's gaze raked Hammond Maxwell's weathered face. No wonder he thought he recognized her! Did you think you saw Ellen, your former bed wench, you white bastard? Is that what you see when you look at me, your guilty memories of my mother?

She was aware that Maxwell's hated blue eyes were still staring at her, but she ignored him, beyond a brief nod of her head when Alex introduced her.

"That's sho' an unusual name, honey," Miz Lucretia Borgia said.

Hammond Maxwell's voice slashed across hers. "You needn't speak, Lucretia Borgia, unless you're spoken to."

"Yes suh," she said and lapsed into silence. But like Hammond Maxwell she couldn't take her gaze from Scandal's face either. Glancing at her, Scandal saw the liquid black eyes deep in tears. Scandal felt her own eyes burn suddenly, and she looked quickly away.

She heard Hammond speaking, insisting that he had known Miss Gischairn somewhere. "She jus' looks that familiar I swear I'd known her," he persisted.

Augusta Maxwell laughed, her voice sweet and cool. "Miss Gischairn is the fresh young beauty every man dreams of in his youth—that is where you knew her, Hammond."

Scandal was thankful when Alex and Augusta Hammond had

finally exchanged all those little pleasantries and bits of gossip passed like trivial coins between old friends. Hammond limped away, leading the small procession. Miz Lucretia Borgia hesitated a moment. Her eyes tear-brimmed, she said, "You sho' am a lovely chile. Lovely. Yo' mammy mus' be mighty proud of you. . . . I do hope you is happy, miss. And take care of yourself."

Scandal's throat felt tight. She smiled, reached out and squeezed the old woman's hand with all her strength, feeling the re-returned pressure. "I will. I promise. . . . And you too . . . you take care."

"Lawsy, I will, chile . . . but it don't mattah about me no mo'. I old in the bones and long in the tooth and 'bout played out my string on dis yere side ob de Jordan."

"Don't say that. You're young. You'll always be young."

Hammond stopped at the door and swung around, bracing himself on his rigid leg. "Come on, Lucretia Borgia, you stop annoying the young lady."

Lucretia Borgia nodded. "Yassah, Masta Ham, honey. I comin'. I comin' right away. Fast as my ole bones will move me."

Scandal stood as if rooted to the floor until Miz Lucretia Borgia had gone through the thick glass doors and disappeared in the darkness. She shivered and clutched Alex's arm tightly. "I want to go home," she said.

In the cab she crouched crying softly into Alex's white handkerchief. "Please, Scandal, tell me what I've done."

"You haven't done anything. I'm just—so unhappy."

"Scandal. Dearest Scandal. Don't. I can't stand it when you're unhappy like this. It tears me up inside."

"Then you'd better get away from me. You'd better stay away from me. I'm not a simpering little doll. I'm made of moods. Hundreds of moods, and most of them miserable. Just like this."

"I know you are, Scandal. I know. I do know about your moods. And I love them all. Each one hundred of them."

28

"You won't believe this," General Butler said. "But I attended this piddling little gathering for just one reason, Miss Scandal—

to get a look at you. I've heard more about you than I have about any other ten women in town. Now that I've seen you, I'll say this. For all their boasting, they didn't do you justice."

"Thank you, general." Scandal lowered her eyes becomingly, if hastily; she was afraid he would read her distaste in their black depths.

For Julien-Jacques Gischain's prophecy had come true—New Orleans had fallen, and the uniforms about the city were now blue.

She tilted her head again and said, teasingly, "I'm afraid you're not very sincere, General Butler. You're trying to turn my head. I might have believed you, in my naiveté, but you call this a *little* gathering. Why, general, this is one of the soirées for which New Orleans is famous the world over."

He laughed harshly. "Well, if it is, I'm damned if I understand what all the fuss is about."

Benjamin F. Butler was the signature appended to the hated regulations set down for the conquered city. He had been a lawyer and prominent Democratic Party leader in Lowell, Massachusetts. He was a stout man with pink skin and squinting blue eyes. His high-pitched voice carried over other sounds in a grating and unyielding way. He laid down the law—the new military law of occupation—to the businessmen of the city. Rumors said General Butler set out his first day in command to make a fortune in various black markets and favors-for-sale. He ordered federal boats to protect his brother while he traded in contraband goods with the Confederates. But the women of the town hated him most—and most emotionally. When four young New Orleans rebels pulled down the Union flag from the roof of the Mint on Esplanade Avenue and dragged it through the streets to the cheers of onlookers, Butler ordered the men hunted down and hanged. When Union troops complained that New Orleans women treated them with contempt on the downtown streets, Butler issued his most famous edict of all—one which exploded all over the United States and Europe and was protested to President Lincoln after being debated in the English Parliament—his "Woman Order." Any woman in New Orleans who insulted a Union soldier would be treated in a fittingly contemptuous manner by the soldier. Mayor Monroe lost his office when he protested the order. General Butler had the mayor not only removed from office, but imprisoned, for protesting. One would think a sensitive man would know he was hated by the subjugated people; if Butler knew, he remained totally insensitive to it. "I'm doing my job," he said. "You people got to understand that."

Scandal stood on the wide circular staircase with its rococo gilt banisters overlooking an enormous dance floor, awed despite the fact she'd been here many times in the past year. She loved the glittering beauty of the gold-and-blue dome and the gently whispering glass chandelier that tossed out fragmented lights like confetti across the crowds of handsome people in their best formal outfits. For her, raised in Wilkes Corners, where a fireplace or a smoke-blackened lantern furnished the best light one saw after dusk, the splendor of this majestic hall would always remain breathtaking. She could not forgive the general for denigrating it, even when she understood he was driven to disparage everything that smacked of the Old South's glory and grandeur. Or perhaps he ran everything down to elevate his own estimation of himself. In either case, she found it offensive.

A salon ensemble played for dancing. At tables or on chairs along the polished walls sat the citizens of New Orleans who for one reason or another could not boycott functions which their hated conquerors would attend, who sympathized with the Union cause—and there were many of these—or who, like Scandal, refused to give up the last pleasures of an increasingly difficult life just because Yankees would be present. "As soon sit down with a nigger," was the answer most New Orleans citizens gave when invited to these parties.

Julien-Jacques Gischairn had retreated to his summer home on the north shore of Lake Pontchartrain. He took with him three of the younger male servants, leaving Scandal in the St. Charles Avenue mansion with a serving staff of six. "What would I do stuck away in the woods all summer?" Scandal asked when he invited her to flee the town with him. She had spent the previous summer there with him, while still under the rule of her tutors, but was unwilling to cut short the season of her triumph.

"If you survive this summer in New Orleans, you'll be begging to get away next year." He gazed at her with a coyote grin. "You'll see. Those loutish Yankees everywhere make life in my city impossible, but any summer is impossible here unless you're a native old webfooted mud-bug. Do you know, child, it rains *fifty-eight* inches a year, and most of it in the summer? Mosquitoes like egrets. Oh, you think I exaggerate. Just you wait until the drainage ditches overflow and stagnate. And Bronze John—that fearful malaria epidemic!—God knows I pray you're spared that. The rain and the mosquitoes and the soured ditches are enough without seeing people vomit black blood and then fall dead in it. Oh, I've seen that. Too often. I always got out even before the Yankees came. Now, you couldn't keep me here."

"Have a good time, Uncle Julien." Scandal kissed him lightly. "I'll see you in the fall—unless I die in an epidemic or marry some millionaire in the meantime."

He laughed. "Do keep your eye on the main goal, girl—an advantageous marriage. That's what it's all about. Don't waste your time on Alex Vigneaux, and for God's sake don't get in-involved with any Yankee, no matter how high his rank. You might as well commit suicide if you marry a Yankee. If you had a love affair with a Negro, it wouldn't damage your reputation nearly as badly."

General Butler's unwavering gaze fixed on her breasts startled her. He didn't care that they were the center of all attention. His squinting blue eyes boldly undressed her in this crowded salon. There was nothing flattering about his lecherous staring; it was insulting, as if he called her a whore in his high-pitched strident voice. When reaction and nerves caused her nipples to harden and stand erect against the translucent emerald-green fabric of her watered-silk gown, she hated herself as much as she despised him.

The general was grinning crookedly. "You can thank me for rescuing you from an evening of boredom."

"Oh?"

"Yes. It must bore hell out of a looker like you to simper and smile at these Southern milksops. Good to be around a man, eh? I'm quite smitten with you, young woman. I look for the best. I buy only the best, no matter what it costs me."

She caught her breath, repulsed and enraged, then forced herself to smile. "You could never afford me, General Butler."

He laughed and shrugged his heavy shoulders, squared by epaulets. "Maybe. Maybe not. But it's reassuring to know you *are* for sale."

"Oh, I'm for sale all right—"

"All you Southern trollops are—"

"—but you couldn't afford to meet the price."

"When I want something, missy, I have ways of bringing the price down. I finally pay what I think merchandise is worth." He stared at her cleavage until she felt his eyes like crawling things on the bared flesh of her décolletage. He laughed again. "Why are you nervous? You must be used to men's attentions by now."

"Few gentlemen treat me as callously as this, general."

"Aw hell, sweetie. I'm just having some fun." He laughed. "Up where I come from, little lady, we know what we want, we go after it. We don't beat around the bush like your weak-kneed milksops down here."

"Those milksops have been giving your people trouble at Bull Run and at Shiloh, haven't they, general?" she inquired.

His face went gray, his mouth pressed into a tight line. Then he laughed and took her arm. "Hell, little lady, we'll be fightin' our own civil war here in a minute. Let's watch the natives dance on their own graves."

Clutching her by the elbow, he led her to the entrance of the ballroom. Standing on the top stair, still gripping her arm, he said, "You need a few lessons in military tactics, missy. Let me tell you, it ain't what happened up at Bull Run or at Shiloh. It's what's happening here. Right here in New Orleans. In the gut of the South's underbelly.

"I can tell you this, missy. We foretold the end of this war within the first week after them snivelin' rebel bastards fired on Fort Sumter. Why, you talk about Shiloh. The rebs just held us up a little there. And only a few days later, the United States Navy under Commodore David Farragut stood out there before New Orleans and liberated it from rebel control.

"Some hotheaded sons of bitches here looted the piers and burned blockaded cotton. They stole hams, rum, liquors, anything they could carry. But even God in heaven was against them scum. Rain put out the fires on the wharves during the night, and I come in and restored order.

"Don't you see, missy, the Union has hit the rebels where they live—in the gut? The city that controls the Mississippi is controlled by the Union Army! We bombarded Fort Jackson. Then Farragut sailed right past them river forts—seventeen ships in a single column of three divisions. Fourteen ships made it and sank eight rebel vessels, including the ram *Manassas*. This here city surrendered the next day. So that's what we did. We showed them rebs we could take their most important port—deep in the belly of their own land! Their most protected city was vulnerable, and it fell! By God, missy, we shoved a red-hot poker right up the rebel rectum."

Scandal covered her face with her fragile fan, concealing her smile and her contempt, but widening her eyes in a look he accepted as reprimand—we can never know what others think, only what we believe they're thinking. Scandal reproved him gently. "Why, General Butler, such an uncouth way to talk—in the presence of a lady—even if she is only a Southern lady."

He grinned, contrite. "Forgive me, dear little lady . . . war itself is uncouth. And I'm afraid the men who fight it can become uncouth, no matter what they were before. War makes beasts of men, ma'am. I pray you can forgive me." No matter what he said, she saw that he was captivated. He said, confidentially, "In July, Commodore Farragut will be honored by the United States Congress and be made a rear admiral. I plan to give a reception for the admiral that will really put this town on the map. I'm planning a court of the loveliest ladies we can find down here for him—and by God, I want you to say you'll lead that parade."

Scandal was spared the necessity of replying by the voice of a bronze-red-haired woman who had for some moments been standing at Scandal's elbow and now stepped forward, simpering up at General Butler. Scandal's mind went blank. She'd been introduced to this woman. She had forgotten her totally; she could not for the life of her recall the woman's name, and yet she'd known for some seconds the intruder waited for her to introduce her to the military commander. Panic completely scrambled Scandal's thoughts. If she'd ever known the woman's name it entirely eluded her now.

"What parade is that, general?" the red-haired woman asked, smiling up at him. She pinched Scandal's elbow. "Well, dear, aren't you going to introduce me to the most vital and attractive man in the hall?"

"Oh, I'm so sorry," Scandal said. "I've forgotten your name." She heard the woman's intake of breath, like the hiss of an asp. "I was delaying—only trying to remember."

"We all know what you were *trying* to do, my dear. That's quite obvious. You were *trying* to keep the interesting and virile men to yourself by monopolizing all their time and excluding other women they might find more attractive."

Scandal stared at the smartly attired woman, helpless and enraged at the same time. She realized suddenly there were persons she could hate more savagely than white men: their white women. Obviously this overpainted, brittle-hard bitch wanted something of the commandant. People who could exist without his patronage stayed away from functions he attended; the others panted after him, as this woman did. Scandal spoke in a soft but deadly tone. "Well. I said I'm sorry. Now I am truly sorry."

The woman's sharp voice pierced like a lance. "Yes, my dear?"

General Butler laughed. He enjoyed this bitter byplay between the two Southern belles, with himself as the prize. He glanced at the intruder, a tall, slender woman, with the memory of fading beauty enveloping her, and a glassy hardness that seemed somehow accented by the diamond tiara she wore like a crown on her dark-red hair.

"Now, ladies." General Butler said. "Don't fight over me. There's enough for both of you."

"I am Manon Levesque," the red-haired woman said with a steely smile. "Mrs. Louis Levesque. Louis is head of the Sugar Exchange, you know." She refused to look at Scandal, this incident a slight she could neither forgive nor forget.

"Oh yes, Mrs. Levesque. I've met your husband. Tonight I'm busy with this young lady, but if there's something urgent you want to see me about, why don't you make an appointment at my office, any day next week?"

Manon Levesque sucked in her breath audibly. She retreated a step. She glared at the general, raked her gaze across Scandal's face. Manon's eyes glittered with hatred. She turned on her heel and strode away across the tiled flooring, her heels clicking, cheeks pallid, fists knotted, her mind already seething and plotting vengeance. . . .

The St. Louis Hotel doormen bowed and smiled, leaping to open the tonneau door of the Gischairn carriage and help Scandal alight.

"Evenin', Miss Scandal," the majordomo said, a large black man with a wide and toothsome smile. "You do looks *très chic* tonight."

"Thank you, Joseph." Scandal extended her gloved hand and Joseph gently assisted her from the carriage. "Don't let my coach get too far away. I hate to walk even half a block on these dangerous streets these days."

"Don't you fret, Miss Scandal. We protect you from these yere Yankee hooligans. With our life if we have to."

One would not have believed the city starved, that only the summer warmth averted disaster for thousands. Hardships of every sort plagued the citizenry. But the street and hotel blazed with lights, with people in their finest—as if the war itself were only an unconfirmed rumor.

The Northern blockade was taking its toll on New Orleans commerce. Not only were the Gulf Coast and the huge Mississippi controlled by Farragut's ships, but all inland waterways as well. Railroads were taxed beyond capacity, and when equipment failed or broke down, no repair parts could be had. Soon the simplest items were in short supply. Wharves along the river rotted. The water lapped over unprotected breaks in the levee. Cargo warehouses stood as empty as a church on Tuesday, locks rusted and windows thick with grime. Food was scarce and prices inflated beyond reason. General Butler's troops were fed first. They ate well. Friends of the general could buy food at black-market prices, but they *could* eat. Others scrounged, or went hungry. Repeatedly, General Butler sent word to St. Charles Avenue that he would "that day" call upon Miss Scandal Gischairn. Scandal managed to stall him, sending back word that as long as her uncle was not in the house as host, her reputation would be irreparably compromised were she to succumb to the temptation he offered. She did not know how long she could deter him, and the invitation to General Butler's reception for Admiral Farragut was a "command appearance." She had been chosen, her invitation assured her, as one of the sixteen young debutantes who would form the celebrated rear admiral's "court" for the evening.

Scandal's gown of pink silk gauze, low-necked, short-sleeved, trimmed with white lace and satin piping, was old. She'd worn it numerous times before; but "making do" was the accepted and popular course these days. She was lovely enough to turn heads when she entered the glittering ballroom.

The first person she saw was General Butler. He was surrounded and restrained by Manon Levesque and several other women and could not thrust his way immediately to where Scandal paused, but his eyes struck against her with almost a physical impact—of cold spittle. She shivered slightly and turned away.

Louis Levesque came at once begging a dance. Scandal let him write his name on her dance card. Across his narrow shoulders she saw Alex Vigneaux grin at her impishly.

The ladies of the court were quietly summoned to the dais. A hush fell over the room. General Butler made a high-pitched, impassioned introduction of the guest of honor. Rear Admiral Farragut appeared on the dais. The band struck up "The Star Spangled Banner." Everyone in the room stood, but the silence spread, tomblike. Farragut's response to the ovation was brief. He reminded them that, like them, he was Southern-born. But unlike some, his loyalties were with his nation. He hoped all would join with him to bring this savage fighting to an early end. At the rear of the hall someone started singing "Dixie," weeping, and was wrestled from the area by Union soldiers.

As if there had been no disturbance, General Butler introduced Madame Louis Levesque, who would present the lovely young belles providing the admiral's court.

Scandal stood among the sixteen young women, like an orchid among daisies. She felt General Butler's eyes on her, anguished with need. She kept her head tilted, did not look at him. As each young lady was introduced by Manon Levesque, the orchestra played an appropriate theme, and the belle was joined by her escort for the evening and promenaded to a place beside the smiling rear admiral.

The group around Scandal dwindled. For some reason she could not isolate, panic fluttered like bees in her stomach. Something was wrong, though she could not yet say what. Her first intimation was in the chilled way Manon Levesque glanced past her each time she read an introduction.

When the fifteenth young woman was introduced, the orchestra played a love song popular that year and she was paraded to meet the admiral and take her place in the colorful court. Scandal stood alone, her heart slugging, empty-bellied. She saw Alex grinning at her, waiting to escort her to the site of honor at the admiral's side.

Suddenly, Manon Levesque turned her back, signaled the orchestra to strike up music for dancing. Manon walked away, going down the steps from the dais to where General Butler stood, stunned, mouth agape. Scandal stood on the dais alone, ignored by Manon, snubbed.

The ugly thought raged through her mind. Revenge. Manon had planned this moment precisely, almost like a military maneuver. Scandal was snubbed, made to look ridiculous, no matter what happened now. General Butler might well silence the orchestra, as he was attempting to do, but the audience got the message: Scandal Gischairn was beneath the notice of Manon Levesque. The woman had had her revenge for Scandal's slight in being unable to recall her name.

Scandal shuddered, looking around. Alex strode towards her, but the last thing she wanted was anyone's sympathy in this moment. She could not bear for these people to patronize her, to smile behind their hands, to laugh in the next week at the memory of her standing like some impostor or intruder on that dais. She turned, heeling around, and then she was running, pushing her way through the crowds. She did not slow down until she raced out on the walk, the night wind from the river chilled against her face. Joseph ran to her. "Miss Scandal, you all right?"

She managed to control her voice. "My carriage, Joseph. Please. I want to go home."

Scandal pressed back in the dark tonneau of the cab. She seethed with rage. She saw clearly that Manon Levesque had been plotting vengeance since that first night she had felt slighted before General Butler. Not even the fact that she had since ingratiated herself and entered the general's most intimate coterie had lessened her need for revenge against Scandal. I know how she feels, Scandal thought, because damn her, I won't rest until that painted bitch pays for this night.

Jumbled, disconnected thoughts spun in her mind. She would go at once to Julien's place on Lake Pontchartrain. No. She could not. She knew better. Julien would not take her in, in defeat. Sardonically, he would send her back here to face her adversaries, to laugh at them, mock them, as he did. Well, dammit, right now she didn't feel like laughing.

Her eyes filled with tears. Rage boiled up inside her. She sat, fists clenched at her sides. The clop of hooves, the creaking of thoroughbraces, the crack of the driver's whip were unreal. Only the savage, arrhythmic pound of her heart had reality for her. Lights from street lamps sprayed wanly across her for an instant, then were abruptly gone, plunging her into darkness. All she could really think was that she wanted Wade. Oh, Wade, where are you? Why am I in this terrible place without you?

She entered the silent old house but did not even consider going to bed. Falling across a mattress to weep was not her style.

She walked into her bedroom, deep in thought, coldly occupied with angered thoughts raging and wheeling inside her mind. She undressed slowly, staring at herself in her full-length mirror, the lights glittering and gamboling across the vales and shadows and planes of her lithe gold-tinted body.

Purposefully, almost instinctively, at least without fully conscious volition, she chose her laciest, most revealingly transparent and fragile silk nightgown. She didn't know precisely why she did this, only that it was meet and right so to do. The pale-beige material did not conceal the pink eminence at her breast, or the dainty dark triangle at her thighs, rather accentuated and highlighted them.

The gown draped along the symmetry of her body, sensuous to sight and touch, and she nodded as if satisfied about something. Abstractedly, she dipped the glass stick into a small bottle of musky cologne, dabbed it at her ear lobes, along the slender pillar of her throat, between her gently rising breasts. Then she selected a matching robe of translucent silk from its hanger and slipped her arms into it. Puffed shoulders of lace, peekaboo bodice of eyelet laces, a soft belt to gather the whispering fabric at her waist while, rather than closing it, severing the lapels across her bust, accenting the sensual beauty and undress of the ensemble.

Wearing soft tan slippers, she prowled the house. She did not admit consciously either that she planned any course of action at all, or that she expected anyone to visit at this hour of the night. If she told herself anything at all, it was that she was simply too tense, too upset, too enraged to sleep.

She crouched in a great wingback overstuffed chair in Julien's library, with a double bourbon over ice, uncut by water.

She frowned, lines creasing between her perfectly arched brows. On the screen behind her eyes she saw Manon Levesque's face in extreme closeup, with all its flaws and painfully concealed betrayers of age. She watched that hard sleek face disintegrate, cut to ribbons by her nails. Scandal smiled tautly, seeing that taut, aging face, ashen with fear, the terrorized eyes staring helplessly up at her. She saw Manon in hell.

Angrily, she discarded the fantasy. It wouldn't do at all. It was entirely too easy on Manon. She would have to learn to hate more efficiently.

When the bell sounded at the front door, Scandal remained unmoved, neither surprised nor disturbed. She sent the butler, protesting, off to his quarters and walked coldly and deliberately across the foyer to answer it herself, her chin tilted, delicate of line but determined of set, her ebony eyes as chilled as ever Manon Levesque's had been.

"I learn from you, Manon," she said under her breath.

She knew who her guest would be, even before she opened the door, but she pretended surprise, shock and some disapproval, mixed and diluted with unseemly and ill-concealed pleasure. "Why, M'sieu Levesque," she said, smiling and pouting at once and clutching at the silk belt rather than the lapels of her revealing robe. "How surprised I am—"

"And pleased, I hope?"

She glanced past him, biting at her underlip. God, Julien would be proud of me, she thought. "Isn't Madame Levesque with you?"

"I thought it best to come alone, under the circumstances. I hope you won't mind too much."

"It's so late. . . . I thought perhaps it was Alex Vigneaux, come to commiserate with me in my—unhappiness."

"I had to come, Miss Scandal." The thin, balding, pot-bellied tycoon stood disconsolate in evening dress, dance pumps and opera cape, holding black silk high hat in both sweated hands. "I am so deeply sorry—about this evening."

"I *was* treated shabbily." Scandal's black eyes brimmed with tears, which she turned aside prettily to conceal. She let him go on standing on the stoop. She held the door slightly ajar—as if on guard against him, and herself.

He sighed, anguished. "I had to come at once and tell you how sorry I am, Miss Scandal. How desolated." His voice hardened, though he continued to smile obsequiously. "How enraged I am at Manon. She has always been selfish and cruel. This is too much. Entirely too much. She has gone too far this time. I don't know if I can ever forgive her this latest indecorous behavior, this unmitigated injury done you. . . . I regret it with all my heart, Scandal." He glanced uncomfortably about the night yard, his coach waiting in deep shafts of shadow. "Please, may I come in? Only for a moment?"

Scandal bit her lip ingenuously, troubled, yet obviously tempted beyond her poor fragile feminine will. "Oh, Louis. I would love to ask you in. But—you know—my uncle is not here. . . . You know how people are. A virile, worldly man like you—I wouldn't have a shred of reputation left."

"Oh, Scandal. I'm old enough to be your father. A man brokenhearted by the brutal misbehavior of his wife—wanting somehow to make amends." His words were decorous enough, but his small eyes in suet sacks of fluid riveted themselves to the fragile écru edging and peekaboo eyelets disclosed at her bosom by errant lapels.

Hesitatingly prettily for some seconds while the aging executive danced from one foot to the other nervously, Scandal nodded at last.

She opened the door and allowed Levesque to enter the foyer. Here she hesitated, as if unwilling, despite her inner wishes, to let him enter farther. She watched him, her eyes brimming with tears and her lips quivering. She had never looked so young, so alone, so vulnerable, so destroyed by casual cruelty. And all the time behind those stricken eyes, she was thinking, shooting fish in a barrel. It was like shooting fish in a barrel. Less than sporting, but permissible if the fish insisted upon jumping into the barrel, wasn't it?

She drew in a ragged breath, as if unable to speak. Stricken, Levesque threw his tall hat and spotless gloves to the polished floor behind him and pulled her against him. He touched her gently, consolingly, patting and whispering, as he might with child frightened and alone in the dark, but even through his concern, she felt the thud of his aging heart, the stiffening at his fly.

"You were so good to come," she whispered. "I never felt so—alone. So abandoned. So hurt inside and helpless. People will laugh at me. I don't see how I can go on like this."

His arms tightened on her. "Oh, Scandal, if there's anything in this world I can do to make up this beastly injury Manon has done you—"

"There's nothing." She shook her head and wept forlornly. "Nothing, Louis, except your friendship . . . and of course that's impossible."

"Impossible?" He shuddered convulsively. "Why?"

"You are—her—husband."

"Oh, Scandal. You're the one harmed. The innocent one badly injured. How could I turn my back on you until this grievous wrong is redressed?"

"Oh, Louis, you are so kind. So kind—and so strong."

She slipped her arm lightly about him—in a daughterly fashion—and led him toward the living room. After a brief hesitation, Levesque put his own arm about her waist, careful that his touch could not be misinterpreted. He was already trapped in some inner confusion because of the totally unusual way his aging parts responded to Scandal's young beauty.

Inside the living room, she paused. She turned her head and fixed her tear-drowned eyes upon him. "Oh, I do thank God for good and kindly friends like you, Louis." She wheeled half away from him suddenly as if she'd said too much, could no longer trust her own emotions.

She heard Levesque gasp. Her turning had thrust his hand over her breast. For a long beat she remained rigid, as if shocked and overwhelmed. She felt Levesque's hand tremble on the supple rise of her silk-shielded bosom. She sensed delightedly the battle waging inside him. He wanted to lurch away, apologizing, and yet the lure of those shapely globes was too exciting, too bewitching, the meat of a thousand orgasmic dreams of this past year. He could only stand, benumbed, gripping the soft, resilient fullness in his paralyzed palm.

"Oh my God, Scandal," he whispered finally in agonized delight when she did not lunge away from him in rage. "You are so beautiful. The very touch—enchanting."

She pulled away now, rigid. Her voice chilled. "M'sieu Levesque, you must not—take advantage—of my weakness. You must be strong. For both of us. We are alone in this house. . . . You must protect me—from myself—as well as from you."

"Oh, Scandal," he whispered, reaching for her, "you have nothing to fear from me. Nothing ever to fear from me. You know I would never hurt you. I would do anything for you. I want only to be permitted to protect you—"

"From myself," she repeated softly, feeling him tremble and glow, his body burning feverishly.

He drew her to the couch and sat beside her on it, keeping his arm about her as if to protect her from unseen dragons. When Scandal sat down, the robe parted even more, falling back not only from her bosom, but from her upper thighs and belted waist. She sniffled, too overcome with grief to notice how delicately and intimately her body was exposed to his anguished gaze.

"Oh, Scandal. I regret that you're hurt. I never want you hurt. You're enchanting. Adorable. Beauty unlike anything I've ever seen. . . . Oh, God, I can't get you out of my mind." His hand touched her silken leg above her knee and slid involuntarily upward, dragging the fragile fabric with it.

She shivered prettily. "You mustn't do this, Louis . . . you'll sweep me off my feet."

He tried to laugh self-deprecatingly, but he was overwhelmed by the heat and supple loveliness of her thighs. "Would God I could—"

She shook her head, sinking back against the couch, breath quickening. "But it's not fair—you're a man of the world and I—"

His breath seared her face. "You're the loveliest creature on God's earth. Look at me . . . I'm shaking all over. Like a boy. Like a young boy. What a fool you must think me."

"I? A young and innocent girl think you—a rich and powerful man like you—foolish? I'm awed by you, Louis. I always have been. But I mustn't let you do this." Somehow he had wadded the gown under his hand until his fingers probed at the bare flesh of her inner thighs. "Oh, you are too strong—too forceful." She bit back a rage to savage laughter. "I can't let you use me—you a worldly man—and then throw me aside."

"Never." He looked as if he might weep in anguished protest against this unfair charge, but his fingers pressed harder between her legs. "Oh my God, never."

Suddenly, she was pressed down under him, in his arms. His hands went over her like fevered talons, thrusting aside robe and gown as if he could no longer endure even this fragile transparency between her body and his avid gaze. He drew her body fiercely upon his hardness. His hips bucked involuntarily. He gasped for breath like an old Wilkes Corners mudfish out of water. She lay shocked by the ferocity of his assault. She hadn't even realized men of his age retained those juices which boiled in response to girls as young as she. His dry mouth kissed her lips, her throat, her jawline, her cheeks, any part of her exposed anatomy he could reach while holding her imprisoned. She trembled in violent revulsion, a quivering he mistook for passion reciprocated.

"Oh dear God," he whispered, throat taut. "I've got to have you, Scandal. Now. . . . Oh, Scandal, I never knew it would be like this—though I've dreamed of nothing else since the first time I saw you."

"But you are a distinguished and aristocratic elder. Old enough to be my father. I can't believe you want me—"

"Believe it. Believe it."

"—and your wife is so much lovelier than I—"

"Oh never. Never."

"—though I hate her. Still, I can't let you do this."

"Manon is nothing, nothing to me." He panted against her face, forcing her with one grasping fist to hold her hips still under his thrusting body. "Why, Manon became involved with this General Butler. Ostensibly, she told me, to ensure my retaining my connections and place as head of the Sugar Exchange. But he has become her whole life. I don't care. I don't care, Scandal! Because all these months, I've been able to think only of you. . . . Let me love you, Scandal. Let me hold your body to mine, your lovely naked body to mine—"

"You mustn't talk this way."

"I can't talk any other way . . . I can hardly talk at all."

"I thought you cared for me—respected me."

He moaned deep inside himself. "I do, Scandal."

"And yet you want to use me—"

"No, God, Scandal, no. I want to love you. To show you how much I love you—"

"You want to use me and discard me. My uncle has warned me."

He sobbed helplessly. "What does that limp-wristed old nancy know about what *men* feel for women?"

Scandal tried ineffectually to draw away. "He says love is love —even between two people of the same sex."

He winced, shaking his head. "Disgusting. . . . But I don't

want to talk about that old maid. Believe me. Trust me, Scandal. Everything that old lace-drawers has told you is wrong. A man—even an older man like me—especially an experienced older man like me—can love devotedly, loyally, unselfishly."

With sudden and surprising strength she wrested free of him. Levesque half fell from the couch. He grasped at her, crying out. She shook her head, her face flushed, though she did forget to straighten her gown over her exposed thighs or to cover her breast, which glowed pinkly above the lace écru edging of he bodice.

"You mustn't do this. You mustn't take advantage of me like this—as much as I might want it. You must not . . . my uncle isn't here—"

"Thank God," he whispered fervently.

"I cannot—I must not—let you come in here and use me—like a—trollop, just because I'm deeply hurt inside—and helpless against your strength—and virility. I must not. I know you are a gentleman. Oh, you are, aren't you? And I like to think I'm a lady, at least most of the time."

"My God, Scandal, you are! I wouldn't love you like this if you were not! You are the loveliest, gentlest lady of them all. But I am a man, Scandal . . . I am driven beyond my reason . . . I've got to have you . . . oh, Scandal, let me. Please let me." He grasped her hand and pressed it down over the prominence bulging at his fly. "I'll do anything to prove I love you. Anything. I'll do anything you ask to prove how deeply I love you . . . you have only to ask."

She drew a deep breath, wounded. "I'd want nothing—"

"I want to give you something. Ask me! The impossible! Anything! Let me prove my devotion."

"You would be paying me—"

"Oh, Scandal, no! Not a payment! The farthest thought from my mind! A gift to prove how deeply I love you. Something you want, Scandal. *Anything* you might want."

She stared at him, all wide-eyed innocence. "Anything?"

He nursed at her exposed breast a moment, then looked up panting. "Name anything; anything I can possibly do for you, I will do."

"No. I don't want to demand—more than you might want to give."

"I want your demand to hurt. It's got to hurt so you are convinced of my adoration and respect and love for you."

She lay still for a long time, letting his trembling, sweated fingers explore the heat of her femininity. She felt ill, but she was exultant in her triumph and she forced herself to smile and part her legs just enough.

"Anything, Scandal," he persisted. "I swear it as God lives. Anything."

"I want her tiara," she said at last, as if speaking reluctantly.

"What?"

"Manon. I want her diamond tiara."

"Her diamond tiara?"

"She owes it to me."

"Oh dear God."

"She's hurt me deeply. I want *her* to hurt. As I hurt." She pulled suddenly away from him and stood up. He stared up at her, wild-eyed, from the couch. "You may come back—with the tiara."

"Scandal! I'll buy you—"

"Manon's tiara. Or don't come back." Scandal shrugged. "I told you it would cost you more than you would want to pay."

Scandal made a late, dramatic entrance at the reception given in honor of General Butler by St John (everyone pronounced it Sin-Jin, which was somehow appropriate) and Carlotta Oberle. Oberle headed the Cotton Exchange. No matter what it had cost, General Butler had made possible shipment of cotton through New Orleans to the mills in New England. St. John Oberle and Carlotta remained in excellent financial condition, though most of the parish existed at starvation levels. Scandal, along with most of the town, knew that Oberle supported a quadroon mistress named Isabel, who lived in the manner of a princess. Rumor also persisted that Isabel had a fortune stashed away in Cuban banks. When St. John Oberle lavished money on her for new dresses, Isabel bought bargains in Congo Square and banked the difference. Isabel might well have been one of the richest women in New Orleans. No one knew if Carlotta suspected her husband's arrangement with his quadroon mistress, but if she knew, Carlotta hid her emotions. She, like most of her friends, was a member of the most sophisticated and worldly social clique in town. This was the compelling reason why Scandal had chosen this fête for her first appearance in public since the heart-breaking debacle at the hands of Manon Levesque during the reception for Admiral Farragut.

Scandal heard the whispers race ahead of her into the salon like a fire in a field. It was more than her appearing in public again—it was her appearance itself!

She swept in through the doors held wide for her by admiring servants, wearing a floor-length red cape and beneath it a daringly cut red gown and red slippers. The form-fitting gown was without decoration, embellishment or frill. Scandal had been able to get material to have it made only after the most discouraging setbacks. Only her distant—and she managed still to keep him at arm's length, even while promising so much more—friendship with General Butler made acquisition of the materials possible at all.

She walked with her head high, taking long steps and swinging an unusual but trend-setting matching tote bag. When she checked her cape, she removed from the tote bag a diamond tiara. Glancing in a mirror, she placed the tiara at a rakish angle on her head. It gave her a go-to-hell look, with meaning she knew would not be lost on the sophisticated company dancing in that brilliantly glowing ballroom.

Getting Manon Levesque's beloved tiara had consumed a few days of time, but it had not presented any of the difficulties present in acquiring the red material for her gown, for example. She had merely told Louis Levesque the price for spending one night in her bed: his wife's prized diamond tiara. Then she had let his fiery hungers make the decision for him.

It had required four days of agonizing, rationalizing, suffering and planning before Louis returned with Manon's tiara wrapped in newspapers. He had staged a bungled robbery—the window was broken from the inside and nothing taken but the tiara—and had consoled the brokenhearted Manon by promising to buy her another when the war ended, when the blockade was lifted.

Rain raged the night Louis brought the tiara to Scandal. She had warned him that when he came with the tiara to spend the night in her bed—she did not even bother to say *if* he came—he was to come stealthily into the garden and hide in the carriage house. Her reputation was at stake. He must call to her from the carriage house and she would permit him to enter through a side door.

She let him stand an hour in the rain. The carriage house was securely bolted—as she had known it would be. Since Yankee soldiers and prowling looters wandered across the face of the city, nothing was safe unless it was triple-bolted. She had stood, hidden behind a curtain, and watched Louis wait patiently in the thunder and lightning and drenching downpour. When he finally was sodden, she allowed him in, pretending sympathy and distress that she had slept so soundly she had not heard him.

She'd tossed the tiara aside as if it had no value for her now and taken him in her arms. He was so old! It was disgusting! But it was quickly over. Not even a pimply-faced boy came to a climax so suddenly and totally. Naked, he had slumped on her mattress then and slept, snoring. She'd wakened him at five the next morning and sent him out again into the persisting rain. She had not even permitted him to kiss her again.

When Scandal walked into the ballroom wearing the revealing red gown and the tiara tilted rakishly on her head, dancers faltered. Even the music ceased for a beat and then resumed. But nothing was the same. Somehow a nightmarish quality flooded the brilliant room. People whispered, smiled and then laughed. Dancing with General Butler, Manon Levesque stopped. She stared, turned a ghastly white under her paint. She did not laugh.

Head high, a faint, impenetrable smile on her lips, Scandal walked directly toward Manon and the general. Manon shook free of Butler's arms. She stared at Scandal, at that diamond tiara, rakishly catching, reflecting every light in the room. She shook her head.

Scandal did not hesitate. She kept walking forward. Manon retreated. She shook her head again. Around her, mocking laughter bubbled and then boiled as in a caldron. She backed away, shaking her head. The laughter rose. Suddenly, Manon heeled around and ran.

Alex Vigneaux caught Scandal's arm. "Dammit, Scandal. I'll never understand women."

"You're not my conscience."

"Thank God. I'd die of mortification. . . . I know you had cause to hate that woman, but my God, Scandal, you've destroyed her."

Scandal shrugged, her smile unflinching. "Then I can live with myself again."

Scandal was having her breakfast in bed—a luxury Gischairn would not permit when he was in town—when an apologetic rap on her door was followed by the appearance of the aging butler. "Miss Scandal, Master Alex Vigneaux is in the sunroom. He look mighty distressed. He say he got to see you, right away."

"Send him up here, Vanson."

"Yes'm." The butler looked doubtful, knowing his own master would chastise him if he ever learned of this matter. But after a few moments, Alex entered the room, rumpled, carrying a newspaper.

Scandal formed a kiss with her lips. Alex didn't smile. He said, "Well, at last, Scandal, you got what you wanted. You are the talk of New Orleans. Infamous. The most notorious woman in the city."

"How nice. And how did that happen?"

"You know how it happened, Scandal. You made it happen. Manon Levesque went home alone from the ball, went directly into her husband's gun room, put a pistol in her mouth and blew her brains out."

Scandal winced and sank back in the pillows. Alex shook his head. "Everyone is talking about you. They say this whole business is too odious to mention, but they mention it. I don't know when they'll stop talking about it. . . . Manon, hard and brittle and self-centered as she was, I don't know if she deserved this. We managed to convince the newspapers that Manon heard a prowler, got a gun, and because she didn't know how to use it, accidentally killed herself. But everyone knows better. They all know she couldn't face the jeers and laughter after what you did to her, Scandal." He sounded sad, not angered.

"You're too good, Alex. Protecting Manon. Trying to protect me. Letting people use you. Why don't you stay away from me?"

"Because you're going to need a true friend, Scandal, whether you think so now or not . . . . I don't know if you're going to find it is so easy to live with yourself . . . after all."

29

French Pines Plantation comprised thousands of acres of silt-rich Delta land between the bayous and the river. It practiced a kind of intensive farming that would not long survive the end of slavery, but in the summer of 1861 it was rampantly productive. Sugar cane flourished lushly, stalks climbing eight and ten feet tall before tipping with curvature under their own weight to form tight green and breathless tunnels between the rows. The tasseled green fields stretched as far as one could see in any direction. French Pines land reached out in breadth and depth the distance a man could walk in a day from the manor house. A low stone fence and broad stone-pillared gates marked the entrance to a winding lane leading through a quiet bower of water oaks to the magnificent Chalet Le Blanc.

Wade was hardly aware of his arrival at the huge farm. He

sprawled, poisoned with infections contracted in the barracoon, fevered, debilitated by starvation, weakened by despair. He felt totally abandoned by man and God. His legs remained in spancels, ankles festered with sores. His arms were linked at the small of his back with handcuffs. He slept fitfully, battered on the boarding of the wagon bed. Le Blanc had stopped regularly on the eternal drive from New Orleans for food for himself and pans of scraps handed out the back doors for the two servants seated with him in the box of the wagon. Le Blanc had not fed Wade. The servants had given him gourds of well water when they tended the horses.

Le Blanc had not spoken to Wade since the sheriff's bailiffs threw him, shackled, into the wagon bed outside the barracoon.

Wade wanted no words from Le Blanc. He had known plantation owners like Le Blanc all his life: men who accepted as God-given their right and power of life and death over slaves and underlings.

Vaguely, through the numbing waves of nausea pounding inside his temples, Wade heard black children run shouting along the shadowed lane, heralding the arrival of the master. "Masta come home. Masta come. Masta come."

Le Blanc cracked his whip sharply and the children fell silent. The wagon was halted briefly in the perimeter around the mansion. Someone called to Le Blanc and the planter answered sharply, "Later. I'll be back up to the house later."

The wagon rolled down the incline to the blacksmith shop in the work area of the farmyard. Le Blanc spoke to the servants beside him. "All right, haul that nigger out of the back and git him on his feet."

The blacks put the tailgate down. They caught Wade by the legs and pulled him out. He had lost at least thirty-five pounds during his incarceration in the barracoon. His beard was ragged, his hair standing wildly about his head.

Nothing was clear to Wade. He saw dozens of black faces in a grinning fringe, through swirling shadows. His legs were too weak to support him. He slumped helplessly to the ground.

The two blacks knelt beside him to lift him, but Le Blanc's cold voice stopped them. "Let the son of a bitch get up by hisself. Ain't nobody going to help him once he's out in the cane fields."

"He look mighty peaked, Masta," a black man said.

"A touch of this whip is just the medicine the son of a bitch needs to git him right up on his feet," Le Blanc said. As from a vast distance, Wade heard the crack of a whip, felt the cut of the weighted leathers across his back. He merely rolled over on his side.

A black man ran across the sand, knelt beside Wade. "He mighty sick, Masta. I help him to his feet."

The whip cracked again and the black screamed in pain and fell away from Wade. "Goddam you, Kite. I don't need you tellin' me what to do. You stay away from that lazy bastard till I tell you to touch him. You hear me, Kite?"

"I hears, Masta." The black youth was still crying with pain from the whip cut.

"And stop that whinin'. Hell, I didn't hurt you. I could as easy have popped out an eye, if'n I'd wanted to. You jus' remember that, Kite."

"Yas, suh, Masta. I remember."

"You shore as hell better. . . . Now you go git on a mule and fetch the vet. Tell Doc Caprice I got a prize nigger I want he should inspect. Tell him he looks white, but he's black. And he might need some attention before I'm through with him today."

When two more whip cracks across Cameroon's back convinced Le Blanc that the new slave could not pull himself to his feet, Le Blanc jerked his head. "You, Tupelo, and you, Merk. Drag him into the smithy. I wants to put a little fancy markin' on him, so's he gits away, folks know what he is."

As the two slaves dragged Cameroon by his heels into the smithy shack, an iron ring was struck several times with a crowbar. The sound rang out to the farthest reaches of the plantation, summoning the slaves. "Want them blacks all to see this," Le Blanc said. "Want them to git it into their thick skulls what happens to you blacks what try to run from French Pines."

As they awaited the gathering slaves, troubled, loitering, fearful, and the arrival of Dr. André Caprice, Le Blanc expounded on the evils and the penalties for those who ran from his farm. "I don't have runners," he said, raking his gaze across the dark faces of his slaves. "I don't tolerate it. A slave runs from French Pines, I bring him back. Either I kill him or I brand him—depending on what I think is best. If he's wild and a runner that nothing can't cure, I put him and me both out of misery. I put a bullet in his head. If I think he's got sense enough to know I mean business, I brand him runner, like we're going to brand this white nigger today. Right, Tupelo? Shouldn't have any trouble with him out cuttin' cane once we brand him, eh?"

"We brands him, Masta, he don't run no more," Tupelo said. He was a huge Negro, thick in the shoulders, keglike in chest and belly, his legs tough stanchions, his bare feet oversized and flat in the dirt. His hair was a tight kinky mat over a receding forehead, ridged brows, deep-set eyes, wide nostrils and thick pink-ridged lips. On his own left shoulder the seared scar of an R stood in bold relief against the chocolate brown of his sweated flesh.

"You had to learn, didn't you, Tupelo? Eh?"

"Tupelo don't run no more, Masta."

The blacksmith heated the coals. From a rack of brands, he brought the R and set it in the white-hot coals. "Get it good and hot, Kenzy." Le Blanc said. "Got to make him feel it, eh, Tupelo? Make him hurt, right?"

"We make him hurt, Masta," Tupelo promised.

Le Blanc delayed awhile longer, then he checked the branding iron and found it glittering to suit him. "Hell, we don't wait no more. Go ahead, Kenzy. Burn an R in the white nigger's shoulder. No matter if he was to git away now—which he won't—that there brand will prove him a black animal and a slave for life at French Pines. Ain't no sense waitin' no longer for Doc Caprice. He'll be along when he can, I reckon. . . . All right, Merk, you hold him down. Go ahead, Kenzy, brand him."

Tupelo said, "Let me brand him, Masta. I brand him good. I mark him right. I know how."

Le Blanc laughed and shrugged. "Sure. Go ahead, Tupelo. You're a good nigger. Now that I burnt some sense into you."

"Yes, Masta. Tupelo a good nigger. He your nigger now, Masta."

Le Blanc laughed and held up his hand. "All right, you blacks. Can you all see this here? Want you all to see it. Want you close enough you can *smell* his stinkin' flesh when it burns. Want you to know. You give me trouble—or Tupelo tells me you give him trouble in them fields—this what you git."

Tupelo took up the brand. He bent over where Cameroon lay sprawled with Merk's knee on his spine. Tupelo waited, but Cameroon did not struggle. Tupelo stared down at the protrate man, unable to believe he was not fighting against this searing iron. "Go ahead, Tupelo," Le Blanc said.

Tupelo pressed the branding iron downward upon Wade's shoulder. The sizzle, burn and stench of cooked flesh smoked up in a gray haze. Cameroon cried out and then slumped unconscious, face down in the sand.

Tupelo replaced the iron on the stone hearth. He stared at the unmoving form.

"Good work, Tupelo," Le Blanc said. "That's why you've

survived in them fields. Why I have made you my foreman of field hands. You do what I tell you and you do it right."

"Is he dead, Masta?" Tupelo whispered, eyes stricken.

"Hell, he ain't dead. But don't fret your burr head, Tupelo. He'll be dead anyway before he leaves French Pines. Ain't but one way this white Nigra is going to leave French Pines. In a pine box. So if he dies now or out in them cane fields, it don't matter. For the rest of his life he will live and regret that he murdered my own dear sweet brother Henri Le Blanc. . . . That's where I mean for him to die, Tupelo, the most horrible of deaths, working 'till he dies in my cane fields. Far as I care, he's got one reason to live, to regret what he done to my flesh and blood."

Dr. André Caprice arrived as the troubled black slaves retreated from the sunstruck bare yard around the smithy. Caprice swung down from his golden mare and Le Blanc greeted him warmly. "You jus' missed the excitement, André. Put a brand mark and the fear of God in this here new white Nigra."

The veterinarian knelt beside Wade. "He's unconscious."

"Well, hell, doc. That's why I sent for you. Give him a dose of something. Get him on his feet. I mean to have him working in the fields tomorrow."

Caprice laughed across his shoulder. "I know you're a determined man, Albert. A man who gets what he wants, but unless you're some kind of voodoo conjuring miracle man, you're going to let this fellow recover a while. He's right on the brink of death."

"The hell he is. He's playin' possum, that's all. He's been masquerading as a white man. Living easy. He'll harden up in a few weeks."

Dr. Caprice glanced up. "You sure this here is a mulatto? He's got none of the signs."

"Listen, goddammit. You jus' do your job as a vet. He's a Nigra. That's been proved in court. And I'll tell you what else has been proved in court. He's the Nigra that killed my brother Henri. So you just bring him around conscious. I'll get him on his feet, or I cut him to ribbons with my whip."

Caprice stood up slowly. "This man—or black slave—or whatever you say he is, is too ill to work. He looks starved, dehydrated, ill with every filth known to man. You got to clean him up, clean out his system. Or you ain't going to keep him alive long enough to get him into your fields. Now I'm telling you this straight, Albert. You can kill him with a whip. Or you can give him a chance to get well. That's up to you."

Le Blanc hesitated, his face taut and gray. He stared, enraged at the unconscious man on the ground. Raging, he drew back his boot and kicked him in the belly. He swung his arm, waving him from his mind. "All right. You, Kite. Help the doc get this Nigra to one of the cabins. You stay with him. You do whatever the vet tells you. . . . I tell you this, Kite. The white Nigra dies, I'll take it out'n your hide. You hear me, Kite?"

Wade swam slowly up through a warm glow of semi-consciousness to the unbearable agony of awareness. He saw the slender veterinarian, with thin, dark face, Van Dyck beard and close-set ears, and beyond him the troubled face of the black man named Kite. Vaguely, he heard them talking, " . . . ill . . . poisoned . . . just let him sleep . . . feed him what he wants to eat—if he ever does . . . try to keep him clean and dry and comfortable . . . and pray, Kite . . . that's really all we can do."

The slim hold on reality slipped away, and when Wade woke again night was deep around his cot. He made out the form of Kite lying on the floor near him. He slept again. For a long time nothing was truly clear. He had no idea how many days and nights passed. He was dimly aware of sunlight, painful against his eyes, the fading of the sun, darkness. Little else had reality. He dreamed that Scandal came into the room. She spoke softly to Kite. She tended Wade. When he caught her hand and tried to draw her to him, she disappeared like the wraith he knew in his mind she must be. Gradually, he became aware of a slender girl who came during the day and cared for him. Her flesh was a light tan; she was beautiful, her black hair caught in a bun at the nape of her neck. She rarely smiled. Her hands were gentle, but she was not Scandal. He would never see Scandal again on this earth. He had to get Scandal out of his mind. He whispered, agonized, "Scandal . . ."

The woman knelt over him. "I Deedry," she said. And then she added in a dead, flat tone, "I Tupelo's woman."

Kite staggered in from the cane fields every night after dark. He ate ravenously, washed in a rain barrel and then slumped in an old cane rocking chair near Wade's bed.

He told Wade that Tupelo and Le Blanc came to the cabin each morning. "They're going to take you to the fields soon," Kite said. "Masta is raging now that you is laid by so long. He say you up soon. Or he git you up."

"They've taken off the handcuffs," Wade said. "When do they take off the spancel at my ankle?"

"Say they don't," Kite said. "We got a few men spanceled at work in the field. Bad. Real bad. Always gittin' caught in the growth, around the base. Grows up out itself. Gets jagged and thick with leaves. Can't be helped. You falls. You jus' git up. Quick as you can—'fore Merk or Tupelo helps you up, with they whip."

"How do you stand it?" Wade said.

Kite shook his head. "I keeps my mouth shut. Much as I can. I works enough to keep them whips off . . . I been here two years. . . . Mostly, the cane-field hands die off in a year or less—they suffocate, lots of 'em, in the middle of the fields. Gets so they ain't no air can get in through the cane stalks. They just suffocate. Or they run yellin', crazy, gasping for air, until they are shot, or fall dead—they hearts just bust."

"But you live?"

"I ain't pridy about it. I was bought at a private auction. I was brought here as house nigger. But I made them Le Blanc folks mad. They put me in the fields. Mostly, they buy from these slave traders, what brings they coffles round here just before cuttin' time."

"I've seen those coffles. The dregs of every plantation. The sick, the crazy, the idiot, the bad actors that can't be controlled—"

"That's what they buy heah. They buy 'em cheap and they work them until they drop dead. Then they throw the bodies into the lagoons—'gator food. Sometimes it's them that die that I most envy. They free at last." Kite shook his head. "Rest of us. Know come daylight we got to be back in them fields, choppin' cane. We cuts ourselves with machete and die, we suffocate and die, we die of heat prostratin' us, or we die of snakebites. . . . Hear Masta laughing one day. He say to Doc Caprice, Louisiana got fifty percent of all snakes in this heah country and that fifty percent of snakes in Louisiana are in these here cane fields. . . . One way or 'nother, no field hand lives very long out in them fields."

Wade awoke one morning to a strangely silent cabin. The sun streamed in one of the windows. Everything was cleaned, scrubbed. There was a sense of tension.

Aware he was not alone, Wade turned his head. Deedry stood beside his bed.

His eyes widened. She was naked. Her slender body gleamed, the soft color of tea roses. Her breasts were full, dark-nippled, her belly flat, the black triangle at her thighs glittering.

Deedry tried to smile, failed. She turned back the cover and lay down beside him on the cot. "I want to," she whispered. "I've looked at you every day and I've wanted to."

He felt her hands caressing, massaging, manipulating. He felt himself respond. Dear God, how long had it been? Not since that morning with Scandal in the Vieux Carré. Scandal. He would never forget her. He would never see her again, either. But even with Deedry driving him wild with her mouth and her hands and her sensual body, he could not get Scandal from his mind. As Deedry drew him to her, working herself in frantic passion, he closed his eyes—and behind his eyes, he saw Scandal's face. . . .

30

"Wake up. Wake up, Brother Wade." Kite's voice quavered. The rail-thin black man crouched over Cameroon's cot. He shook Wade's shoulders, his hands trembling with panic.

Wade opened his eyes. The first livid fissures of false dawn vaguely illumined the cabin room. Still stunned with sleep, his mind groggy with fatigue and lingering illness, Wade stared up at Kite's anguished face, stark in the pink shadows. He moaned aloud.

"They comin', Brother Wade." Kite's fingers tightened on Wade's biceps. "They comin' for you."

Wade barely understood what the black youth was saying. He heard the pound of heavy boots on the cabin stoop. The door was struck hard and thrown open.

Tupelo entered the shack first, a lantern held high above his head. Lances of light flared and danced across the room, bouncing against the bare walls. Behind Tupelo, Albert Le Blanc strode. The aristocratic planter carried a coiled bullwhip. Le Blanc and Tupelo paused in the middle of the flooring. Merk remained standing in the doorway. His face was chilled, expressionless.

"We 'bout ready, Masta." Kite's voice trembled with his anxiety to placate the white man. "Yassuh. We jus now gittin' up. Stirrin' our bones, Masta. Stirrin' our bones. Yassuh."

Le Blanc cursed the black man. "Shut your whimperin' mouth, Kite. I'll ask you when I want to hear from you. . . . You ain't never going to learn, are you, Kite? Never learn to keep your mouth shut until white folks speak to you." He glared coldly at the youth kneeling on the floor, then jerked his head toward Wade, who struggled to rise from the cot. "Get up, white nigger ape. Time to go to work."

Wade tried to lever his body up on his arms, but they were weak and trembled, barely able to support him. He swung his legs over the side of the cot, wavering when the room spun and lunged about his head. He grabbed at the mattress for support, his knuckles gray.

Le Blanc handed the coiled whip to Tupelo. He jerked his head toward Wade, his voice lashing. "Get him up. Get the son of a bitch up."

Tupelo nodded. He shook out the whip. The heavy coil struck the flooring, loud in the morning silence. "On your feet, Snake-brains," Tupelo said.

"Snakebrains. Snakebrains. That's mighty clever, Tupelo." Le Blanc nodded and laughed. He put his head back, laughing. He glanced toward Merk, who stood grinning in the doorway. "We got a new name for our white nigger. Snake. Snakebrains. ... Let's go, Snake. We're taking you to the fields this morning."

Wade nodded. The room no longer spun. His stomach felt nauseated. He bit down hard against the bile gorging up into his throat.

Tupelo stood with the whip poised, doubled. Wade drew a deep breath, held it, and managed to stand up. Abruptly the room skidded and wheeled crazily before him. He clutched out wildly for support and found none. He toppled heavily like a felled tree.

Le Blanc stared down at him. "Give him a dose, Tupelo."

The whip lashed across Wade's back. The coils caught the raw scabs of his branding wale, raking it open. Wade crawled, trying to escape the leather lash. He pushed himself up on all fours, stayed there, his head drooping between his shoulders.

"Look at our fine white Nigra," Le Blanc said. "Don't look so mighty now, does he? Looks just like any other Nigra now, don't he? Eh, Merk? Old Snake will be whining and begging like a whipped cur, most any minute." He stepped closer, his voice rasping. "Get up on your feet, goddam you."

Wade nodded, but was unable to rise. Le Blanc's cold voice hacked at him. "You've laid around here on your tail as long as I'm going to tolerate it. I don't give a thundering goddam what nobody says, you're going to the canefields today." Le Blanc glanced toward Tupelo and jerked his head. The whip, doubled in Tupelo's fist, cracked again. It was like the fire of the branding iron intensified a hundred times on Wade's sensitive flesh, because he was well enough now to respond to pain. He heard Le Blanc's raging as across an incredible and thunderous chasm. "Get up. You're going to the fields. I don't give a damn in hell if you live to get back tonight, because it don't matter to me when you die in them cane fields—today, next year, it's all the same. Because that's where you *are* going to die."

Wade slumped against Kite in the rear of the flatbed wagon. The vehicle bumped and rattled through the rutted lane in the chilled bayou dawn. Ahead of them yawned the silent green sea of sugar cane.

The wagon rolled to a stop. Merk jumped down from its box and shouted at the slaves to roll out. From another flatbed wagon a slave handed out machetes and scythes.

Wade pushed himself off the rear of the wagon and stood wavering a moment. Merk's voice cracked at him like a pistol. "We goin', Merk," Kite said. "We goin'."

As Kite had warned, they did not remove the spancel at Wade's ankle. He moved slowly, cautiously, or the hobble, intended to restrain horses or cattle, threw him. He was afraid if he fell in this slimy mud he would not be able to get up. He was thankful Kite walked closely at his side.

Wade limped with the tail end of the crew toward the lush jungle of matted cane. He back bled, his head spun, but he bit hard on his lower lip, refusing to ask for mercy. The sun blazed, brightly and feverishly orange before eight in the morning. Sweat ran from his matted hair into his eyes and beard, salty on his lips.

Le Blanc had waited only to see Wade placed on the slave wagon, then he had returned to the mansion. For this, Wade was thankful. However, he soon learned that Tupelo was Le Blanc's other self, Le Blanc's eyes, Le Blanc's whip.

The slave at the supply wagon had handed Wade a machete. Tupelo grabbed it and threw it back into the wagon bed.

Laughing, Tupelo handed Wade a scythe. The implement was heavy and awkward, but Wade soon found that when Tupelo and his assistant, Merk, were occupied elsewhere, he could sag for a moment against the scythe, lean on it for support.

Tupelo's big voice raked at Wade. "Masta say you don't git no machete, Snake. . . . Masta say you a dangerous white nigger. Masta say you ain't no-way to be trusted with no knife."

If Wade had prayed for a moment's release from Le Blanc's imposed hell, he did not find it in the fields. He did not see the plantation master again that day. Le Blanc seldom ventured into the sweltering, sun-seared, swamp-soured fields. But Tupelo was there. The big Negro seemed to be everywhere in the vast acreage at once. His raucous voice rode on the stifled silences. One moment, a distant baying, almost at once, a terrible raging over one's shoulder.

"Tupelo learnt," Kite whispered to Wade as they worked. "Tupelo learnt good. Tupelo was a bad nigger. Masta almost kilt him many the time. But Tupelo smart. He found out how to live in these heah fields. He wanted to stay alive, and he learnt. He cunning. Like a weasel. He found out how to stay alive. He learnt he had to be like the masta. Only more like him. Crueller."

Wade watched the huge Tupelo through occluding heat waves. He could not believe a slave could treat his fellow slaves with such heartless, conscienceless inhumanity. Tupelo was far less compassionate toward the other blacks even than the lord of the farm.

Clutching at every moment he could steal to lean for support against the scythe, to quiet the irregular hammering of his heart, to relieve the trembling weakness in his calves, to soothe the dry burn of his throat, to stem the flow of sweat into his eyes, Wade somehow made it through the morning.

He fell often. The new cane stalks grew up out of the dead stubble and hacked-off butts of other years. These sharp, bamboo-like spurs caught his spancels and threw him. He toppled heavily, helpless, his body soon caked with the damp, sour red mud.

Kite ran to him. His voice quaked with fear. He spoke to Wade but stared frantically across his shoulder. "Get up. Get up. Fast."

Using his scythe for support, Wade pulled himself to his knees and, panting, managed to stand erect. He just made it as Merk's whip cracked across his back.

The naked red sun blazed down, simmering rain in puddles, cooking the stubble and cane undergrowth. The breezes ceased as the sun climbed, and the field became an unbearable kiln.

Infrequently, Wade heard someone yell frantically for the dead wagon. Without exception, the black field hands dreaded death and the dead. They retreated from the dying, let them die, superstitiously terrified. Wade watched the mule-drawn tumbrel lumber into the almost impenetrable rows.

The cutting crews moved deeper into the field. The suffocating, breathless heat intensified. The men could scarcely breathe at all under the tall, almost impenetrable roofing of cane tassels. These thick tips formed canopies which kept out any breeze and magnified the dank heat boiling up from the doughy loam. The slaves had to be driven by whippers into these tunnels. They were forced to hack away the stalks in order to breathe at all. Sometimes they could not work fast enough, and failing, they tried to retreat, even against the whips.

Choking and gasping for a single breath of air, the slaves lunged for the open spaces. Escaping the fetid tunnels, they fell to their knees, pounding with both hands at their chests to force oxygen into their lungs. Terror rose as they suffocated. They stayed, crouched and gasping, struggling for oxygen like fish out of water, even with the whips lashing across their backs. There came to be no escape. Death. They welcomed it, courted it, came to look forward to it in anguished longing.

Time, like the sun, seemed to stand still in the fiery midafternoon. The sun seemed to slip from the crest of heaven and then hang suspended there, blazing, blistering, pitiless.

Near where Wade worked a Negro fell dead in the breathless heat and oppressive humidity.

Wade stared at the dead man. A moment ago the man had appeared as strong as any of the workers around him, sluggish, gasping for breath, but no weaker. Suddenly, he was dead.

Kite said, "He lasted a long time. Been heah most two years."

A terrified Negro yelled, "Dead wagon."

The tumbrel clattered through the opened rows. Merk and Tupelo walked in alongside the two-wheeled cart.

Tupelo stared at Wade, surprised that it was not he for whom they called the wagon. "Still alive, huh, Snake?"

Wade didn't answer, watching them. Tupelo gazed at him for some moments, then spoke over his shoulder, loudly, for his benefit, Wade saw: "You niggers. Drag this yere corpse yonder to the lagoon and throw it in."

The black workers shuddered, withdrawing. Tupelo laughed, still peering at Wade in the sodden heat. "Go ahaid, drag him out of here," Tupelo said. "Reckon there ain't no better scavengers than them ole crocs and 'gators in the lagoons." He shook his head, taking up the discarded machete. "Gots to tell Masta Albert to git us some new meat out here . . . cane hungry . . . 'gators hungry . . . got to have new meat."

Wade doubted that he would last out the day. He knew that Merk and Tupelo grinned, betting privately how long the whiteskin could exist in the heat. Somehow when the iron ring clanged, calling quitting time, Wade was still on his feet.

Kite grinned at him.

Wade shivered in the unrelenting heat. The sun had broiled his flesh. Every muscle in his body ached. His hands blistered within the first hour, the blisters broke, watery and hot by noon, the raw sores grew red during the afternoon and by nightfall burned with infection. But he survived.

At the cabin, Wade managed to climb the steps and walk into the front door before he staggered and fell.

Deedry and Kite lifted him up. Deedry had filled a wooden tub with well water. Kite helped Wade undress. He sank into the icy water, which grew warm from the feverish heat of his flesh. Wade felt faintly revived. Kite poured water over him from a bucket. Deedry scrubbed him with a thick bar of lye soap. Her hands were gentle. He tried to smile his thanks. He could not. She did not mind. She understood.

Kite and Deedry helped Wade towel down and pull on Osnaburg pants, a tow-linen shirt. Deedry had prepared dinner, sidemeat, sweet potatoes and collard greens. Wade slumped in a chair at the table. He was too sore, too ill, too exhausted to eat.

Kite nodded toward him, chewing, his mouth full. "You best try an' eat something, Brother Wade. Onliest way you can stay alive in them fields."

Wade stared at Kite. "Do you keep yourself alive—so you can go back into hell?"

Kite shrugged. "Long as I alive, Brother Wade, I got me a chance."

"For what?"

Kite shook his head. He chewed, thinking this over. "I don't know. I alive. . . . Maybe somehow I gits away. . . . I don't know, but I alive."

Wade nodded. He tried to smile. Kite made sense, the only rational reasoning in all this insanity. You stayed alive as long as you could because as long as you breathed, there was some slender hope, and you clung to that.

The cabin door was thrown open. Wade heard Deedry's sharp intake of breath. Kite's fork clattered against his tin plate. Wade turned painfully on the caneback chair.

Tupelo stood in the doorway. He stared at the three people in the lamplit room, his face twisting, his black eyes glittering, as empty and flat as shards of broken glass.

He narrowed his gaze to Deedry's bloodless face. He said, "I been lookin' for you, woman. Didn't reckon to find you hidin' in here with the white nigger."

"I here," Deedry said. Her slender chin tilted. "Ain't hidin'."

"You smart you be hidin'. I come to fetch you. . . . You come home now."

"No."

"You my woman."

She drew a deep breath. She stood up, moved away from the table. She shook her head. "I ain't your woman, Tupelo. No more. I done told you. Weeks ago. Months ago."

Tupelo's hamlike fists clenched at his sides. "Don't make no never-mind what you tole me. . . . You my woman. You come quiet with me. Or I drags you out of here."

Her voice remained chilled, level. "You best go, Tupelo."

He strode forward. He caught Deedry's wrist. She broke free, savagely. Physical violence was nothing new between them. He had hurt her until he could no longer frighten her. He could kill her but she was not afraid of him any more.

"You ain't stayin' here, woman." He snagged at her arm again. Deedry retreated.

She shook her head again, watching him coldly, her eyes dry and empty. "You can kill me, Tupelo. But I won't go back to you. I won't never go back to you."

Tupelo stared down at Deedry, almost helpless. He ruled by violence, in the canefields and in the quarters. When his strength and brutality failed him, he was helpless. He was helpless against Deedry because he wanted her so terribly.

Deedry's gaze clashed against his defiantly. He looked about, raging, frustrated. Then he grabbed her arm again. She twisted, catlike, and broke free. He cursed, mewling and growling at once, and backhanded her across the head.

Deedry spun around and fell against the wall. She stayed there, unmoving. Her fingers dug into the unfinished panels.

Wade pushed up from the chair. He caught up a kitchen knife, but Kite clutched his arm, restraining him.

"He'll kill you," Kite said. "He wants to kill you. . . ."

Tupelo's gaze raked across Kite and Wade as if they were vermin. Then he stared at Deedry once more. He spat at her, turned and charged through the door into the night sobbing.

"Jesus," Kite whispered. "Things wasn't evil enough befo' . . . now he purentee got it in for you."

Wade said nothing. There was nothing to say. Kite had said it all.

Deedry returned at last to the table. She pushed her food about on her plate, but ate nothing. Kite sat for some moments staring through the opened door at the tautly silent plantation night, then he took up a buttermilk biscuit, sopped it in the red-eye gravy. He ate again.

Wade awoke late in the night, some hours past midnight. He lay, staring through the musky darkness. He heard Kite's labored snoring, Deedry's deep breathing. Ravenous with hunger, Wade got out of bed. He found and ate two cold sweet potatoes. Soon his stomach was bloated with gas, twisted in knots.

Sleepless, he rolled in agony on his cot until daybreak. His body ached, numb with pain, his muscles cramped, his flesh cooked by yesterday's sun, but he and Kite were at the foot of the cabin steps awaiting the work cart at six a.m.

Tupelo was like a raging animal, the fury festering in him. He was savagely aggressive from the first moment. No one could work to suit him. He dogged Wade's heels all morning, daring him to rest, to fall, to ask for mercy.

Kite had it only slightly less evil. Because Kite considered Wade his friend, Tupelo hated him fiercely. He drove the slender black youth relentlessly.

At noon, a middle-aged Negro slashed his own arm just below the elbow with his machete, almost dismembering himself, severing the artery.

As the man threw away his machete, crying out, Merk ran into the row. The bleeding man walked in tight, mindless circles, blood spewing. Without waiting to see what had happened, Merk brought his bullwhip down across the man's back.

Kite leaped between them, catching at the whip.

Merk stared at Kite, mouth twisted back from his teeth. "You wants the whip yo' own self, nigger?"

"He's bleeding to death," Kite said.

By this time, Tupelo had arrived, striding in between the workers, shoving them aside when they did not move quickly enough to please him. He caught the wounded black's arm, stared at the mutilated flesh, saw it was self-inflicted. He dropped the man's arm, his mouth twisting, and shoved the black slave away. The man fell to his knees.

The bleeding slave stayed there, trying futilely to staunch the flow of blood with globs of soured mud.

The slaves stopped working, crowding around. Tupelo drove them back, raging at them to return to work. Then he stood impassively, watching the man bleed to death. Blood gushed from the sundered artery with every frantic pound of his heart.

"Think to get out of working, huh?" Tupelo stood over the

bleeding man, unmoved by the man's agony or the sight of his blood. Sweat stood in great marbles across Tupelo's face. His tow-linen shirt was discolored with sweat.

Trembling, mindless with agony, the man stared up at the field foreman. "Get me to the vet, Tupelo," he begged.

Tupelo shook his head. "No. You cut up. You live, you lose that arm. You no good to me. No good to Masta."

The man sobbed. "Help me, Tupelo . . . please God, help me, or I die."

Tupelo shrugged, the sweat streaming down his face from his matted hair. "Don't care if'n you die, nigger. You wanted to git out'n these yere fields . . . you cut yo'self to git out . . . you gon' git out." He nodded his head. "You gon' git out—when you daid. Stub arm ain't no good in a cane field. . . . Nobody wants to feed a nigger what can't work."

The man's head bobbed up and down, frantic. "I'll work, Tupelo . . . I swear. Get the doc for me. Stop the bleedin' . . . jus' stop the bleedin', Tupelo, and I go right back to work. . . ." But the man's voice weakened. His clothing and the ground around him were sodden with his blood by now. He sagged forward on the ground, crying helplessly.

Tupelo let him lie there, writhing, screaming, sobbing, whimpering and finally silent. At last, Tupelo bent over the unmoving body. He nodded, as if satisfied. "He daid." He straightened and yelled for the dead wagon.

When the tumbrel arrived, Tupelo ordered the carcass hauled away to the lagoons.

Wade felt sickness gorge up in him. He was more aware of the horror in which he existed. His mind was clearer. He stared at Tupelo, incredulous. When the newly deceased body was thrown into the lagoon and Tupelo laughed, nodding with satisfaction, Wade's stomach twisted with horror. This was nightmare, played out in blazing sunlight. He had never seen inhumanity like this. No one could have made him believe such heartlessness existed, except that he saw it himself. He'd grown up on a plantation—the farm on which he had been born. He'd visited scores of similar estates. But he was seeing cruelty as he'd never even suspected it was practiced on this earth. And yet it was not the mindless cruelty of a savage black overseer against his own race. What Tupelo did he learned from his own master. What Albert Le Blanc represented, Tupelo carried out. . . . .

Wade stood in the blazing sun, and shivered. . . . .

The other blacks, forced by men with whips to return to chopping cane, muttered, cursing at Tupelo, a low, persistent sound of rage in the breathless heat. The foreman laughed at them. He stood, staring at them.

"I lets you die—if that's what you want. I lets you fools kills yo'self if that's what you want." His voice cut at them, lashing.

They gazed up at him, grumbling. But Tupelo only laughed louder, sweat spraying when he swung his head. "You can cut yo'selves up, kill yo'selves, any time you want. I lets you. Go ahead. Slash away. I lets you. . . . Onliest thing I won't stand for is you to quit working. I know my job. I know what my job is. My job is to keep you mules working. . . . Cuss me, niggers. Cuss me all you want. You jus' keep cuttin' cane whilst you is cussing."

The big man strode back and forth among them, almost as if daring any one of them to attack him. He didn't even carry a whip. His sweated shirt was opened across his keglike chest, as if he bared a target for them. Every man around him held a lethal machete, or a glittering-bladed scythe.

He stared at them, his black eyes savage with contempt. "You heah me, niggers? You heah me and you heah me good. . . . I got one job . . . and I keeps that job jus' one way . . . jus' one way . . . I gits the cane cut. That there's all what matters. How much cane is cut in this yere field and ground in yonder mill. That's all. . . . I alive and I live good—and I means to stay alive and live good. . . . And that means one thing—that means you bastids is gonna cut cane and keep cuttin'. . . ."

31

Suddenly Scandal was notorious. She was the most talked-about female in the crescent city.

People did not quickly forget how Manon Levesque died. Though hundreds perished in the yellow-fever epidemic which stalked in the wake of the early-summer rains and thousands more fled the town in panic, and every news report listed increasing Confederate dead, Manon's death hung in infamy, like some sulfurous cloud. Coupled with her death in every mind was the image of Scandal Gischairn parading arrogantly before the world with Manon's tiara cocked at a hellion's angle atop her black hair—laughter twisting her murrey lips and bubbling in her wicked heart.

Few of the best families remained in the occupied, plague-ridden city during the deadly summer. They propounded any excuse the army would accept as reason to depart the military zone. They abandoned heirlooms, priceless accumulations of many acquisitive generations, and they ran. General Butler and his officers were glad to see them go. Property confiscation was easy when levied against absentee tenants.

Those families who stayed in New Orleans that fearful summer huddled behind closed windows and locked doors against the onslaught of malaria, yellow fever, the swagger of the conqueror, and the terror of looters, official and unsanctioned. Few parties or dances were planned or carried out; there was little to celebrate. There was not much happiness to be found in that ravaged city. No one had the heart or the credit for trivial pursuits. Those who did, for various reasons, host small social gatherings or the infrequent soireé, carefully, calculatedly and coldly omitted one name first from any list of guests: Scandal Gischairn was no longer welcomed among the elite of French or American New Orleans.

She was not received by the respectable families. This was bitter, but far from ruinous. She remained a celebrity; her fragile beauty lent brilliance to any affair; many struggled to be caught in her company. If she wished to go out, she could dance all afternoon among laughing people, every evening find excitement to tide her through any summer night. But this existence was in another world removed from the socially elite, a gathering of adventurers, outcasts, and the infamous like herself. This demimonde pursued her heedlessly.

Often, and increasingly, Scandal stayed alone in Gischairn's silent old St. Charles Avenue mansion, lonely, under self-imposed restraint.

She prowled the house. She lay across her bed and dreamed of Wade Cameroon. After all these months, the pain of loss distracted her still. She felt undone by his desertion. She still saw his abrupt departure as abandonment, cold and calculated. He no longer wanted her. This was certainly made clear by now, and she cursed his memory.

Despite herself, she lived in hope—when that doorbell chimed downstairs, her heart lurched. It might be Wade, even yet! And when it was never he, her grief and rage and love gorged up at once, a spinning froth poisoning her mind.

She wanted him! How gladly she would exchange everything in this house, in this city, this world, to be again in Wade's arms. She had earned her sublimest dreams, fulfilled her most vaunted ambition. The unhappy little girl who dreamed herself free of the drudgery of Wilkes Corners had pursued that dream and made it come true, every grain, every imagined delight, every profit. And she left empty and alone. She had followed a dazzling siren only to find her another painted cheat. She had paid dearly for everything she had, and it was nothing she wanted.

She wanted Wade! She smiled, tracing her fingertip across her lip, recalling the way he had loved her on that trace to New Orleans, the way he had waited until he thought she slept and then tenderly, yet passionately, held her upon him, caressing, fondling, cherishing her body. How could he have tired so quickly? How could he have so casually put her from his mind and walked away forever from her? Oh God, how she hated him.

How she loved him! How she hoarded every inconsequential incident between them, the shared laughter, rages, fears, dreams. They'd had them all, concentrated in time, as if the gods themselves allotted only minutes to their love, but could not contain its depth or its fury.

She bit her lip. On the trail, fighting Wade and her own traitorous heart, she'd boasted she could forget him, she could forget anything she had to forget in order to gain her ambitions.

Her black eyes brimmed with tears. She had believed that fallacy then. She'd been such a deluded fool, she'd believed she *could* forget Wade Cameroon in the glamorous life she planned for herself. Now she knew better. Her heart ached emptily at this hard-learned lesson. She could not forget. She would never forget.

If only she knew how to find him, she would go to him. Now. Running. . . .

The distant doorbell chimed, persistently defying the tranquil house.

Involuntarily, Scandal lurched up on the bed. She held her breath, listening.

It seemed an interminable time. She decided the butler had turned the caller away, whoever it was. Then the discreet knock at her own door. The butler said, "Miss Scandal. A General Butler to see you, ma'am. I tole him you don't no-way receive gen'mum callers unchaperoned in Masta Julien's house. But he walk right in. He say I to tell you he waitin'."

"All right." Scandal exhaled heavily, unaware she'd been holding her breath.

For a long moment she sagged on the mattress, empty, disappointed. At last she stood up and regarded herself critically in a full-length mirror. Her dress was crushed, her hair in disarray. Julien-Jacques would be furious if she received anyone— —even a Yankee officer—in such dishabille. She did not care.

She patted briefly at her hair, brushed casually at her dress and went unhurriedly down the stairs.

General Butler awaited her, standing, in full uniform, in the doorway of the sun parlor. The butler hovered in the shadowed corridor, face taut with disapproval.

The general strode forward to meet Scandal at the foot of the polished stairs. He seemed to have gained weight grossly since she'd seen him last. His jowls sagged; he could no longer conceal his paunch. He lived on the fat and richest sinews of the conquered carcass of this fallen land, and he grew bloated with his success.

She did not smile. The general extended both his hands to her, but she ignored them. After a moment he let his arms drop to his sides, not in the least dismayed, discomfited or disheartened. One thing he had learned in the long months of federal occupation of this parish. He could have anything he wanted in New Orleans. Anything.

"I missed you," he said.

Scandal didn't answer. He drew in a deep breath, gazing at her loveliness. The vague lamplight splashed wine tints across her face and slashed faint shadows over her flushed cheeks. She looked somehow disconsolate and unhappy, but he waived this. It was her fragile beauty that set him afire, made it impossible for him to stay away, impossible to take his gaze from her face.

"What's the matter?" Ben Butler said. "You knew I'd come, didn't you? You can't pretend to believe I'd be put off forever."

"I hoped you wouldn't come—like this."

"My God! Why? I'm a man. I want you. When a *man* wants something, he goes after it, missy."

"When a *gentleman* truly cares for a woman, he does not compromise her reputation, general."

His mouth twisted. "What kind of corn-pone hypocrisy is this?"

"I told you. My uncle is not here. It is not proper—or even decent—to entertain you in this house without a chaperon."

He stepped closer. "You can stop that old-fashioned affectation and fluttery-handed prudery with me. One thing I've learned, *on site*, is that under their pretense and coquetry, every Southern woman is a slut. Most of them, I've found, wear half a dozen crinolines—and no underpants."

She laughed at him coldly. "That's one discovery you'll never learn about me, general."

He did not bother to smile. "I already know about you. As I knew about Manon Levesque. Do you know how long it was—in minutes—before I had her naked on a bed the first time I was alone with her?"

"I don't even want to know."

"They all came to me. They all wanted something. They simpered, they flirted, they stalled, but they fell on their backs quickly enough."

"They wanted something. I don't."

He nodded. "That's because you're young. You haven't sense enough yet to know what you want. Once you've had a man——a real man—and not a flabby old ram like Levesque—you'll know."

"And you're going to teach me?"

"That's right. I've been patient, and I've waited long enough. Too long. My first instincts about you were right."

"Oh?"

"I knew instinctively you were a hussy. A whore. But your fine airs, your expensive feathers, fooled me. So I played your stupid game—while old men like Levesque sneaked in here and bedded you down."

"You're so sure of all this."

"Hell, girl. The whole town is sure of this. No one doubts *how* you got Manon Levesque's tiara. No one doubts *why* Manon killed herself."

"Get out."

"Oh, no. I came here because you wouldn't come to me. You didn't need extra sugar, special permits, visas, official sanctions. Those women who did come to me, without exception, came because they *wanted* something. They were willing to barter their thighs to get what they wanted."

"As you say, I don't want anything."

"There's more." His blue eyes impaled her. "After those cream-of-Southern-aristocracy women went to bed with me *once*—they all came back. Secretly. Sneaking in. Begging. When they already had what they came for—they came back—to *me*. And *you* will."

"I couldn't want anything badly enough to come to you for it. There's nothing on earth I'd want enough that I'd let *you* touch me."

He laughed at her, unruffled. "We'll see about that. You haven't been pressured yet. Your darling uncle has not been *taxed* to the full dollar. All these things because I've protected you. If I removed my protection, you'd be on your knees to me in a week."

Her head tilted. "Until then, get out."

"Don't be a damned fool, girl. Are you really stupid enough to doubt that I can take this house from you, the food from your pantry, the servants from your kitchen? I can imprison you. All I need to do is sign the order."

"On what charge, general?"

"Who needs a charge? I *am* the United States government in this hellhole. You are a Southern slut. If I say you are a rebel spy, you'd rot in jail. If I say you bought a quart of milk on the black market, you'd be arrested, held without bail, without counsel. If I say you solicited for prostitution, you'd be jailed for as long as it pleases me. Please, Scandal, don't push me. Don't be a damned fool."

He caught her suddenly in his arms. She struggled, but he held her pinioned against him, his arms like steel grappling hooks. From the darkness of the shadowed corridor the black servant sobbed helplessly, impotently. Butler ignored the negro as if he did not exist.

"You're hurting me," Scandal whispered.

He laughed, trembling with passion. "A crushed rose smells even sweeter," he said. His breath spewed hotly across her face. Scandal looked about wildly for anything she might wield as a weapon. There was nothing. Rage boiled up through her. She saw his face coming nearer, his features distorted through an occluding red fog of fury.

At first the insistent clangor of the doorbell had no reality for Scandal. The sound was lost in the throbbing of blood in her temples, in the rages pounding in her brain.

It was not until Butler swore, released her, and stepped back that Scandal recognized the chiming of the doorbell for what it was.

Her heart lurched. Perhaps it was Wade. If God still reigned in heaven, it was Wade.

"I'll get it," she called to the unmanned servant slouched in terror against the wall.

Without another glance toward General Butler, who stood erect, getting his emotions under control, Scandal turned and ran across the foyer.

She jerked open the front door and then sagged against it, empty.

"Scandal." Alex Vigneaux smiled brightly up at her from the stoop.

She stared at Alex, wanting to cry in despair. Alex was almost as slender as she and would be far less effectual against an amoral, arrogant man like Ben Butler. She managed to smile. "Oh, hello, Alex."

"May I come in?" He smiled again. "It is important."

She held the door wide. Smiling, holding his top hat in his manicured fingers, his morning coat immaculately pressed and tailored to his slender shoulders, Alex entered the foyer.

He stopped as if struck, staring at Scandal's guest. Somehow, Scandal kept her voice light. "You know General Butler, don't you, Alex?"

Alex nodded coldly. Butler stared through Vigneaux as if the young fop were of less consequence than the black servant shuddering in the sapphire shadows.

"General Butler was just leaving." Scandal's voice was flat, chilled. She remained where she stood, holding the thick, tall front door ajar.

Butler hesitated a taut, silent moment. Then he shrugged and laughed, without mirth or warmth. He took up his gold-braided hat, set it jauntily angled on his head. Then gripping his riding crop as if it were a whipstock, he crossed the foyer.

"You'll remember what I told you?" he said to Scandal.

Her eyes struck against his. "How could I forget?"

"You are very wise. I hope you are as smart. . . . I will be back, you know."

Her gaze did not falter. "I am quite aware that Bronze John is not the only vile pestilence plaguing my poor city."

Butler stiffened as if she'd spat in his face or struck him. His blue eyes clashed against her black ones. After a taut beat, he exhaled and laughed. "I could arrest you for that seditious statement, girl. And jail your dandy little Creole here as witness. I hope I misunderstood you."

Her gaze probed his coldly. "If you misunderstood anything I said, general, I am sorry. Truly sorry."

She found Alex sprawled out on a sunroom couch, his head back and his arms spread wide.

He stared up at her. "My God. When you make an enemy, you go right to the top, don't you?"

She shrugged. "If you are afraid, you needn't stay here."

He came to his feet, instantly contrite. "My God, Scandal. I'm sorry. But I am scared. For you. That man controls everything that moves in this town. We eat—drink—exist—at his whim."

"I'm finding that out."

He caught her hands. "Did he hurt you? . . . I'll kill him. God knows, I don't know how, but I'll kill him."

She shrugged. "You can't kill him—he's a Yankee."

He tried to smile, self-deprecatingly. "I'll think of a way."

"Why should you? Kill him and a hundred more will spring up to take his place, just as arrogant, just as evil, just as vicious."

He put his arms about her, troubled. "What is it, Scandal? I've never seen you like this."

She pulled free and prowled the room. She shook her head, spread her hands, helpless. "I'm just so unhappy. So miserable. I want to get away from here."

"Then do."

"How can I? Where would I go? Do you think he would give me a travel permit?"

Alex sighed. "He might. If you got it before he knew you applied. . . . That's why I came here this morning. One reason. I came to look at you, to touch your hand if I got the chance. . . . But mostly, I came to say my mother worries about you—as I do—alone here in this house, in this town."

Scandal bit her lip, seeing Ben Butler's fat-jowled face clearly etched behind her eyes.

"We both worry about you, Scandal. Mother wants you to come to our summer place. Away from this pestilence. Away from the gossip. Away from the Yankees."

She gazed at him and suddenly nodded, crying. She walked toward him, blinded by her tears. "Yes . . . I want to go. I want to go now."

By noon, the carriage was loaded, the servants had barred and secured all doors and windows in the mansion—ineffectual precautions against the looters and the army of occupation. But it was the ritual observed by every traveler, though they realized they might as well have walked out and left all doors and windows open and unlatched.

The butler and maid sat on the carriage box with the driver. Alex clutched Scandal's elbow and hurried her along the walk through the maze of Julien's flowers, shrubs and plants.

At the edge of the driveway, Scandal hesitated. With Alex trying to urge her into the coach, she looked back, eyes brimmed with tears. Gischairn's home was such a stately, lovely and serene old mansion. She had been as nearly happy here as she had been in her life. Would she find a charred hulk, a ransacked hovel when she returned? Or would she ever return to this place, to the life she'd known?

She shuddered and allowed Alex to help her into the tonneau of the carriage.

The coach moved slowly on the teeming streets. Nightmarish beings hastened about their nightmarish business, ransacking, pillaging, stealing, killing, dying of pestilence. Alex insisted she keep a handkerchief over her mouth and nose as protection against inhaling the germs of malaria and yellow fever. The roadways bristled like littered avenues down into hell. Fever victims buckled suddenly, spewing black vomitus, allowed to die where they fell. Tumbrels, manned by Negroes wearing masks and gloves, rumbled though the streets, carting away the dead. Swaggering soldiers in blue, intimidated by nothing, walked wide around the dead and the dying who sprawled on the banquettes and in the gutters. A thickening, taut silence spread shroudlike over the city.

Scandal pressed back into the coach against the soft rests, sickened by the sight and stench of death. Alex shouted at the coachman to hurry, but the roads were blocked. People waited with their worldly goods lined for miles back from the gatehouse at the northernmost exit checkpoint from the city.

She did not want to look out at the scarred skeleton of the lovely town she'd once dreamed ahead to and which she had found so brilliant and full of lights and laughter. Many stores were closed, abandoned, boarded. Some of those who tried to remain open were looted, windows smashed, doors hanging like broken wings.

At the exit gate, a stout soldier in a blue uniform ordered them out of the coach. They stood in a line, along with the servants, while non-coms searched all suitcases, bags and trunks. Openly, they confiscated any item which intrigued or tempted them. There existed no recourse against this thievery. Even if there had been a chance to recover, the delay would be miserable, interminable, dangerous. These fleeing people wanted only one thing, at any cost—to be granted exit visas as quickly as possible.

After what seemed an unconscionable delay a young lieutenant emerged from the gatehouse. He paused before Scandal. A light summer rain fell, glistening on her cheeks and eyelashes.

"You Miss Scandal Gischairn?"

Heart sinking, Scandal nodded.

The lieutenant continued to smile. "I can grant permits to these other people in your party, ma'am. But I can't give you an exit visa."

"Why not?"

The young officer spread his hands. He continued to smile.

"Your name is on a list, Miss Gischairn. I'm sorry. There is only one way you can be issued a travel permit. It will have to come directly and exclusively from General Butler himself."

Scandal exhaled, defeated. "I'll have to see General Butler personally?"

The lieutenant nodded. "If you want to leave this town you will."

32

Wade wakened slowly, unwillingly, at daybreak. He lay, sore and miserable, and fought against the overpowering fatigue which seduced him back to sleep. He opened his eyes, wincing against the pain of the first lances of pink daylight. For a long moment he lay tangled in Deedry's arms. He moved his arms gingerly, conscious of burning pain in his biceps and shoulders. He raised his head on his pillow and gazed down at Deedry's smooth, dark-skinned nakedness. He felt himself grow heated, wanting her. He cursed himself for it. He wanted only Scandal. Yet he admitted he'd never see her again. And Deedry was close, her adhesive thigh clinging to him, her slender arms across his bare chest. There was allure in her comely body, in the willing way she gave herself, the hungry way she suckled at him, as if she would devour him! My God he was only human, and there was the terrible fascination of witchery about the fair-skinned black girl. Only encased in her embrace, driving himself to her, loving her and loved by her, could he forget this hell in which he found himself.

Good God! He had to get out of this bed before she drained him again, and he was too weak to stagger out to the work wagon. The arrival of that labor cart every morning marked one more day Wade had endured, one more day he'd survived in Le Blanc's cane fields.

He shuddered. He'd thought he would die within the first week of torment in that sun-braised hell. He resigned himself to death, to falling in exhaustion or sunstroke, or worst of all suffocation. He'd seen men die in those fields, choking, unable to get a breath of oxygen. In his nightmares he saw himself fighting to get that one lifesaving gulp of air where there was none, his throat parching, his lungs collapsing. One thing was ordained. He'd die—in Le Blanc's hell—in Le Blanc's way. Tupelo, Merk and the arrogant Le Blanc watched him coldly, with a patience devoid of all human concern, poised like vultures to dispose of his white carcass. Each morning like this when he woke up, his first thought was that he'd fooled them. Hell, he fooled himself.

Well, he had to get up now. He couldn't go on lying here, even though he felt the blood engorging in his staff, the need fulminating through him for Deedry's body, Deedry's loving ministrations. He had to be up and dressed, even though he ached so agonizingly he did not see how he would make it through one more sweltering day in that breathless sun.

He drew a deep, ragged breath. Daily somehow he grew stronger, escaped the lingering and debilitating effects of the illness he'd contracted in the slave barracoon at New Orleans. The guards had told him he'd look back on it as the good old days. He bit back savage, raging laughter.

He turned carefully, staring at the sleeping girl beside him, her breast crushed fascinatingly against the rigid muscles of his chest. If it had not been for Kite and Deedry he would have been dead by now. Each night Deedry prepared the best food available in the most palatable fashions she could devise. To her kindness, quiet devotion, and fabulous lovemaking, he owed his recovery. To Kite he owed the chance to stay alive long enough to see daylight this morning. Damn them all! He was going to live.

He sweated. He had immersed himself in Kite's simple faith—as long as he breathed there was hope. As long as he went each morning into that seething caldron of Le Blanc's cane fields and lived through the heat and inhumanity until the night, there was hope, there was a chance—for something. Neither he nor Kite knew what they hoped for, only that they hoped. This was all he had to cling to, and he kept it vivid in his mind.

He stared down at his own unpalatable nakedness. Grinning savagely, coldly, he wondered what allurement Deedry discovered in his emaciated body. My God, he'd lost weight. The night Le Blanc's detectives had captured him in the St. Louis saloon and thrown him into that Royal Street slave barracoon, he'd weighed one hundred and ninety pounds. The pitiless Louisiana sun had cooked the flesh from his bones. The cotton scales showed him he weighed less than one hundred and thirty pounds. His skin was seared the color of old leather. Veins erupted blue and taut across the backs of his skeletal hands, along his wasted biceps, in his taut-skinned temples. His eyes, sunken in their sockets, stared in wary anguish at the world. Unceasing labor in the cane fields had hardened him, the sun had dehydrated him, dried him like cured meat. He was as hard as petrified stone. Thin cords of muscles rippled across his chest, his shoulders, along his thighs. Dehydrated, fired and fused with hatreds that never receded from the front of his mind, he persisted. He lived.

In his imagination he recalled Albert Le Blanc's hated countenance. His slow recovery—but recovery!—his adapting to the brimstone hell of the cane fields, amazed Albert Le Blanc, but pleased the planter as well. Cameroon's was a life sentence, imposed by Le Blanc, condemning him to hard labor as long as he lived, but death, in those soured acres. Le Blanc had believed it would prove a short imprisonment, ended by a quick death. With some cold pleasure, the master of French Pines Plantation saw that Cameroon would abide. He would persist, along with the strongest Negroes. His suffering would be extended, though the end would be the same. Le Blanc nodded at this, satisfied. Le Blanc did not care how long his prisoner lived, in his earthly hell. . . .

Gently, holding his breath, Wade disengaged his sweat-annealed body from Deedry's and got out of bed quietly, trying not to waken her.

He pulled on his clothes haphazardly, staring at Kite sleeping restlessly on his thin straw pallet.

Wade winced, staring down at the fevered black youth. As Wade grew stronger, he became aware of the way Kite was failing. Kite had already lived longer than most men existed in the canebrakes. Most Negroes died within their first year on cane-field work gangs. Kite had endured for almost three years—while the remorseless sun sapped the last gram of strength from him. Kite had existed on hatred and an obstinate refusal to bend, either to Le Blanc and his hated overseers or to death itself. But Kite suddenly found it harder each dawn to answer the work call; the deadly shadows of the cane fields were closing on him, no matter how savagely he fought against them.

Wade stood, delaying as long as he could before he had to shake Kite awake. Death stalked Kite now in those canebrakes. He'd developed a chronic cough. Where he'd previously eaten ravenously as armor against the killing heat and backbreaking labor of the fields, he barely ate at all now. The food he did force down refused to stay on his stomach. Last night he'd sat at the supper table in candlelight with Wade and Deedry, wheezing, almost unaware of them, staring dully at the floor.

And yesterday, for the first time, Kite had fallen in the fields.

Kite staggered and suddenly collapsed, felled by exhaustion and heat prostration. Hobbled by spancels at his ankle, Wade had run to the boy. Dr. Caprice arrived and, shaking his head, diagnosed Kite's illness as malaria, adding that it was too late to save him and that anyway few recovered from Bronze John. Kite's skin yellowed, turning a sickly bronze.

Wade shook his bared shoulder gently. Kite protested, fretting. "Kite. You'd better get up—if you can."

"Yeah. All right."

"Tupelo will use his whip."

"I'll git up. Just a minute more."

"If you can't make it, Kite, I'll tell him. They can't make you go if you're sick."

"No. No. Don't say nothing to Tupe—I'll git up." The boy struggled on the rumpled mattress, but could not move.

The door was thrust open and Tupelo stood there as the room was flooded with a bright shaft of early-morning sunlight. Wade turned, staring at the overseer.

"Kite's sick today, Tupelo. He can't make it today."

"I cain't make it, Tupe," Kite said, supporting himself on his his elbows. "I cain't."

Tupelo laughed without mirth. "Sure you can make it, Kite. Up and at 'em."

"I too sick, Tupe. I swear I too sick."

"Hell, git up. Or I'll use the tetch of my whip to git you up. . . . You dyin' no-how, Kite. Bronze John's got you. . . . You mought as well work as long as you can. You no good to nobody layin' round here."

Less than an hour after he'd staggered out into the rows of cane, Kite doubled suddenly, dropping his machete into the rich black silt. He cried out, heaving black vomitus. The other Negroes stared at him, stunned with terror. They backed away, crying out, stumbling across the rows, trying to get as far from him as possible.

Stumbling, Wade ran to where Kite had fallen. He knelt beside the boy. Kite's black eyes were white-rimmed with agony.

Tupelo swung down from his saddle horse and strode along the row to where Kite crouched on his knees, clutching his belly and retching up black fluid.

Tupelo stood over Kite, whip doubled in his fist.

From his knee, Wade squinted up at the overseer, who stood with the sun a giant halo behind him. "Kite can't stand it out here, Tupelo."

Tupelo had been staring at Kite, mouth twisted in a savage grin. He jerked his head up and peered, unblinking, at Wade. He gripped his whip tautly, looking as if he'd backhand Wade across the head for daring to speak. Instead, he drew a deep breath, his chest expanding like a puff adder. He spoke in a deadly-quiet tone. "Git yo'self on back to your work, Snakebrains."

Wade remained where he knelt, supported by his scythe, beside Kite in the blazing sun. Kite twisted his head, eyes dilated with agony. "Do what he say, brother." Kite vomited again helplessly.

His sweated face contorted with revulsion, Tupelo retreated a step involuntarily. "Get up, Kite. Git on your feet, nigger."

Kite sagged his head between his shoulders, shaking it from side to side with what appeared his last strength. He jerked his head up suddenly, grimacing with the pain gripping his stomach. "I cain't, Tupelo."

Tupelo motioned sharply with his head. One of the whippers ran forward. Tupelo nodded toward Kite. "Git him up."

The whipper struck Kite across the shoulders with his lash. Kite sobbed and fell forward, face first, into his own vomitus.

Growling, mindless, stumbling over his own shackles, Wade lunged upward toward Tupelo, swinging his scythe as he moved. Rage erupted from the throats of the blacks around them.

The glittering scythe struck Tupelo's shoulder. The big man threw up his arm to ward off the blow and almost lost his arm. The steel hacked deeply and blood spewed.

Tupelo growled. He ignored the slashed and bleeding arm. Like an enraged bull, he roared and pounced toward Wade.

Wade swung the awkward scythe back to swing again. Tupelo caught the shaft of the scythe in his fist. He wrenched it from Wade's grasp as he might yank a toy from a child.

Still growling, eyes red-rimmed and murderous, Tupelo hurled the scythe behind him. Blood gushed down his arm but he was unaware of the blood or the pain.

Tupelo jerked a five-inch knife from his belt as he advanced on Wade. His lips pulled back, baring his teeth and bright gums.

Tupelo dropped his right arm, holding the knife ready to rip upward. His other arm bled profusely and hung uselessly at his side. Unaware of pain, insensitive to his blood pulsing in rivulets along his biceps and clotting on the backs of his splayed fingers, he watched Wade warily, growling deep in his throat.

Wade looked around wildly, backing away. He knew Tupelo had to kill him to keep these other slaves subdued and submissive. As Wade stepped back, a cane stub snagged at his spancel. He staggered, plunged to his knees.

He stared up at Tupelo. If he fell, he would never get up, but he could not run away.

Something glittered beside his hand. For the briefest split in time, he stared at Kite's machete where it had fallen in the cane spurs and undergrowth.

As Tupelo's shadow fell across him, Wade scrambled forward, going under the swinging knife.

Tupelo hesitated as Wade seemed to prostrate himself like a human sacrifice.

Wade's fist closed on the machete. He turned and came upward, swinging wildly, trying only to force Tupelo back and keep him at bay with the shorter hunting knife.

Tupelo thrust at him again, slashing upward.

Wade's machete chopped across Tupelo's wrist before the overseer could draw back his arm. Blood spurted from Tupelo's forearm, and the knife fell from his pain-paralyzed fingers.

Helpless for that instant and blinded with pain. Tupelo stared at Wade, unmoving. In that split second of eternity, Wade could have killed him. God knew he wanted to. Through the haze of heat waves Wade saw the whippers beyond Tupelo, the big man's hand-picked enforcers, led by Merk, running toward them.

Closer, the machete-armed slaves crowded forward, muttering savagely, roused by the smell of Tupelo's blood, the sight of a worker attacking the hated foreman. The murmur swelled like some bloodthirsty roar of a ravening animal. In that instant, the slaves reverted to the bush of their forebears.

They ran forward, incensed by the odor of blood, the savagery of their hatred. They surrounded Wade and Tupelo, screaming and brandishing their machetes and scythes.

Merk and the whippers slowed to a walk. A few yards from where Tupelo and Wade stood over Kite, they hesitated, stopped.

The slaves enveloped Tupelo, closing in on him. Merk stood paralyzed. As if in catatonic trance, he stared at the mindless, rebelling slaves. Tupelo yelled his name, his scream shattered with terror. Merk only shook his head. He looked about impotently.

Suddenly, he heeled around and leaped into the saddle of Tupelo's horse. Face rigid, Merk stared for one taut moment at the slaves swarming over Tupelo. Then he wheeled the animal about and raced it along the narrow lane toward the Le Blanc mansion.

Wade felt himself engulfed as the blacks rushed in around him. They swung their machetes at Tupelo. Hacked about the head and shoulders, Tupelo staggered. He heeled around and tried to run. A slave slashed across his ankle, severing the tendon. Tupelo screamed in unutterable agony.

"Kill him! Kill him!" The voices raged around Wade.

Driven to his knees, bleeding from his head as well as his torso, Tupelo crouched, covering his head with his bloodied arms.

Wade yelled from the pit of his belly, "Stop it!"

For a full second the insensate slaves surged forward. Then they hesitated, machetes raised. They fixed white-rimmed eyes on Wade.

Wade looked around. The whippers stood impotently. Some had even dropped their whips. With Tupelo bleeding and helpless on his knees and Merk in flight, the whippers stood paralyzed. Most of them had suffered in these work gangs. By flattering Tupelo and fawning over him, they escaped the work crews, became part of his elite guard, armed with clubs and whips. Now, with Tupelo beaten to his knees, bloodied, their loyalties wavered.

The slaves stared at Wade, waiting. Wade clutched at that instant of indecision. He threw up both his arms, waving them.

"Merk's gone for the master," Wade yelled at them. The savage muttering ebbed slightly. "We got one chance. We stay here and kill Tupelo, they'll get us." He swung his arm toward the bayous. "We run . . . now . . . across this field . . . to that bayou . . . it's the only way to freedom . . . the only way to stay alive."

Freedom! That magic word ate through even the wildest bloodlust. The gang yowled in approval. A slave ran with a cold chisel and hammer from the supply wagon. In moments, Wade's spancel was ripped free, the bolt broken.

Wade swung his arm toward the rim of the field in the far distance. The slaves ran. Swinging their machetes, they hacked a path through the tightly massed green cane. Some of the guards hurled aside clubs and whips and ran with them.

Wade knelt and tried to lift Kite to his feet. The emaciated black boy shook his head, too ill and weak to rise. "No. Leave me here. I all right now. Get out, brother. Get away."

Wade hesitated. The first bloodhounds bayed distantly at the farmyard kennels. He squeezed Kite's shoulder in his hand, then jumped up and ran.

Screaming, laughing, cursing, the slaves ran as swiftly as they could find or hack tunnels through the tall cane rows. The fields steamed, breathless and suffocating.

The slaves rushed forward in a giant wedge, swinging scythes and machetes. They plunged into the almost impenetrable growth. They breathed, somehow. They ran, hacking a path.

The distant green of cypress and cedar in the bayous beckoned. The slaves kept their heads up, their eyes fixed on that far swampland as if it were a glimpse of paradise. But distances can deceive in sweltering heat. The cool trees, the promise of freedom, seemed to hang like a mirage beyond reach, to recede as the cane rows clotted tighter, like fists about their throats, cutting off the last wisps of oxygen.

The slaves slowed, gasping for breath. Wade stared around. There was no quick avenue of escape open to them. They could only grind to a halt in the thick undergrowth and as one man hack frantically at the cane, clearing a lane wide enough so they could breathe, even shallowly.

Hounds bayed behind them. The sound of the yelping animals carried menacingly across the fields. Some of the slaves fell on their knees in the clearing, gasping for air. Wade yelled at them, but they refused to get up. At least here they could breathe. They were terrified of being trapped, unable to breathe, deeper in those clotted rows.

Wade stared at them. Bloodhounds had reached the end of the lane behind them and now ran yelping across the fields.

"They'll kill you if they catch you here," Wade said.

"Let 'em come." One of the slaves shook his head. He swung his machete up high. Sweat rolled in marbles from his matted hair. He panted, barely able to speak. "Let them dogs come. We chop 'em up."

One of the other men, still on his knees, growled with laughter, nodding. "Yeah. Chop 'em up. Like we chop up the white mastas when they come."

Wade yelled at them. "They'll come with guns. We've only one chance to stay alive. We've got to get into those bayous."

He located the nearest fringe of bayous topping the far rise of the field. He didn't bother to speak again. He ran into a tunnel between the tall-reaching stalks, hacking at the obstructing outshoots of cane.

For a taut moment the other slaves hesitated. The hounds yowled frantically. The slaves jumped up. They crowded in behind Wade, swinging their machetes.

The baying hounds closed in behind them, incensed by the strengthening scent of their quarry.

The fleeing men didn't stop again. They cut a narrow swath, somehow finding a breath of air, driven by the yowling hounds, seeing the cool foliage spreading out ahead.

Wade broke out of the cane field at the brink of the bayou. He hesitated, gasping, his lungs aching. The other men ran out of the cane tunnels behind him. They could hear the dogs nearer behind them now, but they were laughing, breathless but exultant. The bayous stretched ahead—the hope of freedom in those vast, lost swamps.

Panting, Wade swung his arm, pointing toward the deep woods atop a slight knoll. Gasping for breath, knees weak, he ran up the incline. The slaves plodded after him, clutching their machetes. Some of them looked fearfully across their shoulders at the baying hounds struggling in the undergrowth at the brink of the field.

Wade slowed, his heart sinking. A sense of terrible wrong flashed through him. At first he didn't know what had sent panic flashing into his belly—he heard something ahead of him even before he saw it.

Taking long steps, he staggered along the incline. The sound was clear and distinct, unmistakable in the breathless silent heat —the click of shotguns being cocked to fire.

He slowed to a stop, lifting his hand to slow the blacks. They wavered, paused, stopped, holding their machetes ready.

Albert Le Blanc rode out of the beard of the hammock. He took his time, cold, deadly, unhurried. He was flanked and followed by other white planters, all on horseback and all armed. They fixed their guns on the slaves, surrounding them. The revolt was over.

The slaves were disarmed, their machetes and scythes tossed into the rear of a flatbed wagon. Le Blanc ordered them into a long single file. They walked with their hands locked behind their heads.

With mounted men riding beside them on the narrow shell-paved road, they were returned to the slave quarters of Le Blanc estate.

Kite had been brought in by wagon from the cane fields. Kite was dead. They had thrown his body carelessly against a brick wall at the smithy as if it were the carcass of an animal. Sickness gorged up in Wade's belly, and tears stung his eyes. He slumped in the sun.

Dr. Caprice worked over Tupelo on the shadowed table inside the blacksmith's hut. Caprice looked up at Le Blanc and shook his head. "Can save his life, Albert. But he ain't no-way no good as a work animal no more. Severed Achilles tendon. Won't never walk again. Might lose that arm, too."

Albert Le Blanc nodded and shrugged. He did not even glance toward his mutilated overseer. "Patch him up, doc. I'll get a few dollars for him—first slave coffle that passes."

Tupelo sobbed. "Please, Masta. It's me. Tupelo. I your nigger, Masta. Please. Before Gawd, Masta. I work."

Le Blanc shook his head and walked away. He did not look toward the black man again.

Le Blanc strode out into the sun, where the slaves had been herded into a circle. They slouched, terrorized, taut, staring at the ground.

Le Blanc raked his cold gaze across them, his mouth twisted with contempt. "Reckon you niggers think to get the day off because you rioted against me, eh?" He moved his head, staring at the tops of their lowered heads. He shook his own head and laughed. "You men are going back to the fields. Right now. You'll get back to work and you'll stay at work."

He waited, but no one spoke. The buzzing of flies was loud in the tension and silence.

Le Blanc glanced around, found the man he sought, the grinning Merk. He said, voice hard, "Merk, you're in charge. Head 'em out. . . . Long as you make the bastards work, long as you get my cane cut, the job is yours."

Le Blanc turned to move away, then hesitated again. He exhaled heavily. His gaze crawled across the ring of slaves, settled on Wade. Le Blanc's mouth pulled into a twisted smile, as cold and vile as spittle. "You, Cameroon . . . you just *thought* you were in hell, Cameroon. . . ."

33

"Scandal. I'm disappointed in you. I knew you to be an arrogant little baggage, but did you really think you could run away from me?"

General Butler laughed. He looked her over as if she were horseflesh he intended to own. His blue eyes clung and clawed and crawled like fat maggots across the rise of her breasts. At last he forced his gaze upward and met her glittering eyes. His voice taunted her. "Well, I predicted you'd come to me, didn't I?" He smiled, his lips pulling in a brazen smirk. "You've come even quicker than I thought. Quicker than I even dared hope." He nodded his head. "And on your knees, too."

She bit at her underlip. For one of the few times in her life she felt frightened and helpless against unequal odds. She'd heard Butler lock his outer door when he closed it behind her. His orders to his underlings had been specific. He was not to be disturbed under any circumstances.

Though the building teemed with soldiers, supplicants, sycophants and guards, she was effectively and totally isolated, alone with the general as if they were together in some remote and barricaded tower.

"I would not have come," she said. She kept her eyes straight ahead. "But I had to."

"Of course you had to." He laughed. "Do you think I'd let the loveliest tart in New Orleans run away without even saying goodbye to me?"

"I'm not running away." She spread her hands helplessly. A sense of depression had enveloped her at the exit-point guardhouse; it deepened now. He was not going to let her go at all. She had returned here with faint hope, which now she abandoned entirely. Alex, of course, had insisted upon returning with her, but he was barred at the foyer downstairs, as she had known in advance he would be. Poor Alex. He was more helpless than she was. He had looked so slender and ineffectual against the swaggering soldiery downstairs. She had felt a rush of pity for him, even distracted as she was.

General Butler walked around his desk, taking his time like a Great Dane toying with a poodle. He examined the papers which had been sent in with her. He glanced up. "It says here you were taking two trunks, several suitcases and many hat boxes. This sounds like you were running away. I was in your home only this morning. You mentioned nothing about taking even a brief journey." His lips twisted. "Perhaps if you had, I might have facilitated matters for you."

She winced. "For a price."

"No one gets anything for nothing, little girl." His voice hardened. "I told you this morning how deeply, how devotedly and passionately, I had desired you—since the first time I saw you. I also assured you that I would be back to see you, that I would not be put off any more. Suddenly, you are stopped at a checkpoint, heading out, with two trunks, suitcases and hat boxes. It sounds as if you plan more than an afternoon's jaunt along the shores of the lake."

She drew a deep breath. "Alex Vigneaux brought me distressing news, General—"

"Yes. He distresses me. He with his pretty face and limp wrists. I don't know what a hot-blooded filly like you can see in a milksop like that—"

"—distressing news," Scandal persisted, her voice rising over Butler's taunting tones, "about my uncle. Uncle Julien is desperately ill. At his summer place. The doctor says it is malaria—"

"Malaria. That old battleax is dying of Bronze John and you ask me to believe you're dashing off to visit him?"

"If I hope to see him alive, I must go." Scandal lied easily, the words forming themselves smoothly.

"So. That's why you were headed out with servants and worldly goods—for a deathbed visit with your uncle?"

"Yes. That's the truth. . . . I beg you, general. Don't delay me any more. Whatever is between us . . . whatever might be between us . . . can be dealt with—anyway you wish—to your satisfaction when I return."

"When you return. I see. If I let you go now, you will come back to me—of your own volition?"

She nodded eagerly, trying to smile faintly, but not too lightly. "Oh, I will . . . Ben. I swear it. I will. I've been a fool. And I know that. But right now I'm distracted with worry over Uncle Julien. I can't think of anything else."

"I had no idea the old boy was so important to you."

"He's the only relative I have in the world, general. The only one. I am his ward. I am all he has. He lies dying—"

"And with a considerable fortune to leave behind, I believe."

"He's too ill to think about anything like that—"

"Of overwhelming proportions, even considering the confiscatory nature of inheritance taxes—"

"He's very ill, general. He lies dying. I beg you."

He shrugged. "Don't be so impatient. If he's as ill as you suggest, I don't think he will change beneficiary just because you are delayed a few hours."

"He may die if I am delayed a few hours."

"So be it." He shrugged. "Then he will just have to die alone, won't he?"

"Please, general. Won't you, in the name of human kindness, let me go to him?"

He spread his hands, his eyes tracing the outline of her bosom lovingly. "That's up to you. I am not inhuman. I'm willing to let you have the visa you need to exit the military zone and visit your dying, Midas-rich uncle."

"Then let me go."

He shook his head. "But not on the promissory note of your returning to me—sometime—in your gratitude."

She flinched as if he had struck her. "I will come back to you. On your terms."

He came slowly around his polished desk and leaned against it, eyeing her relentlessly, his mouth pulled into a taunting smile. He crossed his ankles, staring at her until she felt an overwhelming impulse to cross her arms across her breasts like the soubrette in some old-fashioned melodrama. "I don't know what you think I am," he said.

"Please, General Butler. I know what your price is. I have agreed to pay it."

"When you return."

"I am distracted with worry about my uncle. You wouldn't demand of me that I—try to—entertain you now—with my mind sick with worry?"

"Wouldn't I? I can tell you what I wouldn't do. I wouldn't accept your promise to pay later. I am a general in the United States Army, girl. I was a lawyer, a powerful and astute politician. One does not get where I am by being naive and trusting and gullible as a fly swallower."

She sagged, her eyes brimming with tears. She kept her head erect, her chin tilted. "What do you want?"

"It seems to me that I told you you would come to me—on your knees. You have come. But you are not on your knees."

She looked about, the gray sunlight at the huge windows, the deep carpeting, the heavy furnishings, the general watching her coolly. "Is that what you want? Do you want me on my knees?"

He drew a deep breath, his eyes clouding over faintly. He touched at his lips with the tip of his tongue. "That might do. For a start."

Her hands at her sides, Scandal sank to her knees where she stood. "I beg you," she said. "On my knees. Please let me go."

"You'll get your visa," he said, "when I am ready."

He straightened and crossed the narrow space between them. He stood gazing down at her, his face flushed, his breathing impaired. He reached out and closed his left hand on the back of her head. She shuddered, but remained unmoving while he freed the pins, letting her hair fall darkly about her shoulders. His eyes had glazed over. His hands shook, but they were rough on her head, pulling her closer. She understood what he demanded of her, what he was going to force her to do. She felt a wave of revulsion burn hotly through her body. She was ill, repulsed, but she did not resist. She dared not resist. . . .

Alex asked her no questions about her encounter with General Butler; she volunteered nothing.

For hours she crouched in the darkened tonneau of the carriage beside him. Her mind spun and struggled in the sour sewer of disgust and revulsion. She tried to tell herself the only thing that mattered was she had her visa; he had let her go, she'd escaped him, and she'd escaped New Orleans. For a little while at least, she was free.

She shivered. Finally, Alex was able to bring her out of the depths of her depression. He promised her parties, horseback riding, swimming in the Gulf, long and lazy afternoons in a world far removed from the sordid memory of occupied New Orleans.

She was able to sit up straighter, to give some fragmented attention to the countryside through which they passed. This did nothing to elevate her spirits. She found only gray desolation in the destitute rural regions. The battles had not scarred this area, but had choked, starved and deprived it. The sons who had marched away from these old homes were now prisoners in some alien union stockade, or were buried in the rocky fields of northern Virginia, casualty statistics. She found nothing but want and deprivation. Wasted, empty-eyed people watched silently as Gischairn's elegant conveyance rolled past, drawn by fat, prancing animals.

She tried to look forward to the excitement Alex promised in a world untouched by the blockades of war. She found herself wishing for Wade, praying for him, lonely and lost without him. She tried to concentrate on the happiness she'd known in New Orleans, all those bright ballrooms through which she'd wafted as lightly as her faint perfume, adored by hundreds of lingering eyes. But all those eyes were Ben Butler's eyes, the hands reaching for her were his rough fists. She cried out and bit down hard on her lip, feeling soiled, degraded.

It was a warm summer evening when they arrived at the Vigneaux mansion overlooking the disputed Gulf, patrolled by Yankee warships, but lying serene and tranquil and aloof. Stepping from the coach into the sapphire twilight, she shivered faintly, not at all reassured by this quiet elegance, and she clung apprehensively to Alex's arm. The stately old home overlooked the gray beach and the darkling Gulf. In a row of elegant chateaus, the Vigneaux manse loomed imposingly, like some unapproachable feudal citadel behind invisible moats.

In the very remoteness of its splendour, the Vigneaux estate looked most forbidding. She could not believe she was welcome here—in her notoriety, in her inner insecurity, Ellen's daughter of a mustee father, a fugitive from Falconhurst. She felt frightened even when the doors were flung open to her and lights and servants spilled out warmly to greet her. She heard the voices, the laughter, the bustling people hurrying to assure her comfort and pleasure, but she felt as if it were all meant for someone else, as if she were an intruder here, barely tolerated. She had the inescapable sense that this luxurious mansion was deserted and she was alone and friendless and lost in an alien place. She pressed closer to Alex.

"Are you all right?" he whispered.

"Don't leave me."

He laughed. "Of course I won't leave you. You have nothing to worry about. Everybody here will love you. Mother has been looking forward to having you here." He laughed again at the look of doubt shadowing her eyes. "Really."

She nodded. It grew quite dark as they left the carriage and crossed the wide veranda into the Vigneaux home, from which brilliant lamps tossed great streamers of cheerful yellow light over the tiles, the gravel, the lawn and the distant hedges. As exhausted as she was, she could appreciate that it was all extremely beautiful, costly, and cared for, that its blurring design was Virginia Colonial, an antique brick chateau reared gemlike in a setting of luxuriant gardens which swept down to the beaches. Alex led her into the foyer. Though the house was crowded with summer guests and live-in relatives, Alex's mother was nowhere to be seen, nor did he remark on her absence. Without his mother there to greet her, Scandal felt the house was barren and cold and closed to her.

Scandal looked around her, assaulted by a babble of laughing voices. She felt intimidated in the great formal foyer paneled in native magnolia and gleaming with shards of lights from lamps and chandeliers which glowed, reflected in the walls, the parquet flooring and the lovely eyes of pretty girls. There was profligate magnificence about this place, this summer retreat peopled with beings dedicated to a stubborn denial of war and hardship.

Ahead of her a broad staircase rose to a less illumined and cavernous upper hallway—as if it were in those dark crannies that the family truly existed with their hurts and their secrets. Despite the noise cascading over her, an intense stillness seemed to smoke downward from the dark corridors and envelop her.

She tried to shake off the mood of depression. It had been a long and evil journey with the sordid business in Butler's office at its outset. She tried to respond to Alex's assurances. She'd been in the house for less than five minutes and yet she was overwhelmed by a sense of oppression and foreboding. She wanted to turn and run across that wide and fragrant terrace, back into the gossamer night where she belonged.

At eleven the next morning there was a knock on her bedroom door as her maid hooked the last eyelet on her pastel-print morning dress.

"It's Alex, Scandal; if you are ready, we'll go in and see Mother for a few minutes before lunch."

Scandal surveyed her reflection in the mirror apprehensively and joined Alex in the silent upper corridor. Along both sides of the hallway stretched many doors, all of them closed and forbiddingly silent.

She warned herself she was imagining obstacles where none existed. They wanted her here, even if she could not convince herself that she belonged. Still, there was no reason to look for trouble in advance. Mrs. Vigneaux, the matriarch of the clan herself, had invited her here; she need not have done it if she hadn't wanted her.

She drew a deep breath. Most of her nervous uneasiness sprang from the fact that she'd never been a guest in so imposing a house. Not even Gischairn's St. Charles Avenue mansion had prepared her for this kind of aloof elegance. At least Julien would be proud of her. She had come a long way from a bed wench's cot at Falconhurst. Julien-Jacques Gischairn had done all he could to prepare her for this moment. It was up to her to carry it off.

Still she felt weak and unworthy.

Alex led her down the carpeted passage to the east wing of the house, which was set aside as the sole province of his mother. Her heart sank a little in her chest and rattled oddly. He rapped at a closed door before he pushed it open and ushered Scandal into a vast, sunlit living room unlike anything she had ever seen before.

Like the lower hall, the walls were paneled in light magnolia, polished to a brilliant sheen so even the sunlight mellowed and blurred in its depth into faint amber. In a great overstuffed armchair, reinforced with pillows and coverlets, reclined an aging woman with white hair, fragile features but chilled undeceived eyes that unreasonably and unaccountably recalled General Butler to Scandal's mind.

The room was furnished with every convenience to allay its mistress's anxieties, if any such existed, to ensure her comfort and to shield her from the real world, daily growing more real beyond her tall french windows. Despite all these expedients dedicated to Mrs. Vigneaux's pleasure, Scandal's eyes were drawn to a book on the table beside the aging woman as the centrepiece of this room, of this woman's life. Mrs. Vigneaux set the tome aside as Alex and Scandal entered, and there was almost a reluctance in her action. Scandal saw by the embossed title on its morocco-bound cover that it was *The Jefferson Bible*. She had never heard of such a book. Mrs. Vigneaux noticed her glance. She reached out and caressed the volume. "You might wish to read this sometime, my dear," Mrs. Vigneaux suggested. "The life and morals of Jesus—taken directly from the texts of Matthew, Mark, Luke and John by Thomas Jefferson."

Scandal smiled faintly and nodded.

"Mother," Alex said, "this is Scandal."

Mrs. Vigneaux smiled, her waxy face creasing. "Of course it is, Sonny. I recognize her from the paeans of praise you've heaped upon her. Welcome, child." Then Mrs. Vigneaux turned and stared at Alex. "Well, go on. Leave us alone, Sonny. We want to get to know each other. Don't we, my child?"

"Of course," Scandal said weakly, unable to imagine anything she desired less.

When they were alone in the silent room, Mrs. Vigneaux gazed unblinkingly at Scandal for some moments. Scandal had seen the same look in the faces of purchasers fingering merchandise in fine stores; she felt less than human; she was a commodity to the older woman. Mrs. Vigneaux's voice flowed, low, level, somehow warm and at once imperious. "I want you to marry my son Alex."

Scandal's lips parted. She stared at the elderly matron, her black eyes wide. Whatever she'd expected to hear, it was not this. She managed to whisper, "What?"

"How old are you?" the aging dowager inquired.

"Eighteen."

"And alone in the world. Except for your uncle—that errant old reprobate Julien-Jacques Gischairn."

"Yes."

"Well," said Mrs. Vigneaux with an air of finality, "it would be a good marriage for you. Excellent. Advantageous. Money. Social position. Security. What else could a young girl ask?"

"I'm not in love with Alex." Scandal tried to smile. "I love him. I do. But I'm not in love with him. I think Alex understands that."

"I believe he does." Those disenchanted eyes, as cold, undeceived and calculating as Ben Butler's fixed on her. But Mrs. Vigneaux's voice continued gently. "I believe love is very much overrated in marriage. By sentimentalists. Fools. I don't think you're that sentimental. I'm sure you're no fool. Many qualities are far more urgent and important in a marriage contract than love. You'll know that by the time you're my age. . . . I hope it won't be too late for you."

Scandal did not answer. Her thoughts spun in her mind. She wanted Wade. Only Wade. Yet common sense counseled her that she would very likely never see Wade Cameroon again in this life. It was almost a year since she had seen him. If Gischairn mentioned Wade at all, it was to advise her coldly to forget him. This sort of marriage proposed by Mrs. Vigneaux—the arranged contract involving finances, security, position—was what Julien had trained, aimed and polished her for. She felt as if Gischairn stood at her shoulder, warning her sardonically to enter this compact with Alex's mother.

Biting back an inner ache of sadness, Scandal managed to smile. "What does Alex have to say about this?"

Mrs. Vigneaux almost smiled. "What indeed? I could arrange many far more propitious marriage covenants for my son, child. Some where both families have wealth enough so the stipulation would be almost a merger. But I am considering Alex's wishes in this matter. We have discussed his getting married. I have told him he must be married—within the year. I have done all I can for him. The best schools. The grand tour of Europe. A most generous allowance. Trust funds. I paid a substitute to fight for Alex in the Confederate Army. I have protected him. I shall go on protecting him. But I am no longer young. I must face my own mortality. He has been my whole life—all my life. I cannot even consider dying until I have made every arrangement for his security. Marriage is a part of that security. I want him married—for many reasons. He agrees to marry. But it is you who must be his bride, or no one, he says. I cannot budge him on that."

"I'm sorry," Scandal said with some irony.

"So am I. There are fine aristocratic Southern families. There are girls I could control. I don't believe I can run your life. Not at my age. . . . Once, I could have, but I am too old, too tired. So, I'll see Alex safely married to you—and leave the rest to heaven."

"You don't care how I feel about it?"

"Not really. I hope you will be happy. But that is of moderate importance to me. I hope Alex will be happy. But his happiness is not my first priority either. I want him married. That is important. I am quite willing to negotiate with you. On your terms. I will make you this firm offer: if you will marry my son Alex, I will pay you twenty thousand a year—as long as you stay married to Alex, for life, if it works out that way. This will be your own money, to use as you wish. Alex needn't even know about it. You could be rich. I am offering you a fortune."

Scandal caught her breath, held it. "When do I have to let you know?"

Mrs. Vigneaux shook her head. "There are no options, my dear. There are a dozen lovely young girls downstairs. If you don't agree to marry my son, one of them will. I'll be quite as pleased with any one of them as Alex's wife . . . only poor little Alex believes he can be happy only with you."

34

The wedding of Miss Scandal Gischairn to Alex Vigneaux was a festive event to be marked in Delta history not only as a ceremony of unprecedented splendor, but as the highest moment of social glamour in the terrible time of military subjection under the hated heel of the Yankee invader. This single moment of exotic celebration was seen almost as one gallant and desperate act of defiance against the mighty Federal war machine itself. Long before the rest of the Confederacy suspected itself totally and cruelly overmatched in this bloody war, New Orleans had seen the final and tragic end. But for one brief hour that amber September day, the victor was vanquished, overcome, defied.

Invitations went out to a select upper coterie of American and French families. From the first moment a sense of daring and excitement galvanized the citizens who existed under the Yankee heel and who had somehow survived Bronze John's latest mindless onslaught. The people closed ranks, rose in an effervescent flush of anticipation, of determination. Any excuse for festivity might have served to unite them, but the marriage of the loveliest, most exciting belle of the parish into one of its oldest families was a catalyst rousing soul-stirring reaction, heart-expanding, electrifying, thrilling. The two worlds of the crescent city for a little while merged as one and turned out in all their faded, ancestral finery.

The overflow of horse-drawn conveyances disgorging wedding guests spilled along the wide avenue and into all the side streets around St. Paul's Church. Such a display of Creole-American pomp had not been seen during the long war years. Coaches of every description, trim and condition settled arow, horses patiently sagging in their traces. The guests began arriving more than two hours early in the sweltering heat, laughing in parties and groups and couples, walking down the shaded avenue. They hurried into the church seeking the most advantageous pews from which to see and to be seen, until the last seat was gone. Latecomers walked as far as a mile, and found uncomfortable perches in an upper choir loft usually reserved for black worshipers.

Few of the guests complained about the heat, though dainty fans swished constantly and strong men sweated tight collars limp. Most poised expectantly for the first glimpse of the bride. Scandal was once more in the good graces of the most exalted family; all had been forgiven, the unfortunate Manon Levesque forgotten. Scandal was now a Vigneaux, or she soon would be. This alteration in her circumstances modified her character and reputation and the public's perception of them in most uncanny ways.

Scandal's sensational return to New Orleans that September coincided with a marked revision of estimation of her; it can be compared to a time when the queen's seamstress evolved as if through some fairy chrysalis into the monarch's regent.

The huge cathedral was vaguely lighted by thousands of candles, illumined by white dresses, white flowers, white Bibles and white faces. There was somehow a blood-red brilliance in the afterglow.

Julien-Jacques Gischairn found a wicked delight in all this pomp and ceremony. It pleased his sense of the ridiculous that these hidebound racists had gathered to watch a *black* girl marry into their prejudiced bosoms. And most bitterly rewarding of all, *he* had engineered this impossible feat. He had taken a kitchen slut, with slurring tongue and rough hands and a lack of all the graces, and brought forth a swan to thrill these fools. He wanted to laugh, but contented himself with a twisted, sweet-tasting smile that was not meant to be shared.

Two arrivals created sensations within themselves and alleviated the heated boredom of the breathless waiting. General G. F. Shedley, the military governor of the state of Louisiana, arrived with his spit-and-polish retinue. Somehow the gold and purple of his authority recalled the laurels of the Roman legions. The federal military establishment was not yet master of the world, but was on its way. Onlookers were jostled, pushed aside, a way cleared for the governor-general, almost as though he were accompanied by flourishing of banners and trumpets. Whispers buzzed in his wake. One knew General Shedley came in deference to the name and influence of the Vigneaux family. The governor must be counted among the friends of the groom. But one saw later at the wedding reception that the governor had switched allegiances: he was sweated with excitement, captivated by the bride, almost to the point of buffoonery. He stumbled over people getting at her, crying out, "If there is anything I can do for you. Anything at all. You have only to ask." But this was later.

General Benjamin F. Butler's arrival was less spectacular visually, but even more stirring for its shock value. Who could have invited him? He was far more than villain incarnate, he was the embodiment of the enemy, he was its cold and swaggering symbol of oppressive arrogance. Necks craned and women whispered behind their fans.

Butler found his place and sat sweated, almost drunk, outraged and totally depressed, between heartbroken tears and savage raging laughter. He could not believe this comedy. He could not accept it. He could not change it. He had been unable to approach Scandal in the days since her return to New Orleans. God knew he had tried to get at her, but she had remained totally unreachable behind the impregnable walls of her uncle's mansion on St. Charles Avenue.

He stared in anguish at that altar where Scandal and Vigneaux would exchange their vows, plight their troth, ruin their lives. That damned little nance! What in hell was Scandal thinking to marry a bloodless, effeminate little popinjay like Vigneaux? Not all the money in the world was going to keep her warm in bed.

The general's red-veined eyes burned, his dry throat ached. He wanted Scandal. He had thought coherently of little else since he had briefly and erotically tested her wares in his office—in exchange for a travel visa. He had dreamed ahead to that fantastic moment when Scandal returned again to the confines of his sovereignty. And now she was marrying into the wealthiest and most influential of the French families.

Damn. His mouth twisted. Perhaps he could demand *droit du seigneur* from Vigneaux. God knew the little pantywaist was going to need help before his wedding night ended.

Suddenly, the mammoth organ sounded, gasped and wheezed into the wedding march.

The waiting was over. There was a final rustling of guests rising in the pews, pressing closer, tiptoeing to see, an awed inhalation. Then a profound silence spread across the auditorium, and moving to the music, the bride came as part of an incredible procession of Creole-French-American feminine pulchritude. One seldom saw so many glorious flowers gathered in one bouquet. But the beauty of all the bridesmaids dimmed and diminished as Scandal, eyes demurely fixed on her betrothed awaiting her near the altar, flowed with the music down the wide aisle on pristine red carpeting.

People caught their breath involuntarily, stunned at this display of sensational beauty. The bride's radiant loveliness burned itself into the memories of them all. For generations they would measure all beautiful brides against the slender sylph who floated, idealized and unreal, before their benumbed gazes.

General Butler caught back a helpless sob and almost choked. He stood straighter, sucking in his potbellied gut as if it were somehow all-important.

Governor Shedley's mouth sagged aslant. His eyes widened. He had attended with some reluctance. He stood entranced.

Scandal's veil was gossamer and served only to accentuate the delicate planes and lines of the cameo perfection of her features. Her dazzlingly white gown was cut extremely low at the bodice, daringly exposing shadowed cleavage and sapphire rise and curve of her breasts to the very brim of their areolae. The ultra-slim waist flowed out in lines of lace and linens and silks, suggesting trim thighs and calves and ankles. She carried a minute white Bible, and she glided like an ethereal nymph in the shimmer of candlelight.

Only the solemn homage to the almost pagan loveliness of the bride remained in the most recalcitrant mind. Dry-eyed, the groom's mother sat in the first pew and thought back over all the expense, the challenge of Catholic dogma, the bending of rules to allow a non-Catholic to marry in the church, the anxieties, the doubts, the questions, the inevitable botches. Madame Vigneaux sighed, gazing at a bride lovely enough for her son. It was worth it, all worth it, after all.

Julien-Jacques Gischairn stared at Scandal's radiant loveliness and didn't believe it, even though he had created and polished it. He blinked away tears. His throat felt tight. How many young girls had he trained and honed and educated and foisted on the socially elite over the past thirty years? God only knew. But of all of them, Scandal was the loveliest, she was indeed his supreme achievement.

General Butler sank suddenly in his pew. He sagged to his knees and choked back sobs he could not contain. He pressed his head down as if he were praying, and maybe he did pray, in his anguish. For months afterward, he would be sitting alone and he would break suddenly into tears he could not control.

The eternal day ended—the reception, the dancing, the long receiving lines, the compliments, the laughter and crying—it all ended, and finally Scandal and Alex were alone in their suite at the Vigneaux summer home. It had been formally closed for the season, which made it all the more an ideal honeymoon retreat.

Scandal teetered on the verge of exhaustion. Despite a cool outward demeanor, the inner fabric of her nerves was tattered after the unending ordeal. She had spent most of the day taut-drawn, in a nervous state of tension. Somehow, she expected the glamorous dream to end abruptly in ugly nightmare—perhaps pregnant, barefooted Hester and the Peavey family would barge into the church to claim her. She alone knew what an impostor she was, how little she belonged in this place, in this marriage.

She was so tired she wanted nothing more than to fall across the bed and sleep. She knew better. Every bride has her nuptial duty. Alex would want to make love to her. He had never been a passionate or even an aggressive lover, but there was the wedding-night ritual. Somehow, she would submit to him—and smile. She would do all she could to conceal her need for Wade, her desperate emptiness; she would make him believe he satisfied and thrilled her. It was the least she could do for him. She could do nothing for herself now, and she owed him that display of devotion, false and empty as it was.

In their master bedroom, Alex prowled before a mirror and surveyed his reflection sourly. He too, was exhausted from the long tense day of ceremony. He ran his fingers through his dark curls and touched at his precisely trimmed mustache. Then he gazed into his own eyes in that clouded mirror, thankful it was not brilliantly lit as he faced himself in this moment of truth. He felt his body wracked with a tremor of anguish and dread. Then he told himself coldly that if he could want any woman he would desire—and respond to—Scandal's wine-tinted perfection.

"Alex?"

He turned to the radiant reality standing behind him. He caught his breath and gazed at the delectable vision. If the world had thought her beautiful beyond words at the wedding and during the reception, he wished they could know how incredibly lovely she was in her transparent gown of lace and gossamer watered silk.

"Jesus." He muttered the oath in an anguished whisper, a despairing curse, self-vilification. The anguish was lost on his bride. She smiled gently and went to him, warmed by his approval.

He touched her lightly, and his brief kiss was without passion, but she was too tired to care, too preoccupied to be concerned.

"Are you tired?" he said.

"I'm all right. We made it."

"Yes. We made it. Thank God. We are here alone at last. . . . I've always wanted you where I could protect you, Scandal, look after you, take care of you."

She laughed at him.

He frowned. "What's the matter?"

She kissed the tip of his nose, teasing him. "You sound more like a mother hen than a—lover—on his wedding night."

"Oh God, Scandal, maybe I am more mother hen than—than lover."

"I don't think so." She laughed. "If you are not a fiery lover yet, you will be before I'm through with you. I know how to please you . . . I know a hundred ways to please you."

"You please me now—as you are—smiling at me—in a thousand ways."

"Wait until I get you on a bed."

He winced, and for the first time Scandal sensed the anxiety in her young husband's manner, an uneasiness that upset her. She knew so little, really! Wade had made love to her. Wade had taught her what love was—but that was love with two lovers vitally in love with each other; there was nothing to give, nothing to take, there was only mutual sharing in every touch, every kiss, every glance. She had not thought her life with Alex Vigneaux would be easy, but she had assumed all the guilt—she did not love him, she was hardheadedly marrying him without love; she was making a bargain she meant to keep.

But she was unlettered in the ways of the world, in the physiological and psychological differences in human beings. In her mind all couples waited eagerly through months of courtship and engagement for this night. She would not have that ecstasy, but she would try to deceive him with the counterfeit of pretense, because as she had told Madame Vigneaux, she did love Alex, even if she was not—and never could be—in love with him.

She had believed he would want nothing more than to remove the shimmering fabric of her downy gown and go immediately to bed. But he hesitated, in a reluctance she found unsettling. She had heard that many brides are timid, demanding that all candles be extinguished before coming out of the closet—but Alex wasn't the bride. She watched him oddly. He seemed to want to prolong their conversation, and yet he yawned in painful exhaustion. His gaze barely touched her nakedness, accented and revealed through the gossamer fabric. He scarcely glanced toward the bed, its pristine white covers turned back for them.

Troubled, Scandal lay down across the bed, her diaphanous gown twisted tightly upon the warm rises and planes of her shapely body. She fought the aching fatigue that threatened to inundate her. She forced herself to smile up at Alex, falsely, invitingly, promising, flirting. She extended her bared arms toward him.

"I'll just have a drink," he said.

She laughed, though the premonition of wrong intensified, quivering like a chill through her. She tried to joke lightly. "Are you afraid of me, Alex?"

"Of course not!" He laughed with her, but his hands shook when he poured a tumbler full of bourbon and splashed in water. "Of course not." Inwardly, Alex winced. How could he admit he was afraid of himself, of his own inadequacy, his sudden and terrible realization of how criminally he had deceived her, and how evil that deception was, magnified in this bower. "Let me have a drink." He turned and gestured with the heavy glass toward her. "Won't you have one?"

She stifled a yawn. "No. Whiskey doesn't really sharpen your senses, darling—it dulls them."

He winced again as if slapped. Maybe that's what I want, he thought.

"I want to be aware of everything that happens this night, don't you?" she persisted.

Jesus.

Putting aside the empty glass, Alex coughed spasmodically. He came to the bed, walking without anticipation, with heavy tread. He met her eyes, but he was unable to smile.

"I love you," he whispered. He ran his hands along her thighs, smiling oddly down at her. He used, as he never had before, gross and salacious words.

She went cold. Then, seeing that he was suffering, she relented. He might need the artificial stimulus of obscenity to rouse him, even on his wedding night, as obviously he'd needed the liquor. She drew a deep breath, tried to smile. "Come fuck me," she whispered, wanting only to please him, to be whatever she perceived he wanted her to be.

She saw him stiffen as if she'd struck him. She felt helpless. What did he want of her? Did he want to mouth bawdy, brothel phrases as if she were a streetwalker while she lay passive, unmoved, chaste and virginal? She didn't know what he wanted. She didn't know what to do.

"Please," she whispered, growing frantic. "Come to bed."

"Yes." He caught the sheer fabric of her gown and thrust it upward over her head with all the gentle consideration of a rapist, but when she lay naked and raised her arms to him, he stood indecisively, looking down at her, his sunken eyes anguished. Then he stared at the gown crushed in his fist and threw it to the floor behind him. He sprawled across the mattress beside her.

Shocked, she found his body fevered. He sweated profusely; his nightshirt was already damp with sweat, stained at the armpits and across the chest. He tried to ignore what was happening to himself and sought her body almost as if forcing himself. His soft hands kneaded the rise of her breasts, the rounded heap of her golden belly, the dainty darkness marking her thighs. Sweat marbled and spilled from his forehead.

She reached for him, found him flaccid. He drew in his breath sharply. His hands tightened on her roughly, as if the friction of their flesh might somehow ignite a fire in his loins.

He sweated, miserable. She whispered to him soothingly. "Relax," she begged. "It will be all right, Alex . . . it will be all right."

But it was not all right. The bride assessed as the loveliest in the memory of the town tried every trick she knew, had read of, heard whispered, or could imagine in her growing desperation. Nothing helped.

The distressing minutes stretched into galling hours, the unhappy hours multiplied. The bed was rumpled, discolored with his perspiration, and like a pit of rocks for her. And nothing roused him.

At last, he shuddered and fell away from her, limp and desolated and defeated. He sobbed suddenly. "I'm sorry, Scandal. I'm sorry. God knows, I'm sorry."

35

The jumbled dawn crept into the room and ended the nightmarish night. Scandal lay sleepless. She'd been overwhelmed with fatigue, but now she was coldly, sickly wakeful, afraid she would never sleep again, and yet she who had danced in scores of Delta dawns was so tired she did not want to move. And though her eyes burned with weariness, she did not shut them as the room brightened into wan pinks and desolate grays of morning before seven.

A clock in the corridor struck the hour, and she lay listening to the strokes of the chimes, feeling something die within her. She wanted to turn over and bury her face in her pillow, to weep disconsolately, weep out the ugliness and the anguish, to cry for all she had lost and all she would never have. But she did not move. Her tangled hair spilled like a dark shroud around her head. She lay listlessly with one slender golden arm dangling over the side of the bed.

She tried to put some sense into what had happened to her. Life had dealt her a shabby and evil hand. She had been deceived by a man she had thought good and kind and loving.

Lacking the courage to admit the truth about himself—whatever that proved to be!—he had played out this cheap and vulgar comedy to deceive her.

She stared at the lightening ceiling, trying vainly to understand the workings of a mind capable of this gross cruelty. Her honesty forced her to admit that she herself was not guiltless. She had married without love, for profit. She deserved what she got. But still the terrible blow to her pride remained, along with sick fears for the future. Her own guilt made Alex's treachery no easier to bear.

When the chimes ceased and the silence settled again in the chilled room, Scandal got up sluggishly from the bed. She found her heaviest robe and, shivering, slipped into it as if to conceal her body, which Alex found repulsive, from Alex, from herself, from God's eyes.

Savagely, she yanked the waist cord and tied a fierce knot at her waist.

Alex still lay, his arm thrown across his eyes, on the bed, unable to speak, unable to face her or the prospect of this dismal new morning and all the empty days ahead.

She walked tiredly across the room and sank upon a brocaded, pillowed bench at the inset windows overlooking the faintly shadowed garden. The ground glistened mistily, the sun winking obscenely in the dew, a frosty chill promising an early winter. The gulf stretched gray and dull, matching her mood. She sat and stared through the paneled windows, trying to think, trying desperately not to think.

Then she heard the whisper of the mattress as Alex got up. He came across the room and sank into a club chair, his head in his hands, dejected and self-reviling. His sweated nightshirt, wrinkled, sweated, and opened with such anticipation last night, now left unbuttoned, unnoticed.

They sat for a long time, quite close and yet withdrawn, two strangers imprisoned together in Eden, cellmates in paradise. At last he sighed deeply and looked up. She heard the crinkle of fabric when he moved in the big chair. She saw that she had not been alone in hell last night—his deathly-pale face showed the havoc last night's farce had wreaked upon him. His eyes were red-rimmed, puffed and sick. He tried to smile, a look which failed into something more like dread.

"I'm sorry," he said quietly. When she shifted on the bench, he raised his hand nervously. "Please don't go! Stay there; I want to talk to you. I've got to talk to you."

Scandal nodded and turned slightly on the bench to face him and watched him with half-closed eyes, her hands folded in her lap.

"Scandal, for God's sake have mercy. Treat me—as kindly as you always have."

She frowned, studying him. "What do you mean?"

He moaned. "Scandal, I've done a vicious thing to you, to me, to both of us. I haven't a word I can say in my own defense. I deserve no pity. I've been malicious. I can't ask anything of you—except forgiveness."

"I don't know—what I'm supposed to forgive."

'Scandal—my dearest Scandal—I never wanted to hurt you. . . . I was pushed into it—almost as surely as you were."

"Why did you marry me?"

"That's what I'm talking about. There was nothing else I could do, even when I knew I might destroy you—and myself."

"Why did you marry me?" she repeated. "You didn't want me . . . not as a wife. You knew."

At this Alex seemed to collapse totally. He sagged forward, his arms between his knees. With a great effort he tried to pull himself together.

"I had many reasons for marrying you, Scandal—reasons that had nothing to do with—my behavior in our bed last night. I guess it all starts with my mother. She's the matriarch of this whole clan, a very strong and domineering person, and I am her only son. God knows some of my sisters are probably stronger than I, but she wouldn't have it that way. I am a Vigneaux. I must live as a Vigneaux, even if it kills me—even if it destroys you. For a long time mother has suspected, with good and ample reason, that I might never marry. As you well know now, I am a person who never should marry. There are such men, Scandal, just as there are strong and vital men, honest and dishonest, libertine and priest. We're all just men . . . they are men and I am something. Only my mother would not have it that way. She was ruthlessly concerned about my reputation in a world where a person's life is subject for public comment, public censure—if you stray from the norm, whatever that is, for God's sake. She loves me. I am sure of that. She wanted to protect me. She was fearful for the family name. There was nothing selfish in her actions. I have to keep reminding myself of that."

He paused for a long beat and then he continued, anguishedly: "I too am cowardly afraid for my reputation. Men like me have secrets which must be kept hidden at all costs. My reputation is precious to me, and I thought first of that, even ahead of you, as dearly as I love you."

"How can you say you love me?"

"Oh, Scandal, how can you think I don't love you! If I didn't love you—with all the strength in my worthless soul—would I be torn apart like this?"

"I don't know," Scandal murmured.

"If rumors started about my *manhood*, Scandal, I could not exist in this world where every man is virile, a warrior, fiercely masculine. I could be ruined, Scandal. That is one reason why I married you."

"Didn't you care what you did to me?"

He spread his hands and sat staring at them. "I didn't even

realize what I was doing—what Mother and I were doing—to you until last night. I lied to myself, as completely as I lied to you, Scandal. I believed my mother's lies. When you and I were married, I would be all right. Everything would be all right, once we were married. I believed that, because I had to. And, too, I knew that mother was *buying* you for me. She promised to make you rich if you married me. I wanted it that way. I wanted you to have all the money you could get from her. Those were all the lies I told myself, Scandal. Those were the most compelling reasons."

"Still, you could have prepared me—you could have told me—about—"

"Could I? Suppose I'd told you and you wouldn't touch me—or my mother's money? I knew I could never marry any woman but you, Scandal. I was afraid to tell you the truth. And besides I believed—I wanted to believe—with my sainted mother, that once you and I were in bed all my problems would resolve themselves and I really might live happily ever after. God knows how I wanted to believe that. I knew I loved you. I loved you then, and I love you now, Scandal."

"In your way." She tried to keep the bitterness from her voice.

"In my way." He nodded solemnly, and his vulnerable young eyes brimmed with tears. "There was more: I wanted to protect you—keep you from rough men with hard lips and cigar breath and callused hands and callused hearts. I did, Scandal! I wanted to give you everything you could ever want to make up for what I can't give you—what I couldn't give you last night. Now I know better. But now it's too late."

There was a long, brittle silence in which Scandal remained motionless. There was so much Alex left unsaid, unspoken, things he perhaps had never even considered. How was she expected to live as his wife, each long hour of every interminable day from now on?

Abruptly, he burst out passionately, "If you can forgive me, Scandal, and somehow forget last night, I'll make it up to you. I'll spend the rest of my life making it up to you."

She signed heavily and stared through the casement window at the brightening morning, the sun burning away the last wisps of early fog. Alex waited, as if holding his breath.

"I didn't know," she said at last. "There were men like you.... I've read about the ancient Greeks who loved young boys. I know about men like Uncle Julien.... But—"

"Oh God, Scandal! I'm not even like Julien-Jacques Gischairn. He's an avowed pederast. I don't passionately desire *anyone*. I don't like anybody. Least of all myself. No. I want no one like that."

She stared at him, incredulous. "I've heard that—priests are like that, but I never believed it."

His mouth twisted. "And neither did I. Priests have their acolytes. Their choir boys. Each other. They have God knows what.... No, I'm not like a priest, either."

She frowned, unable, a healthy, normal young girl with fierce appetities for life itself in all its variety, to understand him, as badly as she wanted to, as urgent as understanding was if they were to exist together.

"I hesitate to say this. It sounds like an excuse, a lie, an evasion. ... Maybe it is, I don't know. I see it consciously as the truth. I have never wanted anyone—male or female—since I wanted a girl named Mozelle with all my heart."

Her head tilted and her heart lurched with compassion at the heartfelt hurt in his little confession. She waited in silence. At last, Alex said, "It may have no validity. I was only a child. Seven years old. I was—as far as I know—abnormally aware of my sexuality, of my penis, my balls, my erections, and the excitement I felt would swamp my mind when Mozelle showed me how differently she was made from me."

"Mozelle?"

He smiled faintly, remembering. "She was the daughter of our cook. She was eight or nine—"

"She was black!"

He nodded. "Ah. The crux of my story. She was indeed black. Beautiful and black and fiery hot—almost as innocently passionate as I."

He laughed bitterly, in self-hatred. "No lovers were ever more ardent than we. Every moment we could steal away, we were together. We explored each other, tasted and tested and probed each other. We were happy together. Maybe we were too happy. Maybe even the gods were jealous. I don't know. We did it dog-fashion at first because that was the way we had seen the animals do it on the estate. We experimented, made discoveries. The main discovery was that we loved each other—and only each other in all the world."

"What happened?" Her voice was a taut whisper.

"What else? We were caught. Stripped bare, put in scalding water to wash away the filth and blistered with a whip. They told me I had to stay away from Mozelle or they would have to sell her and her mother—they could not sell a slave child alone—in New

Orleans. In terror, I agreed to anything! I would not even look toward Mozelle if only they would not sell her! If only they would treat her kindly. Those two things were all I asked, all I dared to ask.

"I stayed away from her. I died inside, for I loved only Mozelle in all the world. My mother preached at me. The others screamed at me. Prayed over me. Threatened me with hellfire. Shamed me. Whipped me when, needing to urinate, I showed an erection. They told me my penis would rot and drop off if I put it in Mozelle's black flesh. I would get warts and go blind and lose my mind. I must never touch a Negro in passion—and white girls were above such ugly and sordid behavior. They scared me. Terrified me. I woke screaming at night, grabbing to be sure my genitals had not rotted and wasted away. They scared me so bad I—I've never had a full, throbbing hard-on in all my life since then. . . . And now after last night, I know I never will have."

She held out her arms as a mother might to an agonized child. Alex fell on his knees and buried his head in her lap. She sat soothing his hair with her palm. She felt his slender body wracked with tears.

"It's all right," she whispered. "It's all right."

He sobbed. "How can it ever be all right?"

"It is. Mozelle made it all right. Knowing about Mozelle made it all right. . . . I know you have loved. Now I can tell you the truth about myself. . . . My love . . . I was guilty, too, Alex. I married you without the love a bride should have for a groom."

"I knew that!"

"But you didn't know why . . . you didn't know about a man named Wade Cameroon."

He glanced up, frowning. "I don't know that name."

"No. He brought me to New Orleans. He brought me here and deserted me. . . . But I loved him from the first moment I saw him. I never loved anyone else as I loved him. I know I never will."

"Why didn't you go to him? Why didn't you follow him?"

She started slowly to tell Alex the story of her strange life. As she spoke she remembered the way she had related her adventures to Wade on the trace to New Orleans and how Wade had wept with laughter, calling it the funniest fiction he'd ever heard. She bit back a lonely, bitter smile remembering. But Wade's remembered laughter made her wary. "I'll tell you," she said now. "But you must promise now not to laugh at me. . . . If you laugh, I swear I'll kill you."

"I don't know anything that could make me laugh right now," Alex said.

She spoke haltingly at first, and told him everything. She began at the fabled farm Falconhurst, where her mother had been the master's bed wench. She followed her mother into exile and rape and death. She told of growing up in the Wilkeses' house as a Wilkes, and working as a slavey when the Peavey family came. She told of tricking Wade Cameroon into marriage and running away with him. She held back nothing. She told him that Gischairn had taken her in, lied about her being his niece and trained her for one thing—an advantageous New Orleans marriage contract.

She waited, but Alex did not laugh. He pulled himself up beside her and held her gently in his arms. She felt the hot splash of tears on her hand. "That's the saddest story I've ever heard in my life," Alex said. "Oh God, Scandal." He held her against him and cradled her in his arms, crying.

36

Alex never contemplated the arrival of that day when he would present himself at Julien-Jacques Gischairn's home seeking help. Too much was implied when one presented himself at the old sensualist's threshold; he had carefully avoided the place as he might any pit of perverted iniquity until Scandal went there to live. But now, needing information he was unable to uncover alone, all other avenues closed to him, he was forced to set aside his natural revulsion for the aging hedonist. Even as he rang the doorbell of the St. Charles Avenue mansion, he wondered how the godless and debauched old roue would receive him. He held his breath, listening to the chimes echo deep within the house. By coming here, he placed himself in Gischairn's debt, a situation he'd carefully avoided as the fly evades the web. There was no longer any choice. He had spent months trying to find the information he needed himself, and there was no one else to whom he could turn.

He was surprised when Gischairn himself opened the front door, shocked at the warmth and pleasure with which the old voluptuary greeted his unexpected arrival. A discomfiting thought flashed hotly through his mind. Perhaps Gischairn believed that he had come to him as convert. His former abhorrence for Gischairn grew out of the aged debauchee's insulting assumption that one day Alex Vigneaux would come to him—as his kind. Alex flushed, hating Gischairn for looking at him carnally and despising himself that his slender and delicate appearance roused homosexuals to immediate displays of interest, camaraderie and overt affection. He felt his face burn to the roots of his hair.

Gischairn led Alex into the sunroom and waved him into a wing-backed chair. The most potent essences in the room were heady mixtures of oriental incense. Gischairn stared at him unblinkingly but inquired about Scandal. "And how is your—bride? Well, I hope." His mouth twisted into a wicked smile. "She hasn't left you, has she?"

Rage flared in Alex, but he controlled his emotions. He shrugged and smiled. "Not yet."

Gischairn appeared neither pleased nor displeased at this information, merely patient like some superannuated spider. Alex's anger raged again. He warned himself he'd come for assistance, not to prove to Gischairn that he was not like him, not one with him, did not belong in the purgatory of his nether world, and never would.

Alex said, "I'm looking for a man named Wade Cameroon."

Now Gischairn's habitually arched brows tilted slightly. "Why would you do a damned fool thing like that?"

Alex drew a deep breath. "Scandal said you knew him."

"Yes. Casually. Briefly. I knew him. He's out of my life. He's out of your life and I'd leave him there."

"I've promised Scandal I would find him."

Gischairn's mouth twisted oddly. Alex hated him. He wanted to hit him but he forced himself to remain calm.

Alex related to Gischairn most of what had transpired between him and Scandal on their wedding night. Gischairn looked as if he tasted some incredibly delicious morsel, but remained silent until Alex told it all. "Scandal told me about her love for Cameroon. Told me that you met him, that perhaps you know what happened to him."

"I still don't know why you would want to find him. Do you plan some *ménage á trois*?"

Alex winced. "I have not looked that far ahead. . . . If you have information which will help me find Cameroon, I will be eternally —grateful." He hesitated, letting the old sensualist make what he would of that. Nothing mattered to Alex except that somehow he make reparation for the criminal wrong he'd done Scandal.

Gischairn shrugged. "Still, I find it odd that even one as odd as you should try to find his wife's former lover."

Alex longed to tell the old man to go to hell, to leap to his feet and stride out of here. Instead, he replied softly, "I've hurt her. I want to make it up to her. I don't care what it costs me."

"How noble. Here he is, the last gallant of the knighthood of the Old South. I find it somehow fitting that it should be you upon whose shoulders falls the tattered trappings of the age of chivalry."

"Will you help me?"

Gischairn's mind seemed preoccupied with something else. His eyes glittered with wicked laughter. "I wondered that Scandal would marry you. I attributed that to her true innocence. I even wondered about your wedding night."

Alex flinched. The price was high, and he was paying it. He had known it would not be easy, it would be costly, but he was prepared to pay. "And now I have satisfied your curiosity."

"But your failure in your nuptial bed didn't surprise me. I anticipated that. I expected maybe when that door-bell rang this morning it would be Scandal, in tears. I was astonished to see you. I am stunned at your mission." Gischairn forced back his taunting laughter.

"Will you help me?"

The webbed mouth pulled across Gischairn's stained teeth. "I don't know if anyone can help you. . . . If I were God I'd erase you and start all over."

"That needn't concern you!"

"Ah! Such fire."

"I need help. I beg you to help me. If not for me—whom you find comic and ridiculous—then for Scandal. If you feel any kindness at all for Scandal, I beg you to put aside your acid contempt and help me."

"Let's not screech at each other, dear boy, like shrews. People will think we're lovers."

Only a savage control of will kept Alex in his chair. He wanted to walk out. He wanted to tell old Gischairn to go to hell, and walk out. He stayed where he was, his face deathly pale.

"Can you tell me anything about Wade Cameroon?"

Gischairn laughed. "Yes. I can tell you he may be fatal to your own domestic bliss. Yes. I can tell you that wherever he is, my advice to you is to leave him there. Leave him to hell."

"I want to find him. I mean to find him. I shall find him. With your help, or without it. It may be easier with your help."

Gischairn waved his arm placatingly. "Oh, immeasurably easier. But let us not rage at each other like two old maids. If you're to find Wade Cameroon then we—you and I—must work together, the most unlikely pair since Quixote and Sancho."

"Just tell me what you know. I'll take it from there."

"I'm afraid it is not that easy, my boy. What I *know* will only raise new questions, throw up new obstacles for you. What I may be able to learn may uncover young Cameroon—at your own risk. I assume no responsibility."

"I ask none."

Gischairn sank back in his chair, reflective. "The last time I saw Wade Cameroon, he had come to me, much as you have come now, asking my help in finding Scandal. She had run away from him. I hired detectives, and I found her. But I never found him again. He let me wait in the bar at the St. Louis Hotel. I found that unforgivable. It was much later that I inadvertently uncovered a reason for his dereliction. I suppose Scandal told you that I arranged that her marriage to Cameroon be annulled?"

Alex nodded.

"I sent lawyers and detectives to the capital at Baton Rouge. There, listed as a newly purchased slave at some plantation, was the name Wade Cameroon."

"What plantation?"

Gischairn shrugged, eyeing him oddly. "Aren't you interested in the deeper implications of this information?"

"No."

"You should be. My lawyers determined that if Cameroon was sold into slavery, this meant he had Negro blood. This means he is black, though he is built like a young Celtic god." Gischairn smiled. "A man of color."

"Cameroon? A Negro?"

"You still don't digest the import of what I'm telling you, do you? We dissolved Cameroon's marriage on the grounds of miscegenation. If Scandal was a mustee, and Cameroon was white, then the marriage was illegal and could be abrogated before law and church. This was our thesis. This was our brief. . . . But let's look at this other information uncovered at that time—Cameroon himself was sold into slavery. This being true, they are both black, and the marriage is legal—and you, my dear boy, may well be guilty of bigamy—of marrying another man's wife. Even if that man is black."

Alex stared at Gischairn's sardonic face. "But to you this is all a big joke, isn't it? You don't believe that Cameroon is black, do you?"

Tongue in cheek, Gischairn shrugged again. "The law says he is black. The law defines a Negro as one with a drop of African blood in his veins. He was sold into slavery. Ergo, as far as the law has been able to prove, he is black."

"And your considered advice is that I leave well enough alone?"

"You didn't ask for it. But that's it."

"Do you know the name of the plantation to which Cameroon was sold—as a slave?"

"I can find it out."

"Would you be so kind?"

"And what will you accomplish with this information?"

"I shall go there and find him."

"And what will this prove? The plantation owner has title to a black animal named Wade Cameroon. What will you do, buy him?"

"If I must."

"You solve nothing. Unless you find proof first that Wade Cameroon is lily-white, you resolve nothing, you merely compound the confusion."

"What do you suggest—except that I forget the whole matter?"

Gischairn smiled. "If I were doing this—and I assure you I would not do it!—I'd first uncover the fact that Cameroon is white. If he is white and the law is wrong, your redress will be facilitated, the annulment remains legal, your marriage sanctified in the eyes of the Catholic Church and the Louisiana social elite."

"Damn you. You still think this is all a joke, don't you?"

"Dear boy! Don't you think it is a priceless farce? Where's your sense of humor, your appreciation of the ridiculous?"

"God knows."

"But it is such a burlesque. I love it. It's beautiful. Ironic. One of those once-in-eternity jokes life serves up to lighten the anguish of human existence. The truest revelation of the falsity and stupidity of the Southern gentility. Let's assume that Cameroon is a Caucasian without a drop of black blood. This makes him neither better nor worse in my eyes, but it is everything in the view of Southern aristocracy. Here we have Scandal, who has confessed to you that she is a mustee. Scandal, born of uncertain paternity to a bed wench at the Falconhurst stud slave farm, sits in the lap of luxury, accepted as the wife in one of the Delta's oldest white families, the belle of white American and French New Orleans *polite* society! And Cameroon, scion of one of the region's finest white families, is shackled and sold into slavery! My God! Don't you see how beautiful that is?"

*

The Vigneaux clan was gathered in conclave. The setting was the large living room of the Vigneaux mansion overlooking the river. The matriarch of the clan sat stiffly in an overstuffed, high-backed chair, ruffled collar accenting the stiffness of her neck. On couches, deep chairs and window seats for the lesser members sat the daughters, their husbands, the nephews, uncles, cousins to the third removal. They were a powerful family. Their position in New Orleans was impregnable. They were five-generation Southerners. They collaborated and cooperated fully with Military Governor Shedley and with the army of occupation. Business took precedence over patriotism. Anyhow, they had never wanted Louisiana to sever its ties with the Union. Financially such a move was wrong; and this made it erroneous in every aspect as far as the least Vigneaux was concerned.

Only two people in the room stood. There were chairs for Alex and his bride, but neither wanted to sit down. Alex stood near the wide french windows overlooking the dark and curving river, the weeping willows, the shaded lawn, the manicured hedges and pallid gardenias.

Scandal stood near a polished Sheraton drum table. She held an envelope in her hand. Her fingers were chilled and trembling. Eyes of the clan were fixed on her, like humorless judges in inquisition.

". . . and that is why I want my marriage to Alex annulled," Scandal was saying. "I have reached that decision, and Alex concurs."

"Totally," Alex said from the window.

"I was afraid of something like this." Gabriel Vigneaux was an uncle; he was executive administrator of the far-flung Vigneaux interests. Madame Vigneaux, Alex's mother, however, was the chairman of the board. Hers was the final decision, the only opinion of ultimate importance.

She sat watching Scandal. She did not laugh, but she looked as if she wanted to, in contempt. "You and I have a bargain, my dear," she said.

"I want to be released from it," Scandal said.

Madame Vigneaux shook her head. "We allowed for this, my dear. I gave you plenty of time to reflect on what might happen to you—once you were married. Your decision, once made, was irrevocable. You know that."

"We can't hold her to it," Alex said. "We must not."

"I'm afraid, Alex, you will have to let me handle this," his mother said. "You have mishandled it. I must repair your bungling. This is not a new role for each of us."

"I don't want you to protect me any more," Alex said.

"Then I must protect you against your own weakness, musn't I?" his mother inquired in that acid tone. "I must protect my family's interests, its good name. Its reputation."

"It doesn't matter what you say, Mother, I want Scandal to have her freedom."

"Impossible. What will we tell the people of this town? That the heir to the Vigneaux name and estates could not satisfy his bride, could not even *perform*? Is that what you want us to tell them?"

"I don't care what you tell them. I'm thinking only of Scandal."

His mother waved her hand. "Scandal entered a bargain, Sonny. With me. She walked into it with her eyes open. We shall expect her to fulfill its provisos precisely as if she had signed some business contract with your Uncle Gabriel."

"Precisely," Uncle Gabriel said.

"Alex," one of his sisters said, her voice kindly. "You know that personal happiness—or unhappiness—is not as important as the family. It never has been. It never will be. You know that. Scandal will have to learn to live with it."

Madame Vigneaux kept her gaze fixed on Scandal. "We don't ask the impossible of you, my dear child. Only that you be discreet."

The others nodded, solemn of mien, in total accord. Scandal stared at them, shocked and angered. "What you're really saying —in your delicate way of saying nothing at all—is that you don't care if I have lovers. You don't care what I do in order to exist in the establishment of your precious family—as long as I am careful and quiet about it."

Madame Vigneaux nodded. "I might wish we did not have to put it in words, child, but yes. We all adapt to life. We compromise. We learn to exist. Not one of us in this room has not had this experience. Not one. You are no better than they. But you are one of them now, and you will behave like one of them."

"We can condone nothing less," Uncle Gabriel said, smiling gently, even sadly, at her. Scandal, looking at the darkly handsome and aging man, wondered what adjustment he had made and what it had cost him. At any rate, it was behind him. He had learned to live with it. He expected as much of her.

Scandal shook her head. "I won't do it."

Madame Vigneaux did laugh now, as she might at a stubborn child. "Well, I'm afraid there is nothing else you can do. . . . You will find us a loving and supportive family, my child. Close-knit. Protective. It will not be the worst of lives for you."

Scandal shook her head. "If you do not quietly have my marriage annulled, I will do it."

Uncle Gabriel's quiet tone reproved her. "Do you for one instant believe we would permit you to publish the fact—or the intimation—that a Vigneaux was less than a virile man? No, dear child. We'd be forced to do anything to stop you."

"Use any excuse you wish," Scandal said, "but set me free."

Madame Vigneaux shook her head. "We won't discuss it any further, Scandal, ever again. You are one of us. That is final."

"The only acceptable reasons for annulment, young woman," Uncle Gabriel said in his even, reticent tone, "are either demeaning, embarrassing or scandalous. They are hurtful to a family's reputation. As much as we might sympathize with you, we cannot permit it. We must refuse."

Scandal opened the envelope and shook out the aged, cracked and scarred document. "Then you may be interested in this," she said. She did not wait, but read from the manumission papers awarded Ellen nineteen years earlier in Benson, Alabama. At first, there was a restless stirring, but a silence washed out over the room, and when she finished reading, there was not a sound. It was as if the clan held its collective breath in tension and terror.

"A Negress," one of the sisters whispered.

Scandal nodded. "I have defaulted on my contract with you, Madame Vigneaux. It was entered into dishonestly. I did not then reveal all the facts about my ancestry. . . . I am now prepared to reveal them—in public."

No one spoke. At last Uncle Gabriel got up from his leather-covered chair and went to where Madame Vigneaux sat as if she had turned to stone. They whispered together for some moments. At last, Uncle Gabriel stood up and returned to his chair.

Madame Vigneaux fixed her gaze on Scandal but did not speak. It was Uncle Gabriel who said, "The annulment will be arranged as speedily as possible, young woman. Go quietly and in good health. Go with God."

37

Alex was able to forgive Gischairn's sardonic and contemptuous attitude. His hatred for the aging sybarite was considerably mollified by the incredibly efficient manner in which Gischairn set about gathering the irrefutable evidence concerning the progenitors of Wade Cameroon.

The old man insisted—as his gift to Scandal—upon hiring lawyers and detectives who combed every legal document extant concerning Heather Hill Plantation, its owners, slaves, history and, especially, the background of the second wife of the master of Heather Hill—Wade Cameroon's mother. Gischairn's immense wealth made the achievement appear easy, but Alex was extremely rich too and he had been stymied at every turn. It was Gischairn's determination, drive and dedication to any task which made the difference, shunted aside all obstacles and brought them one morning in April to the manor house at French Pines Plantation in the loam-rich Delta.

There was small opportunity for conversation between Alex, Scandal and Gischairn in the tonneau of Gischairn's luxurious coach. Each was silent, filled with private thoughts. They listened to the shouting of the coachmen, the noise of the wheels, the rattle of leather and gear, the hooves of the horses. Gischairn had insisted upon accompanying them to Le Blanc's vast farms. He had begun this project, and he would not be content until he had seen it through. He poised on the seat, gripping the head of his cane, looking ahead in cold anticipation.

As for Alex, he found himself grudgingly admiring the old man. Now he was forced to understand vagaries of the roué's strange personality. Gischairn's wealth set him apart. He was a man who was intended by the fates to enjoy a surfeit of life's luxuries. As a young man he had been comparatively wealthy—a matter of inheritance—but almost effortlessly he had multiplied his wealth by thousands. His was a Midas touch, a casual, disinterested ability to turn any investment into astounding profit. He had been involved in every traffic, legal and illegal. He had brought slaves boldly into New Orleans vendues when all trade in slaves was outlawed by the United States. He had never cared for women; he had been mocked; he had become self-sufficient. In time he bought everything he needed—respectability, great power, influence, dread, even friendship. Alex did not yet like Gischairn, but he understood him; he admired him and stood in awe of his arrogant pride and dignity.

He glanced toward Scandal, huddled against the far seat, lost in fear and anxiety. His heart sagged in his chest, twisted and battered raggedly.

Now that he had forever lost her, now that their mockery of marriage had been annulled, he knew how deeply he loved her.

How he loved her! This was not the fiery lust he knew she wanted in a lover, the carnality a woman expected in a man. No, his love for Scandal was far different, far more exalted. Perhaps it was the devotion the knights of chivalry had felt for their ladies. Gischairn had taunted him about being the last of the knights errant, belonging to that extinct species of the chivalrous gentlemen of the old South. Well, maybe the old hellion was right. In the fullness of his love for Scandal, he wanted to protect her, shield her, guard her against the least harm. He would die for her.

Distracted, Scandal crouched in the coach, her thoughts turned inward and edged darkly in terror. She recalled Albert Le Blanc, the cruel and conscienceless man she had encountered on that long-ago trace to New Orleans. She held all the aces; Gischairn had left no stone unturned in providing her with the truth about Wade Cameroon, his parentage, his past and present. But was Le Blanc a man to be swayed by the truth? She regretted that she had not killed him that time he came upon her and Wade on the trail. She had warned Wade then that he would never live free as long as Le Blanc stalked him.

Not many of her thoughts this morning were of the past; they were mostly fearful anticipation of that moment when she arrived at French Pines. Gischairn's attorneys had learned everything about Wade to the moment Le Blanc had purchased him as a slave from the public barracoon in New Orleans. But no one spoke of whether Wade had survived nearly two years in the hell of the cane fields. The cane fields were a death sentence for the slaves condemned to them. No Falconhurst slave was ever sold for such labour; the Falconhurst people were too fancy for such killing conditions. She had heard that if a slave lived as long as a year in the cane fields, he was extraordinary; not blessed, but damned to abnormally prolonged suffering.

Suddenly she was sick with fright. A cold chill shuddered through her and she shivered in the heat. Suppose Wade had died? That was what Le Blanc wanted. He had bought Wade to ensure that his brother's slayer would die the most agonizing of deaths—in the sweltering hell of the cane fields. Suppose after all Gischairn—and Alex—had done to find Wade for her that she was too late? How could she go on living if Wade was dead?

The coach was stopped and had been for some moments before Scandal could shake free of the anguish that enveloped her.

Alex gave her a faint smile. "We're here, Scandal. Don't worry any more. It's going to be all right. . . . We'll get him back for you, one way or the other."

She caught his hand and squeezed it fiercely, trying to let him know how deeply she appreciated all he had done for her in these long weeks.

The coachmen opened the doors. Gischairn alighted first. Then the servants assisted Scandal to the shell-paved drive before the magnificent chateau. Alex followed.

Albert Le Blanc stood on the brink of shade at his veranda. Looking at him, Scandal went weak.

Le Blanc had seen her, of course, but had not yet recognized her. He said, "Welcome to French Pines Plantation. Come in, won't you?"

Gischairn crossed the sun-struck space between them first. He shook hands with Le Blanc and turned to present Alex and Scandal.

Le Blanc straightened. He stared at Scandal. His eyes darkened, but his face paled. "Can it be?" he said. "I had heard you were dead."

Gischairn laughed. "The girl you knew, Le Blanc, is quite dead. Rachel Wilkes is dead. Scandal Gischairn Vigneaux lives, however."

"Vigneaux?" The fact that Scandal had married into the powerful family added to Le Blanc's shock. He recovered his aplomb and invited them to sit in rocking chairs on the shaded veranda. Servants served coffee, bourbon, lemonade and many kinds of small pastries. Nothing was touched by the guests.

Scandal said, "We have come for Wade Cameroon."

Le Blanc's head jerked up, his black eyes clouded, and then he laughed. "Just like that, eh?"

"Just like that."

"It's not that easy, missy. Wade Cameroon is *my* nigger now. For as long as he lasts—out there in my cane fields. I bought him, as I buy many of my slaves, from a public barracoon. You don't want him. If you saw him now you wouldn't want him—what's left of him."

Scandal's eyes blurred with tears. "Still, we've come for him. I hope you won't make it difficult."

"No, I shan't, missy. I shall simply refuse to discuss it. I told you. He's my nigger and he's not for sale." His voice took an almost kindly tone. "Missy, the man you're talking about no longer exists. A big, swaggering mustee, masquerading as a white man, killed my brother. Well, I have arranged his punishment. I set his sentence. He will not escape it. . . . He was dead—as far as you're concerned—when he was captured and thrown into that nigger barracoon."

"Where he was thrown on false evidence supplied by you."

"You're talking technicalities, missy. I'm talking realities. No such man as you saw in New Orleans exists any more. Now, I'm a good host. I welcome you people. We may exchange news of New Orleans, mutual friends, the war, anything you like—except that nigger slave. Either we drop that subject or I must ask you to leave."

"We are quite willing to leave," Scandal said. "As soon as you turn Wade over to us. Mr. Gischairn's lawyers have proved that you falsified information, suppressed information, presented lies slanted as you wanted them to cause Wade's arrest. Once you had him declared legally black, you brought him here."

Le Blanc shrugged and smiled. "I did nothing illegal, missy. The slave in my cane fields is a nigger I bought. He will die there —the death he deserves."

"I am willing to buy him from you."

"He's not for sale."

"I'll pay enough to buy twenty slaves—a hundred of the culls you buy to kill in your cane fields."

"No sense buying fancy animals for killing manual labor. I can't seem to impress you with the only important fact in all this discussion: Wade Cameroon will leave French Pines only one way—in a pine casket."

Scandal winced as if he had hit her. "I can't believe you'd refuse ten thousand dollars for one slave."

Le Blanc hesitated. Scandal said, "You may soon lose *all* your slaves. You won't get a dime for them. The war is going badly for the Confederacy. President Lincoln has issued a proclamation freeing all slaves. What will you do when the Confederacy falls?"

"I don't believe it will. And as I'm sure you know, the proclamation specifically exempts this parish along with the others that have long been in Yankee hands. . . . I do admit that things have been going poorly for us. They've taken some of my best blacks to dig trenches and throw up parapets."

"But not Wade."

Le Blanc smiled sourly. "I told you. Nobody gets Cameroon. I mean to see him die out there in those cane fields. Hell, he's already lived over a year more than any of us thought he could."

"Mr. Le Blanc, I have made every effort—as these witnesses will attest—to deal rationally with you. But I don't believe you are sane. In the face of Lincoln's proclamation, which will surely be extended throughout the South eventually, you refuse ten thousand dollars for one slave."

"All right. Old baboon-face Lincoln may end up freeing my

niggers. But I'll wait to see if he can make it stick."

"I've tried to be businesslike," Scandal said. "You won't have that. You could go to prison for what you have done to Wade Cameroon."

"For Christ's sake, young woman. Whether he's white or black, I bought him as black, and even the union recognizes my right to own him."

"You'll get your chance to tell that in court," Scandal said.

Gischairn spoke then, his voice even and slightly ironic. "She's telling you the truth, Mr. Le Blanc. She is dealing in realities with you now. You see, we have proof of Cameroon's heritage. His mother was indeed born in Martinique—but of impeccably white French parents. This is not too important. The important fact I'm sure is not lost on you. You had this information. You suppressed it. We have proof of that, too. Whether Wade is all you say, you are not guiltless—he is not black as you have falsely sworn. This makes you guilty of bondage. This is a felony, sir, as I am sure you are quite aware. You won't have a chance in hell in any court. Especially not in this state, where Governor Shedley represents the federal government."

Le Blanc sat in silence for a long time. There was in Gischairn's quiet, deadly voice a tone not to be doubted. He seemed to flinch and retreat into himself as if he'd been struck vitally. He did not move. It was almost as if they could see the wheels grinding and spinning in his brain. He had proved himself an arrogant, reckless and willful man. He truly believed himself set apart. That he had demonstrated by falsifying reports on Wade's parentage and going into court with his lies. He was the despot on this land; monarch over all the lives of his family and his slaves. It was not easy for him to accept his own fallibility. At last he glanced up, face pallid and cheeks rigid. "You say you'll pay me ten thousand dollars?"

"We won't pay you anything," Alex said. "We will turn over the information we have to Governor Shedley and let the law deal with your guilt."

Le Blanc kept his eyes on Scandal. "You offered me ten thousand."

She nodded.

"Do you have the money with you?"

Over Alex's protests, Gischairn's footman brought the small chest containing the ten thousand in gold.

"We'll go get your nigger soon," he said. "I want to put this money in safekeeping. I'll order a cart sent round—I don't believe your coach would travel in the fields."

Alex refused to accompany them to the fields. He said he opposed the idea of paying this felon anything; he washed his hands of the matter.

Scandal looked at Alex almost tenderly. It was nearer the truth, she believed, that Alex did not want to be with her when she met Wade again for the first time. He had done so much for her; she was aware he did love her deeply—in his way. She was happy to spare him any suffering. She touched his hand and kissed his cheek lightly.

Gischairn insisted upon accompanying them. He took along his footman. The black man sat in the bed of the cart as it rattled along a narrowing lane into the mudgreen fields of sugar cane.

The heat intensified, seeming to smoke and rise out of the wet loam and silt-rich earth, from the standing red puddles, from the massed jungles of stalks, and from the sweated bodies of the driven slaves.

Scandal felt the sickness well up in her as they approached the work crews. The cart rattled and bumped. Le Blanc did not speak. Gischairn sat straight, looking disdainfully about him.

At last Le Blanc halted the carriage and called to a tall, broad-chested Negro bared to the waist and wearing Osnaburg britches. "You, Merk . . . bring Cameroon out here to me."

Scandal held her breath, barely aware that she was not breathing. Her heart hammered swiftly and then slowly, irregularly, threatening to lose its rhythm, to stop altogether.

After a long time the overseer returned with a thin skeleton of a man in tow. The man's ankle was shackled, and he dragged his leg behind him. He wore a tow-linen shirt, cotton pants. He was barefooted. He was burned the color of strong coffee. He weighed little over one hundred pounds.

Scandal heard Gischairn's sharp protesting intake of breath beside her. Her vision blurred with her tears. Both she and Gischairn expected to find the man they had last seen in New Orleans—another lifetime ago. He had been tall, muscular, happy and laughing. This sun-dried skeleton bore no resemblance to the Wade Cameroon they had known. Le Blanc had not lied about this, but he had failed to prepare them for the whipped and sallow wraith who cowered in the road beside the cart.

Scandal bit back her agonized cries. She stepped down from the seat of the cart. She said, "Wade."

He looked up at her. His sunken eyes widened for a moment, and he stared at her as he had in a thousand lonely dreams.

Then he realized this was no dream. The vision he beheld—a

Scandal a hundred times lovelier than he had known—stood before him.

A sob broke across his lips. He shook his head, retreating.

"Get in the back of the cart," Le Blanc said. Wade hesitated until Merk prodded him with the whipstock. Wade sat beside Gischairn's footman in the bed of the small wagon. He slumped, shoulders round, staring at the ground.

"You son of a bitch," Gischairn said to Le Blanc. "You should be hanged. God knows you should be hanged."

Le Blanc pulled the cart in before the plantation smithy. He leaped down from the boot and ordered the shackle removed from Wade's ankle.

Scandal sat immobile, trying to find any resemblance between this human skeleton and the magnificent man she had married and abandoned.

With hammer and chisel, the smithy removed the shackle from Wade's ankle. Cameroon seemed barely aware of what was happening to him. He stared at the ground.

Unexpectedly, Gischairn's coach rolled down the incline, with the driver and Alex on the box. The coachman made a wide turn. He headed the carriage out and then drew up on the lines.

Alex leaped down from the seat. His face was unnaturally flushed, his hair mussed. His eyes glittered with excitement.

He strode across the bare sand to the carriage. He reached up and helped Scandal to the ground. Then he held Gischairn's elbow while the older man alighted.

Alex said, "Have you got Cameroon? Are you ready to go?"

"There he is." Gischairn inclined his head toward the man standing slump-shouldered.

Alex's eyes widened, his mouth sagged open. "Jesus Christ," he said. He looked at Le Blanc. "You are guilty of murder."

Le Blanc spoke coldly. "You've got your slave. He is guilty of murder, my friend. Let's be perfectly clear about that. He killed my brother. I admit only to being judge, jury and executioner."

As if holding himself in tight leash, Alex said, "Scandal, get Cameroon in the coach. Hurry. You too, Gischairn. I want to get out of here."

"I may as well tell you, all of you," Le Blanc said. "Cameroon is not free of me—he never will be until we settle the matter of my brother's death."

Alex stood with his legs apart, his face flushed, while between them Scandal and Gischairn helped Wade into the coach.

When they were inside the tonneau, Alex drew a gun that none of them suspected he had. Alex fixed the mouth of the gun on Le Blanc. His young face was pale but his voice was steady. He ordered the smithy to shackle Le Blanc to the stone wall.

"You fool," Le Blanc said. "How long do you think I'll stay shackled?"

Alex shrugged, backing toward the coach. "I don't know. Long enough to think clearly. If you are smart, you won't follow us. If you want to live, you will forget Wade Cameroon and pray that God forgives you what you have done to him."

Alex swung up on the box beside the coachman. "Get going," he said. The coachman cracked his whip over Gischairn's fine carriage horses. The coach quivered and then raced across the yard.

Inside the tonneau, Scandal and Gischairn found themselves battered and flung wildly as the coach swayed on its thorough-braces. But Alex did not allow the coachman to slow until they were five miles from French Pines.

When finally the coachman pulled the horses off the road for a rest, Alex swung down and with the gun at his side stared along the backtrail.

"Why do you think Le Blanc will follow us?" Gischairn said.

"I know he will," Alex answered. "Because I stole back the money Scandal paid him for Cameroon. I don't believe one has to buy the freedom of a free man. I don't believe a man like Le Blanc should profit from his cruelty. I don't think Scandal should give up the money she got from my mother. . . . I do think we ought to get to hell out of here."

38

They arrived in New Orleans after nightfall. Not until they reached the lighted heart of the town did Alex permit the coachman to curb the lathered horses. For all the long miles on the highway Alex had sat tensely on the driver's box, armed, watching the backtrail. They saw no sign of Le Blanc. But all of them believed with Alex that the master of French Pines was back there, stalking them. Until the coachman whoaed the horses in the driveway of Gischairn's mansion on St. Charles Avenue Alex did not relax his vigil. He shoved the gun under his belt and swung down with the footman. When the others stepped out of the tonneau, Alex stood grinning at them. "We made it," he said.

Behind the strong walls of the mansion they dared to breathe easily. Once inside its doors, Gischairn again assumed command. All servants were set diligently to work. "There's much to do," Gischairn said. "There's not much time."

They were all weak with fatigue, drawn taut by the thundering ride into the city from French Pines, but now that they were again safe in his home, Gischairn preferred to behave as though the tragic events of the day had never happened at all.

Alex and Scandal insisted they were too tired, too nervous, to eat, but Gischairn scolded them. "Food will calm your nerves. Everything will look better on a full stomach. You're tired because you're hungry."

Supper that night was no simple affair, merely food spread quickly on a table to be washed down with strong coffee. Gischairn ordered a formal meal, and in less than an hour it was served, by candle light, with sterling silver and rich china. Silver goblets sweated with iced water. Liveried manservants served slightly chilled white wine. The food was delicious, and under Gischairn's unblinking gaze both Alex and Scandal tried to eat, like obedient children.

Only Cameroon sagged in his chair, his arms at his sides, his eyes fixed on something none of the others could see. He was unmanned by his rescue, left empty by the utter exhaustion of long months in Le Blanc's cane fields. He found no hope in this brilliant room, among those who loved him. If it had reality, it was the evanescent visions he'd sometimes experienced at night in his slave cabin. He had forgotten he had ever been a white man named Wade Cameroon. He sat dulled, waiting for morning and the work wagon. . . .

Scandal glanced at him. Her eyes brimmed with tears, but Gischairn smiled reassuringly. "He'll be all right, Scandal. He's young—what—in his earliest twenties? He'll come back. He was strong enough to exist in hell, to endure Le Blanc's cruelty. He'll learn to live again."

After dinner, the tempo of activity increased in the Gischairn mansion. A servant was dispatched to fetch a doctor. Other servants were pressed into service attending Wade. He was led into a marble-floored bathroom, where he was scrubbed and soaked and perfumed in hot water. He was shaven, his hair cut, brushed and tended. Gischairn's suits were tailored to fit him by the swiftly working servants. In the midst of it all, Wade sank into stunned sleep.

Scandal sat with Gischairn in the living room. Immediately after dinner, Alex had excused himself and hurried away in one of Gischairn's runabout carriages.

Scandal yawned helplessly, overwhelmed by fatigue, but went on sitting in the deep club chair. She would not sleep if she lay down in bed. Her mind was aswarm with confusions and doubts and fears.

Her heart lurched oddly when she thought about Wade Cameroon. As he had forgotten his existence off Le Blanc's plantation, so she wept inwardly for the handsome and lordly lover she had lost. He had been so beautiful! So fair and filled with laughter, so eager for love. There was little trace of that man in the wrecked hulk asleep upstairs. She did not believe she would ever find that man again. She wanted to cry out in protest. She had been a fool, ambitious, driven, but she had loved him. In the little while they were together he had given her more happiness than she had ever known and she had thrown it away with both hands. She would trade it all for Wade's recovery, for a little while with the husband she had adored in spite of herself. She was sorry for all the wrongs she had done him and she wanted only to be permitted to make it up to him, to atone for her grievous sins against the love God had given them.

Gischairn seemed to follow the tangled skein of her thoughts. He said, "We must get you away from here—you and Cameroon—as soon as we can."

"Do you think Le Blanc will follow him?"

"Don't you?"

She winced. "I know he will. He obsessed."

"He sees it as normal grief over the murder of a younger brother—a wrong that must be avenged."

"He knows that any court of law would call Wade's act self-defense. Henri Le Blanc tried to kill him."

"Albert knows this. That's why he never went into court. He feels he is above the law in avenging his brother's death. He may follow you. No matter where you go. Alex and I will try to get you away quietly. If we can, you may be freed of Le Blanc."

"I pray we can. I love Wade. Not as I did when he was my husband—but as some lost soul who has only me. I have always loved him. I know that now. I know that nothing is the same. It never will be again. But I must do for him what I can."

"I think you're too pessimistic. If you get him to the tropics—

one of the Caribbean islands perhaps. You'll have the sun and mangoes and avocadoes and citrus, bananas and every delicacy from the sea. He'll recover. He'll regain his strength. You'll see. Once you take him away from here."

She extended her hand in a gesture of futility. "You are forgetting M'sieur Le Blanc."

"No. I'm not forgetting anything. I know that we must stop him—and we shall try."

Her voice sounded empty. "He is not a man who can be stopped."

Gischairn laughed at her. "You forget—I'm a bitchy old person who won't be pushed aside. You've got to have more faith. In me. You came here from some country kitchen and told me what you wanted. I got it for you, didn't I?"

"Far more than I ever dreamed."

He nodded, smiling faintly. His diamond earring glittered in the lamplight. "Yes. You got what you wanted. You did it. Not I. I provided only the opportunity. You provided the heart—the fortitude. You were the queen of the Delta for a while. As long as it pleased you. You married into its wealthiest, most influential family. You were accepted by them. You did it all, Scandal. And that's why I know wherever you go, you'll rise naturally to the top. You'll be an outstanding person wherever you are, in whatever company. You'll find happiness if you give yourself a chance."

"But it won't be the same," she protested, exhausted and frightened.

"Nothing is ever the same. But it is up to us to make what we have work—to make it better than what we had."

Her mouth twisted. "You make it sound so easy."

He smiled. "I had to prod you before, Scandal. But you found your own way—with your own talent."

"How can I? I can't make Wade love me again. He doesn't even know me."

Gischairn shook his head. "No. You don't know *him*. He's been deep in hell—without you. You'll have to help him come back."

Her eyes filled with tears. She felt so alone, so helpless. She was so tired and there was yet so far to go—and no signs along the way and no promise that she would ever find Wade again.

She sat straighter, tilting her head to hide her tears, but a shudder wracked her body.

*

The first slashes of false dawn illumined the sapphire skies and turned gray in the lamplit room. They heard the wheels of a carriage and the hooves of a horse on the drive.

Scandal came up out of her chair, her heart pounding.

Gischairn waved his arm. "It's only Alex, my dear."

Alex entered the room a few moments later, walking with quick strides into the pale rim of light from the table lamps. He looked sweated and exhausted. She had never seen such strength of character in his young face, such a determined fire illumining his eyes.

"I don't know if I've done any good," he said. "I went all along the levees, to every wharf where a lighted ship was taking on cargo. Where they weren't I shook Negro seamen awake and asked their destination, the hour of their sailing. I even entered all the waterfront saloons—as long as they were open." He sighed heavily.

"You found a ship?"

"At last. I found a freighter. I met the captain aboard a Cuban ship, the *Cisne Azul*—the *Blue Swan*. A fourmaster out of Havana. They were loading freight before sailing downriver at nine this morning. Their first port of call is Havana on their way to South America. They touch port in most of the islands of the Caribbean."

"Sounds excellent." Gischairn nodded and smiled in approval.

"I thought so. They do carry passengers. I tried to buy passage for Scandal and Cameroon. That's where it all fell apart. The *Cisne Azul* does carry passengers, but because of the war, and the way it is going, the passenger quota was filled up."

Alex paced the room. His shoulders sagged slightly in his rumpled, rain-spotted suit. "I did all I could. I could not force them to agree to take our people. I decided you might be more effective, Gischairn."

Gischairn nodded and smiled. "You were wise to return with enough time for us to get down there by nine this morning."

"You can't force them to take Scandal and Wade aboard."

"I think I can. Though 'force' is probably the wrong word. I won't consider force."

"The *Cisne Azul* is of Cuban registry. I learned it is owned by Yankee-Cuban interests."

Gischairn nodded. "Of course it is, my boy. That's what I meant. Among my many interests is included shipping—especially shipping involving Cuba. I am on the board of directors of the company that owns the *Cisne Azul*. I believe we can approach it in confidence that it will take our passengers."

Alex gazed at Gischairn, awed. "You're a real old son of a bitch, aren't you?" he said.

"It's a learned trait," Gischairn replied.

Ship whistles and foghorns blasted warning that the moment for weighing the *Cisne Azul's* anchor was at hand. Gischairn's closed coach sped along the wharf and pulled in as closely to the gangplank as the blue-garbed soldiery would permit. The piers were brightly sunlit. Soldiers stood guard everywhere against possible rebel sabotage. Sailors ran along the decks of the freighter. From the poop deck an executive officer shouted orders through a megaphone. Noise rose on every side.

Gischairn left Alex, Scandal and Cameroon inside the carriage, its curtains tightly drawn. He hurried up the gangplank and was lost in the crowds of passengers and well-wishers aboard. Inside the breathless coach time dragged heavily. Alex met Scandal's eyes and tried to smile, but even in his smiling he was none too hopeful. Cameroon sat between them, well dressed, even elegantly attired in Gischairn's suit which had been hastily altered for him. He did not speak. They told him repeatedly that Scandal was taking him on a sea voyage for his health, to some tropical island paradise where they would be happy and secure. He did not respond. He seemed either not to hear or not to understand.

"I'll never forget you," Scandal said to Alex. "Your kindness. Your goodness. Your generosity. Your bravery."

Alex was watching tensely through the pinked curtain, his gaze fixed on the gangplank along which Gischairn should issue momentarily.

"Of course you won't," he said. "Any more than I'll forget you." He exhaled heavily. "We truly did love, Scandal, you and I—"

"In our way."

"We loved," he said. "But I was—I am an emotional cripple. One of the invisibly wounded. At least that's my excuse. . . . Our love will last—in the only place where it can persist—in our memory."

Scandal blinked back tears. She did not speak again. Alex turned back to his vigil, eyes studying the busy gangplank in the last moments before it was withdrawn. "Damn," he said. "Where is he?"

At that moment Gischairn appeared at the head of the gangplank, his footman walking ahead of him, politely but definitely clearing a way for his master. Gischairn came down the gangplank, moving quickly against the flow of hurrying people.

He came across the wharf and opened the rear door. He jerked his head toward the black servants, indicating the suitcases and trunks. The servants leaped down to haul the baggage aboard. He grinned wickedly up at the people inside the vehicle. "All right. Let's go. There's some sort of tide at the mouth of the Mississippi the captain says he must make."

Alex sat unmoving for one long beat. He did not answer, his face remained expressionless, but he filled his lungs with air and exhaled heavily. Then he caught Scandal's elbow and helped her alight to the pier. Cameroon followed, blinking against the sun, withdrawn, disoriented and disturbed.

"It's all right, Cameroon," Alex heard Gischairn saying. "No one will bother you where you're going."

Alex flinched at this, somehow not yet assured. But Gischairn looked as if he were totally in command—of the morning, the *Cisne Azul*, the world around him as far as he could see. He motioned Alex ahead of him. The servants went first, bowed under the weight of the luggage, half running toward the gangplank where sailors waited to haul it in. The four of them followed, moving hurriedly through the crowds.

They heard a yell, but in their haste did not even consider that it might be for them. The servants hurried up the gangplank. The ship's stewards took over the bags and trunks.

They reached the foot of the gangplank before they fully realized that Albert Le Blanc stood at its foot, barring the way. He stood tall, face cold and savage, as if he were the wrath of God. He held a coiled bullwhip in his fists.

A hoot of derisive laughter struck them like cold and rancorous spittle. "Now ain't this a pretty sight? Running away with my nigger, eh, little lady?"

The four of them halted. From the lower ramp of the gangplank, Le Blanc stared down at them in sardonic judgment.

"The rest of you can go ahead. Sail off to hell for all of me. I want my nigger. I mean to kill him for running away."

Silence washed across the pier. Armed soldiers stiffened, holding their rifles at ready across their chests. Aboard ship, the seamen and the passengers crowded against the sides, staring down in silence.

Le Blanc's voice rose. "You ready to die, nigger?"

Suddenly, an agonized sob gorged up through Cameroon's throat. He erupted from the distracted trance in which he had passed the night.

Scandal caught Wade's arm, trying to reassure him, but he shook free and lunged toward the man on the ramp.

Le Blanc laughed aloud, pleased. He was ready; he had dealt with dozens of slaves infected with hatred. The whip uncoiled with the speed of a striking snake. It cracked across Wade's shoulders with power enough to knock him down. He staggered but stayed on his feet.

Alex drew his gun and stepped forward. But astoundingly, Gischairn caught his arm. "You can't fight his fight for him, Alex."

Alex stared at Gischairn. "What are you talking about?"

"Let him fight. It's his fight. He needs to find himself. His self-respect. His freedom. His right to love like a man—and live like a man. Let him fight for her."

Gripping the gun, sickened by Le Blanc's savagery with the bullwhip, Alex managed to nod. He stood unmoving, the gun at his side. Through his mind raced one idea, too fragmented and swift to be a thought—*no matter what Le Blanc did, he was going to kill him.*

The whip cracked, a sound that made the strongest man on the pier shudder and want to turn away. Women cried out and hid their faces.

Suddenly from the ship railing a sailor tossed a belaying pin. It fell and rattled hollowly at Wade Cameroon's feet. Wade staggered, sank to his knees.

For one instant, Le Blanc hesitated. His head jerked up. He seemed stunned that anyone would oppose him in his righteous assault.

Cameroon's hand closed over the belaying pin. Cut and bleeding, he came upward. Laughing, Le Blanc tried to break his wrist with his whip, to knock the belaying pin free. The whip lashed across Wade's arm and circled it.

With his left hand, Wade caught the whip. With strength no one would have suspected—the sinews and muscles honed in Le Blanc's own cane fields—he yanked forward.

Pulled off balance, Le Blanc half fell forward on the pier. He fought to yank the whip free. He was being drawn closer and closer and closer to Cameroon. When Le Blanc came within arm's reach, Cameroon struck savagely with the belaying pin.

The heavy weapon caught Le Blanc across the side of his head. The planter's hat flew off, and Le Blanc staggered. A yell went up from the ship and reverberated along the pier. The soldiers crowded closer. A deep moan came up from the throats of the men along the wharf, like animals in at a kill.

Before Le Blanc could recover, Wade caught the bullwhip, yanked it from Le Blanc's grasp and hurled it behind him. Another savage roar rattled the wharves and echoed from the cavernous warehouses.

The belaying pin came down across Le Blanc's skull again. The big man sagged to his knees. Cameroon caught him by the throat. He raised his arm high and brought the pin down. Again. Again. He would have beaten Le Blanc to death, but soldiers and pier police grabbed him, pulled him away.

Gischairn stepped forward. He said, "I want this man arrested. I want him charged with attempted murder. There's not a man on this pier or on that ship who won't swear he attacked Cameroon—with a deadly weapon."

That roar went up again. The police nodded. Gischairn waved them away as the ship's whistle blasted one last call for boarding. "I'll come to the station to swear against him," Gischairn said. He had the bleeding Wade and Scandal by the arm, hurrying them up the gangplank before the police could protest.

Scandal hesitated at the foot of the gangplank only long enough to kiss Gischairn fiercely, clinging to him for a long moment. "I'll miss you, you old demon." She wept.

"Be happy," he said into her ear. "That's all I ever wanted for you."

Scandal clung for another moment to Alex's hand. She did not speak, nor did he. And then she was gone, leading Cameroon up the gangplank to the deck. The big ramp was winched aboard ship, lines were cast off and the four-master drifted away from the pier.

Alex and Gischairn stood side by side in the crowd as the big freighter wallowed awkwardly out into the river. Passengers and crew stood on the deck waving. They stood there until they could no longer see Scandal and Wade.

Then they turned and walked away together, grinning, satisfied with a job well done.

The steward showed Scandal and Wade to a beautiful stateroom. A ship's doctor appeared. He examined, cleaned and bandaged Wade's wounds. He found them deep, but not too serious. "They will repair themselves in time," he said with his strong Cuban accent. He was far more interested in Wade's emaciated body, his thin face. "Have you been ill, señor?"

"He has been," Scandal said. "But he's going to be all right."

The doctor nodded, smiling. "The sun and good sea air," he said. "It will work miracles. It has before, you know." He promised to look in on Wade again later in the afternoon. In the meantime, he prescribed many delicacies and much rest. Scandal thanked him, and he left.

Alone, they found themselves restrained, nervous. Wade sat in a chair, got up, prowled the stateroom. He stood staring out the porthole, watching the lush green land slide past.

Scandal watched him but did not speak. A knock at the door brought her to her feet. It was the captain. He had come to welcome them aboard. As friends of Señor Gischairn nothing was too good for them. Whatever they might desire, at any hour, they need only ask.

Scandal nodded. Then she smiled. "There is one thing, captain."

"Anything, señorita."

"When we are at sea, you can do something for me."

"With pleasure!"

"You can perform a marriage ceremony. For us. I'll spend the time between talking Señor Cameroon into the idea."

The captain laughed delightedly. "If the señor refuses, señorita, you will find every man aboard willing to take his place."

"I thank you all," Scandal said. "But I've learned one truth at last. Nobody else can take his place. Ever."

The captain nodded, smiling. "That is the kind of ceremony I love to perform. The only kind. It shall be done, señorita. We will turn the ship into a fiesta—everyone will weep and laugh with you—it will be a wedding you will never forget."

Grinning and nodding, the captain retreated, closing the door behind him. Scandal stood, not daring to look at Wade. But he had found some spark of his old vigor. He stood, watching her. "Why must we get married again?"

She heeled around and faced him, laughing and crying at once. "Because I let you get away from me once. . . . It will never happen again."

For a long moment they stood unmoving, then slowly, step by step, he came to her. She put out her arms and he stepped close. She closed her arms about his wide, thin shoulders.

"My most dear," she whispered. "My very dearest . . . I've loved you for so long—and with all my heart."

His smile was the faint shadow of his old laughter. "No. I loved you. You went away and left me."

"Only because I was a fool. But I loved you, even then. I loved you from the first moment I saw you."

He stuck his tongue in his cheek. "In that hayloft?"

She nodded, kissing his chin. She shivered and pressed closer.

"Of course. From that moment. . . . I didn't have to let you undress me that night. Our plans to trap you were all made. All I had to do was to scream. They would have forced you to marry me anyway. . . . But I loved you . . . I wanted you . . . that first moment. . . . And I wanted you to love me, then, as I want you to love me now."

"And forever," he said.